A NATIVE SON OF THE GOLDEN WEST

Also by James D. Houston

SURFING, THE SPORT OF HAWAIIAN KINGS
(with Ben R. Finney)

BETWEEN BATTLES

GIG

A Native Son of the Golden West

A Novel by

James D. Houston

The Dial Press　　New York, 1971

To Bob Moesle
who has always laughed the hardest
and in the right places,

And to Jack Christensen
who discovered the Hawaiian Islands,

And to Dick Barrymore
who discovered New Zealand,
South America and the Italian Alps,

And to Dave McGuire
with special thanks for
expert advice in aquatic matters,

And to Neil Rinker
who drowned off Espiritu Santo Island,
New Hebrides, November 1957.

A NATIVE SON OF THE GOLDEN WEST

Prologue:
Trips and Voyages

You could say this trip begins in Oklahoma, about the time Hooper's father decides he's had enough of his dry hole of a farm town and is ready to head west where a man can find steady work, pick oranges, build houses, start a new life, make his peace with the weather. Hooper was in his mother's womb then, conceived in the Dust Bowl, delivered in California not long after their rickety trip from Chickasha to Glendale, via the Painted Desert, the Grand Canyon, and the Colorado River in springtime. Call it his uterine initiation, foreshadow of future trips in old cars through hot deserts and cold mountain passes.

You could say that was the beginning. But it would mean leaving out his two grandmothers, one of whom rode as far as the Texas panhandle in his dad's Plymouth, then took a bus back home. And his two grandfathers. And his four great-grandmothers and four great-grandfathers. They might be closer to the beginning. If we can overlook his eight great-great-grandmothers and his eight great-great-grandfathers, some of whom came from England, some from Ireland, some from Scotland, some from Wales, some from Holland, some from Germany, one from France, one from Denmark, and at least two from Oklahoma itself, before that land became United States Territory, inhabited in those pastoral days by people who called themselves Cherokee (meaning cave people). So that if we really want to start at the beginning we should move back up the western hemisphere toward Alaska, retracing that historic migration across the Aleutians from Kamchatka, filtering through the mysterious Ainu north of Japan, heading inland then past the Great Wall of China toward Mongolia where, some men tell us, all things human have their origins.

You might say this trip of Hooper's began in Mongolia some time back. Take out a map of the world and follow his progenitors across the Bering Strait, through Canada, down the Plains States to the Oklahoma prairie.

Or start from the other direction. Say it's what we now call Holland, or farther up that Baltic coast, three thousand years ago, and some shaggy, fur-covered Neoliths are pushing off in wooden boats for what later men called Britain. Say it starts there, across the North Sea, in one of those conquesting voyages historians and archaeologists have unearthed to hold the years and continents and nationalities together.

Or step forward in time. *It's 1155 A.D. in the Scots highlands. A tribe of mountain men are moving their women and children, their dogs, their shaggy cattle, heading farther inland, following a riverbed toward higher country, to get beyond the reach of these new landholders come up from England, these Normans with their tributes and their oaths of service. They camp for the night near a tribe of kinsmen, and while the two chiefs talk about the way the world is going, the son of the chief of the traveling tribe catches the eye of the other chief's daughter, and these two mate privily in a sod hut near the riverbank where the water's noise will cover theirs, the girl giving birth some months later to Hooper's great-great-great-great-great . . .*

An endless task to start at the beginning. You can see how long it would take and how far back we'd have to go, and it isn't necessary at all. One place is about as good as another. So for now say it's eight hundred years later, the Korean truce talks are still going on, and we find Hooper Dunlap at the induction center the day he reports for his physical.

He tells them that he wets his bed, spits blood, suffers night sweats, hallucinations, and temporary blackout. No one believes this. It's the feet that save him. They are flat and knobbed with cartilage deposits from too many days paddling his board kneeling instead of prone. You could say his first step out is the placing of one of those feet upon the chair. The examining captain, a recent med school graduate who's simply putting in his own two years, touches the knob of this enormous flaked and calloused slab and laughs and asks, "Dunlap, how can you stand to wear shoes?" Hooper laughs and says he can't. And that's the end of it.

A week later he quits college, anxious to anyway. The goals there are too precise. Too attainable. They scare him. He yearns for something improbable he can take real pride in, such as he has seen in the eyes of hitchhikers, and believers in Atlantis, and certain professors around UCLA with no known application for their research.

For a couple of months he saves a little money playing guitar in a Western band four nights a week, but quits that too, for the same reason. Now, as this trip begins, he is two thousand miles from the mainland and ten thousand feet high. He had thought of coming by sea in an open boat but January is the wrong time of year for sailing. In the eleventh hour of a twelve-hour flight he's waking for the fourth and final time. The stewardess smell rouses him, orchid, gardenia, pikake leis of fragrance piped in ahead of time from bowers where dusky straw-hipped maidens smile through dripping ferns.

"Fasten your seat belts, please. We're landing in five minutes."

Hose hiss as she steps past him. Hooper snaps his belt to, sits up to watch the garlands curve atop her ample bosom, the girdled clinging of her hips. His eyes don't follow them. Through the far window, as her hips pass, he sees Oahu coming toward him, black and green of upthrust ridge and old volcanic remnants. It's his first island, and from the air he is sucking at it with his eyes, licking it and lusting for a way to make love to the very outline of its dusky humps, scooped craters, cobalt limes of water over inshore reefs.

At twenty-two he has no plan, no job, no contacts, no one to meet him at the airport, since no one knows he's coming. No announcements. No place to stay yet. Not even anywhere he plans to go first. Well, yes, one address. Though not even that. A name, *Broome*, on a scrawled and arrowed map, with some streets unmarked. Not much to go on. He may not find it at all. And it doesn't matter. He has no intentions in particular. Except this lust, which finally takes its first clear and polychrome shape in a window glance from the circling plane. And down the rolling steps he leaps, like some *Bounty* man leaping from the longboat even before it grinds atoll shallow sand, dousing dungarees and slashing feet on coral in his haste to clutch the chieftain's daughter, the first half-shell of kava.

While other passengers are still rising drowsy to the luggage racks, he's across the asphalt runway, bedroll tucked at his elbow, shopping bag suspended from his fist. Instantly sweating in the new heat he doesn't pause for shade and cool air of the bamboo terminal or the dark girls from travel posters selling souvenirs. He follows a long band of sun glare out the far door to plunge a line of taxi-drivers who, since these are days before Californians invaded by the thousands, approach him. And in spite of his sandy hair starting to be shaggy, his lean ruddy face faintly dusty as if salt spray has dried there, his lank-limbed urgency, and carrying less baggage for this unlimited tour than they carry home in one afternoon from the market, three drivers, not yet admitting that such travelers never have money to spend on them, shout, "Taxi, mister?"

"How much?"

"Two dollah fifty, Waikiki."

"What about a bus?"

"Bus take you way outta the way downtown."

"Where do I catch it?"

So that with nowhere in particular to go, at eight A.M. and time on his hands and on his arms and time sliding down his neck with the humid sweat of a morning warmth he's never felt before, Hooper is sprinting for a bus that will take him to the one place on this island he has any sort of connection with, impatient to find it, mainly to dispose of it and get it off his mind.

PART 1

Jonas

— OR —

The Master of Something

The dog that just ran up the center of the road, galloping along the perforated white line like a maniac, in among the swerving cars, up the street with tongue lolling, black and white dalmatian racing for who knows what, follow him with your eyes and watch him turn completely around and come galloping back the other way, smelling the bicycle of some woman pedaling down the hill. Here he comes, energy lurch, full tilt and total concentration, back the way he just came.

CHAPTER 1

Vines

*J*onas drew the map. It starts at a cluster of rusty metal umbrellas outside a restaurant in Waikiki. Checkpoint two is a Chinese grocery, with arrows guiding Hooper around two corners to a short palm-broken street, and the scribbled words, *Broome's Rooms*. Half this block is an asphalt lot lined with cars. Most of the other half is covered by the Paradise Hotel. One building stands between the lot and the hotel's garage entrance. Outside its ruined hedge Hooper stops and unbuttons his shirt, grabs his nose, to pull the sweat off, and holds it for a moment, the way a kid will jumping off the high board.

The very look of this place pleases him. He thinks of buying Joe a quart of beer. He's running with sweat and the paper handle in his other hand dissolves as he studies a broad frontyard, lushly snarled with tall grass and tasseled weeds. These fuse with vines that cover most of the first-floor windows and tendril up to eaves above the second story. It's an old Victorian house with peaked roof, dormer windows, and one high corner turret. Dusty green and purple panes line the window tops. Their casings, once white, are blistered and rust-spotted. The shingle siding is the same grayish brown as the coco palms rising from the yard—four of them, evenly spaced and, below their curving fronds, bearded with unshorn dead and hanging husks. They're taller than the house's highest flick of warping filigree, but house and palms and yard and vines are all dwarfed by the Paradise Hotel, and Hooper lets go his nose, takes a breath, as his slowly tilting head finally sees it, fifteen stories high, square, pink, and hovering.

The paper handle breaks. His bag hits the sidewalk, *Safeway* emblem up—underwear, paperbacks, swim trunks, face plate for diving. He stuffs it all back in and with this bag under one arm, bedroll under the other, follows the track of split and bursting concrete through high weeds to the stairs, which give a little as he climbs them, spongy, half house, half jungle. The righthand banister is leaning out of reach. He reads again Joe's message at the bottom of the map: "Cheapest rooms in the islands, and the place is never full, sometimes even empty because he won't advertise. If he gives you any trouble, act like you already live there."

Press the bell. A thin buzzing far away. Silence. Hooper waits, watching a stained-glass pane in the front door, sunburst of emerald daggers, ruby eggs, crystal center muted with dust and grime. Porch boards are sending up the morning heat, he can feel it through his slippers, wonders if every morning will be this hot and how long it'll take his blood to thin.

Press the bell again, and hold it. The buzzing dies before he lets the button go. He steps back. The house looks abandoned. The map that brought him here is two months old. He's backing down the stairs when he hears a distant scratching, like someone dragging cardboard boxes. Foot shuffle coming toward him. Door handle soundlessly turns.

Black crack at the jamb. "Who is it?"

"Hooper Dunlap. Are you Mr. Broome?"

"That's my name."

"I've come to see about a room."

"Yep, that's me all right, Jackson Broome."

Hooper raises his voice, leans toward the black stripe, searching for an eye, a mouth. "I said a *room*! I'm a friend of Jonas Vandermeer's."

"Nope. Sorry, young fella. Full up."

The black stripe widens, flash of hatbrim, as the invisible head tilts for a final look, then the stripe is narrower. Hooper says, "Hey, wait a minute!"

"What?"

Louder still. "When I came by here yesterday you told me I could move in this morning."

Slowly the door opens. Hooper sees first a dirty panama hat, thrust toward him, level with his shoulder. Then a pudgy grizzled face, one eye shut and the other squinting up through smudged and spattered silver-rim spectacles. A long scrutinizing pause. The old man shoves his panama back.

"I did, did I?"

"You said to come back at eight thirty this morning."

"Well . . ."

He studies Hooper from foot to forehead, and Hooper studies him: round belly hanging over flappy slacks, ukuleles all across an orange aloha shirt, his fly's unzipped.

"How much baggage ya got?"

"It's all right here."

"Lot a people come over with a stack a baggage. Usually too much for their own good. Cart around more things than they'd use in twelve years. One fella actually had shipping crates piled up on my front lawn."

"Not me, Mr. Broome. I'm traveling light."

Hooper hefts his elbows. Broome nods with something like a grin. "Let's get your key then."

He is heading back into the gloom. Hooper, stepping out of sunlight, is blind at first and follows the shuffle till his eyes begin to see murky walls and, at the end of this hall, blocks away, a haze of stairwell light that sends misty feelers down to mold all motes and shadows and crusted numbers on doors that seem to keep the secrets of centuries of roomers. Broome is fat-shouldered in front of him, dragging his feet as if through deep sand. They are bare, and from their rasp on the unrugged floor Hooper figures their callouses are thicker than his own.

Broome stops at the foot of the stairs, his face in deep shadow under the hatbrim that takes the full gush of a skylight high above. Standing over Broome and looking down at his hat, Hooper notices the shiny brown and bottle blue-green feathers of his hatband, covets the hat for its grim and floppy age, the band for its exotic sheen, shipped in from Fiji or the Marquesas, white man's version of a chief's plumage around the feathershimmer crown of Broome's battered panama.

"You wait here, young fella, don't folla me. You understand? Wait right here till I come back?"

He leaves Hooper standing in the cataract of light, just where the long hall turns right and left, not sure which way Broome has gone, since the high light screens the three corridors from this T center, and all Hooper can see clearly is the frontdoor sunburst flashing greens and rubies past the silent rooms.

He waits a long time, wondering who Broome reminds him of. He hears a door close, and another open, then the scratch of bare feet, and a feather ring sheening as the head backtilts to catch light off smeared lenses, handing him a stack of linen—five sheets, three pillowcases, seven or eight towels.

"Hang onto this and folla me," leading Hooper down the right-hand hallway to its final door, pushing this open to reveal a room filled with amber light. Three sides are lowered bamboo blinds. Against each blind a steel-frame cot, tick mattress rumple-sheeted and olive drab army blankets thrown back as if three roomers just jumped out the three high, wide, musty windows.

"Looks like this room's taken, Mr. Broome."

"Nope."

"Beds're kind of messed up. Clothes in the closet over there."

"Nobody lived in this room for thirty years. Here's your key. Toilet's upstairs."

"No toilet downstairs?"

"I use the toilet downstairs."

"What about the money?"

"Nope. Sorry. Neither borrower nor lender be. Heh heh. Know who said that?"

Broome turns to leave. Hooper says, "I mean the money for the room."

But he is shuffling for the door, as if the very rasp of leathered feet obstructs his hearing, and it closes with a click.

Hooper drops the linen and his gear on a rattan chair and rolls up the center blind, sees the parking lot through camouflage of vines, rolls it down again. He rolls up the righthand blind and sees bamboo like his own a few feet away. This room is one of two projecting from the building like stumps of legs. Roll that one down, roll up the lefthand blind and see, through another mat of vines, a rowboat propped against his sill, and beyond it a rear yard continuing the front—old flowerbeds have merged with weeds and once-lawn, surrounding the house with stalks and tassels, pods, runners, hugging vines that seem both shields and captors. In the middle of all this backyard profusion, Hooper sees a woman who looks as if she's just been rolled in a ten-foot wave.

A big woman, maybe sixty, gray hair matted and stringy and hanging to her shoulders, print dress plastered to her body, standing in high grass with arms akimbo glaring into the parking lot where a boy in overalls is hosing down a car. As if sensing some change in her surroundings she slowly turns her outraged head toward Hooper's window. He drops the blind. She's facing him, squinting against the sun, and for a full minute he stands afraid to move, not knowing why, watching her through bamboo slit and camouflage until, in disgust, she snaps her dripping fingers at the ground and stomps around a corner out of sight.

Holding his breath unawares, Hooper exhales, billows dust off the sill and blinds. He inhales some of it, mixed with greenery odor and salt pungence through the cracks, from Waikiki Beach a block away, and with this musty, sea-spiced breath comes the same sense of all things lifting him, same high buzz of solitude he carried on the plane, same globe of containment, waiting in space, incognito, with everything ready to happen. This coated room, his or not, occupied or not, is the perfect enclosure. Like a man submerged in a diving bell he could stand here a long time breathing and squinting at the stripes of outside leaking through. But now there's a violent rattling doorknob and raucous female demand.

"All right! All right! Open it up!"

He doesn't move.

"I know you're in there! Open it! Open it! This ain't a whore-house!"

Hooper imagines her outside his door, still wet from the hosing. It probably happens to her all the time, that kind of humiliation. She was born to be mistreated. He can't help himself. He shouts, "Fuck you, lady!"

"What?"

Silence.

She screams, "I heard that crack!"

One last frantic rattle.

"All right then! Wait'll I get the key from Mr. Broome. He'll have you outta here in no time flat!"

Heavy feet are pounding down the hallway, then as if through a telephone the desperate cry: "Jackson? Jackson? That fella's back in Room Nine! That garbage mouth! I just caught him peeking out the winda! Jackson? Jackson? Can you hear me? You in there? Open this door a minute!"

Rattling knobs, angry pleas, doors slamming even farther away. Silence.

Hooper waits for her to reappear outside the window. She doesn't. The house is quiet. The world is quiet. Glints of chrome flash through slits as cars move across the lot. He can't hear them. Vines and metal mesh and glass and bamboo screen it out. It's sticky like this. He thinks of opening a window to air the sweat. But he likes the quiet, spreads his sleeping bag over the bunk below this window and stretches out, hands cupped behind his head. He thought he had slept enough on the plane. Now at nine in the morning he's suddenly very tired. Not that heavy muscle, burning-eye weariness from five hours playing music he doesn't much like, for drinkers who aren't much listening. It's some lighter-limbed fatigue of a long struggle ended, some marathon arm wrestle, the challenged arm weary yet floating high and clear from sheer release. He lies here feeling the sweat shape his limbs, thinking he'll have to buy Jonas *two* quarts of beer for steering him to Broome's, and thinking of Broome, who reminds him of someone. Reminds him of W. C. Fields in a way, the raspy voice, the crafty eye. Yet not Fields. No . . .

Hooper's dozing eyes snap open at a rusty creak across the room. The outside screen. Someone is raising the window, an invisible hand so stealthy that sashweights and sliding wood are soundless. But Hooper hears traffic murmur, feels a gauze of cooler air. Then the blind is bulging inward, and one white leg is reaching for the floor. A knotty, lineman's leg, a tackle or a guard. Hooper braces silently, sure it's the mad drenched woman sneaking in to capture him.

Another knotty leg below the wide amber blind. Creak of screen closing. A hidden dial fades out traffic, and from behind the blind, at the foot of the opposite steel-frame bunk comes, not the fishwife at all, but a bleached head and no neck and white slab of muscled back that Hooper would recognize anywhere. He holds his breath and waits.

Jonas stands next to the wall, waiting too, for silence to settle around his entry, knees bent, jutting Neanderthal face, arms thrust out and hanging wide as if the very rubbing of biceps against his corrugated ribcage could give away his hideout.

Then he turns, hurries with flat noiseless steps across the room and is reaching for the doorknob when he sees Hooper. He blinks twice, doesn't stop.

"Dunlap, that bed is full of fleas, ya know."

"Which one should I use?"

"They're all full of fleas."

The door slams. He hears Jonas running down an empty hall. Two minutes pass, during which time dusty pungence revives that thrumming buzz, and Hooper hangs suspended in this last envelope of solitude before Joe returns. He savors it, and savors its end. Just enough, the not to be met arriving, to be found already *there*, emerging, like one of the plants. That was all he wanted to arrive incognito for. He is glad to see Jonas, who will never ask how it happened, yet will find out and spread the word.

He hears a distant toilet flush, and slap of hard feet walking back, then Joe is sprawled in the wingback, flat-arm rattan chair looking at Hooper, who has not moved, who rolls his head now to see Joe's white, peeling, chipped, impassive face. Joe is twenty-one, has lived in the sun for eight years of California beaches wearing no more than he wears this morning, old pair of striped golf knickers trimmed above the knee. And Joe has never tanned. Nor has he burned, or even reddened. The sun can do nothing to Joe's skin but assault each layer till it flakes away and hope the one below is thinner or newer or somehow subject to change. But Joe's skin has never changed, always dusty white, sprinkled with blond hairs and stretched over knots and clumps and welts of muscles hardened in his daily wrestle with the sea.

"The old lady took my key away," he begins. "It was a mistake. I shouldn't have let her have it. But she scares me."

"Broome's wife?"

"His concubine. She hates me. She won't let me near the place if she's in the yard and sees me coming. But if I can once get inside and meet her in the hall I just say, G'mornin, Mrs. Pike, and she says G'mornin back, before she knows what hit her, and I'm in for as long as I can stand it, although I usually only come in about this time every morning. I have to. The guys in all the service stations around here are pissed off at me for using their cans so much. You want to go in the water?"

"Can you get me a board?"

"Where's yours?"

"I sold it."

Jonas jumps up and stands over him, grimacing and blinking. "Jesus Christ, Hooper, why'd ya do that?"

"I needed the money."

Joe shouts, "That was a great board! A fantastic board!"

"I said I needed the money."

"What're you gonna do without a board?"

"Rent one, or borrow one, I guess."

"Shit, you can't rent a board. Soldiers rent boards. Summer coeds rent boards."

Joe paces to the blind he climbed through, studies it, slaps a fist into his palm and observes the action of his triceps in the long mirror on the closet door across the room.

"I really feel good this morning. I feel like getting wet. You know how it feels after you take a good, quick, heavy dump?"

"Sure."

"Well, let's get going then. You can use my extra board."

"Wait'll I change."

"I have to move my truck. The meters start at nine. I'll meet you at the corner." Joe is reaching for the blind.

Hooper says, "Hey."

"Yeah?"

"You used the downstairs toilet."

"That's right."

"Broome told me to use the upstairs toilet."

"There isn't any upstairs toilet."

And in a single silent stride and lift and ducking slide Joe is out the window, dropping into a net of vines, albino Tarzan squeaking shut the rusty screen.

CHAPTER 2

1754:
The Ulster Packet

*T*he *darkest sea in the world is the Irish Sea on a bad night, and this night's dark fell too early, with the weather, making one assailant of the water pouring down from the heavens and the swells bucking up from the deep. They wash the prow of the Ulster packet plowing its way from Glasgow to Belfast, and slosh through the starboard rail where the Reverend James Dunlap stands vomiting over the side, his whole life a shambles and seeming at last to find its full expression in this agony of retching into the void. Behind him lies the disgrace of being publicly named a tippler of Spanish sherry. Ahead of him a congregation on the Irish coast, whose only virtue, so far as he can tell, is its remoteness: chances are they'll never learn the reasons for his coming. And next to him here on the flowing deck, unbonneted, taking the storm full in her face, his wife seems to find some terrible pleasure in the drenching and the fury.*

The Reverend retches, and he's too feeble to avert his cheek when an updraft tosses some of it back at him.

His wife shouts, "Never vomit into the wind, James!"

He groans. A stream of bile lashes up at him. She continues, "But you never were one to learn a lesson, were you. James. Always going the opposite way of good sense."

"For God's sake, woman. Not now . . ."

"And there's the holy man I married. Using the name of the Lord in vain on such a night as this."

"Get away from me. I beg you, go."

"Where should I go, James? Can you tell me that? Back to Glasgow? Back to the manse? To warm my chilled bones by the kitchen fire I never let die in eleven years? Tell me where I should go!"

"Go below."

"You go below," she shouts in his ear, "if you dare. I'd rather be vomiting into the wind myself than go below and see those women's eyes."

"Go to hell then," he groans, but so weakly that it's lost in a great upwash and blast of wind through the straining sails. He retches

again and nearly swallows it back as his mouth and throat fill with
wind and water, and he thinks it would be a blessing to have a huge
wave rise and fill his lungs and drown him where he stands and end
this misery, the sea that's churning his innards would be his savior
then, and he leans a little farther, out away from his wife's mouth,
and toward the water as if to meet its icy dark halfway. But then
thinks no. No. It's sin to covet death. The Lord ends this life's mis-
ery in his own good time. Tonight's vile sea is but His test, His
punishment, foreshadowing of His reward. And if I endure it and
make my way to Ireland, the Lord surely will bless me, my flock
will become the holiest in Ulster, and this sea will fence away the
sinful world and all past mistakes. And if tonight this same God-
driven sea should cast my poor wife overboard into the boil and
blackness, there'd be no time to catch her nor any way to search.
Her very cry would be lost in the maelstrom. Nothing to do but
pray for her pitiful soul. And if then in Ireland the whiskey's as
good as they say, well, a man learns how to be discreet, and we
must all be thankful for those things the good Lord sends our way.

CHAPTER 3

The Farther South the Better

*J*onas won't surf at Waikiki. It's
against his principles. Not only soldiers and summer coeds rent
boards and ride there, but also bank clerks on vacation, paunchy
middle-aged men, canoes full of smirking tourists. Joe doesn't consider himself a tourist. Nor does Hooper. They put themselves in
a different, unnamed category of island visitor. And Joe does his
surfing at Sunset Beach, forty miles through cane and pineapple
fields to the north shore. They drive out there in his Reo, one-time
baker's delivery van, a high metal box fitted inside with bunks
slung from chains, decorated outside with movie posters and cartoons and random inked and painted slogans, and roofed with two
surfboards that jut over the windshield like cannons on a gunboat.

See them shirtless side by side. Next to Joe's white bulging wedge, Hooper is a bundle of sticks, his limbs coated, as Joe often jokes, with "Indian muscles," hardly seen on the surface, but there, and waiting, somewhere next to the bone. Joe is weaving from side to side, ducking and stretching, as the traffic shifts in front of him, to find the best view among all the cracks in his windshield. And Hooper, with one lanky arm on the hot sill, is doing two things at once.

He watches this land they're driving through, brownwood shacks of country towns, and road walls of sugarcane, meanwhile remembering earlier trips after waves in all the old cars they once owned, clanking from Los Angeles north to Santa Barbara, or south to Baja California and Mazatlan, clanking and sputtering and flat-tire cursing as far south as they could get without leaving the land, cars lashed with balsa boards, stuffed with bedrolls and diving gear—rusty station wagons, rickety Model A's, abandoned laundry trucks, and taxicabs, and hearses. They had to be old and battered and barely running. The closer to dead the better. Some had belonged to Jonas, some to Hooper. The most treasured was the car that could travel the farthest on five cylinders, or four; three tires; or no lights. And the same measure applied to houses. And to clothing. And to food. Everything had to be old, or discarded, or cheap, or free.

Hooper's father could never understand this, having been himself, at Hooper's age, starving in Oklahoma, scratching hopeless soil for stillborn potatoes, and how lucky he was, coming west in the pit of the Great Depression, to find any work at all, and then when the war came along to land a job at Boeing. He's a supervisor there, with a fine home in Glendale, and a congregation elder to boot, Brother Andrew Dunlap, a man much respected among those two hundred worshippers, most of whom traveled out with him from the South. World War Two made their dreams come true, the Korean just multiplied their blessings, and Andrew's still feeling lucky about the way things worked out, which is why he has told Hooper so many times how tough it was in those early days, eating cornbread and red beans all winter, hiking barefoot through deep mud to a country school that wasn't always open when you got there. He tells such tales, of course, with considerable pride, having endured it all, and having prospered. And this is what Hooper remembers, the pride, the virtue of such denial. Sidestepping his father's hardwon prosperity—the Chrysler, the deep-freeze—he covets the ragged, the barefoot, and the cheap. But not the suffering. No. Sidestep the suffering too. Be ragged, but the farther south the better: Chickasha, Glendale, San Diego, Mazatlan, Oahu. Always someplace warmer. Someplace where it's always warm, and the fields are filled with available fruit, and the sea with fish.

(OLD CARTOON from late-forties *Esquire*. One-palm desert island twenty feet across, two stubble-faced young men in tattered pants and shirts glare at each other while pulling at the arms of equally tattered, buxom brunette, and one man complains, "I searched yesterday. It's *your* turn to search for food.")

Now Joe is starting to talk about the waves they'll ride today. But Hooper only half listens. He's envying Joe this truck, wondering how he can top, or even match it. The upholstery is bursting, one running board drags, the tires are bald, the horn seldom works, it reeks of oil and unwashed clothes and the pungent resin Joe uses to patch his boards. In Hooper's eyes it is the ultimate vehicle. And he has to admit it'll be hard to beat. He'll just have to wait and see what comes his way. Meanwhile—and this comes to him just as they clear a final rise before the island slopes down to its northern rim—he figures he can at least stay even, since minimum investment and painless self-denial are the first terms of their bond and private legend, by having no car at all. Which Hooper instantly decides to do. And he is so relieved at one-upping Joe by bumming a ride in the very car he covets, and so taken with the look of this new ocean spreading out and up—the appeal water always has for him when the land falls away to reveal it—he yells out the window.

It interrupts but does not stop Joe's loud explanation that this now calmly tropical stretch of sea curves north to Alaska, where earthquakes and winter storms make waves as high as houses, with nothing to stop them once they start until they hit this shoreline. Joe says he's ready for them whenever they get here. They're way overdue, as it is. And Hooper understands the loudness, the urgency in his description. It's the way Joe used to describe Hawaii when they were both back home. These islands have the one natural resource that interests him. Not the coco palms, or the trade winds, or the spirit of Aloha. No. Oahu sits in the path of those northern swells, and it has the reefs that lift them to twenty-five, thirty, sometimes forty feet, shaped right for riding if you can get to where they break, and Joe's one ambition is to catch a bigger wave than any other man has ridden.

Waves have never been this important to Hooper. Before he left, he sold his guitars and his surfboard, not only because he (1) needed the cash and (2) wanted no possession he couldn't carry on his back, but also because he (3) wasn't flying out here particularly to play music or ride waves. Yet now, listening to Joe describe waves he has already caught these past few months, the speed and steeper wall and seething tunnels you can shoot through,

Hooper feels old juices reviving. And when they finally leave the sea road and break through a line of hibiscus flame and wind-tattered palms, and reach the spot, the nose of land that flares out onto lava reefs, and see swells humping blue, molting green across the sandy bottom to peak and break with hoofbeats, curling and clattering and rushing white over inshore placid green, Hooper, and Jonas too, are unstrapping boards and waxing the surfaces frenzied, as if the last wave for all future time is scheduled to break in the next five minutes. They slide down a short sandy cliff, leave the beach, and race for the breaking place, boards aglitter in the near-noon overhead sun, their arms digging in like four adzes chipping at the water.

They swing wide to the left, paddle in behind the break, Jonas leading now, and suddenly stop, drop legs over the sides. Like that oldtime statue of the hunching brave on his sagging horse, they sit hump-shouldered in a lull of surf, and wait, as if this in itself is enough, frantic paddle to end up perched offshore where sunlight ripples from the bottom, and a mile stripe of beach to edge volcanic ridges.

Waiting, silent, and after a while Joe explains the lineup.

"They peak fast, Hooper. It's a fast takeoff, and you better only go right. Until you see how they feel. You go left and it's pretty shallow over there. A lot of coral."

A new set is humping. They watch it. Slyly Jonas adds, not to scare, but just to hone the edge of their sport a little sharper, since for him it isn't sport at all, "Guy cut his legs pretty bad last week on the coral. Water was sucking up into his wave, and the tide was so low the heads were popping out in front of him. He got spooked and fell right into one."

With underwater kicks Joe swings his board around, telling Hooper to try for the first one, take a short ride, and paddle back in time to get the last wave of the set. He isn't that hungry. He watches Joe take the first alone, to see how he handles it. He has never seen Joe make a mistake in the water. Joe always knows where the surf is best, where to wait, when to take off, how the reefs look, and why the currents change.

Joe flattens, waits a moment for the green slope to backtilt his board, then one white plunge of arms and his board is sliding. He jumps to his feet, crouched, cuts right just as the wave center snaps up and over, an exploding tube, and from behind, all Hooper can see is shaggy blond hair shooting along the rim just ahead of each erupting section.

Ten seconds and his board slices back through the wave. Joe is nearly aloft with forward motion channeled into his pullout, white arms spread like wings for balance, feet lightly holding the deck. Then he's flat again, paddling back like a water machine, as if pacing himself by a metronome, each stroke striving to move maximum water, just as each wave ridden is not simply a ride, but another, more perfect step toward what he came to Hawaii to do.

While Joe strokes to push through the next wave before it breaks, Hooper flattens, craning back to gauge it, and the sun beguiles him, the way it glints in tiny sparkles massing toward a flash through the center. He knows the moment to dig is just before that flash, but he lets it blind him, turns late to start and nearly loses the wave. With lean arms whirling he plunges straight into the trough where miraculously he rights his board and spurts from a water cave that thunders shut behind him. He listens to the thunder and the slaps of water underneath him, listens too hard when he should be trimming, so it's a balancing act, one foot flat, the other swinging, both arms flapping, elbows and ears and sharp shoulder edges, red trunks slapping at his legs like luffing sails. Hooper's body is so loosely designed, he has always played it this way, his best style being no style at all, and clowning half the time, except during that brief moment on each ride, which now begins as he finally plants his wild foot, and the slapping underneath him smooths to a hiss pitched higher than he's heard before. This somehow steadies him on a hurtling course, makes his board a blade that would plunge him right into the island if he followed it far enough, steadies his hearing and his vision on a single line, nothing intruding, vibrations of water ascend through the wood, up his legs, to attune him completely.

Snap.

Wave wall is flattening, melting back to plain water. Loss and exuberance fuse, and Hooper leaps yelling from his board, spread-eagled, and splats butt-first in its wake.

Joe is shooting toward him on a head-high wave, playing it like a torero, climbing the wall when the shoulder of froth recedes, rushing to his board's nose as the next curling section threatens. Hooper could reach out and touch the fiberglass edge as it skims past him, Joe's knobby feet like a dancer's soft-shoeing around on the wax-roughened surface, just ahead of bursting foam. Hooper dives under the board and the foam.

Into a moonlight boil. Slowmotion billow. He watches the bubbles surround him in pillows of churning. Drift. Go limp in the tumble. Overhead silence, as wave-front is carried beyond him toward shore. Lime puddles up there. Head for the bottom with a light flutter kick, gliding for wet dunes of absolute silence. He hugs the sand, digging fingers in. Coral heads stand on a reef edge over there. Longlost molars. He starts to swim for them, but his lungs say surface. Climb handholds of water till the ears plink. Air.

CHAPTER 4

The Aroma of Love

*T*hat night back at Broome's Hooper lets himself in by the front door, Joe by the window. Figuring they have already lost enough blood to insects, they leave the three bunks to the fleas, both stretch out on the floor, scratching and regretting their greed. They rode their last waves in ten minutes too late, just as the offshore breeze blew the first swarm of mosquitoes down from the hills, dozens of bloodsuckers, hundreds, thousands, and Joe howling, "Fuckers! Fuckers!" They scrambled for his truck, but it was filled before the doors slammed. Only by crashing through underbrush out to the road and speedshifting to capacity of forty-five m.p.h. could Jonas blow all the bugs away. Then, scratching like apes, they made three burger stops on the way back to town and drank two quarts of beer—Joe's reward from Hooper for discovering Broome's—plus one more of two bought by Joe welcoming Hoop to the islands. Now they're still chafing at welts, and belching, and squirming for position on the tatters of a lauhala mat, Hooper's body burning from his first day in the glare, and here comes a scraping at the screen outside, like a fingernail dragging.

Joe whispers, "Oh shit," pulls his head down into his bag.

A girl's voice softly, "Jonas. Jonas."

Hooper whispers, "Joe. Who's that?"

"Sssssshhh," from the bag.

"Jonas, I know you're in there. I saw you climbing in."

Hooper whispers "Joe" and the sheepish head emerges, lips to Hooper's ear, hissing, "Some girl thinks I owe her ten dollars. She thinks I stole it from her purse one day at the beach. For three nights, no matter where I am, she comes banging around asking for her ten dollars back. I can't get rid of her."

Nail tapping on the casement now. "Jonas? Jonas?"

16

Lips to Joe's ear. "*Did* you steal it?"

"Yes. What the hell am I going to do?"

"Let her in."

"What?"

"Tell her to get in the sack with you. That'll shut her up one way or another."

"I can't do that."

"What's the matter, is she ugly?"

"She's beautiful. One of the most beautiful women I've ever seen. I'm just off women. I'm not having anything to do with any woman at least until the winter swells hit. I can't afford to. You gotta help me."

Knuckles rapping, voice louder, "Jonas, I want to talk to you."

"Tell her to come in."

"Aw shit, Hooper . . ."

"You want to get rid of her?"

"I've got to. She's driving me crazy. I can't concentrate on anything. I'm getting behind in my sleep."

"Tell her to come in. I'll handle it."

"I locked the screen."

"Unlock it and get back inside your bag."

Knuckle rap, loud pleading, "Jonas, I *have* to talk to you right *now*."

Joe creeps to the blind, slips one arm behind it, under the raised window, to the screen latch. "Come on inside then."

"You come out here."

"No, you have to come inside." He scuttles back to his bag.

Hooper whispers, "What's her name?"

"Goldie," and Joe slides out of sight.

Long silence. The screen creaks, bamboo bulges into a picket of thin lines from the parking lot overhead lights. The girl is shadowed next to the wall.

"Where are you, Joe?"

Hooper with his mouth in the rolled-up sweatshirt he's using for a pillow says, "Down here."

"What are you doing on the floor?"

"The beds are full of fleas."

"Is that somebody else?"

"Friend of mine. He's asleep."

"Why don't you turn on the light? I can't see."

"I'm almost asleep myself. What do you want to talk about?"

"You know."

"Well, what do you want me to do? I was so broke the other day I was almost starving, that's all."

"You didn't have to *steal* it. I would have lent you some, if you asked."

"I always forget to pay people back. So it ends up the same either way."

"You're talking funny, Joe."

"I was in the water all day. Why don't you lie down here so we don't have to talk so loud."

"I think I should go back outside. I didn't know anybody else was in here with you."

"He just flew in from the coast. He'll be sleeping for two days. Time change messed him all up."

"I ought to get back outside."

But she's moving away from the wall, and Hooper sees a brief silhouette of snug jeans and fullfleshed arm, shortsleeve aloha shirt, straight hair dropping through the light lines, kneeling, sliding in between the bags.

Gently she says, "I'll *give* you the money, Joe, that's what I really wanted to talk about."

Hooper is lifting his face from the squash of his sweatshirt when the door crashes open, latch splitting past wood, a blinding globe of light, and Mrs. Pike comes hurtling shoulder first across the room.

"All right, Mr. Vandermeer!" she bellows.

Jonas squirts from his bag as if she stomped the end. Dragging it with him he heads for the blind, but gets caught there in draw ropes, frantically yanking. The bobbling light falls on Hooper. Seeing the guilty eyebrows of his slim and burned and unknown face, the girl jumps up into the beam crying, "Jonas," whirling, and Mrs. Pike stops short, her bare feet wide apart, her lamp thrust forward at the end of a bulky arm.

"Mr. *V*andermeer! I'm gonna call the police!"

One last yank, and the blind splinters down around Jonas. He dives out the window dragging bag and bamboo behind him. Swinging her lamp on its hinges like a mace, Mrs. Pike drives Goldie, ducking, across the floor and out the window too, yelling for Joe to wait. Hooper finds himself up on a bunk in his shorts hopping from mattress to mattress trying to evade the wild lashings of her lamp.

"Who do you think you are?"

"I just moved in. Go ask Mr. Broome."

"Mr. Broome, my eye! He ain't a runnin' a whorehouse! Wait'll he hears about this!"

Lashing and bellowing she leaps onto one of the bunks herself. The springs break, the bunk falls apart, and as she lands in a cursing heap on the mattress, Hooper grabs his pants and is into the hall, through the front door, high weeds scraping at his legs. He sprints the shattered path, past the hedge, grabs the door of Joe's truck just as it's pulling away from the curb.

Inside, the girl is kneeling on the seat. "What's going on, Joe? What's going on?"

Joe is hunched over the wheel, his sleeping bag piled around him like a shield, refusing to look at her or speak, glaring at a street he can barely see, through a fractured window spattered with bugs.

Hooper climbs behind the seat, among the boards and heaps of all Joe owns, and squats holding on as Joe swerves the first corner. Goldie pleads, "Joe?"

He won't look at her. He swerves again, speeding onto Kalakaua Avenue, shooting amber lights, and holding tighter to his wheel, as if the great hotels on either side are grandstands full of cheering fans, and this is the Indianapolis Speedway, and he is the grimy, firm-jawed, indifferent Indy winner barreling the final lap in a racing tank of his own design.

Hooper is watching Goldie's profile against the stream of passing lights. She looks about twenty, and looks like a hundred girls he's seen around beaches in California—a slightly Mediterranean cast, the way her tan seems to add a final softening layer of flesh, the brown hair sunstreaked and shoved across her forehead, falling straight past her shoulders—and yet she reminds him of someone in particular, the way her chin protrudes, the way her forehead slants.

Her arm lies across the rotting leather backrest. She's pulling tufts of cotton, asking, "Aren't you going to talk to me, Joe?"

He doesn't answer, doesn't blink, doesn't even seem to be breathing, as if any bodily movement would somehow acknowledge her presence.

Goldie watches Joe, waiting, and Hooper watches Goldie, and during the long silence he senses that she is gradually aware he's watching. Her tuft-pulling stops. As Joe roars past the yacht harbor, Hooper says, "I don't mind talking to you, if Joe won't."

She thinks about this, smiles. "Yeah, I know. You don't mind a bit."

"Trouble is, I didn't get a chance to finish what I was saying."

This strikes her funny. Mrs. Pike goes thundering between them. Goldie starts to giggle. Hooper giggles too, and they are looking at each other giggling, snickering, Hooper wondering again who she looks like.

The harder they try just to giggle, not laugh, the harder Joe steps on the gas, until his truck is going faster than he's ever driven it, somewhere over fifty, stutter and clatter of every bolt straining for its life. Their laughter grows to match the noise, and laughing, Goldie climbs over into the back where Hooper, sitting just in his shorts, has shoved the two surfboards to one side, opening the quart of beer they didn't drink on the way back from Sunset.

On Joe's bunk they sit and quell their laughing with sips of cool beer. Hooper tries to talk but the truck makes such a racket now—struggling engine and running board dragging and death rattle of every fender and door—the words are lost. They laugh and sip till Joe passes Pearl Harbor. When the bottle's empty Hooper stretches out between the chains of Joe's swaying bunk. It's too short for him, and no room at all for two. He tips the mattress off onto the metal floor. Hooper and Goldie pitch from wall to wall as they pile old towels and blankets and Joe's clothes to stop the sliding of the boards. Goldie's still giggling when Joe digs into a soft shoulder on a turn and they're finally thrown down side by side.

She feels his sunburn and for some reason likes the heat and the welts. Cool hands along his back. For one moment, as the truck lurches again, Hooper looks up to see Joe's shaggy skull black against the dim light coming back into the cab off the asphalt, and Joe, hunched and solid, is clearly the master of something—Hooper the novice, Jonas the mentor, stolid, shirtless, wrapped in his own foul sleeping bag, only one thought in his mind from now until what he refers to as "the day," untainted by women, and speedway driver of the ultimate vehicle careening through Oahu's night toward Hooper knows not where, nor now cares, as her buttons dissolve and the pungence of resin from the gallon can at his shoulder becomes the aroma of love.

CHAPTER 5

Sunrise

*T*he body of Jonas has designed an intricate couch among all the springs and lumps and ripped seams of his front seat. Wrapped in an olive blanket Joe borrowed from Broome, Goldie lies next to the boards on a pile of towels and underwear. Hooper covers most of the mattress.

For an instant of confusion and terror he feels strange light on his unopened eyelids, then a moment's fear that he missed his plane or that he's been shipped back to Los Angeles, afraid to find out where he is. But his eyes open in an orange haze, and he remembers, and relaxes the way he relaxed in yesterday's room of musty quiet. Quiet here too, except for Goldie breathing next to him, snoring of Jonas up front.

He wants to think about Goldie. But not now. Wide awake he ought to get outside, feel the full face of this sun leaking in and see where Joe finally stopped. The way the truck tilts they must be hanging off a cliff. It has become a light funnel, this truck, catching orange beams on the windshield, bending them over the sleepers and out the tiny unglassed square in the rear door.

Staring into the beams, Hooper remembers this same moment yesterday, sunrise on the plane, and how, turning from the light to the book in his lap, and trying to read, he resolved then to read every morning, at least a few verses, until it's finished, the book he brought along to read as *reading*, only now feeling for the first time in his life like reading it at all. He tried the first two verses four times, each time stalling on "the face of the deep," each time glancing out his porthole and down at the dark blue face, the drifting eyes and wrinkle-slipping mouth and faraway high forehead belying widow's peak just over the horizon, falling hair perhaps, or no hair at all, just the enormous face backtilted, hair hidden and no telling what was on its mind or down in its deep. Yet how many times had he watched it from sandspits and weedy points and perched offshore on his chip of balsa studying the glints, the distant line and never seen its face at all. Until yesterday. Last shreds of darkness slithered off the blueing cheeks. Face of the deep.

He wants to read on. But his copy now is back at Broome's, perhaps crushed to a pulp under Mrs. Pike and her collapsible bunk. He refuses to let this slow him down. The next line comes to him. He mouths it. "And God said, Let there be light."

Through orange beams glance up at the rusty ceiling ribs, listening.

"And there was light. And God saw the light that it was good. And God divided the light from the darkness. And God called the light day ..."

That's all he can remember. Upglancing he lets his vision blur into the mote-haze that fills the truck, listening for some echo, something there he wants to catch.

CHAPTER 6

Getting rid of Goldie

*H*ooper hears a high-pitched trickle against the side of the truck. Jonas has slithered out the open front door and now gives his impersonation of an alarm clock.

The rear door creaks, and Hooper is looking upside down at Joe's stubbled chin, long dark nostrils.

"Hooper, I gotta talk to you."

Chin and nostrils gone. Hooper digs through swim fins, cans of spaghetti, fruit cocktail, orange peels, old maps and tide charts, dragging loose his dungarees. He hops out, joins Joe on a cliff edge where they stand side by side gazing down fifteen feet to tide wash nudging lava rock—Johnny Appleseed and Alley Oop where the sunlight cuts through dry mountain ridges, and a mud-rutted road threads the low cliff's line above a gurgling tide. One of Joe's front wheels is sunk. The truck kneels.

Hooper watches the sun, trying to hold whatever it was he started to hear. But Joe is so gloomy, watching the water, after a while Hooper has to say something.

"I tried. You have to give me credit for that."

"We'll never get rid of her now."

"Suppose we just drive her back into town and tell her to shove off."

"She's unshakable."

"Insult her."

"Won't work. I've called her everything. I've called her a slut so many ways it doesn't mean anything any more."

"Did you tell her you're off women?"

"She doesn't believe me. She takes it *personally*."

"What about hitting her? You ever hit her?"

"O, I hit her a couple of times. In fact once I really hit her. Did she try to grab your balls last night?"

"Yeah."

"Did you let her?"

"Sure. Why not?"

"That's the trouble, ya see. She's always doing that. One night

22

I woke up and she was in the truck with her hand down inside my pants, and I had this enormous hardon. Before I knew what was happening I came all over the place. I was so pissed off I beat the hell out of her. Then I felt pretty bad because she started to cry, so I let her spend the night in the truck, and the next day she was so chummy and palsy-walsy that I had to do something to really turn her off. That's the day I stole the ten bucks. Now here she is sleeping in my truck again. I feel like flying back to the States."

Joe is in despair, and here comes Goldie climbing out in her jeans, and one button holding her bra-free aloha shirt, brim-eyed exuberance for every phase of every day and season, greeting the sun by feline straightening brown arms into it, murmuring, "Wow."

Hooper does not yet share Joe's utter distaste. When she says it's too fine a morning not to go swimming, he can't deny it. So while Joe leans sulking against the back of his truck munching last night's frenchfries, Hooper and Goldie pick their way down a short cliff still prickled with tiny lava bubbles that cooled a thousand years ago.

At her suggestion—the early hour, the no houses or traffic, the generally silken calm and rustle of ocean lift against the stone—they strip. Slide in. Shock moment of thin chill, then blissful ease. Floating. Hooper spews water the way he figures Huck Finn must've done along the Mississippi, watches sunlight sparkle it and splatter on his chest. Goldie's chest is two slick globes on the morning surface, face to the sky, her chin underlit in the low slant of sun, and maybe this is what he was listening for, this slick hush of light and water licking at Goldie. He is studying this view when she rights herself, catching the voyeur at work, and liking it. And only then, as she backs away with a rippleless stroke, and as Hooper starts to glide after her, does the light change and he sees who Goldie reminds him of.

In the sleeping bag dark of Broome's and for the rest of last night he had taken Joe's word that she was one of the most beautiful girls. As Hooper for the first time sees her face clearly, he doesn't agree. She's beguiling, yes. And sly. And kissable. Beautiful isn't the word. But he understands why Joe would use it. And he's worried now that he has gone too far in helping Joe. Except that her hair is longer and her chest fuller and the skin of her face is smooth, not chipped and flaking, Goldie looks alarmingly like Jonas. Beach time has lightened the hair across her forehead and past her ears, so that frontally she's almost as blond. Her eyes now seem turquoise. Up near the truck he thought they looked green. Like Joe's they pick up the color of the water. It's a resemblance so eerie he is flustered swimming this close, the way her blue eyes follow him. He wishes he'd had a better look last night before everything started.

He turns, breaststrokes away, wishes the big surf had come and gone so he could give Goldie back to the man she is clearly mated to.

But he knows Joe is conserving his juices the way he conserves everything this time of year, and Joe won't even look at Goldie swimming naked on this pristine morning in the world's largest outdoor pool. Joe is glued to his truck door and glowering at the horizon, as if his gloomy gaze, could he hold it long enough, might cause some great wave to rise, roll toward him, break close enough for Joe to study its line, imprint the image on his brain for future reference. That's why they ended up last night on this tip of the island's western corner, farthest point from Waikiki, longest flight Jonas could arrange. But more than that. Hooper knows the spot from maps. It's called *Kaena* (*the rage*, as in raging heat; or, in some legends, a relative of *Pele,* the volcano goddess). Winter waves break here so large and so full of rage and spuming echo of lava roar and so close to shallow reefs that no one has ever ridden them, or even paddled close enough to try, and Joe is feeding on that reputation now, feeding on whatever lurks below the surface, whatever reef or timeless sandbar or confluence of currents and jut of land makes those waves heap so awesome and impossible. He doesn't plan to try them here—that would, by all accounts, be suicide—but he wants to carry something with him from this point. It's a pilgrimage, Hooper learns, that Joe makes frequently, sometimes driving out alone to park in a howling wind and beat on the hood of his truck to drum up surf.

Hooper hears a splash and, turning, finds Goldie's inscrutable smile right behind him. It's as if Joe has sunk out of sight into the old lava floe to spurt up next to him here, Jonas with a suntan, seductively inviting him back to the mattress on the floor between the surfboards and the bunk.

He swims away again, says he's getting out. He eases back to the natural ladder of black rock steps, climbs them, and towels off at the truck, where Goldie soon joins him, glistening, hairslick. Then while the old engine whines and whinnies, they push Joe out of the rut, and they're jolting back the way they came, checking every surfing spot, three abreast in the gas-fume silence.

CHAPTER 7

The Fairest Girl Who Ever Lived in Belfast

*J*amey Dunlap hates everything *about his father's life except the sea which thunders along the cliff below their cottage and which his father has only tasted once. When he runs away to Dublin he meets a man named Dugan who likes him for his glib tongue and brash way, and hearing that Jamey is willing to sail in any direction as long as it's away from Ireland, this Dugan makes him a proposal which, for a small risk, will take Jamey clear to America, with a good piece of cash when he gets there.*

It requires Jamey to sign on a British merchant vessel as a common seaman. They have crossed the whole Atlantic. Jamey has been waiting for the first sign of Cape Cod's outer banks, and now, finally sighting it, he makes his first move.

From beneath his shirt he pulls a small picture frame, the picture covered by an orange cloth, and announces loudly, "Mates, I have here in my hand a picture of the fairest girl who ever lived in Belfast."

The deck is sprinkled with shaggy seamen, barefooted some of them, bare-chested or wearing red and white striped shirts and plate-shaped hats with flat crowns. They all turn, half scowling, half amused. Jamey is a favorite. Except for the cabin boys, he's the youngest man aboard. Sandy-haired, smooth-breasted, a blue kerchief round his neck.

"Not only the fairest," he says, "but also the biggest-bosomed and roundest-bottomed that any of you blackguards could imagine."

"Well, where have you been keeping her all these weeks, Jimmy boy?"

"And let's have a look at the wench," says a great, bearded Londonman, reaching to draw back the orange cloth.

Jamey jumps to a hatch cover, grinning.

"Not only the fairest," he shouts, now that they've all gathered, "and the biggest-bosomed and roundest-bottomed, but in this little portrait I hold in me hand, she's wearing no more than what the good Lord gave her to walk around in. And me poor old father

in County Antrim, could he ever get his hands on her, would call
her the reincarnation of Eve herself and call it the holiest act of his
life could he ever bite a chunk from her white behind."

A lecherous murmur circles the deck, and they all press toward
the hatch cover, where Jamey stands haughty, holding the frame
high overhead.

"Dya want to see it?"

"What dya think? Goddam ya, Jamey."

"What'll ya give me?"

"A bath in the bloody ocean, lad. Let's have a look."

"Aah ah ah. What'll ya give me now? I'm not running a bawdy
show. I'm offering this picture up for sale to the highest bidder.
What'll ya give me for the fairest and roundest-bottomed . . ."

With a roar the men nearest Jamey lunge at him, and he shouts,
"Take care, mates! Take care! One flick of me wrist and she's over
the rail for good—and not a man of ya gets so much as a peek. I
can toss it quicker than the first man can reach."

He makes a move to toss it, and men shout, "No! No! Don't do it!"

In their eyes Jamey sees the hunger of four weeks at sea, and
no hope of touching shore or flesh of woman for another week or
more, and that week might as well be a month, a year. Land already
sighted, and they'll be staring at Boston soon, but with all these reports of looting British ships and tea dumped into the Boston harbor, the captain has already declared they'll unload their cargo and
load whatever's standing on the dock, but no man's allowed ashore
till they reach Philadelphia, and perhaps not even there, till they
see which way the flag flies.

He sees this in their eyes, and knows he has them, and Jamey
aches to glance shoreward to search for what Dugan promised
would be there, but he dares not break his hold on them.

"Then stand back a little," he commands. "Give me some air."

Growling and cursing the men in front push back.

"You're an evil man, Jamey," the big Londoner grumbles, "treatin'
your own shipmates in such a way."

"Fair is fair," Jamey shouts. "What am I offered to have this
lovely vision all to yourself?"

"How can we bid if we haven't seen the picture first?"

"But that's what you're bidding for, mates. I won't ask for much.
But a little something now, to make it worth me time."

"A marlin spike," someone growls.

"Serious now, or over the side she goes."

"A sip of my grog," shouts the Londonman, who's grabbing at his
own beard impatiently.

"Two sips," shouts another.

"Two sips and a thruppence," shouts someone else.

"My share a grog till we make Philadelphia," the Londonman bellows in despair.

The bidding begins to swell around him, and Jamey has a chance to glance over their heads, off to starboard. He sees what he's been waiting for and fans the bidding higher by lifting a corner of the orange cloth to reveal one marble thigh and calf.

From the quarterdeck a ship's officer is shouting something, but such a squabble has grown up around Jamey by this time that no one hears. Three officers are shouting when Jamey finally tears the orange cloth away, holds the picture high long enough for the whole crew to see the girl is all he promised, then he tosses her into their midst, and the seamen are howling, shoving, punching, kicking, climbing over one another to possess her.

Officers are firing pistols into the air and screaming through megaphones, but the crew has gone berserk and do not see the pirates or their ship until the grappling hooks are fast and the merchant vessel's deck is overrun with muskets and mercenaries and despisers of the British Empire, Dugan among them, a fierce-eyed man, who boards in the first wave and thrusts into Jamey's trembling hand a long pistol, with the muttered advice, *"Don't be afraid to use it, lad."*

CHAPTER 8

Leave it up to Joe

*N*o one has spoken for forty miles. It's main street Waikiki again, and Joe is double-parked in front of the Royal Hawaiian, refusing to look for an empty space, trying to decide what to do. There'll be no surfing. Yesterday's swell has disappeared, the ocean everywhere is uniformly flat, all the island's fringe is gone, and not a ripple from here to the horizon, no wind chop, not even a boat's wake, nothing but glass. Such days paralyze Joe. Goldie has paralyzed him too. He is helpless clutching the driver's wheel, and now as he sits here watching in his rearview, long Buicks pull up behind him, wait, honk, then wheel out to pass with a frown, sometimes a curse. Jonas entertains himself with that and idly guns his engine, and soon his truck begins to cough. It hacks and grumbles with one last harrumph and they are out of gas.

Behind them cabs are piling up, honking, busses, convertibles, limousines trying to get into the Royal's driveway to drop off airport arrivals.

Joe utters his first remark since Hooper and Goldie went swimming.

"Fucking cars anyway."

After a while, as the horns multiply, he climbs out, steps between a growling cab and his truck of cartoons and movie posters, and he throws open the rear doors with a clang, searching for his rusty gallon can.

Traffic is tied up both ways now as drivers slow to see what's going on. Joe just plods right through it, chopped golf knickers and no shirt and white face scowling at the pavement heat, a block long diagonal through waiting cars as he jaywalks to a Shell station, so that Goldie is behind the wheel and Hooper has to push their truck to a loading zone next to the Royal's service driveway.

He tells her to wait there, guard the truck, and he's just hiking over to Broome's to get his stuff, hoping as he walks away that Joe will intuitively devise some insult so outrageous that Goldie will disappear forever. And hoping Joe won't. Because there is still something about Goldie. The mirror face. But something more. He sees it in the parting smile. A chummy smile, with a slight jerking of the head. A locker room smile. It's hard not to smile back. But don't give her anything, neither plus nor minus charge. Beg off. If anything, offend her. She's like Mrs. Pike. Born to be reviled and shat upon. Some cutting remark at parting then, just to make her feel bad. Goldie, you have rank breath. No. No, leave it up to Joe. To Joe's impulse. Yes, Joe's in tune with the great pool we're all floating in here. Vibrations from this all-encompassing ocean run through him. *Que sera sera.* Leave it up to Joe.

CHAPTER 9

Ain't Misbehavin'

*H*ooper cuts through Broome's hedge with a *déjà vu* of doing this before, yesterday a warmup, and it's all starting over. That frontdoor sunburst of musty glass rubies, opals and jade is a never-blinking eye that watches a world through renegade weeds and watches Hooper climb the stairs, cross the curling floorboard paint. Silent key slides into the lock and he passes through the eye. Stop. Listen. Wading down the hallway with arms crooked out, he feels his way toward the skylight cascade, sure Mrs. Pike lurks there to catch him when the light first blinds.

Halfway along he stops again, listening for footsteps, hostile breathing. Nothing. Straighten up then, to walk erect and enter like the honest tenant you are.

Something makes him stop again.

Music?

Tinny music.

Faraway strings and reeds. Last breath of Paul Whiteman floating out a window. It fades, returns a little louder, a tiny violin backed by miniature guitars. Hooper's groping toward the sound. Wrapped in those notes there's a *déjà vu* from still another time, and he has to find the source.

At the shaft of light he hesitates, squints both ways. Instead of turning toward his room, he turns left in the direction Broome told him not to go. Violins are half-size in this new bend of hallway, infant guitars grow to tenor-ukes, chunking out jazz changes from the thirties, getting louder, yet strangely receding as door after unopened door passes him in this murky tunnel inhabited by no one else but Hooper. There are no roomers, nor any other rooms, just doors with numbers lining one long corridor where the one-woman vigilante committee waits in shadows to ambush her victims. She is posing as a siren now, and this music is her decoy luring him where he should not go.

The music stops receding. At the end of the hall, light as thin as lemonade leaks from a door crack. He stops there, listening, and feels a little safer. He knows the sound. It's the Quintet of the Hot Club of France, and Django Rinehart snaking around on his gypsified swing guitar. Half a minute and the record's over, an old 78,

29

scratching into the wide loops near the spindle, scratching and scratching and scratching and scratching and scratching.

Hooper waits, can't stand the scratching any longer, nudges the door a few inches, peeks in. He sees Broome half-reclining in a tilt-back red leather chair with footrest, bare feet pointing up and out like a duck's, same thin duck trousers, orange aloha shirt cluttered with ukes, panama hat down over his eyes to shield them from the lamp suspended just above him, on an invisible cord from an invisible ceiling, one of those green-shaded lamps that hang above pool tables, circling his red chair with lemony light, and hard to see anything beyond but the Victrola's scrollwork, its hood tipped back, and the silver hockey puck of a needle weight catching enough light from the lamp to glint where it wobbles with the spinning disk.

"Mr. Broome?"

Steady wheezing, and the needle scratch.

Louder, "Mr. Broome!"

"Yes. Who is it?"

"Me. Hooper Dunlap."

"Hooper. Well . . . run outta linen already?"

"No. It sounds like your record's finished."

"It is, is it?"

"Sounds to me like it is. Want me to turn it over for you?"

"Nope."

"Might ruin your needle."

"Heh heh. My needle was ruined a long time ago."

Broome tips back his panama, flashing its feather hand, and swings his big chair forward so he's sitting up.

"Yes, sir. A long time ago. Heh heh. Just played itself to pieces."

He sits chuckling, squinting past the circle of light into surrounding shadows, as if that long-lost needle is circling him and by fixing his stare he can still see it out there, once in every cycle.

"But you could play that tune for me one more time, young fella, you could do that."

Hooper steps quickly to the Victrola and sets the needle on the first groove. It's "Ain't Misbehavin'." He tries to raise the volume, but the knob turns both ways endlessly and nothing changes. Crank the machine. The record speeds up. Broome eases back to his half recline, drops the panama over his eyes, mutters, "Yep. Yep. Yep. Just played itself right down to the nerve," and a slow fading chuckle.

Next to the Victrola Hooper's eyes start to see the room. At his feet a heap of black ten-inch disks, not stacked, but heaped against the wall, whole and broken ones, dusty, spreading out across the floor like a mound of melting tar. Near the machine a long sofa piled with sheet music, and next to the sofa a small parlor organ, and leaning against the organ a bass fiddle with two strings taut, two dangling. It's a long room with a high fireplace facade in the middle of one wall, no chimney, a banquet room once, now hung like a pawnshop with guitars, ukuleles, fiddles, banjos, mandolins, a balalaika, guitar-harps, and some instruments he can't identify— Siamese squashes, giant all-day suckers from Mongolia. This is the room Hooper heard down the hall, one he's never seen, yet instantly knows. He was planning it for himself before he left Glendale, his own collection of 78s forming not a pile but a thin layer, his own row of strings amateurish by comparison—two guitars, a baritone uke, five-string banjo with a flabby head. A collection long ago completed by Broome.

Needle scratching again toward the spindle. Broome doesn't move. Hooper lifts the arm.

"Mr. Broome?"

"You can call me Jackson."

"Record's over."

"Jack's better than that. Call me Jack."

"Record's over, Jack."

"Some people like to call me Uncle Jack."

"You want to hear this record again, Uncle Jack?"

"Nope. Nope. You can take that needle off. Can't stand all that damn scratching."

Broome tilts forward, his hat slides to the back of his head as if attached to the chair. He seems to forget what he intended to do. Sits there.

"You play these instruments, Uncle Jack?"

Long silence.

"Used to. Heh heh. Most of 'em. Before my needle wore down."

"Mind if I fool around with one of these guitars a minute?"

"Lemme see your hands."

Broome sits with his palms against fat thighs until Hooper sticks one hand into the zone of light.

"Here," he grumbles, "here, here, here. Where I can see it."

Hooper shoves it under his nose, and Broome's head inclines, his glasses slip.

"You know that other fella?"

"Jonas?"

"Not one a his fingers longer than my thumb. Looks like he's been doing handstands on the ends of his fingers since the day he was born. Heh heh. All that's left is ten stubs."

Broome grunts out of the chair and shuffles across the room, lifts a guitar from its wall hook and hugs it next to his aloha shirt with both arms.

"But your fingers can *bend*, young fella. That's the first sign somebody might play sweet. If the fingers can bend."

He hands Hooper the guitar and, standing just outside the light circle, shoves his own hand in, palm down, arthritic, gnarled, warted, horny-nailed, knuckle-bunched.

"I don't play so much any more myself. But you play me something. I'm tired of that damn record."

Sitting spreadeagled on the sofa Hooper tunes up and looks around at instruments emerging from the walls, in among drawn blinds, and looks at Broome standing at the edge of his lemony pool. The way the hat shades his face Hooper can't tell if he's listening, watching, or even awake. Dangle-armed, potbellied beachcomber standing in the shade.

He plucks a chord and listens. Dark heavy wood from the Philippines. Broome says, "You know a song called 'Ain't Misbehavin'?'"

"I know that one, Uncle Jack."

"Fats Waller. 'Ain't Misbehavin'.' Used to have an arrangement of it myself."

"You want to show me how it goes?"

Both gnarled hands shove into the light. Broome studies them. "No. No. Heh heh. Got no fingers any more."

Hooper starts to play the tune, noodling its melody, humming, and Broome begins slowly to pace the outer rim of his circle, humming too, not the song, but something else, some random note flow that is not harmonious yet mysteriously does not collide. They're both humming as Hooper plays the chords. Broome mutters, "Lost 'em in a fight with a Chinaman."

Chuckling at that, and humming, while his tough feet scrape, he shuffles the perimeter. Hooper starts to sing.

> *No one to talk with. All by myself.*
> *No one to walk with, but I'm happy on the shelf.*
> *Ain't misbehavin'*
> *Savin' my love for you.*

"Yep, yep, yep," says Broome after every phrase.

Hooper hums another chorus, Broome hums, and sways a little now. His arms lift slowly almost to shoulder level, as if he's trying to remember a hula. He takes off his panama, holds it by the crown and salutes some imaginary audience.

"Yep. Yep. Yep. Yep. Yep."

It takes him four choruses to pace the circle one time, and he stops where he started. Hooper concludes with a soft arpeggio.

"Well, ya see there, young fella. It's all in the fingers. You play sweet, mighty sweet."

At the light's edge he stands as if dozing, rocking, and from the hall comes a soft clap of hands.

Hooper can't see who it is. Broome rocks, starting to hum again. The clapping continues, pushes the door open, in comes Mrs. Pike, blinking, smiling like a candybox grandmother.

"Very nice," she says, beaming at Hooper. "Very very nice. Isn't it nice to hear real music, Jackson?"

Broome doesn't answer. Humming. Rocking.

"Jackson! I said isn't it nice to hear real music!"

He steps to his big chair, sits, tilts back till his eyes are covered. The wheezing resumes.

"JACKSON!"

"Yes? What is it?"

"I SAID ISN'T IT NICE TO HEAR REAL MUSIC FOR A CHANGE?"

"Yes. Fine. Play anything you want."

She stands next to him for a long time, same blue and white print dress, her gray hair pulled back this time into a bun, staring at his mouth like a dentist getting ready to drill, and listening to his wheeze.

Softly to Hooper, "Poor man's fallen asleep."

She tips her head toward the door, signaling "Sssttt," and tiptoes into the hall, where Hooper joins her, and she tips her head again, ssstting him out onto a back porch of cobwebs and concrete washtubs.

She whispers, "It's his heart."

"Oh."

She looks around as if being followed, before she leans close and whispers, "You ever handle a gun?"

"No."

"You ever think about it?"

"No."

"Well, if you ever do, you let me know, ya hear?"

"Why?" Hooper is whispering too.

"Do you believe in Jesus?"

"In a way."

"You know this Vandermeer fella?"

"Jonas?"

"Ya know what he said when I asked him if he believed in Jesus?"

"What?"

"He said Jesus was a wino. Can you imagine that? I told him Mr. Broome never wanted to see his face around this rooming house again."

"I can't blame you for that."

"You drink tea?"

"From time to time."

"You come down to my room for a cup of tea one a these days. And a sweetroll. Have a chat. Fatten you up some." She pinches the thin skin at his waist. "I was listening at the door, ya know. We could use somebody like you."

"Who could?"

She doesn't answer. Suddenly she tenses like a commando, all muscles tightening into a slight crouch as she listens to something outside, then bursts through the screen door and into the backyard, shouting, "All right! All right!"

It's the boy in the parking lot washing cars again, evidently spilling water onto some part of Broome's yard, and as she approaches he squirts her with the hose.

CHAPTER 10

At the intersection

*L*emonade still leaks into the hall when Hooper passes Broome's door on the way to his own room. Distant wheezing. He thinks of stepping in to play another tune, but moves on. There'll be other times. He knows his way now, has found some limit, crossed some line, run the gamut from the front porch to back, the alpha and omega of Broome's, and he walks with insider's confidence along this dark wing toward the light at the intersection. Having intended to gather up his two armloads of belongings and move them for safety into Joe's truck, he sees now that that would be a mistake, and instead he's planning to put the bunk back together and straighten things some when, just before he steps into it himself, a woman appears in the cascade of light, a tall, swarthy dark-haired woman, vaguely Hawaiian, Eurasian probably, Oriental but not entirely, a Polynesian woman in the true sense of the word—many races. Wearing a muu-muu and standing in the light as if a little confused, as if ready to ask directions of the first person she sees. It is night in the middle of the city, at a usually busy but now deserted crossing, and under the lone street-light stands a beautiful woman lost, looking for assistance, and here comes Hooper, her savior and benefactor, about to ask, "Are you looking for someone?" when she steps out of the intersection and right past him into the gloom behind, leaving traces of plumeria and orchid and gardenia, not like the stewardess carried around her on the plane, but somehow the real thing, juice of real flowers pressed and sprinkled in her hair, causing Hooper to wonder how he must smell after twelve hours in Joe's truck. And watching, he sees her widen the stripe of lemonade and walk through and close the door behind her.

CHAPTER 11

The way things have always been

*A*t the opposite end of this long two-armed corridor divided by the lightwell, Hooper's door still stands open, the way he left it last night, and the bunk frame splayed, sleeping bag trampled, window up, bamboo splinters poking in, reaching for their draw ropes. The splinters mingle with vines outside, and he leans at the jamb pondering where to start, or whether he should walk back and knock on Broome's door and ask would he care to hear another chorus. Hooper wants to play a few more tunes now, he liked the bass on that Philippine guitar, imagines what a new set of strings could do for it, and how that woman, whoever she is, probably part Philippine herself, might like to listen and maybe, hearing some ancestral ring in the mahogany, might even begin to dance, the way Broome danced. Her flowered muu-muu is flickering in the light next to Broome's slow circle of the chair, when the bamboo splinters slide out of sight as if swallowed by vines. Joe's head appears at the sill.

Framed there, blue eyes flicking at the room. Hooper in the doorway sees just the head, the vines, *déjà vu* of scene two from yesterday, but as if Hooper can now see through the blinds.

Joe's urgent whisper, "Let's go."

"Where?"

"I spilled gasoline all over Goldie's pants. She's in the can at the Shell station rinsing them out. C'mon!"

"Where to?"

"How the hell should I know? Jesus Christ, Hooper, let's get going!"

He wants to linger and explore Broome's now, wants to get past this window scene and see what happens next (Broome takes from him the old guitar, gnarly hands go soft against the strings, and Hooper's dancing with the girl, long slow turns in and out of the light; Broome's chuckle; some old Hawaiian song he gives a gypsy rhythm to, and the swing of her muu-muu brushes haired bony leg).

"Soon as Goldie sees my truck gone, she'll head straight here," Joe says. "C'mon!"

No choice then. No time to linger. He shuts the door, locks it from the inside, gathers up and passes to Joe his shopping bag, his bedroll, climbs out after them, and follows Joe who hugs vines until they reach the building's front corner. Hunched like infantrymen they break for the truck double-parked half a block away, creep into the cab, and still hunched as if Goldies hide behind every tree, wait for the engine to catch.

In back Hooper's possessions merge with Joe's, and like yesterday, like last night they are on the road out of Waikiki. He wonders if every day will be like this, manic pattern of morning exits, and will there be no escaping it as long as he runs with Joe?

Shrug. Laugh. Has he only been here a few more hours than twenty-four? No. He has never lived anywhere else. This is the way things have always been, careening Oahu from shore to shore, and it would be nice to settle someplace, but leave it up to Jonas, for the time being anyway, until your blood thins out and you know what the whole island looks like.

CHAPTER 12

Trips and voyages: Today Becomes Tomorrow

*A*lready the pattern shifts.

They're heading south today instead of north, toward Diamond Head, world-famous crater, old home of all the soil beneath these hotels and restaurants, old mouth for lava floes that hissed into the sea, filled it, hardened there, took the force of currents and waves till the black stone started to crumble, changed its color, mixed with crumbled shell, went soft enough for ferns, which grow, die, decay, make soil softer yet, and softer, where coco palms rise, and wait, and wait, sprout fronds and milk pods that spill and seep, or dry and rot, and centuries pass. And it's time for the next eruption, next long lava flow of black which now carries Joe and Hooper right up against the ancient crater wall, and this lava too will crumble, make way for ferns. But not today. No, not while Hooper and Joe are traveling. Today it circles the island with a black ribbon, crosscuts and sections it, black striping through the green, and Joe's Reo could be a tiny fungus, amoeboid by-product, parasite creeping along feeding off the color itself, nosing through it, wherever the stripes go, crisscross and circle, and Joe who thinks he is driving will make side trips down a dirt road toward a beach he wants to show Hooper, where the diving is good, or bananas grow wild. But the creature gets hungry, wants to be back on the track that feeds it. Climb in and turn it loose until Joe wants to stop for another beach or inlet or waterfall. The truck's still hungry. And that's the way their days pass, Jonas groping at beaches, sometimes paddling out a few hundred yards, but sooner or later drawn back to his truck, glued, and his truck glued to the black ribbon that goes where it goes and on this island has no stopping place, just the circle and its shortcuts, and Hooper sticks with Joe, the master of something, while his truck takes them down one shore of the island and up the other and won't stop licking at the road.

Joe's sure that anywhere they stop long Goldie will catch up with them, imagines her submerged offshore with a periscope, tracking. So he doesn't mind the driving, the letting themselves be

driven. See them circumnavigating the island not once, but many
times, shortcutting the circle, zigzag and backtracking. The surf
stays flat and there's no real reason for Joe to stop at all.

Today becomes tomorrow.

Tomorrow the next day.

CHAPTER 13

Think dry

*M*ornings Hooper peeks at his
Bible, flips through Genesis at random and reads aloud while Jonas
drives.

"And Onan knew that the seed should not be his; and it came
to pass, when he went in unto his brother's wife, that he spilled
it on the ground, lest that he should give seed to his brother. And
the thing which he did displeased the Lord; wherefore, he slew
him also . . ."

"There's a lesson in that," Joe says.

"What is it?"

"Don't spill your seed."

"On the ground."

"Anyplace."

"You have to spill your seed someplace," Hooper says.

"Not necessarily."

"Not even in wet dreams?"

"I don't have wet dreams."

"Never?"

"Wet dreams are unnecessary. I have arranged it so that all my
dreams are dry."

"How do you manage that?"

"Control, man. Mind control. Dreams come from the mind, don't
they? Control the mind, you control the dream. Concentration,
Hooper."

"What do you concentrate on?"

"I think dry thoughts, that's all."

"For instance. Tell me a dry thought."

"Well, what I try to think about just before I go to sleep is my running board. It's all caked with mud and shit, ya know, and cracked from the sun, and I hate the whole fucking car, but especially the running board, the way it just hangs there, half dragging, half stuck to the door. Goddam middle-of-the-road piece of equipment if I ever saw one. You wanna keep your sack dry, just concentrate on something like that."

CHAPTER 14

Stay close to the truck

A week goes by.

Daily Jonas scans each view of the horizon for any sign of change in the ocean's face. On the sixth day, when he finally sees something, a flicker in the dawn light that seems to roll shoreward, but becomes, as Joe sprints to the water's edge to watch it, nothing more than that distant flicker, on that day Joe climbs back in and gives himself up to the whimsy and appetite of his Reo. And the Reo, satisfied at last, makes one more lap around the island and out to Sunset Beach again, where it comes to rest.

Joe and Hooper, tired of driving, talk about parking for a while, in the truck, till the big surf rises, or any surf at all; and in the truck for another quick getaway if Goldie finds them; and in the truck in case the asphalt stripe fifty yards away reaches out some night to grab it while they're sleeping and start it on the road back to Honolulu by itself.

Something about this new batch of lava and its parasites, on an island as beribboned as Oahu, you just have to stay close to the truck.

Witness the community Joe and Hooper just joined. This parking space—a stubbled clearing on the low cliff between two battered palms—which a week ago was empty, is now occupied by three other vehicles that function much like Joe's: an old Ford station wagon, the kind with real wood paneling; a La Salle sedan, with a mattress where the backseat used to be, extending into the trunk; and a prewar Dodge pickup, with a plywood shed over its backend. They're all nosed up close to the sandy precipice.

The owners are well known to Jonas. All come from California, all flew over about the same time he did, all are sitting out this unaccountable flat spell with the same apathy of outraged impatience, waiting through January for waves they expected in November. One or two are usually out here, or parked over at Makaha when Joe surfs there. This is the second time in history all four have arrived at Sunset on the same day. The first time it happened they named their mobile community *Sunset Automotive,* and in the breezeless heat of this Tuesday afternoon these are its citizens.

STANLEY MOREHEAD, called Sheepdog, baby-faced and trying to conceal it, not by growing a beard, but by letting stringy blond hair grow down to cover his ears and eyes, with no other part of him covered between the bridge of his nose and the line where his red pubic hairs start. A rotten pair of green satin basketball shorts hang from that line, and these reveal, as he hunkers at the cliff edge next to his station wagon's front bumper, half his buttock cleavage.

BYRON BASSIAN, called Black Bass, a weightlifter in the off-seasoon, has been known to shave everything and oil his body, although this isn't necessary, since his body's always chocolate brown and shining with sweat like a Turkish wrestler's. He combs his black hair back, so it hugs his neck and scoops down and out Johnny Weissmuller style. He's now lying on a blanket on the metal roof of his black La Salle, a beer can balanced on his chest.

WALTER CONQUEST is the only married man among them, and his truck, the pickup with the plywood shed, which was once a community showpiece—mats on the floor, shelves for food—is now going to hell. Walter's wife flew back to the mainland last week to have a baby, at home, where her mother could help. Walter would have gone with her, but the surf was due at about the same time, and she understood, and he is still waiting for both events. Short, balding, husky, a miniature Black Bass bending over a surfboard set on two sawhorses behind his pickup, sanding fiberglass away to patch a tiny hole in the balsa. Sweat keeps falling from his forehead onto the sanded surface, and Walter keeps wiping it off with a red bandana.

Joe's engine coughs and dies. No one moves. Stanley hunkers hypnotized by the sea's absolute blue flatness. Black Bass is a chocolate corpse about to slide into it. The only sound is the ssshhh ssshhh ssshhh of Walter's sandpaper. Fronds hang limp. Joe and Hooper sit surprised by the sudden stopping after all this endless jolt and steady rumble, bodies dazed, eyes glazed, staring at hundreds of miles of nothing.

Sheets of glare bank off the water, bend through windshield

cracks. With no more breeze of motion to cool it, the cab is an oven, and both their backs stick to leatherette, catch puffs of cotton stuffing. Like a water clock, drops of sweat fall from Hooper's chin onto his stomach, run down his belly to be soaked up in undershorts. Still nothing has moved but Walter's arm.

Joe sets a finger on his horn. One feeble note of a distant, dying clarinet trickles away over the cliff edge.

After a while Sheepdog rises, hitches up his basketball trunks. They drop again to his pubic line. Blinded by hanging hair he feels along one fender to the door of his wagon, reaches in, presses the horn—a short waaaaaaa, stifled by dead air and unmoving sea—and hunkers back down next to his fender, like a priest of that New Guinea cargo cult sending out signals for some great bird of an American airplane that landed once in 1944 and will never return.

Joe honks his horn again, tiny echo of Sheepdog's.

This time, after a long interval, Black Bass flexes one pec, sends his beer can tumbling off the roof to land on an overturned skillet. Clank.

A third time Jonas honks, reedier still, as if the last signal-bearing copper thread is ready to shrivel into silence.

Walter Conquest straightens up from his sawhorses, inhales and flexes, strides to the fallen beer can, hurls it at Joe's truck and shouts, "Goddam you, Vandermeer, you told me there was going to be some *surf!*"

To drown him Jonas leans on his horn, and the thin note suddenly blares out OOOOOOOOOOOOOOOOO, then sputters, goes reedy, eeeeeeeeee, and flicks back and forth from treble to bass as circuits open and close under his rusty hood.

To give this some tempo Hooper reaches out, starts rapping on the door with his knuckles, tank tank tank. From the La Salle roof, Bass takes the offbeat with one dark arm's lift and fall—tank (whong) tank (whong) tank (whong).

Again Sheepdog rises, hops up on his own running board and, reaching in, syncopates a waaaaaaaa-waa-waa, waaaaaaaaa-waa-waa over Joe's erratic OOOOOO's and eeeeee's. Walter throws aside his sandpaper, finds two more cans and with one in each hand, like maracas, attacks Joe's back door, ka-plink ka-plink ka-plink ka-plink ka-plink, eight beats to every bar, forcing Hooper out onto the dry grass to double his own beat with both hands open-palmed working on the truck's shady side.

Now Black Bass rolls off his roof. In two bounds he's onto Joe's, on hands and knees pounding with both closed fists, plow plow plow. All this starts the truck rocking. Joe's bassoons and clarinets are barely heard in the crash of hollow metal. He leaves the horn section to Sheepdog, who's still blaring, and starts his engine, guns it till the fenders rattle, bumpers squeal. Then Walter is coming at the back door with a frying pan, smashing with great arc swings of his short brawny arms, and Joe's truck is their common drum, pounding and kicking, Bass on the roof now jumping up and down, Hooper slamming one door back against a fender, all yelling, starting to howl, grunting toward some chant they can't find words for.

At that moment, up the sandy cliff comes Goldie, returning from a walk along the beach, wearing a pair of somebody's jeans too big for her and cinched at her waist with a rope, cocking her head at this spectacle, whimsical grin. Jonas knew she would be here someplace, and now does not hesitate, sees his chance. Engine running, he jumps out and catches her by the knees and shoulders. Before the others have time to stop pounding he has thrown his back door open and tumbles Goldie in.

She tries to laugh it off. "Jonas! What are you *doing*?" Climbing toward him through the reek and rubble.

He slams the door and ties it fast with a snag of rope already hanging there.

Inside she's pounding, her laughing face out the glassless window. "Jonas! Jonas!"

But Joe's around front, climbing into the cab, and up on top Black Bass has found the focus for their chant, shouting, "Goldie, Goldie, Goldie, Goldie!" as he stomps the roof. Little Walter smashing in the truck's sunny side with his skillet shouts, "Goldie, Goldie, Goldie!" And Hooper, and Sheepdog Stanley who joins him at the back door, as they both begin to push, are chanting her name. While Goldie, not daring to stick her head out the square hole now, is yelling "Hooper!" as if only he can rescue her.

He looks up and sees her in there—squared temples, high cheeks, jutting chin—all one shaded sketch of Joe—animal fear in Joe's eyes peering out of Joe's cage, and something Hoop would like to push into a chasm forever is between his hands. Blistering heat of metal feels good against his palms as he earns the right to push harder. For a moment he actually believes a good shove now will do it. He leans to the work, watching his feet and Sheepdog's finding footholds in the stubble, inhales the heady goat smell of unwashed bodies. They grunt the incantation.

Jonas has released the handbrake, jumps out pushing at the left front fender, and his wheels roll slowly toward the edge, pass it, downtilt. Giving one last back-shove as he leaps, Bass leaves the roof, shouting "Gol-deeeeee," and Walter's final skillet swing breaks the skin, punches a hole in Joe's Reo. He too shouts. In rising frenzy all five chant her name. The truck noses down the fifteen-foot incline toward the beach, where it lurches, levels out, finally stops with its front wheels catching the last lick of froth.

CHAPTER 15

No choice

*L*ow tide. Joe's truck is sitting on hardpacked sand. Half a moon coats the world with dim gauze. While the other citizens of Sunset Automotive huddle in Walter's pickup drinking wine and filling his plywood room with cigarette smoke to keep out stray mosquitoes, Hooper and Goldie are embracing again. Near the tideline no mosquitoes buzz. Aside from that advantage, he isn't too happy about this arrangement. But he has no choice.

When the truck stopped rolling they all whooped past it into the water, splashing, grabassing, swimming out a couple of hundred yards and racing in. All but Jonas. He kept swimming. When they got back to shore he had turned parallel to the beach and was still swimming, and when half an hour had passed he had swum out of sight into the afternoon glare, and didn't return until dusk, by which time, Hooper, getting hungry, had been compelled to enter the Reo to forage for food. Goldie was still in there, shaken and brooding. He offered her a peanut butter sandwich, and one thing led to another.

She cried a while, told him how she had hitched a ride out three days ago with Walter, figuring Joe would end up here sooner or later, and how she had slept in Walter's truck, but definitely not *with* Walter, not at a time like this, his wife expecting, and Goldie would hate for any woman to do that to *her*, nor with Bass whom she considers too arrogant, nor with Sheepdog, mainly because, from what Hooper can deduce, he has trouble getting an erection. The tears falling into her peanut butter accused Hooper of somehow suspecting, for instance, that she *would* sleep with Walter, a lack of faith which simply added to her general injury at the hands of those Goldie wanted only to befriend. Hooper was trying to leave with the rest of the peanut butter when she begged him to reveal what Jonas had against her as a *person*. A long moment then of searching the darkness for her eyes, and starting to answer. But before he could speak she was hugging him, begging him to talk to Joe on her behalf, and soon, as if to reward him in advance for this service, fooling around with his swimming trunks. And since in the truck dark he could not see Goldie's face, but could, as she unbuttoned her aloha shirt, see dark curves softened by moonlight trickling in, her slight excess of belly flesh promising tasty excesses of abandon, he is now taking her again, is allowing her to be taken by him, slow and easy so the truck won't rattle and attract attention from the cliff.

Joe is not in the front seat this time, yet Hooper finds himself glancing up at the empty space behind the wheel, as he did that first night. He feels oddly like a traitor. Not for taking Joe's girl again. It's his own vulnerability. He should have grabbed the peanut butter and run.

He listens to the tide slapping outside the truck. Little cups of water splat along the hard sand, yards away.

Slap splat becomes an urgent whisper from Goldie. Answering, he speeds up, and they are rocking together inside the littered Reo. When it starts rocking with them, loose parts begin to rattle. Doors jiggle. Springs squeak. Something clanks in back, like a bumper falling off. He thinks Oh shit, but can't stop now, wouldn't stop. Tide gone. Jonas gone. Hold this hot coil winding inside, wind it tight before he lets it go. Jingling metal fills the gauze-coated night, then Goldie moaning. Hooper knows she's on the edge and tries to hold her there, but squirming hips won't let him. Above them Walter's horn begins to blare.

Doors slam. Two more horns are blaring out over the beach. Waaaa waaaaa, ooogah ooogah. Three starters grinding, and Sunseteers yell, gunning engines. None of this slows Hooper down till the rain of tincans and bottles begin to fall on Joe's roof. By that time Goldie's hips are still. She's satisfied. She giggles, "Those crazy *guys*. What are they going to *do?*"

Hooper doesn't know, just lies here, body glued to hers with the warm night's liquid, expecting skillets, bricks, sawhorses, perhaps all three cars leaping the cliff like a nightmare panzer divsion to crush them into the sand.

But the volley suddenly stops. Doors slam again. The mosquitoes, Hooper's allies tonight, have found and surrounded the revelers, who now slap and shout as they scramble back into Walter's truck, crazed with itch and blinding swirl of insects in the dark, Jonas bellowing, "Fuckers! Fuckers! Fuckers!" Then silence.

Slap.

Splat.

"Hooper?"

"Yeah?"

"Was it good?"

"Sure it was good."

"Did you want to do it some other way?"

"Hell no. It was fine."

"I felt like you were trying to tell me something, toward the end."

"No, it was grand, Goldie. Believe me."

"I like my boys to be happy."

"Am I one of your boys?"

"Oh, you're special, Hooper."

"Why's that?"

"You like to do it the regular way."

"I like to do it all kinds of ways."

"Well everybody else around here has a one-track mind."

"What do you mean?"

"You take that Byron Bassian. He just likes to lie on his back with his hands behind his head and make a girl do all the work. He thinks all those greasy muscles make everybody so hot, all he has to do is lie there and smirk and flex. He's disgusting."

"What about Sheepdog?"

"I told you, Sheepdog's a softie. According to him, he's only been hard once in his life, when he was doing a headstand. The one time we got together, I told him to go into a headstand if he felt like it and we'd see what happened. And he did. And I tried everything I could think of, and *nothing* happened, absolutely nothing."

"Joe isn't a softie, is he?"

"Oh no, not Jonas. Joe just likes to do . . . other things, that's all."

"Like what?"

"Oh, you know. He likes me to put it in my mouth while he kneels on his board and pretends he's paddling. Isn't that something?"

Hooper tries to visualize it. "How do you feel about that?"

"I don't mind. But now he won't let me do *anything*. You promise you'll talk to Jonas for me?"

"I'll do whatever I can."

She snuggles closer. "But you're still special, you know that now, don't you? Maybe next time we won't have those crazy guys around with their beer cans and everything." She giggles.

Next time, he thinks. *Next* time? Jesus.

CHAPTER 16

Sunset Automotive

*H*ooper wakes to the sound of water lapping. The rear door swings open. Where froth drags back around his ankles, Joe is pulling one board out.

Goldie snorts, snoring, naked, curled like a puppy next to Hooper, who tries to feign sleep, hearing anger in the hasty way the door clangs, the way Joe yanks his board. Joe spent the night with Walter. Maybe he's moving out now for good, leaving this truck to Hooper and Goldie and the tide. Hooper can't blame him.

When Joe says nothing, Hooper opens one eye and sees on his face not anger at all. What he heard in the clang and drag was haste pure and simple. Joe does not even look at Hooper or Goldie, doesn't see them, doesn't care. Because yesterday's ritual sacrifice succeeded. Some wave-source heard the frantic drumming and their chant. Jonas now is paddling toward the six-foot swell the sea spirits conjured overnight.

Walter, Sheepdog, and Bass are heading for it too, dropping their boards just past the truck's front end, where the water's a few inches deep. As they pass they peek in the window, curious, but not at all surly, as Hooper had feared, figuring they might for their various reasons hold Goldie against him. No. The rise of surf erases all such petty differences. Only Bass holds a grudge. A small hardly noticeable but niggling grudge. Only Bass was aiming cans at Hooper last night. Only Bass wants to get his hands on Goldie, as he has every night since she arrived, and can't. Walter is being faithful to his wife. And Sheepdog isn't interested, being not only impotent, but a practicing mystic who long ago made it clear that if he's going to copulate with anything it will be the very cosmos itself.

As they move past the truck and toward the breaking surf, follow Sheepdog. Watch him paddle now with a classic Zen commitment to the wave and to the day it's breaking in. Unable to see anything clearly through his mat of hanging hair, he contemplates the breaking place the way a Zen archer will contemplate his target. And just as that archer will hit his target without looking, without aiming, just by giving himself up to the inevitable relationship between bow, arrow, and heap of straw, so Sheepdog hurls himself—the arrow—onto the ocean surface, paddles blindly, full of faith, and somehow arrives at the breaking place at the optimum moment, during a lull between sets, giving himself time to grope around there until he is in perfect position, right next to Joe, who arrived there moments before, not by faith, but by calculation.

Around these two the others group—little Walter, big Bass, lank Hooper on Joe's spare board, and now Goldie, paddling the board of Mrs. Conquest, and wearing Mrs. Conquest's two-piece suit.

Nobody talks. They sit dangling legs in the water, shoulders hunched, silently watching the horizon. All but Sheepdog. He faces shore, certain he'll feel the first wave coming and *know* when to start. He seldom misses a wave this way. Earlier in his career he would assume a lotus position during lulls, fold his legs into his lap and sit there facing shore motionless till the next wave was almost upon him. Then he'd break the lotus and hurl his body at the board, and this very motion, like a loosened spring, would propel him into a wave almost without paddling. It was a legendary stunt, described on beaches from Tijuana to San Francisco. But he gave it up after the day he failed to break the lotus in time and got swamped while his legs were still knotted. Unable to swim or even float, he nearly drowned before one last wave rolled him up onto the sand, a legless beggar, spitting and retching and by that time too weak to break the position alone.

Next to Sheepdog, facing the opposite direction, Byron Bassian sits watching the horizon but also sideways eyeing Hooper. Bass sees himself as an ass bandit of wide reputation. For him surfing is one of several ways to attract women. When parking at Sunset he makes almost nightly raids on nearby towns. Bass will race all the way to Honolulu if necessary to return next day with tales of this *pelt* and that *snatch*. Only Goldie has kept him out here three nights straight. Now he feels obliged to confront Hooper in some way, not in a major way, since Bass isn't very brave, and he secretly admires Hooper for whatever it is he used to woo her. But for his own satisfaction Bass is breathing heavily through his nose, eying him. He looks so tough—long jaw, spread nose, narrow eyes—that when he tries to look tougher, as he does now, by frowning and furrowing his brow, he becomes a huge bashful infant. From time to time he eyes Goldie to see if she knows he is eying Hooper.

But she is eying the skyline with Joe and Walter. Only Hooper notices the Geronimo squint Bass is giving him. The first wave of a new set is humping blue-green and glassy. Four start paddling for position in front of it. Hooper holds back. Bass, noting this, holds back too, flashing him the squint again. Hooper figures this challenge for some test of his wave-riding prowess, and so starts to concentrate on the second wave, building out there now.

When he glances at Bass, to see how he's lining up for the take-off, the squint has become a dark leer.

"From the sound of things last night, old Goldie was going like a kangaroo."

"Better than a kangaroo."

"Did she sit on it for ya?"

"She was so busy I can't remember all the things she did."

Rush of water lifts them. Bass is so distracted by this conversation, he takes off late, finds himself closer to the curl than he likes to be, gets caught in the upsnap, and somersaults into the soup yelling, "Goddam sonofabitch!"

Hooper, forgetting how fast the waves here break, doesn't cut soon enough and loses it too. They both end up swimming for their boards and find themselves far inshore, paddling back together.

It is a way of getting acquainted, this leisurely arm-stroking side by side, fellow countrymen twenty-five hundred miles from home, now losers of the same wave, bobblers in the same boil of white water. Ahead of them a new swell rises, carrying Jonas, and behind him, Goldie. Another common denominator. They exchange fraternal squints.

Bass is leering. Hooper can't quite muster a leer. This Goldie, she's a special case. Tenacious doesn't begin to describe her. She's been insulted, beaten, robbed, doused with gasoline, pushed off a cliff, and still coming back for more. He watches her pursuing Joe across the green wall. She rides perfectly trimmed, a brown, breasted, slender version of Jonas—knees bent to the same angle, palms flared for balance, hair plastered, and water beads clinging to a stern face concentrating on a wave that sends its color to her eyes. The resemblance is heightened by their watery backdrop, by a feature-sharpening sunlight that sharpens Hooper's uneasiness too —dulled last night by dark and lust. It's uncanny. Unnatural. Joe's body and spirit twin. Hooper begins to lose his appetite for the breakfast he's been looking forward to. He has done all he can do for Joe in this matter. He wants to get away. Joe will just have to solve it by himself. Hooper still believes in Joe's ability to devise some way to dispose of her for good. He hates to think what it will have to be. But, *que sera sera*. Leave her up to Joe. Meanwhile he'll keep his distance. From both of them. For the time being anyway. He begins to see that Joe is on one trip, Hooper on quite another. And whatever Joe is master of, well, Hooper will leave that one up to Jonas too, along with his mirror-girl.

Knowing Goldie's persistence, the safest thing might be to leave Oahu altogether, try another island, head for Maui and hike through that old crater, or track the northern beaches of Kauai, where no

one has lived for fifty years. Or try an island even farther south—
Tahiti, Bora Bora, Nuku Hiva, Tubuai. He's dreamed of all those
southern islands. Maybe now's the time. No rush of course. But he
could spend a while in Honolulu checking on boats sailing south.
Yes, there's a plan. And hang around Broome's some. And fondle
that guitar. But when? And how to get back to town?

Well, as some forgotten guru once told him, if you hold your
hand out long enough, sooner or later something will fall from the
sky. Hooper believes in such things.

Celestial gift takes the color of a Hershey bar when they reach
the breaking place and in another lull Bass resumes their conversation. Joe, Goldie, and Walter are far inshore paddling toward
them. A few yards away Sheepdog sits facing the trees. Sheepdog
seldom speaks, and then only in cryptic mumblings: *Allah moves
in strange ways . . . Hark, the herald angels sing.*

"Listen," Bass says, "I got me a little gash over in Wahiawa is the
original kangaroo kid." He humps the air right in front of him.

"She Hawaiian?"

"Shit, I don't fool around with Hawaiians, man. She's Eskimo.
Her old man's in the army over at Schofield. She *never* gets tired
of it."

"I don't guess I've ever seen a real Eskimo."

"Hey listen, Hooper." He glides in close and leans toward him.
"All these other guys are so hung up on waves and all that shit, I
can't get any of 'em to go into town with me to fool around. You
wanna drive over there with me some night? To Wahiawa?"

"Sure. Why not."

"She's got this sister she wants me to fix up. We could have us a
kangaroo *party.*"

"When you want to go?"

"Tonight?"

"Hell yes."

"Whoooo-eeeee!" Bass yells, and whips his board around as a new
wave lifts. He humps his fiberglass a few times, shouts, "I think
anybody who says surfing is better than screwing is sick!"

Sheepdog, just before the wave reaches them, eyes invisible behind his dripping blond veil, turns and says, "There's more than
one way to skin a cat."

CHAPTER 17

Hooper's Ride

*T*heir three boards line up, Bass and Hooper craning back, gauging the time to dig arms in, buddies now, saddle partners, Sheepdog waiting prone, apart, attuned to whatever small vibration change marks the sound of an approaching swell. Now all three paddle, crouch, ride, slide together down the wave's bosom.

Bass is farthest out from the curl, where the ride is easy and there's nothing to do but stand there, which is what he mainly likes, strike a pose, one arm out and one crooked back, thighs flexed for maximum definition, and hold this for photographers hidden in the brush along the beach.

Inside, next to the curl, where white foam chases his board's tail, Sheepdog rides. Like Joe he finds each wave's most critical spot and hangs onto it, where the wall is steepest, the ride fastest, the risks greatest. Sometimes from a distance you can only tell them apart by the hanging hair. But there's another difference. Watching Joe is like watching a precision instrument perform. You admire the smooth play of interworking parts, and it takes a long time to tire of the same perfect movement repeated. Watching Sheepdog is like watching a seed pod blown in the wind. It might land in the right place and sprout, or it might drown in a rainstorm. Sometimes he shoots tunnels no one else would dare attempt, simply because he can't see the danger he's in. Sometimes he's totally buried under tons of white water almost anyone else could have avoided. Jonas never takes his eyes off the wave he's riding. He doesn't trust the ocean at all. Sheepdog lives in constant peril. He trusts the ocean the way an astrologer trusts the stars.

Hooper falls somewhere in between. For moments at a time he can muster Joe's kind of concentration. Then things distract him, his mind wanders, the way his arms and legs wander searching for some gravity center along the wave. And during that peak moment in every good ride, when the sea's tremble climbs through balsa up his bones to bind all sound and sight and motion, then he can believe with faith like Sheepdog's. It never lasts long. The moment passes, belief dissolves into memory. But some moments are longer than others—like this wave's. Already free of Goldie he feels as if he's starting somewhere for the first time, again. This is the one thing he most expected from these islands. Lots of beginnings. A new beginning every day. And this ride is a long, glassy, sharp-edged, tubing birth canal that carries him almost to shore, revives his appetite, starts his stomach gargling for breakfast.

A fine euphoric ride, sharpened by the prospect of whatever morning meal awaits him—peanut butter, pork and beans, pine-apple and cold sardines, anything, it doesn't matter. Gurgling he whirls his board, heads for the break and rides again, grows light-headed with the lack of food, and soon grows reckless, catching waves late, or early, or right on time, with that loose drugged headi-ness you feel as a child plunging in and out of pools all afternoon, you splash and shout at friends and fall off the diving board, finger-tips pucker with the water's warmth. That feeling's channeled into the three or four waves of every head-high set, so delicious that no one paddles in to eat. Lunchtime comes, and Hooper has the rhythm of the day—long ride, paddle back, the space you lose and recover when the white water piles over you, shimmering lulls of endless noon, and the way waves hump, flickering the deep face, shading as they roll, growing into bars of shadow, jumping at sun-light, and then you flatten, no longer timing it. Flatten and go.

The day's rhythm soaks him. Between rides salt cakes him. His cheek skin tightens, eyes burn as he stares at the water rim and at its left edge, Kaena Point, ten miles off, black arm stretched to catch the sun if it ever falls, like another island he can paddle to if this one sinks. Call it another beginning, if this time starts to end. Is-lands, distant promontories always comfort Hooper like this. The islands off the beach at Mazatlan. Catalina out in front of Long Beach. He thinks of Monterey. With Joe he spent a week once in the town of Santa Cruz, where you can stand on beaches and look across the bay toward Monterey, and that peninsula is the ridged and mossy island of your dreams, the somewhere else you can al-ways get to. They were never enough, those offshore islands, just the illusion of beginnings, but better than the western mainland, the country where Hooper felt everything ending. The only part of California he cared about at all was the zone between the ocean and the Coast Highway. He and Joe traveled it north and south for years, a strip a mile wide at its widest, its southern leg the last edge of the Great American Desert, long lip of land soothed at last by cooling sea. From Santa Barbara north, log-strewn miles of empty beach, tide pools, seal country, scattering of resort towns, and mountains sloping to the water. This is what he always wanted California to be, had grown up expecting it to be, kept waiting for the rest of it to become, and it kept becoming something else. He early felt the loss of something he had barely glimpsed, slipping out of focus, something he deserved to gaze on, had in fact been promised, but which began to recede from view the day he was born, not knowing that this is nothing new, it has always been the same, the main difference being that the Pacific's edge sitting where it does, the promise there has been louder and the loss keener for all the voyages halted. So Hooper started gazing at the haze of coastal islands and savoring, among the rock blues and kelp greens, odd hints of tropical cobalt, random currents that sometimes drifted north of Cancer to tickle his leg and glaze his eye.

Now that warmth and color is not just tickling his leg, it is surrounding him, Pacific succulence. He looks at the closest island, remembering his first glimpse of it, from the circling window, beauty spot on the face of the deep, feels again that ache to possess the contour, or be possessed, by island, by the sea contouring it, by beaches where sea and island overlap, the shape itself containing all the rumble chants and stop of time he knows was dissolving the moment Captain Cook's sectioned spyglass first pulled this coastline into focus, if not before, yet refuses to know that, and so begins to dream of other islands, warmer water, softer greens, farther south. This time it's the south you only reach by sea, because if there is such a thing as a country of endless beginnings, there's only one way for him to get there. He can't fly in, or drive Joe's Reo. He has to sail.

"Seen from the sea," (says Melville of Tahiti) "the prospect is magnificent. It is one mass of shaded tints of green, from beach to mountain top; endlessly diversified with valleys, ridges, glens, and cascades. Over the ridges, here and there, loftier peaks fling their shadows, and far down the valleys. At the head of these, the waterfalls flash out into the sunlight as if pouring through vertical bowers of verdure. Such enchantment, too, breathes over the whole, that it seems a fairy world, all fresh and blooming from the hand of the Creator."

Add a dusky blackhaired maiden who resembles no one you have seen before, suckling pig on a spit, wade ashore dripping, and she plucks a hot morsel to place between your lips. Softly bite the glistening fingers. Ten days on the island of Oahu, and these are Hooper's dreams as surf soaks his mind and his unfed body till sundown.

CHAPTER 18

The Getaway

*R*ed-cheeked, bulbous-nosed, curly-headed, round and squat, with a checkered vest hugging his satisfied belly, yellow and white like a hillock of butter cubes, and a golden watch fob curving below his navel, and a swallowtail coat, Abner Dunlap sits at a circular table, looking at his handful of cards the way he'd look at a baby in a crib, both cheeks pushing at his eyes. His chubby white fingers close around a short stack of blue chips, lift, set them noiselessly on top of an enormous, multicolored mid-table pile.

"Raise you another fifty dollars, my friend."

His opponent, a pale, slender, steady-eyed man with a curving black moustache, covers the bet and calls.

"Three queens," says Abner, turning his cards face down on the table, watching his opponent with the same benevolent eyes.

"Let's see 'em."

"Gentleman's poker. I believe that's what we agreed to play."

The man reaches behind one broad table leg, and his arm, when it reappears, is longer by three feet of shotgun. Abner is staring into the twin barrels as if they are binoculars.

"Before I left Fredericksburg," he says, "seems like every other day somebody'd be talkin about how hospitable folks are over here in this part of Virginia."

"We welcome all honest men and good-lookin' women. I'd like to see those three queens."

Circling Abner's eyes are rings of sweat to match the barrel holes. If he doesn't turn his cards over, this man will blow his brains out. Yet if he turns them, he's a dead man too. He only holds a pair of eights. His fat hand slides across the table, stalling.

A small boy in homespun overalls appears at the shoulder of the steady-eyed man.

"Beg your pardon, mister."

"Git away from me, son."

"You own that black stallion out in front?"

"Yeah. What about it?"

"Looks to me like somebody's trying to steal the saddle."

The man's head jerks an inch to see the boy, and in that instant

Abner upends the table, ducking as the gun goes off. The double blast knocks out a big chandelier, and in the crash of crystal and spilling chips and mayhem of startled voices, Abner shoves his shoulder into the boy's stomach and plunges crouching through a side door into darkness. Twenty yards down the alley he cuts between two sheds, hoists the boy to the flanks of a waiting mare, grunts his own wide rump and bulging gut into the saddle, and they are galloping for timber country, swallowtails flapping, watch fob clinking on a button of his butter-cube vest.

Ten minutes of hard riding, then on a ridge above the town he stops, listening for hoofbeats. It's quiet everywhere. From his saddlebag he lifts an oilcloth package, unwraps a large bar of saltwater taffy, breaks it, and hands half to the boy who, munching, asks gummy-mouthed, "You make any money, Paw?"

"No, I did not make any money."

"Didn't lose any, did ya?"

"That's none a your business."

"Why don't you ever win, Paw?"

The town below is a sprinkle of sparks on a black blanket, and along this ridge the only sound for several moments is the snap and crackle of sticky teeth pulling at the taffy.

Finally Abner says, "For the simple reason that very few people in this world have any sense of humor. That man down yonder, for example, not an ounce of humor in his flinty soul . . ."

"Maw says . . ."

"And she's another, Davey. If your maw could see the humorous side of anything for ten minutes of her life . . ."

"Maw says she ain't riding one more mile. Says you're gonna lose every dollar we've got 'fore we even git to Tennessee. Says she's taking the wagon back to Fredericksburg herself first thing in the morning."

Long pause of snicks and taffy crackles. "Davey, you might as well learn something right here and now. A woman will say that every time."

"Say what, Paw."

"Tell you she's gonna go someplace she don't want to go just to keep you from going someplace she don't think she wants you to go."

"Where do you want to go, Paw?"

"One a these days we're going to get to Memphis, Davey. Memphis, Tennessee. Where there's riverboats as big as hotels, and I heard once about a card game there that went on for seventeen days . . ."

Some unseen light source flames the polished cheeks, sends out

glimmers from his fleshy eyes, as if his arcing watch fob catches
every spark from the distant town, channeling one upward beam.
"Why Davey, if we can somehow get to Memphis, Tennessee . . ."

Hooper's Dungarees

*A*t the Los Angeles Goodwill
a long table with a four-sided low railing. From the unsorted heap
of jeans, levis, dungarees, coveralls, and cant-bust-ems, something
about one pair intrigues him—the naval cut, the sturdy thread, the
paleness of long use that links any wearer with times past. Gray
along the inner waistband the name is stenciled, NATHAN MENDO-
CINO. He imagines the trousers in Mendocino's jumbled garage, a
general clean-up, the bundle of useless clothes thrown at a Goodwill
Industries van, and Nathan's wife at the curb, relieved, fulfilled,
hands on hips to watch all that clutter drive out of her life. Hooper
sees Nathan on a giant carrier, Seaman Third Class, when the
dungarees were new, walking from flight deck to chow hall, war on,
and Nate has seen New Guinea, Saipan, Wake Island, Guam. When
they hit Oahu, it's two weeks shore leave for rest and recoup, dungarees hung out to dry, and Pearl Harbor sun bleaches one shade
lighter. Streets, beaches, docks, decks, Nathan moody at the gun
mount while waves fan back from from the prow.

A perfect fit. Beltless loops, metal button tight-sewn two inches
below Hooper's navel. Right hip pocket gone, to leave a blue square
on the pale. Left one holds a black wallet. Thighs uniformly faded,
and from the thighs downward, as the blueness darkens, the color
seems to have drained the way glass slips in old lead-paned windows, collecting toward the bellish bottoms, elephant flaps resting
one edge of each circle, whenever Hooper stops walking, on each
splayed slab of brown flaking instep.

CHAPTER 19

Water Buffalo

*W*hen Bass bought his '38 La Salle from a yeoman stationed at Pearl, the deal included a watch coat wadded behind the seat. As they pull up near the house in Wahiawa, he slips into his watch coat, zips it to his chin and instructs Hooper to get inside the thick woolen poncho Bass sleeps in.

An hour past sundown and ten miles inland, it's sultry. Hooper says, "It's too damn hot for a poncho, Bass."

"Do what I say, man, or you'll die."

Thus bundled they slide through a hibiscus hedge, cross a yard littered with coconut husks, and climb the backporch stairs. Bass raps four times. The door is opened almost instantly by a brown, moon-faced girl who steps back and lets them enter. It's like walking into a deepfreeze. Hooper's throat closes with the shock. Air-conditioners whine from all directions. Every window is closed, all blinds pulled. Arctic currents rush from wall to wall.

As the door latch clicks, the girl throws her arms around Bass's neck. He lifts her off the floor in a bear hug. From that position he says, "Honey, this is my old surfing buddy, Hooper Dunlap. Hooper, this is the little gal I was telling you about, Trudy Tlingsit Mac-Arthur, the sweetheart of the Aleutians."

Trudy giggles, nuzzling Bass. Hooper hugs his poncho close and grunts, "Hi," marvels at the ball of frosty steam his mouth makes, and marvels at the sheer kimono that seems to be all Trudy's wearing.

Bass phoned ahead to set things up. Now Trudy's sister appears in the kitchen, also brown, moon-faced, about five feet tall, wearing a high-necked Hong Kong jacket, bell-cuffed trousers with green, dragon-headed serpents climbing toward her waist. Her name is Blanche. She and Trudy are twins. They flew down together from Fairbanks when Trudy's husband was transferred to Honolulu, and all three live together here. The husband, an army staff sergeant, an M.P. with night duty at Schofield Barracks, has met Bass and thinks he's courting Blanche.

Blanche asks Hooper if he wants a bottle of beer.

Without thinking he says yes, then sees the next ball of frost dissolve in front of him, reconsiders, looks to Bass for guidance. Bass says, "You and Blanche sit down someplace and get yourselves acquainted. Me and Trudy have got to go see a man about a kangaroo."

Still bearhugging her inside the canvas arms of his watch coat, her dangling toes six inches from the floor, Bass carries tittering Trudy through the kitchen and out of sight.

From the refrigerator Blanche pulls two bottles of Primo, pries the caps off. She drinks from the bottle and watches Hooper slyly as her head tilts for a long swallow.

The cold bottle's touch is some final trigger. He starts to shiver. His stomach contracts, which makes him laugh. He can't help it. Blanche laughs and sips again.

"You know Byron a long time?" she asks.

"Not too long."

"You like to play kangaroo the way Byron does?"

"It's too cold to play kangaroo."

"Follow me," Blanche says, bending her head toward the hallway. When she turns around he is staring at the fire-spewing mouth of a green and yellow sea-monster, red flames and sinew tongue licking Blanche's shoulder.

The hallway is a wind tunnel, a cave of wintry blasts that leave Hooper sucking for air when they step from it into a shade-drawn parlor off the front room. There a wide couch is covered with a black velvet map of Melanesia and Australia, and piled with gaudy pillows, silk-embroidered, picturing ports all over the Pacific—San Francisco, Los Angeles, Panama City, Pago-Pago, Singapore—purple bridges, coral skyscrapers, orange houseboats moored in silver rivers.

From across the living room they hear muffled laughter and sounds of furniture moving. Blanche shuts the noise out by closing the parlor door and drawing across it a heavy velour drape. This doesn't shut out the wind. Near the ceiling an enormous air-conditioner is howling down at them, and with the door shut, trapped air begins to circle the room, a tornado that chills Hooper to the bone.

Blanche has stepped out of her silken bell-cuffed trousers. She wears nothing underneath.

"Are there any blankets on that couch?" Hooper asks.

"No blankets. Pillows," she says, bending to arrange them. "You want to lie down?"

"Why don't we get some blankets? We could lie down under the blankets?"

"Too hard to play kangaroo with blankets. C'mon, Hooper, you lie down on the couch. I'll keep you warm."

She moves up next to him, raises his poncho and slides underneath. Her hands as they slip around his waist are still damp from the beer bottle, her nose is a snowflake over his heart.

"Listen, Blanche, I'm going out to the car to get my sleeping bag."

Under the poncho her lips move against his chest, muffling the reply. "Nobody ever played kangaroo in a sleeping bag."

"We can play something else."

"What else?'

"I know some other games."

"What other games?" Lips still cooling his pecs.

"Oh, all kinds. Elephant . . . armadillo . . . jackrabbit . . . water buffalo . . ."

"How do you play water buffalo?"

"I'll tell you as soon as I get back."

"No, tell me now."

"Water buffalo . . ." He ponders it. "Water buffalo is a lot like kangaroo."

"What's the difference?"

"Well, the only real difference is that . . ." It comes to him. "You play water buffalo in the bathtub."

She slides out from under the poncho. "Honest?"

"Sure."

"How?"

"First you have to fill the tub with hot water."

"Oh Hooper, I hate hot water."

"You don't have to get in the water. I get in the water. You just get wet up to your calves or so. Wanna try it?"

"Follow me," Blanche says, pulling back the velour drape.

The circling air, anxious to escape, heaves them through the door. Like a blizzard-bound prospector, Hooper lurches upwind, following her to the bathroom. Once they're inside, the door seems to slam by itself, sucked hallward by the hurtling winds.

This room, all tile, is the coldest yet. But steam now is rising from the tub. He drops his dungarees, throws his poncho in a corner and jumps in, reveling in the sting of heat.

Blanche unbuttons her Hong Kong jacket, slips it off, climbs onto the toilet seat, and reaches for a knob that turns the air-conditioner to FULL, to clear away more of the steam. Already she's perspiring, like the tiles.

To evade this downswirling breeze, Hooper submerges as much of himself as possible. Blanche leans over the tub and kisses him.

"What should I do?" she says, moon face next to his, brown hands touching each rim of the porcelain tub.

"First climb in and let your feet get used to the water."

"And then?"

"Start saying water buffalo."

"Water buffalo."

"That's it. Louder."

"Water buffalo. Water buffalo. Water buffalo. Water buffalo. Water buffalo . . ."

CHAPTER 20

Other Beasts

*W*hen Hooper steps back into the wind-tunnel hallway, the door beyond the living room is still closed. It sounds as if someone is in there jumping up and down on bedsprings the way Bass trampled the roof of Joe's truck. Hooper doesn't want to wait. Bass will be heading back to Sunset to wake the others and spread the news of his conquest. Hooper is heading the other way.

Through the kitchen then, and Blanche snuggling next to him, naked, saying, "More water buffalo, Hooper?"

"Plenty more water buffalo."

"And elephant next time? You didn't show me the elephant."

"Yes, elephant. And antelope. And rhinoceros." Reaching for the back door.

"And polar bear?"

"Sure. And jackrabbit."

"And armadillo."

"And giraffe," he says, as the outside heat pours in.

"And kangaroooooooooo," is Blanche's loud and hopeful prophecy as the door slams and Hooper breaks into nighttime trade winds scenting through the Tlingsit palms.

CHAPTER 21

Galloping on

On the dark road out of Wahiawa, bedroll and patched shopping bag spirited from the La Salle, a ten-day's beard and no shoes now, but soaped and bathed and groin-sated, Hooper inhales pineapple ripeness off the fields till two drunk Hawaiians pick him up, pass their wine jug, laugh and scratch heads when he says he doesn't care where they're going. They drop him outside a bar at the edge of Honolulu and he catches a late bus to Waikiki where at last, in the sultry lush of vines at every window, humidity so high it could rain indoors, loving the warm and the sweat that rolls off to soak his bag, he lies on the floor of the room no one has slept in for thirty years and dreams of Eskimos.

He dreams of totem poles and skin-covered huts. He dreams of Cherokee tracking buffalo, and white men galloping past the herd with rifles, potshotting creatures they don't want, demolishing the herd, galloping on.

CHAPTER 22

Goldie's ride

SURF was formerly SUFFE, hence probably a variation of SOUGH (from the Middle English SWOUGH, the Anglo Saxon SWOGAN, *to sound*), a soft low murmuring, ruffling sigh. Which is what Jonas—Anglo Saxon himself, descended from hairy Frieslanders pushing boats through the shore-break and oaring hard to leave the swog of surf behind—has listened to from the beach and from the water and from inside his truck, the sighs, the murmurs, the soughing surf. It lulls, until you finally don't hear it at all. That constant ruffle becomes a coastal

60

silence. Two weeks of this, of chest-high waves, or none at all. Then overnight they jump from zero to six, by afternoon from six to ten. Today they're breaking twelve to fourteen, and that sigh has become a moan, the murmur a growl, and Joe is offshore now waiting for a wave he knows is coming, the wave of the day. You might say he hears it humming toward him, a couple of miles out, thick fifteen-footer to carry him to dinner before the mosquitoes hit.

Joe feels very good now. He's ready. Goldie's gone. There's nothing to do but wait. And waiting, he congratulates himself on last night's brainstorm. It came to him in Walter's pickup, while Goldie slept alone in the Reo, still parked on the beach below. Joe roused everyone early, before the tide started in, lined Sheepdog's wagon and Walter's pickup side by side on the cliff, with ends of greasy tow ropes attached. On hands and knees he scooped wet sand from around his tires, bunching towels and sweatshirts there for traction. He looped both rope ends around his axle. Then the three engines started grunting. The Reo began to move, four bald tires spurting foam and wet sand, eight more spinning in the stubble, with Joe shouting, "Pull it! C'mon, pull the sonofabitch!" As his rear-end cleared the loamy ridge, one rope frayed, broke, Joe's truck lurched toward Walter's, and Goldie, pushing from the bottom, was nearly crushed when the front end swerved. But Sheepdog was out of his cab and yanking like a Volga boatman, while Joe still shouted out the window, "Pull those fucking ropes back there!" Finally righted, with four wheels in the clearing again, he didn't switch the engine off. He swung around, commanded Goldie to get in next to him, and they raced to Honolulu, arriving just as Joe's bank opened, where he withdrew the cash he'd been saving for his own flight back to the States. They drove to the airport, and he bought her a one-way ticket to Los Angeles, tourist class on a plane leaving at noon. Goldie, who had nothing to carry but the jeans and aloha shirt she wore, stood weeping at the gangplank. Joe was merciless. He put her on board and sat in his frontseat sipping at a quart of sauterne till her plane curved out of sight beyond Diamond Head.

By two o'clock he was back at Sunset. After four good hours in the water, he's waiting for the last one now, and waiting is deliciously simple. Life is simple. His only remaining obstacle is flatness. But flatness too is gone. These two days of rising surf is the month's third pulse. And Joe's hopes are up. His cock is up. His stomach is tight, knowing this pulse won't decline. It will grow for a day or two more, till the waves he's been waiting for climb over the horizon groaning with their own bulk and rush.

This morning on Walter's radio the newsman reported earthquakes in the Aleutians. Small-craft warnings are out. A new rip is running along the beach, and another runs straight out from shore toward the break, as if pumped from a great pipe under there. Signs. Portents. Shock waves pushing into the north Pacific are already giving southbound shape to ice water moving past the bergs, not the water moving, but the shape itself, fanning out, picking up speed. Some of them will hit Wake Island, some New Guinea, some Antarctica, some hit nothing, but swing around the Horn or south Australia and roll on till they dissipate, shape giving out, settling down weeks later, limp, finished, flat. But one band of these oceanwides will hit Oahu, pile up on reefs out there, piling till there's more water than the shape can hold, and Jonas knows no man yet has ridden a wave as large as the one he'll ride when the quake shocks and high tide and storm that's due all hit at once.

Joe knows the story of Shorty Baker, in fact heard it from Shorty's lips, and stored it away in his catalogue of wave lore, crossfiled under B for Baker, S for Sunset, C for close-out. It was late in '54, the first year in modern times anyone tried the winter surf out here. Shorty was the pioneer, the same way he pioneered Makaha a few years earlier, and is said to have pioneered the Tijuana Sloughs right after the Second World War, riding an oldtime redwood plank. According to Shorty, in December of '54 it just came up all of a sudden, overnight, bam, the biggest waves he'd ever seen. Shorty and two others got caught in a close-out set, and the rips started carrying them north, a mile or so in the direction of Kauai. Shorty knew the reefs and currents well enough to get everyone back to the beach, but it took two hours of hard paddling to make it, all of them vomiting their guts out, curled up on the sand and too sick to walk. And Shorty later admitted that none of them took off on the biggest waves that broke that day. Being out there among them was enough in itself.

Joe also knows the story of Holoua, a man of Kauai, whose house was washed out to sea in the great tidal wave of 1868. Tearing a plank from the wall of his living room, Holoua is said to have ridden the next wave, a fifty-footer, back to shore. This is, of course, only a legend. Even if it were true, Joe figures Holoua most likely rode the wave lying down. Which in any case wouldn't count.

Jonas knows all the stories, likes to tell them, and hear them told, and to know that soon he too will be remembered in the backends of station wagons, all along the running boards of old limousines around the coastlines of the world.

Free of Goldie, and knowing that tomorrow will probably be the day, it's hard for him to sit on his board in the late sun, grim-lipped and squinting, with his legs adangle, and appear not to listen to

Walter Conquest naming the next wave for the eight-pound boy his wife bore yesterday in Redondo Beach.

"I'm gonna ride this fucker for Jeremy," Walter says. "He's over there paddling around in his crib, and his old man's gonna dedicate this next ride to his kid, and call it a day."

Flattening then, Walter digs for the swell behind them, hurtles past Joe and Sheepdog and Bass, and drops to disappear below the curling hump. Joe turns a cheek to the pelting spray blown over the wave's back by offshore wind.

CHAPTER 23

Walter's ride

*N*o fancy footwork for Walter. Steady as she goes. It's the same with every wave he rides, from two feet high to twenty, take a bead and shoot it, straight as a surveyor's line he measures the wave, never too high on the feathering crest, never too low in its trough, never too far ahead of the break to lose it, nor too close to the curl to get smashed. Walter, you might say, on any wave he rides, is a fixed point of unadorned and respectable safety, around which the others circulate, and as he rides this ten-foot wall he has a dream.

Paddling for it he feels his new son Jeremy crawling up his back, eight-pound fish of a natural-born water baby, tiny hands barely gripping Walter's shoulders when he rises to the crouch with the wave slope lifting. Once in position he stands erect and it's Walter showing Jeremy the way. The speed's juice, the taste of salt feeds the infant. With each yard of forward hurtling, Jeremy seems to grow a little, hands finding strength to clutch the shoulders now, and legs grown long enough to take a foothold each side of daddy's hips. Solid father bears the new weight easily, likes the test, and leans a little forward, shifting slightly, front knee flexing as the boy continues growing on his back.

Soon young arms clasp his neck, bone-hard and sturdy, and the lean legs reach around his waist, locking ankles there. Wave wall threatens to topple, and Walter resumes the crouch, arms low, as if reaching for his board's rails, and the boy then seems to climb a little higher, kneeling along the almost horizontal ribcage. His hands pull hard at Walter's forehead. Then Walter also kneels, as the wave's last section cracks around him. Since he's riding this one in, he wants to milk it. He points into the white water, and the boy on his back's so heavy, with tough knees pushing at the ribs, Walter lies prone. Belly hugging balsa he rides the churning foam shoreward, with Jeremy on top of him, standing now and finely balanced.

CHAPTER 24

Bassian's ride

*B*lack Bass leaves Sunset for Trudy's most nights about seven. Tonight he gets back at twelve and falls asleep with his hand in his crotch. At 3:30 A.M. he is jolted awake, the way your eyes sometimes spring open in the darkness to a strange and sudden sound. Upright on his mattress and eyes wide with listening, Bass strains, and what he hears is silence. Deep silence, as all the sets and cycles offshore coincide in a lack of sound that's louder, in its brief quiet, than the two days of steady roar.

He waits, craning to see out his windshield, and hears a faroff sizzle, mighty teakettle getting ready to scream, rising to its rush and a clattering explosion of whole ocean breaking at once, as the cycles recommence. And Bass knows by the sound that this is it, loud signal of the swell everyone's been waiting for.

Everyone but him.

Before dawn he's into his front seat and backing across the dewy lot, stopping just long enough to pee, hitting leaves he's afraid someone will hear. He sprays around in search of sand. Then he's driving like a fiend for pineapple-fenced-off inland peace of Wahiawa, and as he nears it, feels his penis swelling with relief at successful getaway, great happy erection, more for escape than for anticipation. Through the back door of Trudy's igloo before anyone there is up, and outside the bedroom he hesitates with sudden fear the husband's home. But upon hearing Trudy's message, he climbs right back into her bed, in fact right between Trudy and Blanche, since they sleep together when not otherwise occupied, for the warmth. They snuggle next to him, thick dark arms of Bass reaching to enclose them both, unsure in the half-light which twin is which and not caring, all three free of early morning worry, after this telephone call which just came in from a friend of Trudy's, informing her that Sarge has, for lo these many months, had his own thing going on the side, his night duty being a non-military assignment, and secretly Sarge has been thankful that Trudy too has something steady to keep her out of more general circulation.

CHAPTER 25

Not much to say

*T*wo hours later and the sun's up, but still behind the mountain, three trucks at Sunset Automotive and six boards scattered, waiting, like rifles in a gun room before the alarm goes out. Oyster light of post-dawn tints them, two boards up against Sheepdog's wagon, one on the ground, two on sawhorses next to Walter's pickup, one at the cliff edge, resting on its skeg, uptilted. In this lot of dented cars and charred scoops of campfire and tincan litter and rotten clothes hung from limbs in the breezeless morning air, these boards gleam like armor, like firetrucks, like shipboard cannon. Every deck is waxed for surefootedness, every onetime hole now patched and waterproof, everything else can go to hell but the boards stay sleek, slabs of balsa finely rounded, sheathed with fiberglass.

Now Joe and Sheepdog and Walter come tumbling from the trucks to stand among these boards, rub eyes, stare at the waves that have made sleep impossible. The ocean's sigh and murmur that become a moan and growl is now a howl and grinding roar, and this isn't surf any more. It's a hissing stampede avalanche of water walls erupting. The waves breaking a second time, fifty yards offshore, are the size of those they rode yesterday—now the first barrier to push through. The outside break is something none of them has ever seen before, except in pictures, and the pictures lied because they don't make the sound, or show the heave of a whole ocean in front, behind, on all sides of the great waves that seem to be the purpose of all the rest.

There isn't much to say. It's what they've been waiting for. They stand in a row along the cliff for thirty minutes, watching it, timing the sets, stony-faced. Then Sheepdog and Walter, like deputy sheriffs called to duty, grab two boards from the armory, and kneel in the dry grass fiercely waxing their decks.

Jonas tries to fry some eggs, but can hardly squat over the tiny fire. He's shivering with morning overcast, leaves the eggs to blacken in the skillet, and reaches for his board, waxes it, leads the others down the cliff path. They wait ten minutes for a short lull to let them past the inside break, Jonas all this time squeezing at his sphincter to keep his bowels from falling out. Finally three boards hit the water, splat splat splat.

The current along shore is a river now, as wide as the beach. Beyond it the surface chop is almost breaking, and the white water after each big wave breaks is as high as the cliff they park on— speedup of a continental glacier burying territories in its push.

CHAPTER 26

Sheepdog's ride

*T*hree is always the magic number, Sheepdog tells himself, paddling out. All good things come three. Bad things too. Trinity is nonpartisan, and three any way you look at it is the one to watch. Three blind mice. Three bears. Three strikes you're out. Three little words. Rubadubdub three men in a tub. Three times this month the surf comes up. Today's the third day of the third pulse. I'm third man paddling behind Joe and Walter, and every third stroke I push a little harder. One— two—THREE. One—two—THREE. I will wait for the third set after we get out there, and I will take off on the third wave of that set.

Three cars pull into the clearing just about the time the surfers reach the takeoff zone. Joe and Walt join Sheepdog in letting the first two sets roll through untouched, looking them over, every wave a twenty-footer and no one anxious to try till they see how these look up close. This gives the new arrivals time to hop out and set up cameras. Tripods on the cliff edge, telephoto lenses. One man, in hooded sweatshirt, is making a movie. Another is looking for a sports feature to sell the Honolulu paper. More equipment is on its way. Shutterbugs and spectators.

The third car, a Model A sedan, carries three surfboards strapped to its roof and three more Californians who've been mainly riding at Waikiki and who would remain for a long time today sitting in this car, contemplating these outlandish waves, were it not that the third set is humping out there and someone has paddled over right in under the peak and has barely missed getting swamped by two waves the size of department stores and now seems ready to actually try for the third, from a position that would only be taken by a blind man who couldn't possibly perceive what he's getting into. He's starting too late, it's going to break on top of him. They leap from the car and run to the cliff edge waving, shouting, "No! No! No!" One runs back to blare the horn waaaaaaah, waaaaaaah.

None of this reaches Sheepdog. He only hears the rumble all around of waves broken and threatening to break, he only knows that the third one is ready now, so it's three hard strokes, and three strokes more. It's one—two—three, and one—two—three, and one —two—THREE, and the wave of his choice scoops Sheepdog to its high crest.

Below him there's no slope. A sheer wall. The wave lets go. The blond board plummets. White water's roaring above him before he hits the trough.

On shore the new arrivals are cringing with the hurt. Their faces contort, watching him hit the bottom. He seems suspended there, floating, and the whiteness itself is suspended above, giving him one saintly moment of terrible grace, tiny brown body upright and waiting, with palms out from his waist, not Christ-like, but as if to say, "You see? You see?" before the tumbling wave falls all over him like ten thousand sacks of wet cement.

CHAPTER 27

Joe's ride

*O*vercast today, oyster sky turning pewter, the first lick of water at his instep and Joe's scrotum draws, he has to hold his face together. Flesh feels old and loose and useless. Water colder than he's ever known it in the islands, starts him paddling fast to keep warm, warm the chest. Pecs tight with little spasms as he hits the current that sweeps him toward the break. Easy to get out there now. Too easy. Double hard getting back, if you have to swim. Slow down then. Don't paddle too fast. Save the calories. Save the arms for getting into waves fast. Get out fast too, on the first few rides. Less chance of losing it. Won't have to swim so much. That's what wears you down. Shorty said four out of seven is a good average in surf this size. Make four, swim for three, you're not doing too bad. I can beat that. One thing at a time. First, get the takeoff wired. Then the long wall.

He watches Sheepdog's Kamikaze drop, later sees him bobbing far inshore, boardless and hacking at the foam, trying to swim for it. On the fourth set, Joe tries a wave, like looking down a canyon, cuts a halfmoon as he slides under, up, over the top and out the back. Test flight. He paddles toward the takeoff zone again, still shivering, still cold and rubbing palms as he waits out there for Walter, who took the wave behind him, and made it. Sheepdog is far down the beach, evidently dogpaddling against the rip, two hundred yards below the clearing, and still no board in sight.

By midmorning five more riders have paddled out. Two paddled back in after a few halfhearted tries. Two took wipe-outs—neither as spectacular as Sheepdog's since no one dares get that far into the curl—and decided to swim for shore. One man remains out there with Joe and Walter, a Hawaiian named "Horse" who works at Waikiki Beach.

The clearing has filled with spectators, lenses, more boards and battered cars. Down the coast road a quarter of a mile, where the trees open up, there's another patch of cars, people perched on hoods with binoculars, a touring bus parked, a score of cameras, narrow-brim straw hats.

Joe's shivering has stopped. He's finding the rhythm now. And it's easier to try the big ones when you know shutters are clicking, reels are whirring to record it all. No more legends. These rides will be preserved. Still shots to blow up later and measure with calipers.

Horns are honking too, all the time. It's a way for spectators to get into the act. Cliff-watchers can see farther than someone in the water, so when a set starts to build, you send signals. One honk means take the wave right in front of you. Two means wait for the next one. Three honks means wait for the third, it's the biggest, looks the best.

The swells are five feet higher than when Joe first paddled out.

And they're growing. Each set seems bigger than the last, seems to peak a little farther out each time. Now a new set rises, and Joe and Walter and Horse paddle toward it, paddle hard, not to get caught when it breaks. On shore everyone is honking in unison ONE, ONE, ONE, which means the wave following is either too big or will break too far out to reach. Horse and Walter swing into position. But Joe thinks to himself, "Fuck all those assholes," and he paddles up the face of it, pushes through the slapping crest, drops to the valley, with a glump of his vital organs, arms driving into water marbled scummy white from back foam. He hears the horns again, blaring ONE, ONE, ONE, pleading Take *this* one, for Christ sake. Again Joe paddles toward it, climbs the front, and blinks salt water out, craning. From its spuming crest he sees the third bulging toward him, and beyond that the fringes of a fourth so big it's already frothing, and beyond those stand others, like endless Himalayan ridges, clouding the horizon.

He sinks into this valley, thinking "Close-out set," figuring three will have to be the one, and doesn't notice that all the horns along the cliff are silent. He sees the spot he wants, ten yards away, digs for it till the wave is bulked above him, jade green, foam-veined, cupped with silver from the graying sky. He swings his board, curved palms stroking for speed, looking back to judge the time, up and up and up to see the top. Stroking. Hard. Hard. Harder. A breath-grabbing lift, an instant glance down the deep well of it, then a thirty-foot fall

p
  l
    o
     w
      i
       n
        g

to the bottom where his board catches, spurts out across the curving wall, and Joe knows he has it, hears the sharp clean hissing as it steepens and knows he can't make a mistake. Thunder of the first peak behind him. Loud tunnel thundering shut, while in front of him it opens still wider, endless, expanding before it contracts, green-walling, tingles all the flex, and poise, and stinging him with salt spray.

And so intent is Joe upon the speed and balance, he doesn't hear the horns that now begin to bellow, choral triumph of squawks and beeps and waa-waa-waas. From the clearing sweatshirted girls are yelling. Sheepdog is leaning on his horn and yelling, "Go Jonas! Go go go!" Grown men are shouting at the ocean. Engines roar. A

Minnesota husband at the tour bus turns to sun-hatted wife, "That fella's having himself quite a time out there."

Quite a time, yes, and going all the way, flawless ride, milking it because he knows it'll be the day's last. He rides a hundred yards, and as it dwindles from thirty-plus to fifteen or so, just before the great swell grades out too flat to ride, jumps to another moving from the west, renegade heap of backwash about to break, and takes that ten-footer the other way, toward the crowd, now frenzied with delight, and makes it almost to the beach before he drops to his knees, board still moving, and starts to paddle for a five-foot lick of shorebreak that carries Jonas right up onto the draining sand, where wellwishers have already run down to meet him, cameramen pushing in close with expensive lenses to get every moment of this fantastic ride, from takeoff to beach-walk. And Joe, as if he's all alone somewhere in the South Pacific, bends and gathers up his board, and starts his slow stroll back along hard sand to the cliff path, dragging feet in the tide rush, glancing seaward from time to time, checking it out, ignoring all the hands extended, smiling once as he climbs the path. Without drying off, while the cameras whirr and snap, he breaks out a long can of Danish sardines, keys it open, sitting on his caked running board and begins to eat them one at a time, his long-awaited breakfast, dark grease dripping off his wrist, running to his elbow, dropping to the hairy thigh.

CHAPTER 28

Tableau

*O*ne of the photographers, a bulky Chinese-Hawaiian, pushes forward now, three cameras stacked up in front of his purple aloha shirt, and looking for a feature lead. He moves Sheepdog in next to Joe, and Horse next to Sheepdog, and next to Horse, Walter, who has just washed in after losing his wave. For ten seconds they're lined up like this, alongside Joe's Reo, and the man shoots it: Horse for the local readers, Joe on the running board leering above the jagged lid, Sheepdog holding three balsa chunks in his arms, Walter on the verge of bending to vomit, yet, when the pic appears next day on the sports page of the *Hono-*

lulu Advertiser, above the caption, SURFING ANYONE?, Walt looks like a well-tanned West Point cadet out of uniform and holding a brace.

CHAPTER 29

Rain

*A*fter that everyone stands around awhile to watch the waves that follow Joe's. No one in the water now. They call that wave the close-out. It may have been, for surfers. Some kind of climax. But for the ocean, it's just a start, an opening up. That wave has loosened whatever locks or regulators hold the sets together and hold the surface flat against itself. Spectators and toweled-off riders watch waves grow until the sets give way to gray, heaping turmoil, the whole ocean torn into mammoth lashes leaping, tossing far as anyone can see.

White-gouged water goes grayer still as rain begins to fall. And with the rain the spectators start to disappear, first into cars, to watch the waves a while longer. They watch an ocean that seems finally fed up with the coastline that has been getting in its way so long, watch it lunging at the beach, swallowing sand, tidewashes pushing ever closer to the trees, toward the cliff base below the clearing. They watch this even when the rain begins to drum on car roofs and river down windshields faster than wipers can wipe it off. Even though no one is out there to ride it, everyone sits and watches.

And no one will ever ride such waves as these, unless he wants to be dropped offshore by helicopter and try one maniacal takeoff into oblivion. No board could paddle through it now, the waves are unreachable, and unsurfable if reached, and everyone knows that Jonas has caught the biggest ridable wave of the day, of the season, the biggest ridable wave that anyone here has ever imagined.

Thus a celebration is in order. It is, the general feeling runs, as organizers scurry from car to car in the thickening mud, a day to remember. But not out here at Sunset, where the action is clearly over, and the rain soaks through the metal and upholstery to dampen clothes and spirits. No, the celebration will be elsewhere, and cars start groping out toward the road, forming there a caravan of station wagons, pickup trucks, touring sedans, two more Grayline buses that arrived just in time to give the folks aboard their round-the-island money's worth—all these wave-watchers caravaning out, quite slowly at first, as if reluctant to leave the spectacle, then speeding up as slick wheels find the suction of the glistening road.

Last to leave are the vehicles of Walter and Sheepdog, glintless even when wet. Conferring, they've agreed there'll be no more surfing here today, but beyond the mountains leeward beaches might be free of rain, someplace like Makaha could still be breaking perfectly, and if not, at least there might be sun. Let's head that way, recuperate, think about it. Walter has an extra board.

They drive out, ragtaggle cabooses to the general wagon train of exiting. Only Joe remains, sitting on the fender of his truck, refusing Sheepdog's invitation to come along. He mainly wants some time to stare and let his mind empty, and he knows from the look of the water all around and above him there'll be no surfing anywhere.

The sea, as if it can't pummel the land enough with these mountainous swells and tumbling tides, has sent all its surplus water skyward to fall from above, while the wind sizzles over offshore wave tops in great gusts, making the rain, too, wavelike in its force and rhythm. It isn't cold. Just suddenly the wettest day of the world, this whole island now drenched from point to point, every beach awash with the north swell and drowning, heavy water from the mountains rushing toward the lowlands, and lowlands already soaked, sending it out to sea, and the sea, balking, bulges up at the rivermouths, bulking, forcing water back upstream to growl and foam below the bridges.

See Jonas, soaked, step out of his trunks and sit naked, stubble face into the wind, underwater, middle depths of an ocean whose level just climbed two thousand feet, and no one will escape it but the handful of passenger planes that got off the ground in time to take word back to the mainland that Oahu has just gone the way of all Atlantises.

Trips and Voyages

*O*n the street two Japanese motor-cycles blap and sputter, two old buddies cruising on a summer morning. They stop outside and honk and circle each other a few times, then they blap away down the sea road, blue workshirts flapping in the wind they make, luffing at their backs. These old buddies, old Joes and Hoopers, long returned from those long-ago voyages, they make noises till they sputter out of sight.

PART 2

Broome

OR

The Veteran of Something

Take a trip to North Bloomfield, old Sierra mining town called "Humbug" by the first disappointed Forty-Niners who pioneered the place, in 1851. It boomed thirty years later. Three thousand miners in the pine forest. No one there but a ranger now, a tame doe, a couple of families who like mountain life, and an old man named Charlie, born in North Bloomfield in its flush time, mined it, retired there, ninety and piling in his yard the limbs and twigs last week's snow broke off the trees. A native son of the golden west. Charlie already has his grave picked out, down in the cemetery half a mile away, where most of the graves say "Here lies Margaret O'Neil, died North Bloomfield, 1876, a Native of Ireland." And "Here lies Anton van Buskirk, died North Bloomfield, 1888, a Native of Holland," And "Here lies Richard le Duc, died North Bloomfield, 1882, a Native of Marseilles."

CHAPTER 30

Any Man, Any Boat

*H*ooper wakes early, resting cool-limbed in a six-thirty silence, and pulls from the shopping bag his reading for the day, having reached Chapter Seven. Untold millennia have passed, generations come and gone, now Noah and his children and his two of every species are floating through the deluge, while Hooper reads ". . . the waters increased, and bare up the ark, and it was lifted up above the earth. And the waters prevailed, and were increased greatly upon the earth; and the ark went upon the face of the waters . . ."

Reflecting, he sees it as the greatest escape act of all time, finds a new admiration for the man who, at six hundred years of age, could pull it off. He hums a chorus of "Let's Get Away from It All," rereads the passage and a few verses more, to make sure they did in fact make it through the rain and wet upheaval to a world the water had swabbed and freshened.

Then with the ark still afloat and old Noah out there at the tiller, sloshing down some ancient curve of earth, Hooper is up, dresesd—which is to say, into his shorts and a wide-brim straw hat that for thirty years has kept free of dust a circle on the dark floor of a portable cardboard closet—he is filled with pancakes and coffee, and on his way to see a man about a boat. No man in particular. Any man. Any boat.

The Hawaiian-Chinese harbormaster tells him, where he first stops, "Big liners sail alla time. But no boats right now. Too risky with the weather. Maybe look around those sheds, though, if you want. Alla time somebody down there getting ready to sail someplace."

In the first boatshed a slender young man with his head shaved is flinching as sparks from a welding torch arc back and singe his bare arms and legs. When Hooper enters, the man flips up his metal mask and, grimacing, listens to the questions with manic eyes, then answers, "Yes. Yes, I *am* getting ready to sail. Soon. Very soon. I have thirty more drums to weld up, and I'll be on my way. You want to crew? Well, yes." He steps back and appraises Hooper's build. "Can you weld?"

"I can learn."

"Yes. Well, the plan is basically this. I'm welding together about two hundred empty fifty-gallon drums, and with that as a base I can sail anywhere in the world. Anyone willing to assist me will, of course, automatically become part of the crew, thus part of the movie we're filming along the way. I'm calling it *Kon Tiki U.S.A.* An innovation on Heyerdahl's voyage, using oil drums instead of balsa logs, you see, to prove that any American can use what have become native materials to do anything he wants to do. But these drums are quite expensive. Now if you are willing to invest in, say fifty or sixty drums, at three dollars each . . ."

In the second boatshed, an unpainted hull is overturned, and next to it, on an overturned nailkeg, sits another young man. Hooper thinks he recognizes him—about Hooper's age, blond, tan, stockier, pressed khaki shorts supported by a plaid stretch-belt.

"I'm looking for a way to crew south," he tells Hooper. "Someone said this guy's boat might be almost ready, and I'm waiting to talk to him. He's supposed to be back any minute. Say, didn't you go to UCLA?"

In the third boatshed stands another Californian, a few years older than Hooper, sandpaper dust sprinkled in his blond arm hairs. Hooper calls him a skipper-type, no-nonsense out at sea, wins any race he enters, now smoothing a long mast, while he studies Hooper with an eye half impatient, half whimsical, as if he's answered this question too many times, or perhaps is reminded of himself before he could afford to own a boat.

"I'm trying to put her in shape for a cruise this spring, hope to start around the first of May. I doubt that you'll find anybody leaving much earlier than that. Only chance you'd have of sailing anywhere right now is the *Le Hua*. She's a passenger yacht, takes luxury cruises between here and the Societies, and big enough to handle rough weather, if it comes. She's berthed downtown this week. Most of the crew's Tahitian, but the owner hires from Honolulu once in a while. Or just for the hell of it you might try the *Blue Dolphin*, big two-masted seventy-footer couple of berths this side of the *Le Hua*. Can't miss her. Prettiest boat in the ocean."

Aboard the *Blue Dolphin*, padding its scrubbed and empty decks, Hooper sees no one around. He touches a spoke of the polished wheel, calls down a companionway, listens, descends to a mahogany saloon, red plush carpeting, where fifths of bourbon, gin, vodka stand open, strewn across the bar. On a dark leather couch built into one corner, a balding man in tennis shoes and polo shirt sits holding a glass. Pictures of dolphins decorate the walls, and pictures of other boats.

"Sit down, my friend," the man says. "What are you drinking?"

"Nothing, thanks. Sorry to bother you."

"Nonsense, nonsense. Weather like this, a man needs a little something. I'm having Jack Daniels on the rocks."

"That'll be fine."

The man walks unsteadily to the bar, as if this ship is rolling with a heavy swell.

They sip, rattle their ice around some. The man says, "Well, what's on your mind?"

"Looking for a boat that might be sailing south sometime soon."

"Aaaaaaaaah. Crewing to Tahiti, is that it?"

"Down that way. The *Blue Dolphin* going anywhere?"

"The *Blue Dolphin* never goes anywhere any more, my friend."

"Why is that?"

"I wish I knew," he says sadly, staring into his whiskey. "I wish I knew."

"Are you the owner?"

"I only wish I knew."

Two berths away, aboard the *Le Hua*, a tall hatchet-faced man in a white linen suit stands with one shoe down a gleaming companionway, yells to a stripe-shirted Polynesian high up a mast, yells to a lift-truck driver on the dock, then turns to Hooper, the shrewd eye appraising him almost desperately. They step down, for protection against a new squall blowing toward them.

"You done much sailing?"

"All my life," Hooper lies, having sailed from Santa Monica to Catalina a few times, and in and out of the Newport harbor, and once from Newport to Ensenada, vomiting that time over the taffrail while his fun-loving skipper offered him salami sandwiches, glasses of lukewarm chocolate milk.

"You scared to go aloft?"

"I love it."

"Got a passport? A visa for Tahiti?"

"I can get one."

But at the passport office the next morning, the worried Japanese woman says, "There's just no way we can process your passport in less than two weeks—and that's rushing it."

"My boat sails in three days."

"I'm terribly sorry."

And at the French consulate: "*Mon ami*, visas are not produced by vending machines."

At a tiny wharfside restaurant Hooper curses red tape and bad timing and he's brooding over the noodles in a bowl of saimin soup, when a derelict slides onto the stool next to him. He has ordered soda crackers to sprinkle on top of his noodles. The derelict reaches for a cracker and begins to talk.

"You ever done any traveling, pal?"

"Some."

"I been all around the goddam world."

"How many times?"

"No telling. I been everywhere."

"What's your favorite spot?"

"My favorite spot, pal? Galveston. Galveston, Texas."

"Why Galveston?"

"Why? I'll tell ya why." He grabs another cracker. "The radio stations down that way. I'm nuts about the radio. I listen to the radio every chance I get. There's a station down that way, it comes across the border from Sonora or someplace. They advertise things you wouldn't believe. Lawn furniture in the shape of cactus plants. Life-size statues of Judas Iscariot. I got me a room down there in Galveston crammed full of stuff you wouldn't believe. I live for that town. Been there and left and gone back so many times it makes me dizzy to think about it."

Hooper looks at the man. He does seem to be getting dizzy where he sits. His eyes have glazed over, his head bobbles as he stares past Hooper, through the greasy window, across the street, out across the oil-slick harbor, toward who knows what antenna and wavering frequency. A wasted, stubble-chinned rag of a man who takes another soda cracker and continues.

"Merchant seaman, that's what I am. Oiler, steward, you name it. Take the Gulf run every chance I get. Trying to get back there right now, but I jumped ship so many times they keep kicking me out of the union hall. You ever think about going to Galveston, bud?"

"Where's the union hall?"

"You pull in to Galveston, you can see it from the gangplank—sort of a yellow building, with a big green sign . . ."

At the maritime hiring office, a trim, wine-faced, blue-eyed and blue-jacketed little man tells Hooper, in a quiet, weary Bronx voice, "I'm sick and tired of you punk kids showing up here trying to sail around the goddam world. We got men in this union fifteen years and trying to get berths outta this port right now. What am I supposed to do with *you*, for Christ sake?"

Shove me up your ass, mister, this isn't MY idea of a way to travel.

"Any way I can get into the union?"

"What the hell do *you* think?"

CHAPTER 31

A Tattooed Lobster

*H*e learns the *Le Hua* will return by Easter to make another southern run. His only hope, so it's one more trip downtown to fill out passport and visa forms. He applies for seaman's papers too, although he wouldn't care to use them—since it's wind he wants to move him, not engines—and he doesn't expect them to come through anyway. You need contacts, someone inside the union boosting you. Hooper has no contacts. Everyone he knows is on the bum. Except Broome. Who owns property. Should he use Broome as a reference? Why not? Grinning as he writes the name. JACKSON BROOME, Address, Broome's Rooms, Honolulu. Deciding then to speak to Broome about voyages. Anyone who's arrived in these islands has to know *some*thing about the sea, made at least one trip across it or over it or under it. And old Broome, well, he has a look about him—the veteran of something. Yes, Hooper thinks, as he wades in for a late swim in the dwindling rain at Waikiki, let's go talk to Broome.

In Broome's backyard there's an outside shower, for washing off sand and brine. It's cooler than the rain, which finally stops, after two days pouring, as Hooper wades ashore. Cooler than the ocean, it falls into gravel that's one bare patch in the knee-high jungle. Leaning against this hard, nozzleless stream Hooper stands among vines and tassels and studies the rowboat propped against his windowsill, bleached, split. Near it, almost buried under vines, lie eight or ten moss-spotted oars. Over the backporch roof hangs an old fishnet, its rotten corks dripping. Across the yard he sees paddle boards —white, like a lifeguard uses—and another rowboat that seems to have fallen apart, two jaws of decaying teeth flung permanently agape.

A slim breeze nudges while he leans against the water, watching cloud cover turn maroon from a horizon slit the gone sun's rays slip through. Now that he's searched and found himself stranded till Easter, he leans against the time in front of him too. In the lee of this house, in the company of these hulks and untrimmed bulge of a decade's greenery, he thinks he won't mind waiting a while for the *Le Hua* or whatever other boat it might be. Where he stands, the long ragged hedge blots out most of the parking lot. Chromium door glints might be fisherman torches across some still lagoon. And bounding the yard's far side, the Paradise Hotel is so high and wide, and darkened now, you don't have to see it there. In this quick-falling dusk it could be a vast mauve beach spreading to infinity.

Toweled off, he lifts the screen, climbs through the window, and once inside, reaches back out to wring his shirt, his swimming trunks. Then he's heading down the hall toward the room of the man who keeps that garden for the likes of just such as Hooper to enjoy.

No blinding shaft of sunlight now. Ink indoors. He finds a switch. High above, some bulb from the twenties sluggishly opens its eye. One of those clear-glass, thick-red-filament bulbs, and all it does is make the hall below it darker. Hooper gropes, listening again for noises, and he soon stops, hearing what sounds at first like a distant foghorn. Is it a recording? Or is it Broome humming to himself. Or groaning in his sleep.

Hum or groan or house-spirit winding in the dark overhead, whatever it is becomes a grunt, a chair leg scraping. Hooper creeps forward through the gloom.

"Uncle Jack?"

A slice of lemon light, thin wheezes, then light blocked by the pudgy body, the cocked hat.

"Boys . . . boys."

Hooper's sprinting down the hall. "Uncle Jack!"

Broome is hunched against the jamb, sucking air in broken rasps of rancid breath.

"Boys . . . I can't . . ."

Hooper stoops, tries to get an arm around his neck. "C'mon. C'mon back inside."

The old man tries to chuckle, contorts, and chuckle turns to rattling cough. "A pain. Right up here." He jerks loose one arm and, with his forefinger, draws a circle on his chest. "Pain, boys . . . can't breathe." He bends forward sucking air.

Catching him off balance, Hooper swings him around, guides him back inside the room, inside the yellow circle, up next to his leather chair, tries to ease him onto it.

Stubbornly Broome grunts, between wheezes, "Nope . . . nope . . . can't lay down."

Hooper gently tries to force him.

"Rather stand. Nope . . . nope . . . easier to stand . . . easier to breathe."

Broome's built like a left guard, hard to move without cooperation. Hooper asks him what he wants to do.

"Back," he grunts. "My back."

"What about your back?"

"Vicks."

He leans forward, staring at the floor bewildered, gasping, and between gasps trying to laugh. Again Hooper nudges him toward the chair. Again Broome finds roots through the floorboards, deep in old soil beneath his house.

"Vaporub. It's on my desk."

Opposite the parlor organ, just outside the light pool, his desk is a murky tangle of calendars, notepads, receipts and checkstubs, newspapers, underwear, packets of rusty mandolin strings—a roll-top desk with papers bursting from dozens of pigeonholes, spilling from two tiers of open drawers. Digging through, Hooper finds the big Vicks jar, more by smell than by sight. It's opened and sending out menthol.

Seeing it, or perhaps smelling it coming, Broome begins to re-move the thick coat-sweater he wears at night. He wants the Vicks rubbed into his back. Hooper reaches to help him. Broome jerks his shoulder free, grunting.

"What about your doctor, Uncle Jack?"

Broome is half out of his first aloha shirt and struggling with a second—yellow, covered with names and contour maps of all the Hawaiian Islands. Keeps jerking his shoulder each time Hooper moves to help.

"Doctors ain't worth a damn."

"We'd better call somebody, Uncle Jack."

"Heh heh . . . yes . . . well, you call Nona then."

"Who's she?"

"Number twelve . . . upstairs . . . she'll know."

Hooper doesn't want to leave him. He's still wheezing, coughing some, but seems to breathe a little easier, naked to the waist under the wide green shade. Face dark beneath his panama. Across his fat white back an enormous tattooed lobster, blue and green, with red eyes and claws. Something on his chest too, but Hooper can't make it out. Fat white back waiting for the Vicks.

"Will you be okay for a second?"

"Can't miss it. Top a the stairs."

Into darkness, round the landing, up the long flight, and find there a door already open. In the doorway, backlit, the tall woman he saw last week, same dark hair. No muu-muu. A grass skirt this time, feathered anklets and wristbands, and necklaces of shells and polished seeds catching glow from some soft light inside the room. Behind her he sees fine lauhala matting in the floor, a high wooden drum, brown and white patterned tapa cloth hanging from a far wall. She is reaching for her coat, on a rack near the door.

"Nona?"

"Yes."

"Mr. Broome is having trouble breathing. Bad pain in his chest."

"Oh my God. Where is he?"

"In his room. I just found him."

Down the black stairs, Nona leads, slowing outside his door. Hooper watches grass-covered hips move into the light, where Broome still stands barebacked and panamaed.

"Uncle Jack, what happened?"

"Vicks, Nona."

"You've already run out of pills?"

From Broome, grunts and wheezes. From Nona, pained exasperation as she scans the littered room.

"You didn't throw them away *again*!"

"Vicks . . . Vaporub."

She sees the jar, scoops out a fingerful, and begins to apply it in wide greasy circles, between his shoulder blades, polishing the lobster's head.

Gravelly aaaaaaaahh of contentment from Broome. "That's it, sweetheart, that's it."

"You know you're going to kill yourself."

"Nope . . . fella has to hate life to do that . . . I just hate pills . . . rather have a back rub any day."

He winks at Hooper, coughs. His body bunches around some pain, then relaxes. Nona's arm works under the light. She's six feet tall, but next to Broome, five foot five and hunched to take the Vicks, she seems huge, a giantess descended from Hawaii's race of kings. Onstage here, in the hard light of Broome's circle theater, she could be two hundred pounds of eight-foot matriarch bending to her task. Another scoop and long graceful fingers smear the ointment, level the old man's breathing, fill the room with eucalyptus and camphor trees. From his pores the rubbing dredges a thin gray scum, bordering her wide circles. No telling how long he struggled with the pain alone, but now, through the heavy skin, his bones and thick muscles seem to be relaxing.

"Feeling better now?" she says.

Long silence.

"Heh heh."

One arm reaches to tilt the hat back, light falls across his mouth, a grin through short whiskers, a crafty eye watching Hooper.

"Only one thing'd make me feel any better than I do already."

Nona tosses dark hair, a smile cutting her frown of concern.

"By now," she says, "I guess you know Uncle Jack has a one-track mind."

"Evil's in the mind of the beholder, sweetheart . . . heh heh . . . I'd just like to hear ole Hooper play me another tune on that guitar. That's all I'd like. Could you do that for me, Hooper?"

He looks for some decision from Nona, since she seems to know what Broome needs. But she passes it back to him with another quick smile—questioning, surprised.

"Sure, Uncle Jack. What's your pleasure?"

"Anything you like. I don't guess you remember an old tune called Sister Kate. 'I Wish I Could Shimmy Like My Sister Kate'?"

"One of my favorites," Hooper says.

"It is, eh. You oughtta see Nona here try the shimmy. Heh heh. She can show ya how that song goes. You wanna do the shimmy for Hooper?"

"Some other time, Uncle. Just keep quiet. Let me rub this in good."

Hooper has taken the Philippine guitar from its wall hook and sits on the sofa, with his high knees jutting, strumming, humming, searching for a key. In a few moments Broome starts to hum, and when Hooper begins to sing, Broome is taking short shuffling steps around the yellow perimeter again, bare feet scraping as they inch. Staying close, taking each tiny step with him, but soundlessly, her toes and tendons and thick pads of heel and sole settling each time against the floor, Nona follows, swinging one brown arm in mentholating circles. Hooper's feet, wide, flat, asphalt-scabbed, keep the moderato ragtime, pat-pat-pat-pat pat-pat-pat-pat:

> *I wish I could shimmy like my sister Kate.*
> *She shivers like the jelly on a plate.*
> *Momma wanted to know last night,*
> *Why all the boys treat sister Kate so right.*

Humming again in his unaccountable counterpoint, neither harmony nor disharmony, Broome creeps, mutters "Yep. Yep." Hooper holds the dark wood against his chest and feels its bass notes ringing, loves the wood, the ebony fretboard old and broken-in, yet not worn, the musty smell rising from its soundhole with each vibrating chord, as motes of disuse float away to coat other instruments.

> *Every boy in our neighborhood*
> *Knows that she can shimmy and it's understood,*
> *I know I'm late, but I'll be up to date*
> *When I can shimmy like my sister Kate.*
> *I'm shoutin',*
> *Shimmy like my sister Kate.*

He plays a chorus, working through licks he's done so many times he doesn't have to think about it, and watches Nona, around whose wrists and ankles crimson and blue-green feathers sheen to match the band of Broome's old hat. With each inching step her straw skirt flashes, whisks her legs. Hooper figures she's a couple of years older than he is, twenty-four or twenty-five, although it's hard to tell, one of those lineless Polynesian faces that could be anywhere between twenty-two and almost forty. She could be an illustration from *Captain Cook's Voyages*, except that her chest is covered, and she is so much else besides Hawaiian, a fine composite of every arrival on this coast since Cook himself anchored, and stayed. A delicately prominent Celtic chin, with jaws that flare a little, like a Guamanian's; lips defined by a sharp ridgy line and drawn toward fullness but stopping short of the thickness you often find in islanders, Her cheek skin is pulled close against its bone's curve in the Asian way, yet the eyes are only faintly Asian, black, wide, ovaled, remembering Asia at the outer edges where lids meet in a tiny tail flicking upward. The pupils aren't entirely white. They're tinged faintly brown, against skin darkened by pigments from Luzon or Samoa, but also by frequent sunbaths on the hot sand, lubricated with Johnson's Baby Oil.

Hooper sees her watching his hands. Their eyes meet briefly, and she smiles again, a broad strange smile, as if reading his mind. He starts to sing, can hardly keep from laughing.

Broome chuckles with them. Grunts of phlegm punctuate his humming. Since Hooper was here last, the hill of 78s next to his Victrola has spread lavalike across the floor, into the light. Broome cuts his slow path through this black layer.

Hooper has sung a third chorus when Broome stops shuffling, just past the record heap, tips forward slightly as if the pain returns. Hooper half rises to help. But no. The old man's only bowing, toward his gallery of instruments, turning his head an inch to the right, bowing again with a little waist english, then turning back an inch to the left, nodding into cobwebs, dangling strings, sprawl of black instrument cases.

"Yep. Yep. Yep. Yep."

It takes him a minute to greet all corners of his long room, while Hooper and Nona watch. Hooper tries to see what's tattooed on his chest, but shadows and thick white hair obscure it.

Finishing, Broome frowns, as if annoyed that the music's ended. He reaches for his yellow aloha shirt, rejecting Nona's hand with a shoulder jerk, refusing all help. She gives him the orange one, splashed with ukuleles. His coat sweater. At last he sits down in the leather chair, grumbles with the effort, reclines till his bare feet make a V upsticking.

Panama shoved over his eyes, as if nothing has happened to upset his endless rest, Broome says, "Didn't I tell ya, sweetheart? Didn't I tell ya this Hooper plays sweet?"

"Yes you did, Uncle Jack."

"What else did I tell ya?"

"You said you were going to give him your guitar."

Broome slides his hat back past his nose and squints at her.

"And did y'ever hear Jackson Broome back out on his word?"

"No, I never have."

The hat slides down again. "All ya have to do is play a tune for me once in a while, boy, and you keep that guitar till I ask for it back."

Out of courtesy Hooper protests. Broome seems not to hear. Nor does he hear Hooper's thanks, but seems now to be dozing into a long silence that Hooper finally breaks with a big bar chord—loud, pleased, testing the guitar's strength, like a man will slap the flank of a newly acquired mare, yet grateful, and eager to fulfill the bargain. He's ready to ask Broome what else he wants played, when Nona moves toward the phone, to get herself excused from work tonight, and wishes Broome would *let* her call a doctor. Broome chooses to ignore this suggestion, upon which Hooper makes it clear he can sit with Broome awhile, spend the night if need be, nothing else planned, nowhere to go, no one to report to. And Nona's face, which has been closed with worry, hearing this, now blossoms. Hooper is so taken with the openness of her huge smile, the vulnerability and sudden rush of color and warmth, that he sets forefinger against his lips and steps with her beyond the door.

In the shadowed hallway, lit on one side by half a door's diluted lemonade, and on the other by the high non-light above the distant intersection, he stands closer than he intended, smells again gardenias and orchid fragrance the Vaporub had overpowered. The near lack of light makes her brown neck smoother, darker, her hair black as ocean on a dark night, blacker than the night itself. He wants a handful of it. He wants her exotic face. She still wants to call a doctor. Hooper tells her it might be best to forget about that. And those exotic eyes peer, trying to get a better look at him.

She seems about to argue, but then leans back against the wall and confesses that Hooper is absolutely right. Doctors only make Broome worse. He throws tantrums, plays possum, stiffens like a corpse in his tiltback chair. If sent to a hospital he refuses all food, wets the bed on purpose, clamps his mouth shut like a little boy,

grabs for nurses when they aren't looking and tries at every opportunity to sneak, crawl, roll himself out the back door in a wheel-
chair, and once got so far as a taxi stand six blocks away, where he
was waiting for a cab, before they caught him. No, Broome is a
man who believes in home remedies and no one can do much for
him until he loses consciousness, which isn't likely tonight, since
his attacks are usually months apart. But in case Hooper needs
some help Nona will be right next door, on the second floor of the
Paradise Hotel, in the "Mauna Loa Room," where she dances five
nights a week. Tonight she'll come home right after her last show.
Hooper says he'll be waiting up—a notion she doesn't object to.
Before she hurries off, it's one last anxious glance through the door
at upstuck feet, and in that moment of standing close, silent, sharing
their burden of the old man's quirks, Hooper thinks he could lean
and kiss her, but doesn't, remembering the aftertaste of his sudden
coupling with Goldie, the recklessness with which he followed Bass
into Blanche's house and the impossible conditions for loving *her*.
Gun-shy, in short, yet savoring the abundance of women in his life,
he has, for the moment, time and detachment to weigh his options,
a cavalier ease.

She slips into darkness and his ease dissolves. "He who hesitates,"
the gospel says. Imaginary arms grope after her. Like the last flash
of an ending dream, she reappears an instant later, farther away,
under the old bulb's dim glow, grass swaying as she hurries, feathered anklets jouncing out of sight around a corner, the only sound
a whisk of straw, tiny click of shells and seeds, the front door's slam,
and behind him the old man wheezing, "Hooper?"

CHAPTER 32

A Golden Goose

*T*hese are the songs Hooper plays
while the old man reclines humming unknown melodies from his
private songbook:
    "Ida, Sweet as Apple Cider"
    "Alexander's Ragtime Band"

"Up a Lazy River"
"Mean to Me"
"Mississippi Mud"
"I'm Sittin' on Top of the World"
"Ace in the Hole"
"Button Up Your Overcoat"
"My Gal Sal"
"Me and My Shadow"
"When the Red Red Robin Comes Bob Bob Bobbin' Along"
"After You've Gone."

Then the humming dies. The breath seems to rise steadier and from deeper in his pebbled lungs. Hooper sets aside the guitar and quietly steps to Broome's desk, above which hangs a photo he's been looking at while he played, looking all around this room, seeing its profusion thoroughly for the first time, now that his eyes can penetrate beyond the lit arena—the scattering of clocks, some electric, some handwound, some dead, all pointing a different hour; in among the instrument cases and song sheets, a sprawl of nautical equipment, rusty binnacle lamps, rolls of sailcloth, hatch covers scratched and scoured by endless stormy tides. And then this photo, dusted over, of a trim little yawl, with a man wearing Broome's hat, about Broome's size, maybe twenty pounds lighter and twenty years younger, standing on the deck with one arm resting on a halyard.

The steady breathing stops. The hat doesn't move.

"Why'd ya quit playing?"

"Looking at this boat here on the wall."

"Heh."

"She was a beauty."

"That music soothes me, Hooper."

"Just resting my fingers."

"Yes . . . well, you take care a those fingers too."

Hooper sits down on the sofa, legs stretched, and leaning back with the guitar tilted against his chest, starts to strum.

"Can't read the boat's name, Uncle Jack. What did you call her?"

No answer.

He raises his voice. "I couldn't read the boat's . . ."

"*Golden Goose.*"

"That's a pretty good name for a boat."

"Old sayin I heard once from a Chinaman."

"Is that all there is to it—golden goose?"

"Heh heh . . . fellow who told me this was the scrawniest, raggediest heap a nothin you could ever imagine, didn't have a nickel to his name, and walking around down by the city hall passing out little engraved cards. I don't know where he got 'em, but I took one and paid a lot of attention to what it said because it told me something I had just about decided was true."

A long silence, during which Broome seems to doze again.

"Well, how the hell does it go?"

"What?"

"The old saying."

"The old saying . . . yes . . . was printed on a little card that said, 'If you leave your mouth open long enough, sooner or later a golden goose is bound to fly in.' That's been my motto ever since."

A pretty good old saying, thinks Hooper. He decides to make it his motto too. It describes a way he's felt for most of his life. In tribute he opens his mouth, closes his eyes, sees flocks of geese heading his way at this very moment, and wonders how he will keep from choking on good fortune.

Broome requests "Girl of My Dreams." Hooper starts to sing it. But halfway through, the old man starts talking again, the goose story has reminded him of another episode, and that one of another, and in a garrulous, halting monologue his mind starts reeling back, reaching perhaps for days when all these songs were new and he, not Hooper, was playing them. Slow chords background the jumble of times and towns, then stop again while Hooper stares long at more old pics Broome directs him to, buried in drawers, fallen behind the sofa, brown clippings mixed in with canceled checks and half-finished letters to debtors and creditors long gone. Hooper studies these while the old man mutters, recollects, damns and chuckles and seems to liven with the telling, as if his spasm loosened something else beside the phlegm. Old eyes are gazing past the creamy circle, and this is more or less what Hooper learns.

It's a bleak night in January five years before the First World War. Jackson Broome is holed up in Philadelphia, Pa., a sometime banjo player, barber, steeplejack, circus roustabout, twenty-four years of age and reading a letter from a brother who has ended up in Honolulu, six thousand miles away, asking Jackson why should a man freeze his ass off in the winter and sweat his balls off in the summer when he doesn't have to? Jackson, ass frozen, begins asking around—bars, hotel lobbies, paperboys. No one can give him an answer, so he signs on a merchant vessel out of New York, and a year later he's working as a banjo man in a sailor's bar on Hotel Street.

His brother Walter, a sax player who'd sailed over with a ship's orchestra from San Francisco, gets him the job. And it's here that he meets Luella Pike, in the summer of 1914, a handsome blonde from St. Louis, Missouri, ex-wife of a drummer who was thrown overboard in the Honolulu harbor with all his drums and mallets and drowned trying to swim his equipment back to shore. She ended up waiting on tables in the same bar and working part-time in the tattoo parlor next door.

She offers Jackson some art work at a discount, so one day he stops in to have a lobster tattooed on his back. Luella apprenticed to a master tattoo artist from the Philippines, is assigned the claws and parts of the tail, which Jackson wants curved around one of his sizable hats. Anxious to do a good job she invites him to her room where the light is better.

Bending shirtless in her kitchen, the stocky, supple Jackson soon feels real fingers where the claws should be, creeping toward the nipples on his chest, and her own nipples, suddenly bare and warm, are massaging the zone where the large front claws will join the body.

The tropics being what they are, a month later these two are married. Since Jackson doesn't want her working, she quits waiting on tables, but she won't give up tattooing. She likes it, says it's something she can fall back on. Jack is jealous of every biceps anchored, every calf engraved. He imagines more intimate requests. Accusations are made. Luella weeps. After eight months of this they're divorced.

He tries to have the lobster removed, but the Philippine master says it's impossible. So he has her tattoo across his chest in bulletin type,

THERE IS NO LOBSTER
ON MY BACK

Two years later he marries Luella again. They're going to sail to the South Seas, just the two of them, he will work as a musician if he has to, and she can set up a tattoo parlor if she wants, or maybe they'll just sail on around the world. But Luella gets pregnant. They cancel the trip. Then she miscarries, loses the baby. To cheer things up on their first anniversary, she decides to commemorate the event by tattooing JACK and LU on Broome's bare buttocks—to which he consents, spread nude on the kitchen table, until she jabs one needle in too deeply, breaks it off in there, being out of practice, and that, in a sense, is the last straw. They divorce again, more or less friendly, and when Broome opens his rooming house, Luella is his first customer. This happens of course years later.

Meanwhile Jack and Walter have put together an eight-piece group they call THE BROOME BROTHERS TROPICAL ORCHESTRA, Walter on lead sax, Jackson on steel guitar, the flat-lap kind, with the whining strings, and Walter's Chinese-Hawaiian wife Leilani on vocals. They start playing the big hotels around Honolulu, travel twice to Hilo, with stops on Maui, and on Molokai, Leilani's home island, and finally get a booking in Papeete one winter, an assignment Jack has been angling for. But this time Leilani develops a kind of gout, brought to a head by overeating at the luau in honor of their sailing, thus she can't travel by sea for several months. At the same party Jackson falls on Walter's tenor sax, bending it like a beer can.

The postponement works out well enough. This is the winter they sign with Decca to cut a few records. And they go on to become one of the most popular bands in the islands. In time they write a song together called "You'll Never Go Hungry in Hawaii," which is such a hit during the first years of the Depression that Jackson gets out of the music business entirely, buys some rental property in Waikiki, and decides that if he's going to see some more of the world, it's now or never.

He has just acquired a little yawl, twenty-seven feet, perfect two-man sailer, bought it for peanuts, from a shipper who lost everything in the Crash. And on that very day he runs into the shriveled man passing out cards with an old saying engraved, reads it, and runs right back to the harbor to paint the golden letters on her prow.

All he needs now is a partner. Luella, whom he's hired as concierge, for old time's sake, offers to sail with him. She even takes it upon herself to sneak down and decorate the boat's cabin with a little red trim around the windows. Surprising her there one morning, on hands and knees, red-fingered, dungareed, Jackson rips his shirt open and reminds her of the inscription on his chest.

She says, "Why won't you let me love you?"

Upon which he kicks in all the windows of his yawl's cabin.

By the time those are patched up, his brother Walter has died of a heart attack. Overwork. Four cars, two boats, two houses, eight kids to feed, plus Leilani, now the size of a yawl herself. So Jack sticks around till the shock wears off, settles Walter's affairs, and gets engaged to Luella one more time. She moves into his rooms for six months, but clings so tightly that he leaves her there and moves down to the harbor to live in his boat for a while.

With one thing and another, years pass, and he hasn't sailed anywhere but out to Diamond Head and back. On December 7, 1941, if the bombsights had been aimed at Waikiki instead of Pearl Harbor, the pilots would have seen Jackson Broome on a paddleboard, gliding around in the sunshine belly up, fifty-three years old and content with what remained for him, neither frozen ass nor sweating balls, but time to bask and swim, and his own choice piece of Polynesian real estate, with on one side a view of the beach and on the other a view of the mountains.

Then the war is over, passed him by. Roomers drift in and out of his life. Before the war it was tourists mostly, looking for a "different" place to spend two weeks or a month, a few permanent roomers, musicians, entertainers, old cronies. After the war Broome pays less and less attention to his clientele. He can take them or leave them alone. The musicians now are usually out of work. The steady roomers are servicemen looking for a cheap place to shack on weekends. Prostitutes down on their luck. Winos. Beach bums. There's a man still living upstairs, Hooper learns, who claims to own the original Spanish land grant to Malibu, California, whose rent has been accumulating for fourteen years toward the day when his claim is honored. Broome doesn't care. He has never needed the money. All he wants now is peace and quiet and this castle he has moated with vines and underbrush.

Yet look what they've gone and done to him. For years he lived upstairs in the big room now inhabited by Nona, a large second-story hexagon which, from the outside, Hooper recalls, seems added to the building as an afterthought, where one of the roof corners would have been, hanging over the yard, projecting upward almost as high as the peaked roof itself. Glass on six sides, for an all-directions view. When they built up the beach front they managed to close off the fabled lagoon, but the sunset still poured into every evening sky to color Diamond Head. Then they built the hotel right outside his favorite window, and it was just too much pink wall for Broome to stomach. He moved downstairs, inside his fortress of drawn shades, his pale ring of light. And the next thing he knows developers are trying to buy up his land, his piece of comfort, pestering him to death to get him to sell. They own the parking lot next door, tycoons who moved in from southern California to develop a chain of them all over Honolulu, and now these dealers tell Broome he's a public nuisance keeping property values down the way he does. This is what blocks his breathing, makes his chest hurt, strains his heart when they come around badgering him. Just this afternoon some heavy man in a see-through white nylon shirt, sweating like he'd just flown in from Phoenix and wasn't used to the humidity yet, came telling him if he didn't accept their offer they could have this house condemned. Broome chased him down the hall with an oar, stopped as the front door slammed, and leaned gasping at the jamb, crept feeble back to his leather chair, collapsed.

"Dirty sonofabitch," Broome mutters. "If I was your age, boy, I'd've beat him to the floor."

Broome is trembling at the memory, sitting up stiff-backed, grizzle chin jutting toward ghosts and memories of younger Broomes still circling the dark perimeter. Hooper sees one of them, the steel guitar player, pressed aloha shirt snug across his barrel chest, stepping from the bandstand at intermission into the arms of some drunken six-foot Texan whose wife has been making eyes at Jackson. The Texan starts shoving, and Jack, with a deft twist and sidestep, breaks his wrist. Hooper wishes he had been here this afternoon when the fat man showed up, catch him at the door before he even passes through the jeweled eye, toss him into the tall grass designed to befuddle all such men, and watch him scuttle for the gate.

"How often do they come around here, Uncle Jack?"

Broome doesn't answer. Hooper watches the stiffness slowly melt, the tremble eases. Sit back, feet lifting.

"Bring me that picture."

Brushing off dust with his hat Broome gazes long and silent at the framed photo in his lap and finally says that this *Golden Goose* not only was but still is a beautiful yawl, and berthed not twenty yards off at this very moment, in his back shed, up on blocks, suggesting in his whimsical manner that maybe now's the time for him to sail away, before they haul him off in a dump truck with the front stairs. At the very least maybe he and Hooper should take her out for a shakedown cruise sometime soon, see if she can still do her stuff.

Heh heh. The Broome chuckle. But this time his eyes are wet. It could be merely rheumy strain in the prolonged light. More phlegm in the throat now, though, fluttering under the chuckle. Eyes start to water heavily as his throat closes. Hooper finds himself nearly crying at the old man's helplessness and stubborn will, wants to aid him any way he can, half believes they *could* make a getaway together, blurts, "Sure, Uncle Jack. Why *can't* we take her out?" thinking he and Joe, or Bass, or all three, can drag the boat out of there and tie it to the Reo and pull it down to the harbor and figure out a way to strap Broome to the deck and take her out for a run. Maybe a little patching ahead of time to make her seaworthy again. If nothing else, wouldn't it lift the old man's spirits. Bring along Nona too, to see to his needs while we man the lines and the tiller.

"What do I do to get into that shed, Uncle Jack? Is it locked?"

No answer. Wheeze. In his lap the *Golden Goose*, half covered by the featherbanded panama. Around his eyes wet rings, and the smile from his last chuckle still on his lips, bent. Hooper sets the hat over the forehead to cover the eyes, listens a moment to his steady breathing, then grabs a flashlight from Broome's desk and steps out into the hall.

CHAPTER 33

Jonas has to see this

*T*hrough the back porch, past dark smells of ancient soap chunks fallen behind the tubs, across a patch of high grass, he shoulders the door of Broome's rear shed which, as his flashlight flares, he finds fastened with a coil of rusty wire. Untie this and step out of thick night air into an atmosphere even thicker, with moisture, fern silence, still and viscous. Hooper stops just past the doorway, lets this thickness cover him, slowly shines the dim light around.

The shed floor was planked once, but these planks are compost now, squishy to the foot, too soft to send splinters through his callouses. Among the planks, ferns have climbed to the hull's waterline, dark, wide-leafed ferns sprouting up and out and down like a wake of petrified green spume surrounding the boat. Spars and sheets of cobwebs connect the boat to all corners of the rotting walls and roof. Hooper pushes these away as he inspects the hull, once blue and gold, now rust-scarred, paint-chipped, dry rot, keel-pitted, layered with old barnacles. You couldn't read the name unless you knew what you were looking for, the letters have mostly peeled off, and what's left crumbles at his touch. He climbs a ladder still propped against the the hull and stands at its top. All the brass fittings are green, seem to glow with wet. One cabin window is broken, cabin door hangs open, spider webs in there, an insect stronghold, mold has covered the unholstery with dark velvet lining. Dust is piled on top of that. Dust layers the deck, and the coiled ropes have molded, varnish cracked. The masts are rolled in canvas on the deck, and the canvas too is velveted with mold. Hooper stands at the ladder head like a treasure diver, hundreds of feet down, examining some hulk that sank straight to the bottom and settled to sit through all these damp and silent years waiting with the stoic patience of the derelict—to be discovered, or not to be. He inhales deeply. No movement in this shed, no sound inside, or outside, for a long moment.

Hooper holds his breath, and holds it. His exhale, and a distant grind of traffic, break the spell.

He climbs down and heads back to the old man's room, where he takes up his vigil, on the sofa, with the dark guitar, pecking aimless at its frets, and waiting for tomorrow when he can air that shed out and start to work, and waiting for the Mauna Loa Room to close.

He glances at a clock, at another, and another. On shelves, sills and tabletops, rings and squares of time surround him: 8:24, 2:10, 6:45, 3:01, 9:56. No matter. Just listen for the door. Think of ways to keep out penetrators. So Broome can rest easy. Like he deserves. Like he's doing now.

Hooper floats above the sofa, with everything beginning once again. His head slouches to the backrest, languid fingers fretting, thinking Jonas has to see this. Joe will shit his pants. If Joe's truck is the ultimate vehicle this has to be the ultimate boat. Brush out the cobwebs, scrape off the mold, patch the hull, varnish the mast, drop her in the water, she *has* to float (his own eyes close), she *has* to go like hell.

CHAPTER 34

Where's the pool, sister

*B*utter-cube vest stained and faded now, red hair rusting toward white. He still wears a watch fob, but no swallowtail coat. The day's too humid for that, hot Sunday here in Nashville, and he rocks through it on his hot front porch, hears river water lap beyond the trees. It's not the Mississippi. He ran out of money before he saw those Memphis riverboats. Call it the Cumberland, not a bad river for this part of the country, and as he listens to it, waiting for the singing to start, a man in shirt-sleeves walks up to the porch rail, says, "Howdy, Abner."

"Howdy."

"I got ten dollars says he won't do it."

"Hate to take that much from ya, Tom."

"Even money?"

"Even money."

Abner makes a note of this.

Tom says, "When'll we know?"

Mournful glance. "That's up to Davey."

"You goin down to the baptizin, Abner?"

"Bleev I'll just set a spell."

"Better come along, oughtta be a good crowd watchin." Tom winks, pats his hip pocket pulled tight and shiny.

Abner thinks about it. Sitting and not sitting seem equally hopeless pastimes. He grunts forlornly out of the rocker and joins Tom, strides along next to him toward the river. They can hear singers on the far bank, their gospel joy floating up over the trees. Abner follows Tom through a heavy thicket, sliding down a soft dirt embankment to the last brush line above the water, where four other men in shirtsleeves and wide suspenders squat, passing flasks of corn whiskey, snickering.

Abner squats, takes a long pull from Tom's and finally turns his eye to the sight he can scarcely face: his own son in a black suit, black tie, squishing through mud now toward the water's edge, ready to baptize his first batch of penitents. Not twenty-one years old and already boiling with fire and brimstone, and Abner so sick at heart he has hired a buxom girl from out of town to get in line and do anything she can think of to fill Davey with another kind of heat. Abner's giving even money and forty-eight hours for Dave to prove himself. And he already knows he'll have to sell his horse to pay off these cronies squatting with him here.

Seven new saints have joined the singers on the bank when number eight, the last, reaches for the young preacher's hand. She wades in behind him, water darkening her gingham. Little eddies push it at her legs, and she leans on his arm, breathing heavily, gazing up at him as if the fullness of her spirit is ready to erupt and spill out over everything in sight. He plants his left hand firmly at her lower back, and with the other pinches her nose, instructs her to hold on. And she does—one arm squeezing his waist, one hand around his raised wrist, so that he's pulled forward, nearly falls in on top of her as he intones: "I now baptize you in the name of the Father and the Son and Holy Ghost."

Up she comes, gingham clinging, small shadow at her navel, and great nippled pumpkins bulging at the wet cloth. She hangs on the preacher's arm, pressing close, about to faint. On the muddy beach the female voices dwindle, quickly cease, while the tenors and basses sing out louder than ever, drowning the spatter of guffaws from the far bank thicket.

The girl goes limp against him, and Davey has no choice but to hold tightly if he is to keep her from sliding underwater again. As he starts to drag her toward shore, her body stiffens. She groans. She begins to twitch and squirm. When he tries to relax his hold, her knees seem to buckle. He grabs her tighter still, and she is writhing inside his redfaced and desperate embrace. Her groans grow louder. She begins to chant, "Oh brothers. Oh brothers and sisters."

Davey stares down at her eyes shut tight, the agony of her bunched brow. The deep valley between her heaving breasts seem to depict some terrible darkness the girl is struggling with.

"Oh brothers and sisters," she cries. "I see ... I see ..."

Davey shouts so the whole congregation can hear, "What is it, sister? What is it you see?"

"I see sinners!"

"How many, sister?"

"Hundreds. Hundreds and hundreds of sinners!"

Her dripping body is alternately limp and arching stiffly against him. Dave is wet to the shoulders now himself, splashing and shifting his feet to stay balanced. The congregation watches this strange offshore dance in dumbfounded silence, while Dave shouts, "What are they doing, sister?"

"I see hundreds of sinners ... waiting ... and waiting ... and waiting ..."

"What for?"

Her eyes snap open, she rears back, compelling him with her gaze.

Loud and slow, spreading her arms, she says, "It's a great big pool, brother. Biggest pool you ever saw. Maybe it's a lake. So wide you can't see the other side. And it's all lined up with sinners, waiting ... waiting ..." Her bare arm stiffens, darts toward him "... waiting for you!"

"For me?"

"Waiting for you to come and wash away their sins!"

"Tell us where it is, sister."

She turns from him, free of his grip, standing to her waist in the eddying stream. She looks all around as if searching the trees for an opening, a path.

"Sister," Davey shouts, "where is it?"

She wades toward the bank like a sleepwalker, eyes wide, chest thrown forward, strands of dark hair stuck to her neck and ears and forehead, a wild visionary shouting back at him, without turning around. "I see it! I see it! The spirit's gonna lead me there, brother!"

She passes the knot of astonished singers, her arms out and her head uplifted. "The spirit's gonna lead me this very day. And if any man of God wants to follow ..."

Davey has been watching her haunches pull the cloth taut with each step up the sloping path. Knees lifting, he splashes out behind her now, shouting Hallelujah.

It takes him ten minutes to change his clothes, pack his saddle-

bags with Bibles and hymn books. With the girl saucer-eyed sitting in his saddle, and Dave behind her, astraddle his horse's flank, fresh black suit and straight as a pillar holding stiff curved palms to her tiny waist, they trot out of town. His small congregation watches from the church steps—some appalled, some envious, some uplifted by this proof of holy forces moving in their midst.

Ten minutes later, by another, less traveled route, Abner and his pals trot out of town in the same direction.

One hour south and west, Reverend Davey and his guide plunge into maple forests, reach a small clearing where afternoon light cuts yellow slices in the still air. She draws the reins. Hoof clopping stops.

She listens for a while, doesn't move.

Davey waits, feels her ribcage rise and fall.

The horse snuffles.

At last she says in a throaty whisper, "This is it, brother."

"What is?"

She climbs down, stands barefoot in soft grass as Dave dismounts, trembling. "I don't see any pool here, sister. I don't hear any sinners."

She steps close to him. He glances down into that deep valley. No more darkness there. Slanting sunlight fills it, rounds and polishes the hillocks burnished with sweat. They seem to transmit heat to his face and neck. She takes his hand and leads him away from the horse, toward a cool nest of fallen leaves in among a tight ring of trees.

"Where's the pool, sister?"

"Close your eyes, Brother Dunlap, and wait. Like all those sinners are waiting. Close your eyes and listen to me."

He does. The closed eyelids jerk and quiver.

"The pool is here, brother. We only have to look for it. Within. Does not the Scripture say, The kingdom of heaven is within you?"

"Yes. Yes."

"And this pool, it too is within us. Within you. Within me."

"Of course. Of course."

"And we find it by probing. Within. As with a rod."

"A rod?"

"First we kneel down. Like this."

"Yes."

"You touch my waist again, as you did in the river. Like this."

"Yes."

"With both hands."

"Yes."

"And I touch your waist, brother."

"Yes."

"And we move very close to each other."

"Yes."

"And we must move as one person."

"Yes."

"Now open your eyes and look into mine."

"No."

"Brother . . ."

"I have seen the pool."

"You will feel the pool swelling inside you . . ."

"No. I too have seen the pool, sister! You were right!"

"Press me closer. We must move . . ."

"It is exactly as you said."

"Now we must lie down, brother."

"No! We must stand and praise the Lord. Oh, sister, it is just as you said. I see the pool! I see the sinners! I see what I must do!"

Half reclining she pulls at his arm, reaches a cool hand to stroke his chin and neck.

"Next to me here, Brother Dunlap, lie down. I am the pool into which you must sink."

But Dave is on his feet shouting Hallelujah into the thousand maples. His eyes spring open, blazing with new vision.

"Stand up, sister! Hurry! Now we must ride! I see the road, I see the pool!"

He is pulling her to rise, she is pulling him to lie down. Their sweating hands slide apart. He stands above her.

"Sister, ride with me. There is already too little time."

Then he's running for the horse. She yells something about his manhood. Twenty yards away, with their backs against a rotten stump the gamblers are sipping and digging one another in the ribs —all but Abner, who watches his son mount the waiting and saddlebagged mare, slap the reins, and gallop farther down the road out of Nashville, sound and sight of him disappearing into maple woods.

CHAPTER 35

Among her souvenirs

A door clicks. Hooper wakes, listens, wants it to be Nona, looks to see what time it is. 11:57. 3:04. 8:21. From far down the hall, as if it's a sound tube, he hears small stationary footscrapes. It's Mrs. Pike standing out there taking off her shoes. She's just come back from prayer meeting.

He's up to head her off at the murky intersection, beneath the smoldering filament.

"Evening, Mrs. Pike."

She grabs his sleeve. "Where've you been? I been looking all over for you."

"What's the matter?"

"I have to talk to you."

"Right now?"

"Have a cup of tea."

"I can't, Mrs. Pike . . ."

"Call me Luella."

"Luella."

"You can take out five minutes for a cup of tea now. C'mon."

Moments later they are sitting in her room, Luella on the rumpled double bed in her trenchcoat, Hooper on a straightbacked wicker chair. They're waiting for the water on her hot plate to boil, and he is looking around astounded by the size of the room, high-ceilinged, with one paneled alcove she uses as a kitchen, and a windowed one facing the yard, featuring a pair of french doors. She tells him these haven't been opened in many years. Outside the underbrush has grown up thick.

A table full of blue candles of various sizes lights this tête-à-tête. At one end, on a purple velvet cloth, sits a neatly ordered collection of needles and tinted jars, and above these, tacked to the wall, altarlike in the candle's steady glow, a chart of designs: anchors coiled with rope, American eagles, words like **MOM** and **ESTHER** twined round with pink roses on blue stems.

Her walls are hung with souvenirs like that, framed photos, beer mugs, medallions, and articles cut from the paper. A greening silver trophy stands next to her hot plate.

101

Now pouring water over Hooper's Lipton's sack, Mrs. Pike wants to offer him a position.

"It'd be just the ticket," she says.

"What would?"

"For you to be president. Young fella like yourself is just what we need."

"Who?"

"The Property Council. We ain't had a president since Mr. Coopman died. He played piano down at the Mercy Tabernacle. Fell right over on top a the keyboard one night with the worst crash and plonkety plink you ever heard. Drank himself to death is what it was. He was too old anyway, if you want my opinion."

"What does it do?"

"The tabernacle?"

"The property council."

"Oh, it decides about the property."

"Who else is on it?"

"Anybody living at the rooming house *can* be on it. The thing is, Mr. Broome just can't take care a things no more. I'll give you one example. Every time I go outside now that fella over there in the parking lot tries to *squirt* me. And I know somebody's put him up to that. They don't give us a moment's peace. Don't you think that's a awful thing? Woman my age can't even walk along her own driveway and out to the sidewalk without getting squirted by a hose?"

"That *is* an awful thing."

"Well," she says loudly, with a palm thrown up, as if something has been settled.

"Why don't you squirt him back?"

She looks at Hooper hard for several seconds.

"That's just what I mean," she says. "If you'd be the president . . ."

"Being president isn't really my line at all, Mrs. Pike."

"Luella."

"Luella."

"Listen now. Don't you move."

She gets up, crosses to her dresser, takes from its top a hand grenade. Holding this in her open palm she stands in front of Hooper, looking at him significantly, waiting for his response.

"What are you going to do with that?" he says.

"I found it upstairs."

"It doesn't have a fuse."

"What?"

"It's been de-fused."

She squints past him, as if mentally adding a long column of figures.

Hooper stands up to leave. "It would make a good paperweight."

"That's what I've been using it for."

She sits down wearily, looks at her teacup.

"I ought to be going," Hooper says.

"You haven't finished your tea."

He tells her about Broome.

"Oh dear Lord."

"He's okay now. Breathing easy."

"Why didn't you *tell* me?" suddenly glaring.

"I started to . . ."

She's elbowing past him. "Somebody has to stay with the poor man."

"I know it. I'm just on my way back . . ."

"No, no, no. You go on to bed. I know just what to do."

"I don't think there's much to do but sit with him. No need for you to stay up . . ."

Hooper tries to step in front of her. She shoulders him up against the jamb. "Don't you tell me what there's no need for in this house, young man!"

"Mrs. Pike . . ."

But she is into the hallway. He watches her striding toward the doorway's square of light, sees her suddenly stop, barrel body silhouetted there, spun silver glowing off the top and sides of whirled hair. She tiptoes in.

CHAPTER 36

Sometime after Midnight

*T*here's no use fighting her. Hooper decides to wait in his own room and listen there for Nona's return. He opens his window, lies down on top of his bag to concentrate on every outside noise. Each passing engine, faint palm rustle, footfall on the sidewalk. It soon hypnotizes him. Against his will, at the long day's end, his eyes close again. He sleeps.

A NATIVE SON OF THE GOLDEN WEST

In Broome's room, where the light never changes, so that there are no more dawns or dusks, the old man wakes. His habits fit no planetary pattern these days. Under yellow light his eyes flick open like a hippo's in the sun. Without moving he spots Luella, sitting on his sofa, head thrown back, sucking air.

After a while he hears the front door open, hears bare feet padding his way. The door to his room moves. He shuts his eyes, begins wheezing.

Nona stands over him, looking down, stands for a long time, and feels her veins and muscles humming, both light and heavy, weary and euphoric, with the fast walk home, lonely in the sudden silence of her movement stopped, expecting Hooper to be here, yet glad for this solitude. The old man looks comfortable. For the first time in years, it seems, no eyes are watching her.

Hooper's replacement is comfortable too, next to Hooper's guitar. Nona figures Luella chased him out of here, and she doesn't hold it against him. She figures he must be in his room now and thinks of delivering the guitar, but can't remember which room it is. So, carrying the guitar to a rattan chair outside the light pool, she sits.

Through all the songs she's danced tonight she hears again the zany tune he played. She's thinking of the musician in him. His size too, a height to match her own. And a lingering trace of the preacher he had almost become, Eagle Scout vestiges that seem to say, I am trustworthy, loyal, brave and honest. But mainly the musician. He has a light touch that pleases her. Call it a taste that runs in her family. The men she grew up with are all guitar players, ukulele masters, bassists, drummers, the women sweet-voiced and hula-famous. It's a family of performers webbing all these islands, from Kauai to Hilo. See her sitting here unwinding all the hip and hand patterns she wove in the Mauna Loa air tonight, clearing her head and her lungs of smoke and leers and groping hands, sailors and camerabugs and nightly invitations to free pink ladies, screen tests, now wondering about Hooper and his affection for Broome, and keeping an eye on the old man whose piece of her clan is but a small appendage, great-uncle without issue, who taught her half the songs she knows.

CHAPTER 37

Hashimoto

*M*orning light, filtering through vines and clogged screens and bamboo strips, is uniformly amber. No wind to trouble it. No dust to sprinkle it. Nothing to alter it until a shadow stops outside one window. An eye against one bamboo slit. Hooper's eyes pop open, wide awake, and fix upon that other eye.

"Who is it?"

"Pardon me."

"Who the hell is it?"

"What's the number of this building?"

"I don't know."

"Is this where Jackson Broome lives?"

"Yes."

"Aaaah. And is he home today?"

By this time Hooper's up, drawing back the blind to find a small brown Japanese man leaning over bushes—green twill slacks, short white sleeves, narrow-brim sporty hat, clipboard at his waist. Out at the curb Hooper sees a new Chevvy with the circular crest on the door.

"No. He's not at home. Can I help you?"

"I'd like to speak to the owner of the building."

"We had to rush him to the hospital. I'm his nephew. Watching the place while he's gone."

One blink behind hornrim glasses. The man steps back, sizing up Hooper's no-shirt, peeling shoulders, bleached brows.

"I'm sorry to hear that your uncle is ill. My name is Hashimoto. I'm out here from the building inspector's office. We're compiling a report on all the older buildings in this area that are substandard."

Hooper, leaning on the sill, takes his time replying. "What makes you think this building is substandard?"

"Well." A condescending smile. "We get reports in . . ."

"From who??"

"It's part of our job."

"This happens to be one of the finest buildings in Honolulu."

Another blink.

"One of the finest in the Pacific Ocean."

"I'd like to have a look around."

"That's impossible. Not until Mr. Broome gets back."

"When will that be?"

"Couple of months. Maybe longer. He's in pretty bad shape. He wouldn't want anybody poking around without his permission."

"I guess he wouldn't mind if I just looked at the outside. I'm halfway around already."

A smug hopeful smile and Hashimoto takes one step along the driveway, toward the rear yard, gazing upward skeptically, as if the warping eave might crash down at any moment.

Sharply Hooper says, "Yes he would."

"Pardon me?"

"Mr. Broome would mind very much if you walked around the outside."

"This is just a routine . . ."

"He minds very much having uninvited people even stepping on his property. He values his privacy."

One long leg comes out the window. Hashimoto stops.

"City ordinances authorize . . ."

"I don't care about that."

"What?"

Hooper hops down among the creepers, hands on hips.

"You get away from here."

"Now wait a moment."

"I said get away from here. There's nothing wrong with this building. Go on. Move."

He steps out onto the driveway. He's a foot taller than Hashimoto, forty pounds heavier. The little man retreats, clipboard at his stomach like a shield.

"I'm doing this for your own good. Mr. Broome would be cocking his shotgun by this time."

Over the Chevvy windowsill Hashimoto shouts, "You'll be hearing from my office about this."

"I hope it's an apology."

CHAPTER 38

The man in
Green Pajamas

*J*ust as the car grumbles away, Luella rounds a corner of the building on her way to the mail-box.

"Who was that?"

Hooper tells her.

"Oh dear Lord."

"What's the matter?"

"Heaven and earth."

"What is it?"

"Don't you dare tell Mr. Broome. The poor man would have a fit."

"I know it."

"Why can't they leave us alone?"

"Somebody's after the property."

"Merciful Jesus. You mean he might come back?"

"Maybe. I guess we ought to be prepared for something like that."

"Oh dear God."

"We have to keep those guys away from the house."

Her old eyes open wide, as if Hooper is shoving a pistol at her bosom. Her hands, hanging, seem ready to fly over her head. He wants her to make some outrageous demand he can mock, or counter. He waits for her to recover. She just stands watching him with victim's eyes, murmuring Merciful Jesus.

He blurts, "You've been living here for thirty years. Don't you have some ideas about how ..."

The eyes crinkle to slits again. "Don't you raise your voice to me!"

"I'm just trying to ..."

"I don't care what you're trying! Don't you talk that way to a woman three times your age!"

Two floors above them a window is thrown open. A man sticks his head out, a skeletal man wearing green pajamas.

"What the hell's all the racket?"

She ignores him, stands staring past Hooper as if waiting for a jet plane to take off, for the thunder of its engine to pass.

The man turns red, screams, "I said what the hell's all the racket down there?"

To Hooper she mutters, "I think I have an idea."

The window slams, causing a shade in the room below to fly up, slapping. A shadowy figure rises behind the screen grumbling, "Jesus Christ Almighty."

Hooper follows Luella up the front steps and through the jewel-eyed door.

CHAPTER 39

The Captain in the Attic

She leads him to the light-shaft intersection, up the stairs, along the hall past Nona's room, into a wing of the building he's never visited. Something up here slows him down, the age, the floating silence, the light, so diffused by all the angles it has to make to reach this far, it seems to come from nowhere at all. Second-story doors seem even older than the ones below, longer shut. The nearest bears a small sign, DO NOT DISTURB, that looks tacked up once a dozen years ago and left. The tack has browned a ring around itself against the yellowed cardboard. The top and bottom edges bend outward, heated by a sun they've never seen.

Farther along, another door holds a message on a piece of blue notepaper Scotchtaped above the knob. The tape is dry and wrinkled. The note says, "Be right back."

As they make another turn in the hallway, Hooper hears a tiny creak behind him, turns, sees the man in green pajamas emerge, look both ways furtively. He doesn't see Hooper. He creeps bandy-legged to a door three rooms along and disappears.

Hooper follows Luella up a short flight, through a low door, into an attic room that seems as long as the house is wide, and illuminated by whatever light can force its way through dust piled against the panes of two dormer windows. The panes are diamond-shaped, inside oval frames, and dust rests in the bottom angle of each diamond like silt on a river bottom. The long attic looks like a cos-

108

tume shop, or the prop room of a theater. It's piled with furniture, wicker mostly, rotten matting, bedsteads, fringed lamp shades. One giant basket is filled with green glass fishing floats. There's a dressmaker's dummy wearing a sea captain's coat, and a sprawl of hats —rain hats, straws, derbies, top hats, stetsons, sou'westers, fezzes, pith helmets, sombreros.

Mrs. Pike pushes her way through cartons and old trousers and kneels in front of one of the windows, waving back cobwebs with a painted fan.

"From here," she says, "we could spot them coming easy." Foxy-eyed she turns to see how he receives this.

Like a bombardier he leans above her peering down at the walkway, thinking of sandbags, buckets of ice water.

"Yes. Yes. And then?"

"Well . . ."

Her eyes go wide again. The assaulted. The holdup victim. In this filtered light, a long silence. Her mind has obviously gone blank. Her face is frozen, and her eyes seem slowly to be glazing over.

It's contagious. Hooper feels his own eyes glazing. Hours seem to pass. They sit there eye to vacant eye. Then something comes to him.

"Listen."

She blinks in terror. "What?"

"I think I have it."

"Have what?"

"Suppose someone contracted a terrible disease."

"Who?"

"What about you?"

"Oh no ya don't."

"I don't mean a real disease."

"I'm not catching any kind of disease. What are you up to anyhow?"

"Do you ever drink tea in the morning, Mrs. Pike?"

"I wish you'd stop calling me Mrs. Pike."

"I'm sorry."

"Not as a regular practice."

"I'm sort of in the mood for a cup of tea."

"You are?"

"I think if we could sit down over a cup of tea we could work this out."

"I suppose there wouldn't be any harm . . ."

"It doesn't have to be *you*, necessarily, who gets the disease."

"My Lord, *that's* a relief."

"Probably ought to be Uncle Jack."

"Now you listen here, that poor man already has enough trouble in his life."

"He doesn't even have to know about it."

"Then how . . ."

"Let's go put the water on the hot plate."

"My room's a mess. I ought to run down there first . . ."

"I'm not particular. Couldn't be much different from what it was last night."

But she is scrambling past him, kicking hatboxes aside, toppling a stack of magazines.

"Just give me five minutes," she says, ducking out the door.

CHAPTER 40

Watering

Scheme cooking, Hooper takes his time, tries on a yellow satin vest that flatters his shoulders in the dusty mirror. Wearing this he ducks into the hall, rounds the first corner just as the door to Nona's room opens and she steps out, in a short blue kimono-like beach wrap, carrying a towel. A bright haze from inside her room drifts through the flimsy cloth, dream light. She is the girl of his dreams returning, and he would keep it that way, stand and stare, devour the curves from a distance, while her back is to him, bending to lock the door. But turning, she spots him, and he has to move on down the hall, with firm tread. Don't want to look like a lurker. Greet her with confidence.

"Nona."

She's cool, unruffled. Her mindreader's smile. "Good morning, Hooper," as if expecting him to meet her here.

"Looks like you're going swimming."

"It wakes me up. Want to come along?"

He doesn't hesitate. He doesn't lose a step. They walk downstairs without making a sound, Nona soft-footed by nature, Hooper by design, regretting this slight to Luella, but reminding himself she's used to it, born to humiliation, sudden loss. Their scheme can wait an hour or so, Luella can wait. Every scheme and creature on the planet Earth can wait, as long as he can follow diaphanous Nona through the skylight cascade, toward the frontdoor's particolored sunburst, shine from it pouring toward him through her blue kimono.

Past the hedge they walk a few yards in silence, matching long strides, Hooper suddenly timid, uncertain what to say or do. Something is definitely wrong. Something is missing. Something should be here which isn't. And yes, of course, it's the old man's fault. It's Broome that's missing. Their common problem, their bond, third figure in their promenade, and without him, this gap, this vacancy. Well, fill it then. Tell her about the boat.

"After you left last night, Uncle Jack started talking about that boat of his."

"Boat?"

She's never heard of it. He tells her how the evening went, the songs and stories, and how he plans to patch up the *Golden Goose*, take Broome out for a sail. They are on the beach by this time, and Nona has to stop, right there on the sand, big swarthy girl blinking back sudden tears, telling Hooper nothing could make her uncle happier. The way her eyes glisten, he is nearly crying too, upwell of gentle lust, and warmed by his own generosity. She holds him with these eyes, and he has to do something. Take her in his arms, or take to the water. He grabs her hand, leads her loping over hot sand to the tide line.

Wade in together, feel its cooling ledge. Thighs gone. Loins caressed, eased a little with the tiny jolt, another kind of satisfaction. Bellies gone. Ledge at your chest and lean against it, gentle push of unbreaking swell, its coolness giving with the weight, and swim easy breaststrokes, then sidestrokes, facing each other, eyes meeting, glancing off, sizing each other up, as arms scoop like an aquacade team, affinity for water a strong bond between any two people, supplanting Broome now as common denominator, and Hooper relaxes on his side of the river they make, its current streaming between them, delighted to see that Nona displays neither fear of the water nor a sense of being brave about it, the way so many mainland girls do upon entering the ocean, their faces saying, I don't particularly want to do this but I will. Goldie of course was an exception. A water girl from the start. But there was that taint about Goldie. Shadows across his heart. Not so with Nona. No shadows. No taints. And quite apart from that, when it comes to water, a girl from the mainland will always run second to an island girl. Grace of the natural element. When you're a native son, such things are important. You want a girl who'll go swimming with you, diving with you, all the ways of watering with you. Which may be true on any coast where the climate's right and sand plentiful. But for a native son of the golden west it's an absolute necessity.

Below them now blurred coral wavers. A hundred yards away eight people in a red canoe, first load of the day, lean forward with a plump lazy swell that lifts but doesn't catch, and passes on, without breaking. Around this canoe new sailors from Pearl paddle out, Schofield corporals on rented boards, and wait, or stroke madly for other frothless ripples. Past the boards, past the canoes, out to where the sand stops and green water merges with cobalt, bottom tilts away toward canyon deeps, Hooper and Nona float awhile, holding long comradely talks under the sun spinning up over Diamond Head. They talk about music, and show business, and California, and what they like for breakfast, and Nona's family, and the way things are going in the islands.

"I love to swim out this far," she says. "The hotels shrink almost to nothing."

"Midgets," Hooper says, "Monopoly pieces."

"From out here you can see how high the mountains really are. You can stare at the ridge and not even see the hotels."

He stares at the ridge line and Nona's right, all the hotels melt to blobs, squashed by that high green prehistoric profile, this bottom sloping away below them being old volcanic mountainside sliding on down to the seafloor, hotels appended to its long descent like white snow-mounds at the treeline, which can only melt or avalanche into the rivers that made them.

He stares at that and at the girl who saw it, and he is very hungry. His groin is swelling with a hunger for all these things at once, for the woman who can see things the way he likes them to be seen, and for that mountain ridge, the old island hunger, some way to swallow the entire island, or be swallowed by it, by the water that spawned it, and a simultaneous yearning for those sausages and honeyed biscuits already flavoring the pancake kitchen around the corner from Broome's. Hungry for some way to make love to everything at the same time, he tells Nona he is starved, and she says breakfast is her middle name, and eight minutes later they are on the beach taking turns toweling off with Nona's towel.

CHAPTER 41

The Lover's Meal

*A*fter waking under clean sheets, slow coming to life in the warm morning arms, the shower together, the dressing, the sunshine and head-freshening walk to the restaurant, with bodies still joined, reluctant to part, till the table finally comes between, and the food, and the smells, breakfast is indeed, for morning lovers, a mighty savory dessert.

If you had seen Hooper and Nona there at Johnny B's, grinning at each other across the table while they ate, you would have sworn they were lovers rising late. Not so. This meal is not dessert for them, but foreplay.

Hooper in his yellow vest, Nona in her flimsy beach coat, and between them plates of sausages, scrambled eggs, coffeepot, side order of french toast, syrup decanter, honey jar, and biscuits and butter patties melting. He's never known a girl who could eat this much, with such gusto, and yet such style. Goldie for example is a wolfer, like the men she emulates—half a hamburger in a single bite, half chewed, and mustard gobbing down her aloha shirt. But Nona, who can actually keep ahead of Hooper, appears to be taking her time. Gobbling, he watches her cheeks flush, her brow breaks into a passionate sweat, her eyes shine dreamily, as if she's in heat. And of course she is. Every meal's a luau, and Nona the voluptuary forks it in.

Hooper feels incredibly lucky. Even five years from now she won't be the same. He remembers Broome's account of Nona's grandmother, sweet Leilani, two hundred twenty-five pounds of aloha when she died. Nona has the frame that will carry all that and more. But right now, at this point in time, there's something about her. Chance in a million. Six feet tall. A hundred and forty. Her flesh and bones seem to him to have an optimum proportion. The way he feels today it's true of everything else about her too. He gets the idea that he will make love to her before the day is out. He must. This table full of food has settled the matter. They are both high on coffee fumes and sausage tang and saltwater tingle from the long swim.

"Nona, do you realize that at this moment your flesh and bones have reached a sort of optimum proportion?"

113

She giggles.

"I mean it."

In a puddle of syrup she is sopping up the last of the french toast. Hooper signals for the check.

CHAPTER 42

Hold it hold it

*B*ack at Broome's they are tip-toeing up to the second floor. Hooper whispers, "Nona, this is very strange."

"What is?"

"I feel like we have been out on a date or something, followed, you know, by a meal of some kind or other, and now I am taking you home. In the classic manner. Seeing you to the door. Except that it is only around eleven o'clock in the morning. I guess you're used to that. But it makes me feel . . . sort of upside down."

"What makes you think I'm used to that?"

"Well, you say that your afternoons are taken up with practice and rehearsals and lessons, and that you need a long rest before you go to work, and then you dance most nights. That pretty much leaves mornings, doesn't it? I mean, you must have a lot of men asking you out to breakfast."

She shakes her head. "Very few men ask me out to breakfast."

"Why is that?"

"I get up early for a swim almost every morning. Most of the men I meet don't want to go swimming before breakfast. But they feel funny eating if I've been in the water and they haven't."

She has opened her door. She steps to a turntable just inside the room, switches it on, drops the arm on a record already there, say-ing, "As long as you've seen me home, you might as well come in for a minute, if you want."

Having been all this time prepared to do just that, Hooper now finds himself stuck at the threshold. Where she's standing her blue wrap is backlit from hard sunlight coming off a mirror, darkening the line of her waist and ribs. He wants to say something clever just now, seductive and definite. But he blanks out. He's a jellyfish

114

dangling in front of her, upside down. All those glances he stole on the beach and in the water, at her hips, at her cleavage, don't count. He's seeing her for the first time and can't help staring at her body's outline inside the sheer. She doesn't move, seems fixed in just this spot, on purpose, mirror pre-set for the tantalizing effect. His eyes flick from her face to the room behind, sparkled with things glinting in the mirror-bouncing light. Fresh-watered leafy plants, guitar strings. All the gourds and drums and shell necklaces he saw glowing shadily last night, for these few glimpses, toss the sun like morning surface of a wide bay.

He can't think of anything but that moment when they stood like this outside Broome's door in the hall downstairs, that moment suspended until now.

The record player comes to life, filling this silence with chunkety drums, Tahitian guitars, and Hooper, startled, declares, "You know, I almost kissed you last night."

"I know."

"And on the beach."

"Yes?"

Unnerved. Plunging on. "Why didn't I?"

"You were probably scared."

"Why would I be scared?"

"A lot of men are scared of me."

He chuckles foolishly. "I'm scared as hell right now."

"You see. It's my size. Big woman make big trouble."

"It's crazy." Another chuckle. "I can hardly talk."

"You're shivering."

"I think it's that kimono."

"My jacket?"

"I have ..."

"What?"

"An uncontrollable urge."

"To?"

"Touch it."

"And you're afraid of what will happen if you do."

"I think so. Yes."

"You want to know what I would do if you touched my kimono?"

"What?"

"I would have an uncontrollable urge to touch your yellow vest."

His hand rises, stops in midair, a floating glove.

"Touch," she says.

Hand to her shoulder, slide it slowly halfway down.

She reaches, strokes the yellow satin on his chest, making Hooper laugh.

"Does that tickle?" she says.

"Tingle."

"Still scared?"

"Yes."

"What's the matter now?"

Her eyes begin to glisten, the way they did on the beach, as if she's going to weep, or laugh at him, or has just finished laughing, and this glistening gaze starts Hooper's eyes blinking again with the same wet sheen. Fleshy heat settles on his arms and face, some hothouse atmospheric skin covers the two of them, and the right gesture now, almost any gesture, or word or look could take him past her, into the room, door closing soundlessly. But staring into Nona's eyes, he sees the room around her growing, spots of light merge, space extends behind her, massive aureole which, just below the eye level, outlines her dark figure like a fire, light spreading, walls recede, the door would close, Nona would become the door. He dares not move beyond where he stands right now.

This fear dries his eyes. Behind her the light spots separate, give way again to darker spaces in between—the mattress on the floor, one sheet thrown back, mats around it, floor-to-ceiling tapa cloth. Hooper's sweating. He wasn't ready for this. He wants the old man to come grunting up the stairs and step between them, referee. Or the table of food heaped high again. Or the ocean, safety zone of separating water. He wants to get away, but can't remember where he is or what he's doing here. Directions merge.

Nona turns toward the record player to switch the volume down, widening the space between them. He steps into the room, sees nothing but the shoulder he just touched. When she bends, fooling with the knob, he stands behind her, for an instant holding both hands above the wide shoulders, hesitating, weak with ardor, dread, finally takes both shoulders.

She doesn't move.

Slide slowly down the silky arms again, this time to her wrists.

Above guitars and plocketing drums urgent voices rise, the hurtling pace of mallets and tomtoms and festival song makes slower every movement in the room. Nona's hands take his and cross them on her stomach, where the belt of her short kimono is. He waits and breathes deep, inhaling floral scents that seem to hover wherever she goes, salted now, and with underwater motions lightly tugs at either side of the one-looped knot. It gives with the tugging, till the belt ends hang free in his amazed hands, lapels held only by the friction of overlapping cloth.

The drums speed up as his movements get slower, still feeling at each moment that the next will carry him beyond some marvelous and deadly point of no return, yet how to proceed with caution when the groin aches and Nona's not just waiting any more. Her head tilts back, pliant, searching for something to rub against. He offers his cheek and takes each kimono edge and peels it open, and lifts, and lets it drop to lauhala mat, then hands again against the fine thickness of her stomach draw her gently back, face plunged into the midnight hair. Hands slide up and down the long full body, belly, thighs, and tearing loose the swimsuit top. As if that touched some final switch she whirls and lunges, smothering his face and his fear.

Her bed is amber from the bamboo light. Into its pool of tinted sheets they fall, squirming, pressing all along each other's length, their hands reaching downward. Their lips search everywhere for salt, each lick of salt, each press of palm a claim on that zone of flesh. Then Nona's sliding down to where their hands are, out of sight beneath her black hair sprawl, and Hooper's world turns to oil and honey, with that underache like the waking after sleep, sun not quite up, and you want to hold it just there, below the horizon, light fringe quivering, threatening to spring, that fine moment has to be suspended. All the slippery moments—wave ends, coastal vistas, dawns and setting suns—how to keep their sweet ooze from slipping away, to let the juices run but never spill, how to keep these thighs of Nona always warm against his temples, seeing only dark heat and moisture, blood drumming with the plock-a-plock-a-plocket from Tahiti, honey running with it in his veins, and Nona squeezing at the tap, squeezing, twisting, turning to draw all of it out of him, pulling at it, pulling, and Hooper yearning into her delectable flesh, dreaming hold it hold it hold it.

CHAPTER 43

He reckons not

*H*ot wind blowing down from Kansas, dust through town that would choke a bedouin, and Benjamin Dunlap has never been so thirsty. His eyes are dry, his nose is dry, his tongue is dry, his liver is dry. Slack leather reins are splitting with the dryness. And his wagon planks so hot they'd probably catch fire, any one of them, at a single match flame.

On the seat his wife sits belly-swollen, silent, eyes permanently half-shut, waiting to see what he's going to do. Three other Dunlaps whipped silent by the heat, wait in the wagon's bed, in among the bundles, the boys hiding under straw hats, the girl like her mother, bonneted.

Benjamin waits too, for something to come to him. He sucks at his cheeks, looking for spit. He has half a mind to rob the bank.

Dusty boot on the step-down and he scowls at his kids. "Yawl sit still till I git back, ya heah?"

Quick, challenging glance at the wife, but she's staring at the horse's flaked rump.

Benjamin steps out from the shade they parked in and heads up the deserted street, into the wind. No one out here now but him, dragging boots through summer dust, tugging at his gallus buckles. One pair of overalls, one blue shirt, one old hat. He'd like a new hat. Two dollars would do it. Changes a fella's look, a new hat. One a them cowboy hats, with the crown blocked.

He jaywalks up the main street, and finding his direction as he strides, heads straight for a place called George Meeker's, which appears to have a good view, on the opposite corner, of the Fort Smith, Arkansas, Security and Trust.

Meeker's is a restaurant with a bar, and only one person inside, sitting at a table, fanning herself with a menu. Thirty-fivish woman, her waist still intact, and enormous breasts that Benjamin can't help staring at, thinking how Nell never was much in the chest, even now, seven months along and leaking milk.

"Bar's closed," the woman says.

"Why's that?"

"Mr. Meeker tends the bar, and he ain't here."

"Yawl Mrs. Meeeker?"

"Yes I am."

"My money's good, Mrs. Meeker."

"Mr. Meeker'll be in about four o'clock."

He shoves his hat back and grins. "Ma'am, by four o'clock I'll just be shriveled up like bacon in the sunshine. There won't be nothin left. A glass of brandy, Mrs. Meeker. That ain't gonna hurt Mr. Meeker's feelings none, you pour me out one glass a brandy."

She looks at him over the top of her undulating menu, sees him staring at her bosom again, seems to like that, says, "No, I guess it won't. Yawl go on over there and pour it out yourself and just put the money on the bar. It's too blamed hot for me to even git up."

Benjamin behind the mahogany bar, and as thirsty as he is, finds himself taking his time unscrewing the bottle cap, selecting a glass.

*Mighty nice here in a shady room. Big-bosomed woman to talk to.
He glances over at her, and she's watching him carefully as the
brandy trickles. Shot glass brimming, and his head tilts, Adam's
apple popping from the straight leather neck. He gulps it all.*

*Twenty-five cents on the bar, and he pours himself another, easy
trickle while he lets the liquor already inside him send cool flames
to the ribs. This second glass he sips. Reaching in his pocket, he
finds one coin left and knows by the size it's a quarter and wonders
if Nell has any money stashed away. Always does, he thinks. The
way her mind works. In his moment of hesitation he steals another
glance at Mrs. Meeker and sees her waiting, menu-fan suspended,
till he smacks the quarter down. The menu moves again. Plainly,
money's the only thing she's interested in. He squints out the window toward the bank.*

*"Fella ought not to carry around too much money with him at
one time, do you believe, Mrs. Meeker?"*

"Mr. Meeker never does."

*Benjamin gulps the second brandy, says, "I believe I'll mosey on
over to Security and Trust."*

*He feels very good now, stepping back into the raw sunlight.
Down over his eyes he pulls the old straw and briskly crosses the
street, pausing once on the bank steps to scan the sidewalk, empty,
baking in four directions.*

*Just inside, an electric fan moves air around but doesn't cool it.
Two clerks on duty, he can see, and one teller's window open. Two
customers there ahead of him. Benjamin joins the line, peering over
two sets of shoulders at a small bag of cash a stocky man is de-
positing.*

*Just that much, he thinks, just what that man's carrying in his
pouch, and shee-it, I'd be, well, I'd . . . sees himself scooping up that
bundle and scooting out the door so fast no one can believe it's
happened, then he's down a sidestreet, getting back to their wagon
from behind, and unhitching the horse with two flicks of strap and
halter and lickety-split along main street and out of town he goes,
riding bareback, the way Indians used to do, maybe swing by and
pick up Mrs. Meeker, for the company, she'd never turn down a bag
full of money. They could gallop all the way down to Texas, buy
up a few head of cattle there and run that into such a piece of hard
cash he might just build a big ole house on a bluff somewhere up
above the Brazos and sit out on the veranda, watch herds of white-
faced heifers mooing and moaning as far as he could see. It wouldn't
be any trouble to send back for Nell and the kids then. They'd still
be setting right there in the shade where he left them, planted,
waiting in the wagon. He'd just send a horse up on to Fort Smith,*

*back it in between the poles, hitch it up and bring 'em down to the
ranch—the B.D. spread, he'd call it. Yes, he might do that, and
then again he might not. Sometimes it's hard on the family, when a
man got his start robbing banks. Maybe just leave 'em there. And
send money back.*

"Can I help you?"

*Benjamin sees the teller in front of him, staring up over rimless
spectacles, under a green-brim eye shade.*

He repeats, "Can I help you?"

*Benjamin's right hand slides up the faded thigh of his overalls,
to his hip, where the side-buttons close and where a pistol might
hang. He rests the hand there, as if pondering weighty matters.*

"I reckon not."

"What?"

*Hand on hip, and throat suddenly so dry he knows he'll choke if
he speaks, Benjamin stands staring back at the man. When it looks
as if he doesn't intend to say anything else, the teller peeks around
him, sees the lobby empty and shuts the window. A cardboard sign
flops over its top, fanning one tiny ripple through the heat,* RING
FOR SERVICE.

CHAPTER 44

Interim

*A*t noon Hooper reports for
his appointment with Luella. From Nona it's one aloha kiss
(ALOHA—good-bye, hello, I like you, I love you, welcome, come
again, don't go away; all affections, mild and strong), a light embrace, and head downstairs to find not outrage but ancient feelings
hurt, seemingly beyond consolation. Her voice cracks as she tells
how five poured cups of tea went cold, and finally the entire pot,
and she, waiting, emptied her bladder twice, from drinking them
all in order not to waste it, tea in the morning being, in any case,
an unfamiliar practice. It is only when he mentions the Property
Council that her spirits lift. Still faced with that long-suffering
glance, however, the face of neglect, which he knows well, the
mother's face, doubly pathetic when the woman wearing it is child-

less, and imagining her staring at the steam and then into those steamless cooling cups, Hooper recklessly agrees to run for president, his instant regret sweetened only by the genuine smile of elation she spills all over him.

Another pan of water boils, and they resume the strategy conference. Nona is summoned. She is dubious. But Hooper takes charge, says he'll handle this. Plans are drawn up.

Then Nona leaves for rehearsal, and Hooper heads for the boathouse.

And so the day passes.

And eight other days.

During which time:

a. HASHIMOTO makes his report.

b. LUELLA from dawn till dinnertime stands watch by the dormer window.

c. GOLDIE receives from her father in El Segundo a check for her return flight to Honolulu. He says he'd never stand in her way.

d. ANDREW DUNLAP receives a five-hundred-dollar bonus for inventing a more efficient way to hoist a jet engine from hangar floor to fuselage.

e. JONAS and SHEEPDOG, near the northwest corner of the island, curse the world and each other.

f. WALTER CONQUEST, alone in his truck on the opposite shore, puzzles through a chess game in which he is his own opponent.

g. THE MAN WHO OWNS THE SPANISH LAND GRANT TO MALIBU, CALIFORNIA, drinks heavily.

h. HOOPER, with occasional help from Nona, hoes down ferns, drags spider webs off rafters with an old shirt, begins to scrape the *Golden Goose*.

i. THE MAN IN GREEN PAJAMAS wants to know what the hell is going on.

j. BLANCHE, reading in bed, with a movie mag propped against her upraised thigh, drops a long cigarette ash on the head of a red dragon climbing her leg, and in the instant before her flesh feels it, the dragon seems, to Bass, to be actually breathing smoke.

k. NONA is the subject of a dream in which Hooper is sailing the *Golden Goose* alone through unidentified waters, and finding himself running before a steady ten-knot wind, he lashes the tiller and moves forward. The bowsprit is one of those sometimes found on old whaling vessels, in the shape of a woman's head and torso, leaning over the water. He stretches out on top of her to contemplate the wake veeing back from his prow, and beneath him the bowsprit gradually comes to life, first warming to the touch of his naked body, then wriggling as his hands explore the underside, then its paint-chipped hair goes shiny, and as he enters her from behind, the dark face half turns with a smile of erotic satisfaction.

1. UNCLE JACK recuperates, in fact seems completely recovered after Hooper stops in one night to sing a song the old man had forgotten, making him so happy he laughs outloud, first time anyone's heard Broome laugh that way in years, and laughing they sing the second chorus together:

> *Oh what a time I had with Minnie the Mermaid*
> *Down at the bottom of the sea.*
> *I forgot my troubles, there among the bubbles.*
> *Gee, but she was awfully good to me.*
>
> *And every night, when the starfish came out,*
> *I'd hug and kiss her so. Oh.*
> *Oh what a time I had with Minnie the Mermaid,*
> *Down in her seaweed bungalow,*

Broome: *Low*
> *Down in her seaweed bungalow.*

—SPACER—

*O*LD CARTOON: A one-palm atoll. Ragged, potbellied, smirking lecher writes HELP in the sand, in tiny letters the size of his teeth, while ingenuous fellow refugee, her torn blouse exposing cleavage, points to search planes on the horizon.

CHAPTER 45

Jonas returns

*A*fternoons it's too hot to work in the shed. Now Hooper is finished for the day, heading back to his room with a binnacle light, which needs rewiring. Opening the door he finds Jonas sitting on a rumpled bunk staring at a picture frame. Hooper has heard several accounts of Joe's ride. It's already a legend. But he hasn't seen Joe in two weeks. No one has seen Joe.

Hooper says, "What's the picture?"

For a few more moments Joe stares, then turns it around. A big glossy eight by ten in one of those gold-rims you buy at Woolworth's, that come framing a photo of Robert Taylor, or of Bette Davis in her thirties. This one holds a picture of Goldie. It could be a picture of Joe.

"She's a fantastically beautiful person," Joe says.

"Where did you get it?"

"She sent it to me. I have a mailbox down at the main post office. I stopped in there today and found a package with this in it."

"Was that all?"

"And a long letter. She says she's been thinking about me so much she decided to come back to the islands. She also said hello to you."

"When's she coming back?"

"She sent the letter about a week ago, but I just got down to my box today. I think she said it was sometime today."

"What time?"

"She said six, but she didn't specify A.M. or P.M."

"You're not meeting her?"

"Hooper, have you ever been in love?"

Hooper sits down on the opposite bunk, glances again at the golden frame. "I've got some wine under the bed. How about a pull?"

"I'm all fucked up."

Hooper spins the top off a half gallon of bad burgundy. "Here."

Joe glunks deeply, lets it settle.

He says, "You ever hear about a place called Sacred Falls?"

"I've seen the sign."

"I went out there with Sheepdog."

"It's supposed to be a nice spot."

"It's okay for a while. We stayed there three days."

"What were you doing? Here. Try a little more of this."

Joe glunks and passes it back to Hooper, who glunks, and Joe seems to relax a little with the sour wine burning in his gullet. But something's wrong. Hooper can't help staring at him, trying to figure out what it is. He has never seen Sheepdog's eyes very clearly, but he imagines these eyes studying the jug label are much like Sheepdog's.

"I hung around Sunset for a couple of days after everybody left, watching the surf till it died down. Then Sheepdog came back by, said he was on his way to Sacred Falls. So I tagged along.

"The thing you have to realize about Sacred Falls is that it is a fantastically beautiful waterfall, very high and narrow, that drops down one end of this gorge. You hike back in there, and it's all mossy and crowded with ferns, kind of damp, and the water foaming up at the bottom of the falls. And the mosquitoes there are so fucking thick you can almost climb to the top of the falls on their backs."

"And you guys stayed in there for three days?"

"Sheepdog did. I lasted two. It was his project, ya see. He decided his biggest problem in life at the moment was dealing with mosquitoes, and that it was mainly a matter of self-control and willpower, and that he could will the mosquitoes to leave him alone. So he picked the most infested spot on the island and hiked back in there to test his will. Let me have another pull on that bottle."

Hooper glunks and passes the bottle and waits.

"It was murder, man. We were both riddled. I mean, every inch of us was covered with horrible welts. For two days we concentrated our asses off, but finally I couldn't stand it any more. I had to get out of there. I spent the whole next day in the water, submerged."

"What about Sheepdog?"

"He claims that on the third day it started to work. He says he actually generated anti-mosquito vibrations and that those fucking mosquitoes started to retreat, like someone had built an invisible wall around him."

"That's amazing."

"Is it?"

"Do you think it's true?"

"Who cares?"

"What do you mean, who cares?"

"What difference does it make?"

"If it's true, a guy could go anywhere he wants, any time of day or night."

"So what?"

Hooper stares at him, doesn't know what to say.

"I've spent the last two days beating my meat. I couldn't stop. Isn't that disgusting?"

"Kind of. If you spent two days at it."

"I was thinking about Goldie."

"You want me to drive out and see if I can find her?"

"She'll get into town some way. I'm gonna stay here and look at her picture and work up a big hardon and just hold it till she gets here, and see what she does."

"I'll leave the wine by the bed."

"Hooper, I have to ask you a question."

"Yeah?"

"It's kind of a poll I'm taking."

He waits, watches Joe pull again on the jug.

Joe's question: "What was the happiest day of your life?"

"The happiest day of my life."

"Right."

"That's easy."

"What was it?"

"The happiest day . . ."

"Was when?"

"Let me think a minute," Hooper says.

"Think all you want."

"I'd say it was . . ."

"No hurry. No rush. Take your time."

"Well, it would either be . . ."

The door flies open. Luella is standing there with bulging eyes, cobwebs veining her silver hair like a snood. She can hardly deliver the phlegm-coated message.

"Hooper! Hooper! They're here!"

CHAPTER 46

Hashimoto returns

*T*his Chevvy is bigger, four doors instead of two. The crest on the door is bigger. The driver is bigger. Hashimoto rides shotgun to his boss, Harry Staples, chief building inspector. They step past the hedge and stop, as Staples reads the red-lettered sign on the door.

"Quarantine."

"That wasn't here last time."

Staples scans the front of the house with hands on his Dacron hips. "Condemned would be more like it. Jesus. You sure somebody's living here, Hash?"

"Somebody had to put up that sign."

"Probably that smartass who ran you outta here."

"He did say the owner was sick."

"That sounds like horseshit to me."

Staples leads the way, husky, cherub-faced, kicking at loose shards of path with puzzled disdain, the way you try to kick loose a dog turd stuck to your shoe.

He tries the bell, hears nothing, raps loudly, and they wait, Hashimoto a little behind him, noting on his clipboard the generally perilous condition of the porch—stairs rotting, threatening to collapse, banisters out of reach, one board fallen through, others buckling.

At the second rap they hear footsteps. The door opens. Black crack at the jamb. Hooper's voice. "Who is it?"

Staples squinting. "Are you Mr. Broome?"

"Mr. Broome is very ill. Maybe you didn't see the sign. The house has been . . ."

"Quarantined. So I see." From Hashimoto's clipboard Staples takes a document. "We don't like to pester a man when he's sick. But this house is supposed to be inspected. It's a standard procedure. I think Hash explained that to you the other day, or tried to . . ."

Hooper opens the door a few inches. A white surgical mask covers his face from nose to chin, tied behind his head with strings. He's wearing a longsleeve white shirt, pale rubber medical gloves, some white wingtip shoes he found upstairs.

"The doctor just examined Mr. Broome this morning. It looks like he has smallpox."

"What?"

"He'd never been vaccinated. Must have come in off a ship from the Orient or somewhere. It's very rare, but that's the only disease the doctor said would account for his symptoms. He asked everyone who lives here to stay inside for two weeks. It's pretty contagious."

Staples steps back from the door, pulls at his fleshy skin, inhales deeply and looks at Hash, who blinks once.

"You wouldn't have the doctor's name handy."

"He was a specialist," Hooper says. "His card's right here . . . a

Doctor . . . it's either here or somewhere . . ."

"We'd have to have his verification to postpone this thing much longer," Staples says.

Hooper is dragging through his pockets, stalling. Softly, to Staples, Hashimoto says, "We could still check the outside all the way around, even if we can't go in."

Staples grunts, keeping an eye on Hooper's groping hands, squinting at the mask. Hooper says, "That might not be such a good idea, ya know."

Staples, "Why not?"

From somewhere down the hall come muffled noises that sound like struggle, chairs scraping, voices trying not to be heard. The inspectors peer into the tunnel.

"This may sound farfetched," Hooper says, raising his voice, "but Mr. Broome has the habit of urinating in the grass. Every inch of open space here has probably been peed on by him at least once or twice in the last seven days. It's a bladder condition of his. You walk around here much at all, you might get something on your shoes or cuffs that could, well . . . smallpox has an incubation period of one to two weeks."

Involuntarily they glance down at their shoes, scrape them on the porch boards. At that moment the distant shuffle become a stifled shout, then a door thrown open, and Broome's loud growl, "I know who's out there, goddam it! Now let go a me! Get outta my way!"

"Uncle Jack," Nona pleads, and "Jackson," whimpers Pike. But the growl gets closer as Broome, cursing and railing, appears under the skylight at the foot of the stairs, hat cocked and arms dangling, a welterweight in his corner, spoiling for the bell.

"Uncle Jack," Hooper shouts, "stay away from here!"

This only starts Broome on his way again, toward the porch.

"Is that him?" Staples says.

"Who?"

"The guy with smallpox."

"He's delirious," Hooper says, "out of his mind with fever."

"Holy Jesus!"

"We've been trying to keep him under control . . ."

Halfway there Broome shouts, "You get the hell off my property. You just get the hell away. I know you. I know what you're doing here!"

Staples and Hash are backing down the stairs. Broome now straddles the doorstep.

Looking up at Hooper from the path Staples says, "It's a bad time to press you. But if this house isn't inspected pretty soon, Mr.

Broome can be fined. I think you ought to know that. There are city ordinances involved . . ."

Broome shouts, "You lousy bastards with your goddam ordinances. Get away from here! This is my house and my land, and the only inspector around here is *me*!"

He's trembling, frothing thin strips of saliva. Wild-eyed he leans on the door jamb for support. Hooper tries to help him stand. Pike and Nona make a cluster of helpers reaching for the old man. He tears free and starts down the steps, grabbing at the banister. A chunk breaks off in his hand and he nearly falls into his geraniums, recovers, brandishes the rotten board.

"Go on! Go on!"

The man in green pajamas now is leaning out his upstairs window, shouting along with Broome. "Jesus Christ! What the hell is it *this* time?"

A bald man Hooper hasn't seen before has walked around from the side of the rooming house, carrying an open newspaper, and stops to squint at the commotion. He wears a shoulder-strap undershirt and appears to have been sunning himself.

At the edge of the parking lot stands the uniformed lad with the car-wash hose, letting its stream run limply into the hedge, while around him half a dozen people wait smiling, ready to laugh, or run.

Beyond the curb Jonas has crept into the street side of the Chevvy's backseat. At the last minute Hooper instructed him to rifle their car for loose papers of any kind, which might later be studied for information, or destroyed.

Hashimoto, terrified, has just touched his twill rear to the driver's seat, backingin. As he slides past the wheel, to make room for Staples, and hunches to see through the curbside window, Joe drops out of sight behind him.

Staples, on the path, is fearful too but not quite ready to flee. He watches the old man stagger toward him, casts a hard glance at Hooper, who returns it, glaring over his surgical mask. Staples wants to talk, get something arranged. Broome is backing him toward the hedge when, on the shattered pathway, one of his bare toes catches a shard. He stumbles, falls into high weeds halfway between Staples and Hooper.

Staples stiffens then, uncertain. Hooper leaps off the porch, followed by Nona, and Mrs. Pike who is screaming. "See! See! See! You satisfied now?"

And Staples, "Look. I'm . . . sorry . . ."

Hooper and Nona kneel next to Broome, to lift him, one on each side, and Luella is heading for the gate with the banister chunk, bellowing, "Didn't you hear what he said? Get away! Get away from here!"

Staples has no doubt she'll whack him if she has the chance, and he ducks into the Chevvy without a word, starts the engine, pulls off quickly, he and Hashimoto staring straight ahead through the windsheld, Jonas huddled on the floor behind them, with Luella following their exit path, lineman's knotty calves sprinting over asphalt.

She raises both arms and raises her volume, and appears to be driving their car down the street with invisible bullwhips, yelling, "You better run, you sonsabitches! And don't you dare come back!"

CHAPTER 47

He always knows what he wants

*T*he spectators chuckle at this, until the car disappears around a corner. While they watch Luella slowing down, finally halting half a block away, Hooper has both hands under one side of Broome.

Inert weight won't budge. Over the top of his mask he looks at Nona, sees composure give way to helplessness, then to terror. A timed and mighty heave is needed to raise him from the weeds and toward the stairs, and Hooper then wants her to lead, her family after all, not his. He would lurk forever behind this white gauze, the Lone Stranger, riding into town and right back out again, before or after the rustlers have been caught, he doesn't much care, as long as some kind of stand appears to have been made. But now Nona's terror is mixed with flickers of accusation, caught in a brief glance of straining eyes. She has never been too pleased about the quarantine scheme, and Hooper sees suddenly that she blames him as well as Staples for what's just happened. He wants to shout out something brutal. Restrains it. Has to salvage what he can.

With the miserable certainty that they are pallbearing Jackson to some final crypt, he's backing toward the porch, Nona not-crying, and this is not it. No. Up the stairs, and this just isn't it at all. Bring back that globe of his own high solitude, two miles up there waiting in space and time and void, everything ready to happen and nothing in front of him but two lines diverging to infinity, no one to meet him at the airport, no one to know he's arriving, no announcements, no place to stay, not even anywhere he plans to go first, well yes, one address, though not even that, a name on a scrawled and arrowed map, with some streets unmarked, not much to go on, he may not find it at all, and it doesn't matter, the name on the map is blurring fast, there's only a hat, floating in a yellow puddle, made of fine-woven straws, maybe thirty to an inch, and its fat band thick with feathers of those tiny birds they say Kamehameha and all the chiefs before him had cloaks made from, using only the rarest, from right underneath the wings, plucking armpits of forty thousand birds for one cloak, and this, upon the chief's death would be wrapped around him. In the long narrow hull of his war canoe they'd carry him back up some lava tube to the island's core and hide him, and the skin would dissolve, and the hair, and toenails, but not the feathers. Unless the volcano wakes to flow again and fill the grave canal with running flames, the feathers will survive, along with the teeth. It's forbidden to remove them. There's a curse on anyone who violates the dead. But there is also magic in the teeth, and in the feathers, in anything that's been to death and back.

"My God, Hooper," Nona cries. "Hold onto him!" Her eyes are wet with bulging tears, face contorted, straining.

Her voice rouses Broome, who may have been injured in the fall, or may just be dozing. He begins to squirm like a caught fish. By the time they reach the lightwell he won't let himself be carried another inch. They set him down. He staggers, refusing aid, through the shadows and mote beams, apparition lurching for the doorway. His bare feet never leave the floor, they scrape it, as if he's wearing sandpaper blocks.

The yellow circle is his goal, and with one last lurch he falls against his long chair, climbs into it, knocking off his panama. He leans to pick this up and starts to cough. Gags, like a man who has swallowed wrong, lungs full of water. Can't stop gagging. Whole fat body bucking with each cough, and his face goes scarlet. Under wet yellow hair his scalp is scarlet.

Nona grabs the phone.

Broome protests this, even through his gagging. While she's dialing he jerks his hands at her, groping for the wire.

Hooper tries to hold him back and feels a rush of energy tougher than the spasms, feels that anger in the old man's arms. Some of it travels into Hooper's, the outrage. He would take Staples by the throat . . .

Into the phone Nona's saying, "I need a doctor and an ambulance. Please. As soon as possible."

Hooper says, "Hang up, Nona."

"Yes," she's saying, "it's an emergency."

He lets Broome go and takes the receiver. "I said hang up!"

He moves to replace it, but Nona grabs his wrist. They're wrestling for it.

"Hooper, that's crazy!"

"He doesn't want a doctor! You know that!"

"He's dying this time! I know he is!"

"He's not going to die."

"He's in bad pain," Nona pleads. "Isn't that enough?"

"He doesn't want a doctor!"

"He doesn't know what he wants!"

"He always knows what he wants."

"Hooper, look at his face."

The scarlet's gone. All color has drained away. A pallor now, face of ghastly dough under the poolroom shade, and at this moment Luella appears in the doorway crying "Oh good Lord" and "Merciful God."

Broome's trying to speak.

Hooper says, "What is it, Uncle Jack?"

"My hat . . ."

Nona's grip on the phone goes feeble.

"Gimme my hat."

Hooper takes the receiver and cradle and carries these while he stoops for the panama, covers with it the plastered strips of yellow hair.

This seems to soothe Broome. A long deep breath. He holds it, finally wheezes.

"Rum."

"You want a rubdown with the Vicks?" Hooper asks.

All three make moves toward the chair. One stubby hand upraised stops them.

"Rum! rum rum rum rum rum."

Hooper to Nona, "Where does he keep the rum?"

Tears coming, "He shouldn't have anything that strong."

"Goddam it, Nona!"

"Behind the Victrola."

He finds half a quart of Australian rum and a grimy shot glass and pours a little into the glass, holds this to the old man's lips.

Broome swigs back a small swallow. Something jerks him upward, some twist of pain, or throat burn. He squints hard into the gloom beyond his perimeter of light, eases back. Color returning now, pink in the nose, moles brown again instead of cancerous gray. He lifts his head signaling for another swig.

Hooper provides it and sees the hand holding the shot glass to Broome's mouth trembling. Hooper's shaking all over, nearly spills rum on Broome's orange aloha shirt before the old man drinks. From the doorway Luella's muttering steadily, "Oh dear God," and "Merciful Lord," and "What are we going to do?" And Hooper's eyes are suddenly wide, seeing, as if through a magnifying glass, unswallowed liquor trickling through tough chin grizzle, becoming a brown delta with no outlet but short whiskers sponging it up. In one hand a shot glass, in the other a quart bottle, in his armpit a telephone, all so heavy to his weakening grip he fears he'll lose his hold on everything, wants Nona to walk over and hug him back together. But she is watching him with a look somewhere between misery and hate.

From the bottle he takes a long slug of rum, then shoves it toward her.

"Here, we could all use some of this."

She shakes her head, doesn't speak, as if afraid of what will be released.

Tiny phlegm voice startles them both. "C'mon, sweetheart . . . (*cough*) take a pull. It'll warm you."

With one slow hand he adjusts his panama.

"Hooper's right, ya know. Heh."

"Don't talk now, Uncle," Nona says.

"Yer old uncle ain't gonna die. Not right now anyway . . . Ain't no inspector can come out here and inspect Jackson Broome to death. Heh heh."

With each sentence the voice gets louder, the throat clears. He's grinning again, seems almost ready to laugh.

"No sir. I'm the only one who decides when Jackson says aloha. And I'll let you know when that day's comin'. . . ."

He winks at Nona, holds the eyelid shut.

"So you shouldn't be looking at Hooper that way. You oughtta be swinging him around the room. He saved the day, didn't ya know that? Without old Hooper out there sticking his finger in the dike, why we'd be right where we been all these months, just sittin' back here worryin'. Hooper, would you do Jackson one more favor?"

"Anything, Uncle Jack."

"You call somebody down at the phone company . . . right now . . . and have that goddam thing disconnected."

Hooper does it.

Broome says, "Ole Hooper . . . heh heh . . . he takes the goddam bull by the horns. Why, if I was you, Nona, I'd drink to that. Yes, I would. Fact a the matter, I think I'll have another pull on that jug myself. Like you say, sweetheart, it's strong. But that's what a man needs when it's time to celebrate."

CHAPTER 48

Goldie returns

*J*onas reaches a stealthy hand for the door handle, eases it down. Just before the light turns he throws open the door and leaps. Hunched commando-style, as if evading sniper fire, he runs back along the white line between rows of cars waiting to cross. Staples, intent upon the light, doesn't see who it is and can't give chase because the light now flicks green. Behind him horns are honking. Hash, craning back, is thrown against the seat as Staples bucks cursing into the inter-section.

Joe dives through a hedge and somersaults to his feet, running in deep greenery till he hits an alley behind one of the big hotels. Through the service entrance and into a dark storeroom full of hotel linen, he hides for half an hour.

When he steps back through the hedge, Goldie is standing there on the sidewalk in her jeans and aloha shirt as if waiting for him to return from the men's room. She looks hungover from a four-day drunk. In her dark brown face the rings of darker brown around her eyes seem patched on.

Joe stops next to her and watches the twilight traffic stream, letting his eyes follow individual cars till they drive out of sight.

After a while she says, "Are you glad to see me, Joe?"

"I'm all fucked up.".

"What's the matter?'

It's a couple of minutes before he answers. He starts to tell her about Sacred Falls. When he finishes the story the streetlights are shining. He still hasn't looked at her.

"Oh Joe," she says, "I'm all fucked up too."

When he doesn't respond she goes on.

"At least I was. But I don't think I am any more. Listen. Flying back to L.A. was the worst thing that ever happened. And the best too, in a way. It was like death, Joe, that trip to the mainland. You know how when you're dying, your whole life is supposed to pass before your eyes? That's what happened to me. And I saw what a terrible mess I've made of everything. And I decided that I would wipe the slate clean—that is, as far as my own sense of guilt and sadness and inadequacy was concerned—and I would just start over. And it was fantastic, Joe, it really was. At just that instant the stewardess came by and asked me if I wanted a cup of coffee. And I said Yes. And she asked me if I wanted cream and sugar. And I said *Yes*. And she asked me if I was enjoying my flight. And I said YES. It was so beautiful, a beautiful moment, don't you see? Everything positive, everything balanced. And I knew then that I had al*ready* started over and that the only thing to do from then on was to stay open, open to every possibility. Don't expect anything. Be ready for everything. I realized that I am a person who waits to see what is going to happen next. And that was fantastic relief. All my life I have worried about not knowing what was going to happen next. Now I know I don't really care. Whatever happens is what *should* happen next. Isn't it fantastic how things work out?"

A long silence.

Finally Joe says, "Then you forgive me?"

She looks at Joe with astonished and worried eyes. "Joe, are you okay?"

"I told you, I'm all fucked up, Goldie."

She throws her arms around his neck. "Oh Jonas."

His eyes burn from watching cars all this time without blinking. At her show of affection he squeezes hard, causing his eyes to water.

In his ear she says, "I want to make love to you, Joe."

He still hasn't moved or looked at her. When he doesn't answer, she draws her head back.

"Is that okay?"

"Sure. I guess so."

He puts an arm around her waist and back through the hedge they step, into nighttime greenery.

CHAPTER 49

Sing a song
while you're

*I*t's dark when they emerge from
the bushes. Arms around waists, nuzzle-nosing all the way, they
walk back to Broome's, approach the wide window in the usual
manner, carefully, since the house at night has never been anything
but silent as a sunken ship, and Joe knows any crack of twig or
spring squeak reverberates to the roofbeams.

One leg and his head are in when he hears something he's never
heard here before—laughter loud enough to cover anybody's entry,
and raucous music, from the back of the house. Goldie clambers
through behind him, and they follow the sound to Broome's half-
open door, where they discover what has become a victory party,
involving not only Broome who reigns from his red-leather chair
in the center, and Hooper still wearing his white medical outfit,
gauze mask hanging to his chest like a surgeon's after the operation,
and Nona, and Mrs. Pike, but also the man in green pajamas, and
the man who owns the Spanish land grant to Malibu, a swarthy,
obese, and slick-haired fellow who was drunk when they called him
downstairs and is now passing out at the foot of the Victrola,
sprawled among old records, blocking the cloth-covered speaker
with the flesh that heaps around his neck and shoulders.

Jonas, peeking in, sizes up the situation and would creep away
unnoticed, preferring to brood, and also to keep Goldie concealed.
But Luella spots him. The others spot him. A cry wells up. Luella
rushes at the doorway and Joe is too terrified to run. He shuts his
eyes and braces for the assault. Her widespread arms reach out,
engulf him, lift him off the floor in a bearhug.

She squeezes, shouting, "*This* is my boy!"

Old 78s have been spinning on the turntable, pulled at random
from under the fallen body of the fat man—Django, Red Nichols
and His Five Pennies, the Magic Ukulele of Barney Keauau. Now
the song is "Everybody Loves My Baby." Luella swings Joe across
the room to its twobeat:

> *Everybody loves my baby*
> *But my baby don't love nobody but me . . .*

Arms pinned, Joe is carried to Broome's side, where she plants him. "This is my *boy!*"

Broome grins up at him, "You must be thirsty, young fella."

Joe looks around at the ring of flushed faces, sees Hooper coming toward him with a milkshake glass full of something pink.

"Try the specialty of the house," Broome says.

"What is it?"

"Called the Inspector's Lament."

They are all drinking Inspector's Laments, a blend of guava nectar, pineapple juice, crushed ice and Australian rum—all but Luella, who prefers her rum in a cup of Lipton's having modestly accepted just a taste when Hooper first passed it around, but by this time not objecting when, though her tea is long since gone, he periodically offers to freshen her cup.

"And what about your friend there," says Broome, the genial host, "would she care for a glass?"

Goldie is standing inside the door, masking fatigue with her sunniest smile, suncheeks of mahogany and apricots haloed faintly with apricot fuzz, clean teeth flashing the smile of a girl who knows her face is, if nothing else, able to produce a sunny one, and she'll do that much for you every chance she gets.

Hooper is awash with well-being, heady with success and his veins full of rum. He's so glad to see Joe back he'd run up and hug him too, if Luella weren't in the way. Also glad to see Goldie, relieved she seems to only have eyes for Jonas. Whatever it was in her he fled from, it holds no attraction for him now, at least not tonight, not here. He will keep his distance, of course. Can't be too careful. Especially with Nona present. Hooper gives them a benevolent smile. He feels truly paternal about this reunion, even though the look on Joe's face is anything but that of a lover in the company of his beloved. As he thinks of it, Hooper has never seen Joe willingly in the company of any girl. Something has definitely happened to Joe, something has gone out of him.

A toast in Joe's honor might help. They have all toasted one another several times. Hooper is about to propose it when Luella's grip on Joe's arm tightens. Her limp grin tightens too. She squints hard at Goldie, trying to place her.

Hooper intervenes. "Jonas, isn't this the sister you've been telling me about?"

Joe's blank, impassive eyes regard his for fifteen seconds, giving Hooper the impression that bullets have been fired through Joe's pupils, leaving these two pale blue holes.

"Yes," Joe says at last. "Everybody, this is my sister Goldie."

Luella rears back, scrutinizing. Then she rushes over to Goldie, drags her toward the light. "My, isn't this lucky. Did you just get in?"

"Yes," Goldie says, wary but still smiling.

Luella holds both her hands, glancing from her face to Joe's, smiling like a relative. "I believe you *do* favor Jonas some."

Hooper seizes the moment, shouts, "I think it's about time for another toast."

"Yes, a toast," the others echo. "Another toast."

The man in green pajamas shakes awake the man who owns the land grant. "C'mon, c'mon, we're toasting again."

"To Jonas and his sister Goldie!" Hooper cries, lifting high his milkshake glass.

ALL: "To Jonas and Goldie!"

From Joe a begrudging grin. Apricot cheeks from Goldie.

LUELLA: "Yes! Carried away in the devil's chariot and come back now to tell the tale."

Hooper yells, "Hear, hear."

"Hey hey," grunts the fat man.

Everyone drinks, sips, guzzles. Until now Joe has been a hero missing in action. They demand from him an account of what happened in the car. What did he find.

JOE: (*stone face*) Nothing. Cigar butts. Sandwich wrappers.

HOOP: What did they say?

JOE: Nothing.

LUELLA: Nothing?

JOE: Total silence.

HOOP: They were speechless.

JOE: Stunned.

LUELLA: I think this Jonas deserves a medal. (*She slaps his right pec with the flat of her hand.*)

HOOP: A medal of honor.

MAN IN GREEN: (*drinking deeply from his milkshake glass*) A goddam Purple Heart, if you ask me.

BROOME: What about Hooper? Don't leave Hooper out of this.

MAN IN GREEN: A goddam Purple Heart for both a the bastards.

HOOP: No. No. Purple Hearts are only for men who get wounded.

MAN IN GREEN: What about a *green* heart then, for Christ sake?

Broome's gnarled hand darts up into the light. "Wait a minute. Wait a minute. I've got a better idea."

They look at him.

"Everybody sit down."

They sit, all but the fat man, who is trying to get up. The man in green pushes him over onto his side, hissing, "Cut it, cut it." And the fat man slumps back against the Victrola, head in his hands, groaning like a stricken grizzly.

"Turn off that damn record player," Broome commands.

Nona lifts the arm.

BROOME: What we're going to do is . . . heh heh . . . dedicate a song.

ALL: A song. Yes, a song.

BROOME: . . . to everyone. (*Spreads his arms.*) A song for everyone here . . . my roomers . . . (*phlegm catches in his throat*) . . . my . . . family . . .

Sudden silence, uncertainty.

BROOME: Which I am going to sing.

Low rush of encouraging noises.

BROOME: And while I sing I want Nona to dance it.

Small round of applause while she rises from the floor and makes of this an introductory hula dancer's bow.

BROOME: And Hooper here is going to play.

Guffaws from Joe and the Man in Green as Hooper lifts from its wall peg the Philippine mahogany guitar.

HOOP: What'll it be, Uncle Jack?

BROOME: You'll feel it. Easy changes. Just gimme a vamp in G, about like this.

On his chair arm Broome pats out two bars, moderato, and Hooper picks it up, with a G-2-3-4, A seventh, D seventh, G-2-3-4, A seventh, D seventh. Broome sits up. To another spatter of applause and aaaaaahhs, his piping, reedy one-time baritone begins to sing the song that made him rich and famous:

> *You'll never go hungry in Hawaii,*
> *It's a tropic wonderland.*
> *There's plenty of fish and poi for every island boy,*
> *There's bananas on every hand.*

Nona's wearing her red muu-muu which, under the yellow light, looks orange. She glides up in front of Broome's chair so he can see her, begins to act out the lyrics, hand to her mouth for the opening line, arms spread wide for the second, pressed palms wiggling fishlike, while her hips keep the rhythm. Broome leers, watching her, winks, reaches a toe, as if to lift her dress. She backs up, mockscolding with a finger.

> *You'll find passion fruit in the mountains*
> *And coconuts in the sand.*
> *Oh you'll never go hungry in Hawaii.*
> *It's a tropic wonderland.*

On the last line Broome touches his hat brim, vaudevillean making a stop-time exit. Amid loud cheers he leans back grinning and winds his arm, signaling Hooper and Nona to keep it up. Hooper plays, faking the lyrics, while Goldie, Joe, Luella, and the man in green hum along or throw in phrases they remember.

Nona moves up close to Hooper now. Since his first slug of rum they haven't spoken to each other, separately tending the old man, separately sipping Inspector's Laments. This chorus will be a reconciliation. She's dancing it all for him, smiling down, eyes full of heat. It brings the rum's heat, already warming his neck and face, springing to the surface. Her hips wade in close to his eyes, and he scans her body, as if seeing it and wanting it for the first time. Without effort she glides back. He watches her hands. Keep your eyes on the hands, the song about the hula dancer says. That's where the message is. Fingers supple, stroking air, beckon, offer, pluck fruit, extend it, hands pulling on invisible lines. A thin cold current cuts through his flood of lust, a sense of what it is these undulating hands would draw out of him, something he's certain isn't there. If his head were clearer he might sort out the terms of his reunion. But his head is not clear, each moment it's fuzzier. Hips swell toward him again. That tiny current, brief and shapeless, is swallowed up.

Foolishly they grin at each other. He plays louder. Nona, answering, dances harder. He speeds the beat. She speeds up with him. He slows it way down, retards to a no-tempo, talks the lyrics. Nona becomes a kelp stalk, catching every underwater whiffle. A Latin stroke starts her shoulders shaking. Calypso turns her into a jiggling Jamaican. He tries flamenco, a country blues, a pseudo-banjo picking the high frets. She dances like this is an arrangement they have rehearsed for months. The others stop singing. Hooper isn't playing the song any more. He's changing chords and tunes and tempos too fast for anyone but Nona to follow, playing whatever comes into his head. It has become a little contest. He's trying hard to find something she can't catch. Each time she catches it he reaches farther, genuinely hoping to throw her off balance. Each time she catches it he wants her that much more.

The man in green pajamas can't stand this any longer. He jumps up and skips out in front of her. He's about Broome's height, but gaunt, six inches shorter than Nona. With arms overhead and feet planted he begins a very rudimentary bump and grind, chewing lasciviously on his lower lip. Luella, seeing this, and already swaying along, grabs Jonas, starts to carry him around the room, shouting, "C'mon. Let's dance. Let's dance!" Joe struggles to get free, but she has him in an octopus grip, his white face pushed up against her great bosom, muffling his cries of protest.

She sweeps past the Victrola and drops the arm onto the record still spinning there:

> *Everybody wants my baby*
> *But my baby don't want nobody but me,*
> *It's plain to see.*

Hooper stops strumming. The man in green is forcing Nona back toward the sofa. Goldie, in a sudden moment of junior prom formality, is waiting for Hooper, the only male unoccupied and still conscious, to ask her to dance. Glad as he is to see her, Hooper does not, under any circumstances, want Goldie close to him. He moves toward Nona, intending to cut in on the man in green. At just that moment Nona has moved toward Hooper, to escape the meager hips she knows will soon want to cuddle hers from behind. Their bodies slide together, as if choreographed to, and they stand feet knees thighs chests touching, rocking to the barrelhouse piano while the man in green, whirling, spots Goldie, halfway to her feet in a move that was aimed at Hooper. But the green man has her by the waist, a salivating lecher, and the girl who expects nothing, remains ready for anything, gives him a laugh and two hands on his bony shoulders. Before the song ends, Luella lifts the needle to its outside groove again, the song starts over, and around they go, Goldie and the green man counterclockwise to Joe and Luella, along the yellow rim that circles the old man's chair, kicking and tripping over the man who owns the land grant, who seems lodged in everyone's path.

Hooper and Nona, off to the side, locked close, sway, hug, kiss, let their hands explore.

NONA: (*Lips to his ear.*) Look. Uncle Jack is falling asleep.

HOOP: Right in the middle of the dance floor.

NONA: I think that song was his limit.

HOOP: It might be a good time to get out of here, let him rest.

NONA: We probably shouldn't leave him.

HOOP: He'll be okay. What he mainly needs is peace and quiet. If we leave, maybe the others will. We could take the party upstairs and just check on him from time to time. You want to go upstairs?

NONA: (*Pressing against him.*) Yes. But not with anyone but you.

          (*They kiss, rock together.*) You were right, Hooper. There's no use fighting Uncle Jack. I've never seen him as lively as he was tonight, having such a good time.

He holds her close, strong, silent, till the record's over. Then, arms around waists, they pass Broome's chair, pause briefly, glance down, moving on toward the edge of his light circle, Nona in her orange-red muu-muu, Hooper's gauze mask dangling, white shirt, white ducks, white shoes. He is carrying his guitar. Luella catches his arm.

LUELLA: (*Happily.*) You better get your speech ready.

HOOP: What for?

LUELLA: I haven't had a chance to tell you the news.

HOOP: What news?

LUELLA: You got elected.

HOOP: I did?

LUELLA: We'll have a meeting sometime next week, the swearing-in and all.

HOOP: How many votes did I get?

LUELLA: Oh, it was a secret ballot.

Nona is pulling on his arm, whispering. They move on, out of Broome's circle. The others freeze, and a spot follows Hooper and Nona, moving stage left, till they reach a mattress on the floor. They help each other undress.

NONA: (*Unbuttoning his trousers.*) These white ducks look funny on you.

HOOP: I kind of like them.

NONA: They make you look like a sailor.

HOOP: I *am* a sailor.

NONA: I don't usually like sailors.

HOOP: Why not?

NONA: I don't know.

HOOP: Sure you do.

NONA: Why then?

HOOP: You tell me.

NONA: It's because Al thought he was a sailor. He always wore ducks like that around the house. Trying to go tropical.

HOOP: A phony.

NONA: A *real* phony.

HOOP: (*Trying to make a joke of it.*) Is that why you got divorced? The white ducks around the house all the time? *Long pause. Naked, he sits next to her, on the mattress.*

NONA: Partly.
Hooper waits.
He just got tired of me.

HOOP: I can't believe it.

NONA: He managed the club, remember. It was the first place I worked. I was very young. He was about thirty and very handsome and surrounded by dozens of beautiful girls.

HOOP: (*In the manner of W. C. Fields.*) None as beautiful as you, my lovely.

NONA: One day he just sailed away. From all of us. He was still trying to be a sailor.

HOOP: The sonofabitch. The dirty bastard.

NONA: Sailors always sail away. That's why I don't like them.

HOOP: Well, I'm not a sailor then.

He rolls the white ducks into a ball, throws them off-stage.

NONA: What are you?

HOOP: (*Embracing, easing her back onto the mattress.*) I am the president of the property council.

Eagerly they fondle each other. As the next scene begins, over-lapping the end of this one, the light on Hooper and Nona quickly dims out. Joe and Goldie move toward Broome's chair, pause there glancing down at the top of his hat, then step toward the pool's edge, Goldie in her jeans, her creased shirt, Jonas in golf knickers. Luella catches his arm.

LUELLA: You and Goldie be sure to stop in for a cup of tea now. You know where my room is.

JOE: We sure do, Mrs. Pike.

LUELLA: I wish you wouldn't call me Mrs. Pike.

JOE: Luella.

When they step outside the yellow ring the others freeze and a spot follows Joe and Goldie. Arms around waists they move slowly stage right till they reach a mattress on the floor. Goldie's framed photo hangs on the wall above it. They undress and lie down. Joe stares at the ceiling. After a long silence Goldie speaks.

GOLDIE: Talk to me, Joe.

JOE: What about?

GOLDIE: Anything. I don't care.

JOE: All right.

GOLDIE: All right what?

JOE: I'm going to ask you a question.

GOLDIE: I love questions.

JOE: What was the happiest day of your life?

GOLDIE: Oh, that's too easy, Joe.

JOE: What was it then?

GOLDIE: Oh, that's a cinch.

JOE: Okay.

GOLDIE: The happiest day of my life.

JOE: That's it.

GOLDIE: . . . was the day . . .

JOE: Yeah?

GOLDIE: Gimme a minute to think about this, Joe.

JOE: Sure.

GOLDIE: There have been so *many* happy days, it's hard to . . .

JOE: Just pick one and tell me about it.

GOLDIE: But the happiest of all . . .

JOE: Was . . .

GOLDIE: Was to*day*, Joe! Seeing you again!

JOE: Be absolutely honest now.

GOLDIE: (*Up on one elbow.*) Or maybe it was yesterday.

As the next scene begins, the light on Joe and Goldie slowly dims out. The man in green pajamas pulls the man who owns the Spanish land grant to his feet, gets a skinny arm around his fat back, drags him into the lemony pool, past Broome's chair, where he stops, hunching to get a better hold. Luella touches his arm.

LUELLA: You be careful now. I don't want no vomit on that stairway carpet or up there in the hall. Never can get that smell outta them rugs, ya know.

MAN IN GREEN: Careful as we can.

They cross the perimeter and exit into shadows, the fat man groaning miserably. Luella sees them to the door, then remains there, out of sight. We see only Broome, centered in the pool of light, reclining in his tiltback leather chair, under the wide shade, his panama over his eyes, band of it flashing flecks of red and green. From the Victrola comes a scratchy rendition of "Ain't Misbehavin'." A lead trumpet takes the first chorus, after which we hear Luella's voice.

LUELLA: Well, wasn't that fun, Jackson?

VICTROLA: *No one to talk with . . .*

LUELLA: Jackson, I said wasn't that *fun*?

VICTROLA: *All by myself.*

LUELLA: Jackson, I know you're awake under there.

VICTROLA: *No one to walk with . . .*

I can't remember when we've had a honest-to-goodness party around here. Can you?

VICTROLA: *I'm happy on the shelf.*

Course the older ya get, the easier you have to take things.

VICTROLA: *Ain't misbehavin' . . .*

It ain't none a my business, Jackson. But I have noticed that those spells of yours are coming closer and closer together. And if you don't make some effort to do something about it, well, there isn't going to be anybody to blame for what happens but you.

VICTROLA: *Saving it all . . .*

I've never seen a man look as near death as you looked this afternoon, if you want to know the truth. And what did you do about? Call a doctor? No sir, not Jackson Broome. No, he dragged out the old rum bottle. Sat around drinking rum when you should have been under a doctor's care. It's pitiful, Jackson, that's what it is, just pitiful how a man your age can carry on like that. Do you realize that you have never once done anything that somebody else asked you to do? Never once in your life. If you can think of a single example, I'd very much like to hear about it. Jackson? Are you listening to me?

A two-chorus clarinet solo.

When she speaks again, her voice is cracking, trying to hold back the weeping, yet let whoever's listening know that it can start at any moment. From this point on, the yellow light above Broome begins very gradually to dim.

Jackson, that Hooper would drive you down to the clinic for a checkup, if you don't want no doctors coming over to the house. I mean, I've heard you say more than once it's a waste of good money having doctors over. Hooper wouldn't mind driving you down there. Jackson?

VICTROLA: *Don't go nowhere. What do I care . . .*

Ever since that inspector came around here the first time I been so worried I get sick to my stomach. I *do.* Heartburn. Gas. We ought to *both* go down and see the doctor. I believe there's something wrong with my eyes. *Eight-bar piano break.*

Jackson, did you hear me? I said there is something wrong with my *eyes.* I very nearly fell down in the street this afternoon, just walking back to the house. My head started swimming and I had to stop and lean against a tree and just stand there and hold my eyes closed. (*The quaver in her voice breaks into outright weeping now.*) And I felt so . . . so useless out there, Jackson. Standing up against that palm tree and couldn't even walk, let alone see. Why, another person coming along right then could have . . . taken advantage of me some way, and I'd've been powerless to stop him. Powerless. It was one of the worst moments of my life.

A long pause, vocalist scat-sings, while Luella weeps, letting it all out. When she speaks again her voice, broken by sobs, is smaller, receding.

Jackson, are you listening to me? I said this afternoon was one of the *worst moments of my life.* I've got to go have my *eyes* examined.

The record ends and the needle is scratching its spindle parabola. Scratching and scratching and scratching and scratching and scratching. Luella's weeping turns to sniffles, her voice continues to recede.

Jackson, that record's over with.

Scratching.

You want me to lift that arm off the record?

Scratching.

Listen here, Jackson, I know you inside out, and don't you think I'm gonna walk over there and lift that arm just so you can jump up yelling and scare the life out of me.

Scratching.

I can listen to that racket as long as you can, ya know.

Scratching gets fainter, fading. Luella's voice fading too.

I ain't touching that record arm unless you ask me to.

(*Voice far away:*) Jackson?

(*And farther still:*) Just tell me yes or no.

(*A tiny signal:*) Jackson?

Gone.

The yellow light's so dim now all we can see is the chair's faint outline, silhouette of Broome's behatted head and feet upsticking. The needle still scratches thinly, and above it there rises, as if from behind closed doors, a tinny reprise:

Like Jack Horner, in a corner,
Don't go nowhere, what do I care . . .

Reprise fades but scratching holds. After ten seconds the lights gradually brighten, rise to full intensity. This takes thirty seconds. Three more minutes pass. Then Broome stirs. One hand shoves back the panama. He wiggles his bare feet. The chair tilts slowly forward. He sits for a while under the lampshade, confused. Finally he eases his feet to the floor, stands up. Bent forward he scrapes his way to the light circle's edge and stands there, with his back to the chair, facing the audience. A small spot lights his face. For a minute he stands wheezing, catching his breath, needle still scratching in the background. At first he speaks very slowly, with effort.

BROOME: That was . . . heh heh . . . what you might call . . . a close one. I could feel it . . . everything getting . . . dark . . . darker . . . sinking . . . And I couldn't do a damn thing about it . . . Nope. Just had to stretch out and . . . let it come. Man gets my age he can't do a hell of a lot

about anything. So I let it come . . . Felt like somebody
was down there with a long rope, just reeling me in,
winding me in that rope . . . slow and easy . . . and I
just let him wind and reel me on down. And then . . .
and then he changed his mind. I guess . . . heh heh. Yes,
sir. Changed his mind. Moved on down the beach somewhere, looking for some other poor bastard to scare. He
didn't scare me none . . . Betcha that's why he changed
his mind. Jackson Broome ain't scared to take his leave.
Take it or leave it alone. . . heh . . . You know what? I
wish that damn Jonas would stick his head in my door
right now. Damn kid makes me laugh . . . Dozed off this
afternoon, woke up and there he was, standing in the
doorway looking at me. I looked at him and he said, Mr.
Broome, what was the happiest day of your life? Well
. . . heh heh . . . nobody ever asked me that one before.
I closed my eyes and acted like I was falling asleep
again. After a while I opened 'em and he was still there,
telling me, No rush, no rush. I said something like, Once
I had four different girls on the same day, two in the
morning, two in the afternoon. But that Jonas, his face
didn't budge. He's serious. He says, Be honest with
yourself, Mr. Broome. I closed my eyes again and
finally did doze off and later on he was gone. But I kept
thinking about that, the happiest day of my life. Yep,
I thought about that one. And if he showed up right
now I'd tell him . . . I'd say . . . well, I was about to say,
Today. But that'd be wrong. That would be a lie. I hurt.
There's no way around it. I hurt all over most of the
time, and I hurt a lot. But so what. Shit on it, that's
what I say. You learn to live with it, that's all. Luella
pissin' and moanin' all the time about her aches and
pains. Women always miss the point. Never seen it to
fail. Happiest day of my life? Must've been . . . oh . . .
heh heh . . . when I was around Hooper's age . . . more
or less. You never know it at the time, a course. Out
there with nothing to do but fart around. I'll tell you
this much. Whenever that Hooper comes in here, he
makes me want to cry. He's so much like me at that
age, I can't hardly stand it. Not much idea what he
wants to do. Just out here farting around. The way all
of us wish we could do all our lives. Matter of what you
can get away with. I've always thought that was the
main aim of damn near every man I've ever run across,

to fart around as much as possible. Sooner or later a woman'll come along, though, and throw you off course. It'll happen to ole Hooper. I can see it coming, saw it in that look Nona gave him when he handed her the rum bottle. That's the way it starts. And I could warn him. I could say, Hooper, Hooper boy, I can see it coming. But it wouldn't do any good. Nope. You can't tell a young fella very much he doesn't think he already knows. Oh, there's lots of things I'd like to tell Hooper. But you get my age, your mind wanders. Gets hard to talk about any one thing for long. Hard to get up the effort. He'll do all right. Out here farting around. He's good at it too, I'll say that for him. Some fellas never *do* get the hang of it. Women get hold of 'em too early. But ole Hooper, he must've learned something from his dad. You want to know the truth, that's the man I feel sorry for. Hooper's dad. Hooper's out here hanging around an old bastard like me, singing songs and helping me here and there, doing things his dad would probably give a leg to be doing with his own son. And that makes me want to cry too, if I think about that poor sonofabitch, Hooper's father. Ah, but then what do I know about it. Putting myself in another man's boots. When I never had a son of my own. Who knows. Maybe Hooper's dad kicked him out of the house yelling, Go ye into all the world and fart around to your heart's content. Or maybe there's five other boys in that family, and Hooper's dad is surrounded with sons playing guitars and banjos. Well . . . heh heh . . . I could cry about that one too. But I won't. Nope. Not Jackson Broome. The trick is, to keep the show on the road the best way you can. *Non illegitimus carborundum*, as they say. Don't let the bastards grind you down. Sing a song while you're farting along. So here's one more chorus before I turn in for the night.

Oh you'll never go hungry in Hawaii,
It's a tropic wonderland.
There's lots of shrimp and rice in this paradise,
There's pineapple of every brand.

While Broome sings forestage, five scenes are illuminated behind him, one by one, until all are lit in a kind of pentacle around the old man, beginning at stage left where Hooper and Nona are hotly making love. Behind them and halfway to center stage Luella sits next to her kettle sipping tea. Directly above her, on a raised plat-

form, the man who owns the Spanish land grant to Malibu, California, lies slumped on the floor. A few feet along the same platform the man in green pajamas is sitting up in bed with a magazine, masturbating. At stage right Joe and Goldie lie asleep in each other's arms. The curtain begins to close.

> There's kalua pig at every luau,
> There's guavas to beat the band.
> Oh you'll never go hungry in Hawaii,
> It's a tropic wonderland.

On the last line Broome lifts his panama.

CURTAIN

—SPACER—

Trips and Voyages: May 27, 1933

Green Plymouth gathering insects that swarm across the road from grove to grove, snick snick at the windscreen, and Andrew Dunlap squints past the casualties, focused not on spattered glass but on all-surrounding greenness, roaming it with his eyes, glimpsing road once in every pendulum swing of his sturdy head. For four days out of Chickasha it was nothing but sand country, scrub brush, cactus, gas fumes and radiator plumes, blackstring highway wobbling up to heaven with the heat he kept thinking he had left behind. Hotter still and hotter till they found themselves in Needles, where his wife sat up and whined, "Is this California?" Sweat pouring off them both, pale noonday desert sky, Andrew said they had just crossed the state line. The Indian in her should have been able to take it, even then. But the white girl in her won again. Her spirit broke. She wept and fell into a damp sleep and hasn't said four words since. No great loss to Andrew. He drove and waited and finally, outside San Bernardino, the land began to turn from buff toward yellow toward green, and the greener things looked the faster he drove, till he thought he could actually smell salt air, even through his gas fumes, and the beach thirty miles off.

148

This has maddened him, this sense of destination. He guns his engine, grips his leopard-spotted steering wheel. Around a curve the sun pours straight into his eyes and he reaches for the visor. It breaks off in his hand. He throws it out the window. Plymouth sputters on past orange blossoms, past those rich hills in the distance, each glimpse of them a promise, every turn of land promising —what? Squint harder. Something. Everything. The very look of spring meadow hills rippled with fulfillments he'll come back to as soon as he touches the limit of the land.

Five days graininess of red weary eyes turn to liquid. A cooling wash drains through him. The groves thin out, give way to towns. In Santa Monica he follows signs to the seawall, row of high palms, turns his engine off, lets out a whoop, and shakes his wife.

"Just look at that!"

Circled eyes slowly open. "What?"

"The whole Pacific Ocean, Naomi. Isn't that somethin'?"

Wan half-smile "It's nice all right."

"Nice, shoot! That's the biggest piece a water you're ever gonna see. C'mon. Let's go swimmin'."

"I thought we was going to Alhambra first. You said they was a congregation there . . ."

"We're goin back to Alhambra quick as I go swimmin'."

"Andrew, we ain't got much money left. And I'm mighty tired. And you don't know how to find that place, let alone in the dark."

"We'll find it. C'mon now."

"And you ain't even got a swimmin' suit."

"That don't make no difference. Shoot, honey, this is God's country. Look at them palm trees. You can sit here, or you can come with me. But I'm going swimmin' right now, this afternoon."

The eyes close, a short breath, long-suffering smile. "Maybe I'll git my feet wet then." Pause. "Might be nice to cool my ankles off."

In the sand Andrew drops his shirt on top of his boots and socks. He rolls his khaki trousers to his knees and wades in. From mid-forehead to Adam's apple he's the color of rust, from Adam's apple down he's white as a turnip, white feet pausing for the tide froth, the blood shock of cold. He keeps wading, another pause when the cold grabs his scrotum, then he dives a clumsy dive under one small wave and comes up grinning, black hair stuck to his forehead. He turns and waves to Naomi, up to her instep in wet sand, and she waves back. Her other hand rests on the belly full of child Andrew knows will be a boy. As he turns to dive again, he decides that among all the things he'll teach him—how to saw wood, how to prune trees, how to pray—he'll teach him how to swim in the ocean, and they'll swim together. Like this.

He bends low, shoves his face at a hedge of white water, comes up hooting, ducks his head into the next one, then belly-flops over the next, cavorting like a kid, and Oklahoma is a bad bad dream, thirsty land full of thirsty people can't be real when there's all this water in the world. Hateful wind and months of watching crops sucked back into crumbling, parched soil—all that, and the days of driving, wash off him with the dust, and quick as Naomi gets rested up there's dozens of things like this they'll be doing. Park out by the orange groves and just breathe deep for thirty minutes or an hour. Walk to the top of the greenest hill and see how far they can see, count the trees between here and Mexico.

Again he turns and sees her standing in the same spot, staring down where water licks her ankles below the lifted skirt. The way her dress falls across motherly bosom, the fine smooth melon of her six-month belly, the way late sunlight catches hair she hasn't combed since Flagstaff, catches cheekbones under downglancing eyes, Andrew wants her, right now, on the sand, or up there against the seawall, back from the breeze, anywhere, as long as it's right this minute. The way to celebrate it all is rising in his groin, and he looks, yearning, letting it rise and swell in the cool water, and he knows she won't let him till after the baby's born, thinks it's shameful, and can wither him with a week of accusing looks if he shows any sign of lust during this, her delicate time.

He wades farther out, chest-deep. The water's comfortable now. He shoves one hand down behind his belt, cursing his wife, his one-fourth Cherokee woman, cursing her for that in particular, the Indian buried in her. Out of the largest congregation in Chickasha, where he very nearly had his pick, being song leader, Sunday school teacher, and six feet tall, Andrew chose Naomi. Deep among his reasons was the belief that Indian women are all hot-blooded. He knew Naomi was saving her heat till after she married, and he married her with the secret hope that unspeakable mysteries would soon be revealed to him. He waited for this to happen, and he waited, and is waiting still, but the only Indian secret Naomi has revealed so far is how to sit in one place for a long time without talking. A warm bedmate is the best she can be, and these months even that's denied him. Fine, upstanding. Indian giver.

Hammering at her now with his wet right hand, he wants someone more agreeable to share this celebration. He conjures up the Cherokee girl who smiled at him one afternoon on the road into Muskogee. Why didn't he stop that day, or smile back? Dark, full-lipped, full-blooded. The kind you hear about, will dance with you when it's time to dance. When you've come a long way, and feel like it's time. To dance. To celebrate something. Suppose I did stop.

Yes. And smiled back. It was evening time. And the road deserted. Close the door. Throw her long shawl off. The black braid unraveling and. Indian woman. Let her dance. Yes. It's time. Let her. Let her show you. Let her turn. Indian. Let her. Let her. Show you. Indian. Woman. Let her.

PART 3

Dunlap

—— OR ——

The Lovers of Something

Watch a spider dropping from a porch beam, searching for a place to anchor his web. He drops slowly, his limbs wiggle and flex, he seems to be constantly feeling for something in the air he moves through. And the only thing that holds him suspended there between where he started and his first anchor point is a length of fine line which he himself produces while he looks. Unless the light is right you can't see this lifeline at all. He appears to be floating.

CHAPTER 50

Some things
you can't explain

*W*aterfalls of morning drench Hooper where he stands, beneath the skylight, shirtless. He feels the pressure like a fine mist against his skin, his morning shower. It's early and the light is new, not sunlight, since the sun's out in front of the house. This is sky. All the light above the house is funneled through that square above him, into the darkness and not spreading from there, but following its funnel right down to the floor. Hooper stands inside it, looking first at the front door, its beads of green and red and opal sparkle through the gloom. He looks at Broome's door, closed. The old man seldom leaves it now, just sits back there, inside a room that seems actually to recede from this intersection a little more as each day passes, music getting farther and farther from this centerpost. Hooper realizes that he hasn't seen Broome for a couple of days, overlooked him in the excitement of their current plan, which wouldn't even be a possibility were it *not* for Broome. Yet Hooper can't take the time. He is not a tender of the halt and lame, the elderly and sick, he is not a good Samaritan, nor a bad one—just time enough to pause these few moments under the light shaft and glance at the distant door, glance up the stairs toward the one he just closed, where she's dressing now, leaning forward to cup the breasts, arching to catch the fastener. He would sprint back up to watch that much of it, pang of regret for rushing out so soon and missing one of the finest moments of any day, but turns instead toward what used to be Hooper's door. His shopping bag's still in there someplace, near the spot where he found this wide-brimmed straw he's wearing.

It's weeks now since he slept there, not since before the victory party, spending every night with Nona, and many late afternoons, and each hour savoring what seems to be the last delicious moment in her tropical nest. Doom's inevitable, in the shape of Hash or Staples. A call, a letter, a mortar shell lobbed in from the parking lot, over the hedge from secret gun emplacement (new Buick rolls in, as if to find a day's parking, stops mid-lot, where roof rolls back, telescope barrel noses slowly skyward, penis of destruction lobbing shells one by one through the roof, through the windows, splashing through the sheets of Nona's bed and through the floor to splinter old violas and mandolins). So far a month has passed and nothing at all has happened, no calls, no letters, no return visits. Triumph has turned to complacency. The property council has never convened. Luella has deserted her attic lookout post. The quarantine sign has curled in the heat. Yet clearly this is just the moment extended, between the time the great arm releases and that chaotic instant when the shit finally hits the fan. And Hooper's resolve, if anything, has taken definite shape, found its energy in the throb of blood he felt pumping through the old man's arm when his face turned scarlet, and this energy now pumps directly into the *Golden Goose*. You might say he is building a getaway vehicle for all of them, before the shooting starts, for all the inhabitants of this doomed mansion. Under Hooper's command Joe and Nona and Goldie have all been working on the boat.

Their tools come from a splintered workroom under the house—planes, chisels, saws and wirebrushes, cans of polish, rusted buckets tightly sealed and sometimes full of usable paint. From Broome's apartment come the folded sails, the old lines and fittings. Goldie the girl who expects nothing was as ready for this task as any other. Jonas, formerly the master of something, is now Hooper's first mate. The *Golden Goose* will be their ark, their arc, their time-capsule, their mobile hideout. And if Hooper ignores old Broome this morning it's only because he intends to save him in the end.

He steps out of the shower of light and heads for Joe's door, knocking, shouting, "Joe! Joe!" And when Joe says grumpily, "What?" throws it open to announce "Lift up thy rod, and stretch out thine hand"—Hooper's daily reading having brought him to the middle of Exodus, and this morning, before jumping out of bed he read aloud to Nona how the Israelites arrived at the shores of the Red Sea, the fearful dilemma of enemy troops behind and deep waters ahead. Upon uttering Jehovah's words to Moses, Hooper threw back the sheet and told her, "The time has come, Nona. I feel it in my bones."

In minutes they are all out there, ripping off the doors and most of the wall of that one-time garage, then standing back to consider how best to secure the boat to Joe's truck and also admire their handiwork, now that the morning light, for the first time in twenty years, shines full upon her.

The boat has become exactly what they hoped it would. The heavy oak keel has been painted sky-blue to the waterline. The hull is planked, and painted yellow-gold, horizontal plank lines striping through it. On one side of the prow the name in gold leaf has been repaired. On the other Nona has drawn a longnecked goose in flight. The paint sharpens the line of the hull, which, about six feet back, begins to cut under abruptly, so that the bottom is something like a dinghy's. The rails, walnut-stained, shine with varnish. Between the rails the washed deck wears a film of watersoft splinter hairs. The low square cabin is yellow-gold too, with two of its portholes gone. Aft of the cabin you step down to a pair of facing benches padded with the original cushions, sun-cracked, white where mold was scraped away.

Joe has never mentioned this boat to Hooper. His opinions, like his sweat, seldom come to the surface. But Hooper could tell, the first time he brought Joe out to the shed, by the bunching of his bone-white jaws, the lowering of his lids, as if ready to doze, that Jonas knew he had been one-upped. No land vehicle Joe might ever discover or contrive could run in the same class with a water vehicle like the *Golden Goose*. Hooper knows Joe hungers to sail it, not particularly for where the boat might take him, but rather, at least right now, in the beginning, for the sailing in *it*, to have the pleasure, while afloat, of ignoring its defects, its retarded look, to ignore inquisitive glances from passing immaculate yachtsmen.

This is a taste they all share, it seems—until this day when Hooper decides it's time to haul her down to the harbor for a shakedown cruise. Amid their general enthusiasm Nona's is the lone voice of caution, asking quietly, apologetically, during this moment of reverent admiration, "Do you really think it's ready?"

"What?"

"You said yourself the running lights . . ."

"Running lights are for sailing at night, honey."

". . . flicker on and off like a Christmas tree."

Impatient Hooper shoves his wide-brimmed straw hat back. "We're not going out at night. All I'm talking about is a couple of hours this afternoon."

"The engine isn't much good either."

She smiles, glances around at Goldie and Joe to see how they're taking this. Joe smiles back benignly. Goldie looks a little worried.

"We'll get it started," Hooper says. "It'll get us out of the harbor."

"What about the gas tank?"

"What *about* the gas tank?"

"It's pretty old."

"I imagine it's about as old as the boat."

"Don't you think it looks . . . rusty?"

"If we have to we can patch it."

Her brow knits.

Hooper says, "We'd have to tear out half a bulkhead to put a *new* one in."

"Can I ask you about the sails then? You said you were going to get some new sails."

"I wanted to. But we just don't have the cash for it yet."

"You think the old ones will hold up?"

Charitable Hooper, closing off debate, "Well, that's what a shake-down cruise is all about. I mean that's what we have to find out. Sooner we know where the kinks are, the sooner we get to take Uncle Jack out for a ride."

"I'm only thinking that if the sails happened to tear, or anything else went wrong—all kinds of things can go wrong—wouldn't you need the engine, to get back to shore?"

"Shit," Joe says, "we can always get back to shore."

With a beatific smile Goldie says, "It'll sail, Nona. It's too beautiful not to."

Hooper feels a surge of affection for Goldie. Whatever else you may say about her, there's a girl who'd never give a thought for faulty running lights. Just mention a launching and Goldie's up on deck begging to ride the bowsprit all the way to the harbor.

He sees Nona watching him, smiling her mind-reader's smile now, as if possessing special knowledge, island secrets, eyes full of glisten, aloha, morning affection in the high green grass, and lineless face composed, at ease.

She's right, of course, in a way. But still, there's plenty of time for the finishing touches. Hooper is a little disappointed in her. All these weeks he's been thinking what a fine companion she'd make on board. For a month of humid forenoons he's been watching her work, daubing and whittling at the incalculable hoard, with those slow submarine movements, as if impeded by deep fluids, which were in fact the air's own moisture in the shed, coating Nona's body with a glistening film to shine in the half light. Strong arms on Nona. Nothing delicate about those wrists and shoulders. Graceful is the word. But not delicate. Make a good sailor, has been one of his frequent thoughts. Carry her weight.

But something has changed. Just in these last few days. Something starting to taste a little sour. All the sweetness, that honey, that juice squeezed into his life by the same underwater giant who has a fist around the root of this island, squeezing juices upward into every living thing, making greens greener, blues bluer, reds sometimes redder than the eye can bear—all that rich juice now is the faintest bit sour. Hooper is like the man sucking at saliva to get the taste out of his mouth, then swallowing it, continually swallowing.

Perhaps if he could explain one thing to Nona, that taste might disappear. In this matter of the *Golden Goose*, he would like to remind her of the yellow Desoto with no windows but a front one, that carried him and Joe all the way north to San Francisco one winter, out of gas just as they sighted the Cliff House and probably still there, salt-eaten ruin now. Tell her about the Model A with no horn, no lights, no brakes, no license plates or hubcaps or windshield wipers or floorboards or bumpers, that took them nearly to the Mexican border, where they traded it for a hearse with six out of eight cylinders working, transmission screaming back at a world that had so neglected it, and drove that on south to Guaymas, barely, but nonetheless all the way. It's a great comfort to know from experience that vehicles can serve you like that if you will let them.

But how to explain it to Nona?

Well (slapping palms on dusty thighs, the time has come, stretch out thine hand) some things you can't explain. You just have to prove them true.

CHAPTER 51

It'll start

*B*y nine o'clock they're on the road, boat lashed to Joe's rear axle with tow ropes. The tires on its traveling frame are flat and so rotten they won't hold air, but there's no use buying new ones for this one-way, one-time trip to the harbor. So at five miles an hour they grind down Kalakaua, late entry in the Jackson Broome Small Craft Parade—Nona driving, Goldie on the truck roof waving, Hooper and Joe stepping along, one on either side of the hull, flagging cars to pass. Joe scowls back at spectators, Hooper hopes the tires won't shred and tip the whole rig over. The boat itself behaves very much like a goose wobbling down toward the water.

They want to get it launched by noon, mainly because Nona has remembered a two-thirty rehearsal she can't afford to miss. Hooper swears they can make it and works like a galley slave all morning. But it took them forty-five minutes to get to the harbor, and there was still the mast to step and the boat to rig. Some screws were missing, and a turnbuckle, and one of the blocks wouldn't roll, and what with one thing and another, it's two o'clock before they know it, and Nona has to catch a bus back to Waikiki.

Hooper tells her she can skip rehearsal once.

"I wish I could. But we're putting together a new show."

In her eyes that flick of accusation, like the time they lifted Jackson from the weeds, as if it's Hooper's fault she has to go to work at all.

And this is part of the sourness. Nona's job. Or rather Hooper's lack of one. He's almost out of money now, having spent most of what little he had on this boat, and cautious with what's left. Nona, for instance, just paid for the turnbuckle, since today he's short of ready cash. She pays about half the time now when they go out for breakfast at Johnny B's. And does so with an enormous smile, makes a joke of it. But he knows she's starting to resent it, sees herself abused, and he resents her resentment, sees himself standing here at this very moment prickled with sweat, hands begrimed, knees scraped, working overtime on her behalf, for Christ sake, and now this look, this little duel, as if there's a difference between her work and his and somehow he has fallen short.

Well, be generous. He *was* a little hasty rushing out here all of a sudden.

"Listen, Nona, we'll just wait till tomorrow. What the hell. By the time we get her ready it'll probably be too late today anyhow."

She says there's no use waiting on her account. Take the boat out today, and tomorrow too. Hooper is so eager to sail, so caught up in this headlong race to get the goose, for no particularly urgent reason, after a month of low-keyed tinkering, into the water to*day*, that he lets her turn and start to walk away.

But something in her parting statement nettles him, some petulance, around the edges of her nose, some niggling barb he has never heard in her voice before. Though he knows better, knows he should write it off to the heat, or to her temporary disappointment, and let it pass, he does not. He's just touchy enough himself, after the long morning's plunge toward this deflating moment to yell, "Hey!"

He steps toward her. Before she turns he sees, from these few feet away, how the blue sleeveless jersey shapes her smooth back by hiding it, falls straight from wide brown shoulders to a light fold

160

collected at the waist, behind the long black hair, and catches light, shifting with her stride, and oh, whatever else he was going to say, it is now the case that she is much too beautiful to let run loose, even as far as the bus stop, past those gap-toothed satyrs mending nets over there at the fishing dock.

Catching up he takes her arm. "I'll drive you."

Too late. Her eyes are filling with tears.

"What's the matter?"

"Nothing."

She blinks them back.

Matching long strides they walk in silence to the Reo, climb in. Resin pungence, fruit peels rotting. Hooper fools with the starter. Clunks and sometimes tiny groans of engine turning over. Nona can't help laughing. Hooper, challenged, pumps the gas pedal, shifts into neutral, yanks the choke.

"It'll start."

It does, finally, engine exploding, settling into its pattern of hacks and stutters.

Backing up, Hooper says, "I've never seen you cry. Tell me what's the matter."

"I told you it's nothing."

"Look, we're not taking the boat out today. I've made up my mind."

"Oh that doesn't make any difference, Hooper."

"What is it then?"

"It's just . . ."

She looks at him, as if frightened of what's in her mouth, and asking him to somehow pluck it out, throw it over the side so they can be lovers again.

"What?"

"Your attitude."

"Toward?"

"It's like you don't really care about Uncle Jack's boat."

"Oh shit, Nona. You know that's not true."

"Then maybe it's the way you care. I don't know. Everything you do . . ."

"Jesus Christ! We've spent all day trying to get the fucking sails up. And if we *find* any leaks in the goddam gas tank, it takes about fifteen minutes . . ."

"It isn't just the gas tank. I'm thinking about . . . oh, all kinds of things."

That look again, that anxious, wide-eyed fear of can't help saying what's coming next, or what saying it will lead to.

"You care so much about Uncle Jack and all that. But you'd be willing to take him out in a boat that's only half ready to sail, and . . . if anything went wrong . . ."

"Goddam it, Nona, that isn't true either. That's why we're checking it out ahead of time. What's the matter with you anyway? I've never seen you like this."

The tears let go, Nona sitting straight and tall, just the great backflood released.

"C'mon. You haven't told me what it is yet, have you."

"Nothing."

"Tell me."

"Everything."

"What."

"I don't feel right."

"Why not?"

"My period's late."

Hooper is trying to pass a bus parked in front of the Royal Hawaiian, concentrates on this, just a glance at Nona.

"By how much?"

"About a week."

"That's not so late."

"I'm very regular. I can't ever remember being late."

"Well, it's nothing to get upset about."

"All right, if you say so."

"It'll start."

"Can you guarantee it?"

"You don't have to get sarcastic. All kinds of things can make a period late. There's no reason to get . . ."

"There you go again."

"What do you mean?"

"Letting things slide."

"Now wait a minute."

"It'll take care of itself. Right? Don't change the gas tank. Don't take Uncle Jack to the hospital. Don't do anything about a late period."

"You know what you sound like today?"

"A bitch."

"A mainland girl. A southern California female."

"Maybe I'm just a female. Maybe deep down we're all the same, did you ever think about that?"

"What's that supposed to mean?"

Crying again. "Oh Hooper, some things are so hard to say." Breaking down. "But if you don't say them, they burn inside you . . ."

"You better say it then."

"I keep getting the feeling ... that you don't care about *me*."

"I care about you more than I've ever cared about anyone."

He reaches to pull her over next to him, but she doesn't want it that way.

"I can't help feeling it isn't me you care about. It's some idea of me, some idea you think I am. Maybe I'm imagining this, Hooper, because I'm so afraid of it happening again."

"Of what happening again?"

"What happened with Al. He never once saw me. All he saw was a dancer, a chorus girl, an innocent Hawaiian maiden he could use for a while and throw away. His island girl. I deserved it, I guess, because I saw him the same way. He was my rich mainland *haole*. And you are so much different from him I am almost ashamed to talk to you this way. But I don't want to be used, and I don't want to be anybody's island girl. I want to be me. Nona."

They are double-parked in front of the Paradise now, engine running. She grabs his hands, pulls up close to his face.

"Look at me, Hooper. Look at me hard. In my eyes. Who do you see?"

"I've never seen anyone but you."

They sit for a long time like that, till a cab behind them starts to honk, and Hooper doesn't know whether he has lied to her or told the truth.

CHAPTER 52

The Captain of his fate

*I*n the water by four o'clock, Hooper and Joe and Goldie, and the engine, when it finally catches, gets them nearly to the breakwater. There it sputters and dies. Then a puff of wind, breath of the phantom goose that flies above its namesake, gets them past the breakwater, as the mainsail picks it up, and they scoot out into the bay.

Offshore the wind freshens. They beat into it a while, west and south, getting the feel of the boat. Hooper at the tiller is turning over in his mind various legends he has heard about ways to start the menstrual flow, and generally brooding about what's to be done, trying to sort out Nona's message. He keeps ending up with too many pieces, too much to juggle. He wants one single thing he can hold before his eyes and say, This is it.

The cruise provides exactly what he's looking for. As they sail farther and farther from shore, the pieces gradually merge. In the sharpening spray their edges blur. His mood lightens. He concludes that she's just upset, and overreacting, and time is mainly what's needed here. A man can't change the way he is overnight, after all. And absence makes the heart grow fonder. Facing into the spray he lets it cool him and clear his head. He studies the wake fanning back. Exactly what a man needs at such a time. This is the way it should always be, captain of your fate, and everskimming, feel the ocean in your hands.

The wind has picked up. They are close-hauled now, barreling under it. Hooper cleats the mainsheet and orders Joe to cleat the jib, and glances back at the receding shoreline to savor the space they've already put behind them and this rush of new speed. At that moment a sudden gust hits. The boat heels sharply, with a great pop, like waves sometimes make when they break so fast the foamy air spurts out. Joe and Hooper are yelling at each other, grabbing for the sheets. Too late. All that wind is rushing through space where the sails used to be. The jib has split at the luff, the main is shredded. Behind Hooper the mizzen sends a lap of canvas whipping to cover his face like a scarf.

Half a minute later the sails are ripped and sheared as if a dozen drunken men have been at them with knives, and the *Golden Goose* is coasting to a stop about two and a half miles from shore, just like a surfboard, after the frantic paddle through shorebreak and line of swells, reaches the flat breaking place and makes its sudden halt to wait—except that here no waves approach, no mighty force to drive them back to shore. The steady wind whizzes through their ragged banners.

Jonas and Hooper look at each other. Hooper is in charge. He blinks. Joe squints off toward the horizon, asks, "How much gas do we have?"

"Enough."

"You want to bring in the sails?"

"Fuck it."

Hooper goes below, to try the engine. It whines and whinnies. He tries it half a dozen times. It won't even turn over now.

CHAPTER 53

One of the boys

*U*p on deck he looks at Joe again. Nona isn't absent after all. Her presence and prophecy are heavily felt. It burdens the moment, which otherwise wouldn't be heavy at all, if anything a cause for merriment. But Nona is Hooper's girl, and she is the one who delivered the warning, and all this will have to be explained. It adds a weight that is sadly unnecessary. It weakens the position of Hooper the Captain. It brings new, needed strength to Jonas the Crew.

You could call this moment the first step in Joe's recovery program. Since the days he rode the biggest wave he has been out of balance, disillusioned, even from time to time considering suicide, like an executive fired from a very good job. His goal in life, fulfilled at twenty-one, Joe became the most aimless of men. Goldie caught him at his vulnerable time. He took her back in weakness, for the warmth. But something here on the drifting deck brings it all home to him, the danger inherent in the female presence. Women spoil things. Add to this his brief, new feeling of the sea, sense of entire ocean as perhaps the largest wave of all, and Joe could be young Samson the day his sideburns grew long enough to finger again.

Goldie feels it, some nearly visible current circling the deck among the three of them, Joe's need to stretch new muscles, Hooper's need to regain whatever he has lost.

She breaks the silence. "Isn't that a launch over there about half a mile away?" She starts to wave. "Hey! Hey! Hey!"

Joe and Hooper, for lack of any better solution, yell and wave too. They tear the jib apart and make a long floppy flag, toss it up and down between them like a jump rope, hurl it back and forth.

No response.

Joe says, "What the fuck. I'll *swim* over there. I feel like a swim anyway."

Before they can answer he is over the side and stroking through a light chop, white arms smacking water with furious ease.

Hooper watches him take the first fifty yards, and silently curses the sails, and Nona, and his luck, and lack of money. Now they won't even be able to get across the goddam harbor.

He steps down and sits on one of the benches, elbows back, face up to let the sun bite his cheeks. Five o'clock, two and a half hours till dark, a warm breeze and steady rock to the boat. His main wish at the moment is for a bottle of cold beer, and he supposes things could be a hell of a lot worse than they are.

Goldie says, "I love to watch Joe swim."

He ignores her. Conditioned response. For a month he has been carefully avoiding Goldie, overlooking her, keeping between them the distance a commander maintains from his troops: *See if you can find another bucket somewhere, Goldie... That's a good bit of work there.*

She says, "He has such a fantastic body."

SPIT. SPAT. FLAPPETY TATTERS.

Hooper looks up at her, posing next to the mainmast, running one hand silkily up and down its varnish, and can't help remembering those nights they spent in Joe's Reo, mornings waking next to her, and a very keen pleasure he tried at the time to suppress, and tries now to suppress, just a flash before he tumbled out the door, of her smell and color, the way the greasy sleeping bag twined around her, blond hair spread across debris, the creases in her aloha shirt. He sees her grabbing chunks of bread and wolfing these in huge, half-chewed bites.

"Do you think the body is important, Hooper?"

No harm in talking to her. It's only when Joe's around that her face unsettles him. The truth is, it can be mighty comfortable with Goldie. She knows how to be one of the boys.

"What do you mean?" he asks.

"In personal relationships."

"Sure."

"I love to touch Joe's. It's absolutely free of hair, you know. His upper body anyway. His chest and stomach."

"So is Nona's."

"She has a fantastic body too."

Hooper nods.

"Is she pure Hawaiian?"

"She's part Hawaiian. Part Irish. Part Chinese. Part everything."

"I wish I had a figure like hers."

"You're doing all right."

"She makes me feel flat-chested."

"Nobody could ever say you were flat-chested, Goldie."

"Joe does. Joe makes me do pushups every morning. He says my pecs are bony. He says pecs are a woman's most important feature."

"Pecs count."

"Joe says if my breasts ever fall he'll drop me like a hot potato."

SLAP. SPAT. SPIT. SPAPPETY.

"Does that sound like love to you, Hooper?"

"It sounds like Joe."

"Haven't you known Joe a pretty long time?"

"Five or six years."

"Has he had a lot of girl friends?"

"You're the only one he's ever stayed with for more than one day."

"Really?"

"I think he stayed with one girl two days in a row once, because they got stuck somewhere when his car broke down."

"I'll bet you've had a lot of girls."

"Hundreds."

"Seriously. Have you ever been in love, Hooper?"

"It's hard to say."

"Aren't you in love with Nona?"

"I don't know. I think so."

"People usually know when they're in love."

SPIT. BLAP. SPAPPETY. SPIPPETY.

A long look between Hooper and Goldie, out here in the breeze and dark sunshine.

"Goldie, there is something on my mind."

"Yeah?"

"And I feel like I can talk to you about it, you know, friend to friend? I feel like we have been through a lot together, you and me, in a funny kind of way, and like you will understand."

She is deeply moved by this confidence, winking back sudden wetness. Another silence while Hooper gathers his thoughts, gazes out across the water, watching Jonas halfway to the launch now, steady stroke, tiny white pistons in the distance.

"Suppose for a minute that you are a guy."

"Okay."

"And you have been going with this girl for a while."

"Okay."

"And suddenly she tells you that you have never really looked at her, that she is just an idea in your head and you have never really seen *her*. What would you do?"

"I would tell her that she is being self-centered."

"Why?"

"Because she cannot stand to have only part of your attention."

"What if that doesn't satisfy her?"

"I would get rid of her. You have to be tough, Hooper."

"But suppose..."

"Listen," Goldie says, "I just realized something. I think I understand you in a way I never have before."

"What do you mean?"

"You're just like me."

"How's that?"

"I mean I'm in love all the time. But in a very special way."

"Yeah?"

"Because I love Joe. But I also love you. And the *Golden Goose*. Even the man in the green pajamas. I am in love with the whole world and everybody in it. And I think you are too. And it is unnatural for people like us to be exclusively in love with just one person at a time."

Hooper considers this.

"Now you may think what I'm about to say is pretty terrible. But that is why I think if we ever do actually take a trip to Tahiti or someplace in this boat, it would be so fantastic if just you and me and Joe could make it, just the three of us."

"Hold it, Goldie."

"Does that sound decadent?"

"It sounds impossible."

"I just want everything all the time. Like right now I..."

"Okay, cut it right there."

"It's so sexy out here . . . it's like at the beach. I go to the beach and I want every built guy who comes along."

"Joe's going to get to that launch in a minute, and they'll be starting back over here to rescue us. So just knock it off."

"The sunshine, and those little laps the water makes up against the hull. It makes me want to take off my clothes."

"Save it for Joe."

"Hooper, I have to be absolutely honest with you."

"Never mind."

"I am brazen and horny, and I am going to do anything I can think of to seduce you. I am going to take off my shirt and show you my body."

"I'm going for a swim."

"I am going to prance around the deck in my dungarees. It's the sunshine, Hooper. It drives me crazy."

"Jesus Christ."

"I am going to let my hair fall down around your ears and get my skin so close to yours you can feel how warm it is just from the heat waves. Do you think my pecs are bony?"

"Goddam it, get off of me."

"I know you want me."

"You're unscrupulous, Goldie."

"We have to *do* it, Hooper, out here on the deck, in the sunshine."

"Look. The launch is coming about."

"Oh shit."

"C'mon. Put your shirt back on."

"There's still time."

"Later, Goldie."

"Promise?"

"You're depraved."

"Do you hate me for it?"

"Why can't we just be friends?"

"A good friend will do it to you when you're horny, Hooper. That's what friends are for."

He is watching the launch pick up speed. He can see Joe's golden head, backlit, catching the sun like a saint's, actually making a halo. Hooper observes it with amazement, with excitement. He's a little giddy now, teetering. Joe seems coming not only to rescue him from this afternoon's fiasco, but from things in general. Instant absolution from Saint Joe, powering across the water on magic pontoons.

It is a vision strangely ominous. Saint Joe's head, which should be upright and steady for this mysterious approach, is bobbing like a puppet's. His halo cuts an electric pattern in the air. The man piloting the launch is bobbing too, keeps falling forward over the wheel, causing the launch to swerve, so that its path toward them is jagged, halting, one of leaps forward, sudden tacks. The man's head seems curiously familiar. Next to Joe's luminous one, it is dark, actually black against the sun. As the launch pulls alongside, Hooper sees that the man at the wheel is Black Bass.

CHAPTER 54

The girls are lonesome

*B*ass is wearing a huge red and white aloha shirt. Dark glasses cover his eyes. He and Jonas are laughing so hard they can't stand up. Bass manages to switch off his engine just before he joins Joe on the deck, where they both roll around kicking their feet and screaming uncontrollably.

It turns out, as their laughter subsides, as they begin to raise up on feeble elbows, daubing tear-drenched eyes, that what has amused them is the look of the *Golden Goose*, rocking out here all blue and gold in the setting sun, with her sails cut to ribbons. It also turns out that they are getting drunk on the martinis Bass began to pour as soon as Jonas climbed aboard.

Now Hooper and Goldie have boarded the launch. They are all laughing at the miracle of this reunion. While Bass mixes the third round, they are sprawled around the red leather cabin trading accounts of how both their vessels happened to end up side by side. Bass explains that he has landed a job with a wholesale boating supply house, as a stock boy and sometime salesman, and that this launch belongs to his boss's wife, who happened to pass out in the double berth below decks just before Jonas showed up.

"A fantastic piece," Bass discloses, leering, sotto voice. "And the old man treats her like a horse turd."

He distributes the drinks. Handing Hooper his, he winks lewdly. "Hey, old buddy. You checked in at the kangaroo club lately?"

Hooper, sipping. "I been keeping busy down in town."

"Some a that citified stuff."

"It's the best."

"Listen man, I haven't been out to Wahiawa in damn near a month. I bet those Eskimos are getting lonesome for their old stud. You wanna pay a visit?"

"What about the boss's wife?"

"Who? Lorraine? Shit man, when she goes, she goes out for the night and most of the next day. It's pitiful. I mean she is the kind of lush that brings tears to your eyes."

Hooper is letting the first trickle of gin run through him, and watching the sunset pour through Plexiglas, one of those incredible Hawaiian sunsets, so brilliant and sharp-edged and luxuriously tropical it persuades you, for as long as it lasts, that every dream you've ever heard of paradise might still come true. Enough in itself to make a man forget the future. The alcohol warming his stomach sends a delicious surge of self-pity rising to his head. It mixes with the lust Goldie triggered. Vague regrets that he didn't take her while he had the chance. But he's glad now. It would have been a mistake. With Goldie it's always a mistake. He knew he was saving himself for something. Gazing into Bass's sweat-filmed and grinning face Hooper suspects that Wahiawa might have just the kind of solace he is looking for.

CHAPTER 55

The return of
Water Buffalo

*T*hree martinis later they are back at the harbor, boats moored. Bass leaves Lorraine in the double berth with a note telling her where he'll be tomorrow. Piled into Joe's truck they rattle out of town toward the center of the island while Bass, full of sympathy for their misfortune, tells Hooper he can get him a job at the supply house and that with a little sweet-talking probably finagle him a good set of sails at a discount, maybe on credit, depending how Lorraine feels the day he mentions it.

Savoring these promises, Hooper is a new man. He would return to Honolulu and look for Nona, tell her how old sails and useless engines can be blessings in disguise. He would meet her after work and win her back with the news. A delicious reunion. The timing will be perfect. She'll be expecting him, and if he isn't there she'll grow a crust to protect herself for when he *does* show up. He doesn't want to have to break through that crust.

But now Joe is slowing outside the hibiscus hedge. Hooper is like the diner who has eaten so much his stomach hurts and punishes himself by ordering a hot fudge sundae. With self-disgust and lascivious visions he helps Bass dig through the truck's debris for sweatshirts, jackets, scarves, raincoats, anything to keep the four of them warm.

As they break through the hedge and cross the yard, kicking coconut husks aside, Joe is wearing a knee-length olive army winter coat, buttoned and belted. Goldie wears a pair of Joe's jeans to cover her own, plus a bleach-mottled sweatshirt and an old YMCA towel around her neck, workout style. Bass, thinking ahead, grabbed the big navy-blue watchcoat from his La Salle before they left. Hooper, thinking ahead, grabbed Bass's poncho, and wears that now, above a pair of purple sweat pants, and some logger's boots. He is still thinking ahead, wondering how it will go with Blanche, whether it will be the bathtub again—Blanche did not, when all was said and done, much go for the tub—or will he have to warm their love nest some other way.

Bass knocks.

Moments later one corner of a checkered curtain flips back, moon face peering. Trudy opens the door, trying to look petulant.

"You mean, mean, mean, mean, mean man. Where you been?"

"I been working, making money for my sweethearts. Look here what I brought you." From one pocket he lifts a quart of Beefeater's gin, from the other a quart of Cutty Sark.

"Oh Byron, we don't need that stuff any more."

"What do you mean?"

"C'mon and see."

They file into a kitchen filled with steam. It's billowing from two great pots on the stove. The walls, the ceiling, the sink tiles, the uncurtained windows are wet with droplets of condensing vapor.

Through this cloud another moon face appears. Half of it, at the sight of Hooper, becomes teeth and joyous mouth.

"Water Buffalo!" Blanche exclaims, and throws her arms around his neck.

She and Trudy wear identical flimsy seagreen, see-through harem pants, necklace loops of rainbow beads, plum-covered vests joined at the front by small silver chains, nothing underneath.

Trudy has shut the door, and Hooper is suffocating, soaked with sweat. Blanche's weight is more than he can bear. Gin wearing off, head starting to throb. Regret creeps through his veins like cooling metal.

He pries Blanche loose. Her smile contracts. Be nice to her then. How many times in your life does a girl throw herself against you?

"Hi, Blanche. What's cooking?"

"Elephant ear."

She grabs a pair of tongs, reaches into one pot, lifts out an enormous green leaf, limp and smoking. "You're just in time for dinner."

"Elephant ear is supposed to be poison," he says.

"Not if you boil it twice," says Blanche.

"It's Sheepdog's recipe," Trudy says.

Blanche adds, "The yard is full of it. We're living off the land." She takes Hooper's hand. "C'mon out here where it's cooler."

They troop into the parlor. The couch is still there, with its velvet map-blanket of New Guinea, Australia, the Solomons, its embroidered silk pillows from Santiago, Hong Kong, Yokohama, and Portland. And it is cooler there. But not by much. Incense has replaced the air-conditioners, sticks of it burn everywhere, held in the folded palms of tiny golden buddhas, making thick air thicker, choking the room with spicy sweetness. Hindu temple music quietly jangles from a record player in one corner. Candles light the room, and staring at one of the candles, where it stands on a low draped box, sits Sheepdog, in the lotus position, hair to his cheeks, abdomen bulging and contracting in slow motion as if responding to some pulse of pressure in the air between himself and the candle.

Jonas moves up next to Hooper. His face has never been anything but white, or near-white, or stubbled white. Now it is deep red, and Joe is ripping buttons in his haste to get his topcoat off. "What the fuck is going on?"

Hooper asks Blanche, "What happened to the air conditioners?"

Seductive smile, as if those memories arouse her. "After Sarge moved out, we couldn't afford them any more. We couldn't pay the electric bills." Patting Sheepdog's head she adds, "Anyway they're unnatural."

Hooper looks at Bass, who grins, strips off his watchcoat, shrugs, implying Take it as it comes, and a moment later he is flexing like a Turkish wrestler, body glistening as Trudy slides an arm around his slippery waist.

"Everybody sit down on a pillow somewhere," she says. "I'll bring in the food."

As she wiggles toward the door, Bass, a chocolate sultan, grabs one seagreen flank.

Body reek fills the room, sharp smell of sweat-drenched wool blends with incense. Sheepdog's diaphragm stops for a half a minute while he blinks, absorbing the environmental change.

Goldie has thrown away her towel, her sweatshirt. She had a hard moment watching Blanche greet Hooper, but now she has shrugged that off. Trying to match the effect of their open vests, she unbuttons her aloha shirt and fans her stomach with its corners, swaying to the music, smiling, waiting.

Blanche is helping Hooper out of his poncho, unknotting the string that holds his sweatpants up, widening the waist by sliding tiny fingers past his navel. She unties his logger's boots, slips them off his feet, adds that smell to the room. She pulls down his sweatpants, runs a hand along his hairy calf, says slyly, "Has—ti—ni."

"What?"

"That's from the Kama Sutra. It means the elephant."

Trudy returns carrying two large platters, on one a heap of dark green pulpy mulch, on the other a long red fish, cooked in the skin and still sizzling.

"Ulua," Hooper says, recognizing the fish.

"Va—da—wa," Blanche answers, with amorous eyes, giggling, hugging his arm.

"Blanche caught it off the rocks," says Trudy. "Isn't that something?"

Ooooohhs and aaaaaahhs rise up around the steaming dishes. Bass carves. Trudy scoops the mulch out onto plates, along with

173

rice, cups of green tea. Food for everyone but Sheepdog, who isn't eating. He has been fasting for the past three days.

Hooper envies him. He is starting to feel hungover. The red fish has no taste. The mulch is ugly. It could be lethal. The incense is stifling. He needs to start drinking again. Or get outside. Or back to town is what is really on his mind. Behind a royal palm outside the Paradise.

Next to him Blanche is squirming, murmuring a slow list of Kama Sutra creatures, aphrodisiacs, ways to bite and scratch and titillate and fill your partner with uncontainable desire. Her shiny fingers hold a chunk of white meat, lifting it to Hooper's mouth.

He jumps up. "Joe, I have to get out of here."

Joe, gagging on his first bite of mulch, says, "Me too."

Trudy says, "Don't you like the food?"

"I just can't eat," says Hooper, "funny stomach."

From where he sits crosslegged on an orange pillow, Bass the sultan grins up at them. "Your loss is my gain, old buddy."

"I still want to talk to you about that job."

"Consider yourself hired, man."

"Wait for me," Goldie cries, leaping up from the floor.

"You go fuck yourself," Joe says.

"What's the matter? What did I do?"

"Just get fucked, that's all," Joe says. She jogs to catch up as they head for the kitchen.

Blanche's smooth brown face grimaces with disappointment. She says, "Sheepdog, Sheepdog, why are they leaving?"

A long pause, while the temple music jangles, then the back door slams. "Fools rush in where angels fear to tread."

CHAPTER 56

At the Intersection

As if searching for a cab, she pauses outside the swinging doors, stands on the top step tall and swarthy. Men turn to look at her. Hooper, in the shadow between two thick-trunked palms, is one of the lookers, like the time he first saw her, under Broome's skylight that first day he played Broome's guitar. A spot shines down on her from one of the trees. She seems confused, as if ready to ask directions of the first person she sees, and yet she's unapproachable, unhelpable, untouchable. Hooper savors this tremendous distance between Nona and all the men, including him, who look, the armor she seems to wear that keeps everyone back. She's the girl of his dreams, the woman he has never seen, yet recognizes instantly and wants, the difference this time being that there's no doubt he will have her. It's another beginning, but with all the preliminaries out of the way. That's what's so delicious about reunions. Beginning again.

She doesn't move until he steps out of the shadow, and then doesn't move until their eyes make the separating air electric. She glides down the stairs, and in the driveway he catches her, she catches him. Their lips close the space between, press to bring the bodies closer, all questions lost in the long, liquid kiss. Murmurs slide past the edges of the kiss, "I'm sorry, I'm sorry," Hooper's words, Nona's words.

Cab drivers are watching this, and hotel guests now stepping through the door. He rushes her down the driveway, between the rows of palm trunks and jungle flora, around the corner, through the hedge, up the porch stairs, pausing there to fumble for a key, snickering while urgent hands and lips and legs fumble. A violent kiss sends them crashing up against the door, which opens at the impact. They tumble through it, laughing. And trying not to laugh go careening down the hallway, bouncing off walls, ancient doorways, up the dark stairs to Nona's room.

CHAPTER 57

The floating sheet

*A*fterward he is stretched out watching her and wondering about the single sheet that covers them, the way its lightness rests on leg and chest hair, freshing skin. Somehow it is Nona's doing, just like the great peace settling on him now, making nothing else count, no plan, no other pleasure, no other person alive or dead. And there is no other warmth, or fragrance, or flesh but hers. What preceded was a kind of battle, the flesh lunging to join furiously, drawing back to lunge again. This aftertime is the true joining, two becoming one in the silence, in the warmth against warmth, too spent to draw back, content to merge, lean, lie, loll, languor of luxurious mating in the long peace that follows the frenzy, with a magic sheet for magic moments.

He regards the way it hovers, weightless. He has never seen or felt one like it. He searches for an explanation. It must be that Nona is the only woman he's ever been to bed with. Yes, of course. Why hasn't he thought of it before? The others flicker past. In cars. Backseat and front. In state parks. Sand dunes. Porcelain bath tubs. But never in a bed such as this, with window shades to soften the light, and music, and sheets.

Take Blanche, grinning at him from the soapy suds, hands and arms running with suds as she splashes. Take Goldie, prancing in her dungarees, sail tatters flicking at her legs and shoulders. Goldie on the spotted mattress, wriggling darkly inside Joe's Reo. In that darkness the truck becomes a deserted beach. Heavy waves rock it. The girl becomes Marie from Pasadena, resembling Goldie, except she liked to do it in a sleeping bag, wouldn't have it any other way. "So cozy," says Marie one night, "with everything inside the zipper." And that bag was a big improvement over night fields of bare sand. Sand at night can get as cold as snow. To wrestle a girl in the cold sand is nothing but punishment. Underneath the pier, and underneath Hooper in the sand-flavored snow lies Jo Ann, a deacon's daughter. Above them the pier's barnacled underside, kelp heaped against the pilings, rubble the tide forgot, rusty damp of metal plates corroding in the fog. Jo Ann weeps, "No, Hooper, not until we're married," while she grinds at him with her still unzipped pelvis. "We *will* get married. I want to marry you, Jo Ann. We'll get married tomorrow." He reaches to unfasten something, groping her hips for a snap. Panicked fingers dig at his arm, the hips dry-hump like a belly dancer's, lascivious and writhing, yet taut as a flexed muscle, guarding her zipper. "Don't Hooper!" Hands under his shirt, down his back to the buttocks, where she grabs to push against them. He has never straddled a girl, and never felt this kind of pushing. He can't control the swelling warmth. His white pulse spurts. She feels it, knows what's happening, pushes harder still, for any throb to penetrate the cloth, spreading it around, and his greasy flash of pleasure just deepens his rage at the waste, thinking Goddam it Jo Ann goddam it to hell, while her fingers still dig fiercely at his flank, her hips writhe helpless. "Oh Hooper," she cries, "I'm *so* sorry, I'm so *sorry.*"

Such a small sound she makes now, coming from that tiny fog-night picture blurring. Such a long time back. All that aching buried in the cold sand, while Hooper, buried in this featherbed, sinks deeper in its plushy down of a thousand golden geese.

Jangle trucks and stuck zippers are rusting in the distance. Nothing here but this sheet cocoon and luxury of Nona loose against him. No more Jo Anns. And no more Goldies. Pray there won't be. Would she drip poison in Nona's ear? Hooper, vulnerable, imagines blackmail, forced to take Goldie at regular intervals in ever more squalid surroundings, just to keep her quiet. Intolerable. Forget about it. Forget about everything. This is perfect. Nona's face turning seems about to speak, perhaps to ask again the question, Look at me, Hooper. Look at her, yes. But don't talk. Close her mouth. Words will spoil it, always spoil it. Hold it hold it. Stop thinking. Don't move. Hold her close. Float beneath the floating sheet. Listen to the music. Ancient voices. Stuttering drums. The woodblock gallops. Centuries pass.

CHAPTER 58

Plink

*T*wo years after the Second World War Andrew and Hooper sit side by side for the drive to church. Hooper's as tall as his father now. Their faces echo, the way son's and father's do, similar, yet opposite, something in the straightness of the nose, the chin knobs, Andrew's face rusty, his blue eyes finely coated with rust, Hooper's tan and smooth, his eyes brown, Cherokee shadows at the cheek.

A heavy silence hangs between them. Andrew is counting his blessings, a weekly habit that gets him in the mood for worship service: good health, a solid house, plenty to eat, Boeing on the move and Andrew's on the Boeing team, just promoted from senior mechanic to wheel assembly foreman. This is their last Sunday in the '38 Dodge. Next week it's the brand-new four-door.

Counting his blessings he glances at Hooper, who stares moodily at passing houses. Andrew begins to count his misfortunes, part two of this Sunday meditation, taking the bad with the good, so that inevitably he enters church wearing the creased face the congregation expects of its leaders.

Fourth son in a family of nine, with generations of vast families behind him, child-rich brothers and sisters spread from out here in Glendale clear back to Tennessee, and Andrew went and married a woman with a weak womb, who bore him one son and had to quit. It's hard facing those brothers of his when the families meet every five years or ten, in Albuquerque or Salt Lake, and stand their broods together for the crowd-scene photo. It isn't Andrew's fault. Nor Naomi's. She would if she could. She didn't order the weakness. Not even God's fault, since all things created by him were perfect once. If anything's to blame it's the species itself. Riddled with flaws. Trials. Burdens. And one son is better than none at all. So the least you can do is pass on the comforts that you, growing up, scarcely dreamed of, comforts of the flesh of course, but more important, those eternal ones, comforts of the afterlife, available to any man who can learn to behave himself these seventy years or so. And the first step toward that afterlife, well, that is what's on Andrew's mind this morning, that act of faith which any man who loves his son would encourage at the earliest opportunity. Witnessing that one act would reduce all these other blessings and misfortunes to sounding brass and tinkling cymbals.

"Hooper, I sent your mother on ahead with Sister Winslow because I want to talk to you about something I been meaning to talk to you about for a long time now."

Hooper stares out the window, closes his eyes.

"Boy reaches a certain age, it gets time for him to start doing the work of the church." Pause. "Know what I mean?"

"I guess so."

"There's work to be done and you can only put off doin' it so long. There's prayers to lead. There's communion table to wait on. There's ushering to do when people are coming in to the service."

He glances at Hooper, who sighs with boredom.

"Now nobody can do the work of the church until he is baptized. That's what it comes down to. You are fourteen years of age, Hooper. It's about time you started thinking about these things."

"What about Jesse Bullington?"

"What about Jesse Bullington?"

"Jesse didn't get baptized till he was eighteen."

"Jesse Bullington had only been coming to our church a year when he got baptized. Before that he went to the Methodists. Fact is, Jesse Bullington is a convert."

"Then what about Jesus?"

"Jesus?"

"Jesus didn't get baptized till he was thirty."

Andrew feels his face turn to rhubarb. "That's a special situation.

178

Jesus was the first man to ever get baptized."

"But if we're supposed to follow his example ..."

"Your great-grandfather, David Dunlap, was baptized when he was twelve and devoted his whole life to the Lord's work. By the time any boy reaches fourteen and knows right from wrong ..."

Andrew is disgusted with himself. Raising his voice when he wants to sound benevolent and Christ-like. This isn't the way it was supposed to go. He looks at Hooper, whose face is still averted. Andrew searches for some phrase to end this, to change the mood, to reconcile. Can't find it. Lets the sentence hang.

In Sunday School Hooper is wishing his mother came along for that ride. She never allows the frontal attack. She comes in from the side, and likes everyone else to and never really say what's on his mind. Like this morning's breakfast, looking sideways over the toaster: "Brother Dailey won't be with us no more after today, Hooper. He's moving up to Fresno to a new congregation. He's a mighty good man, and we sure will miss him. I guess he's been preaching here as long as anybody you can remember, hasn't he? I know he thinks an awful lot of you. It's sure nice having a preacher you've known awhile when things come up you want a preacher to do."

With his mother he can answer from the side and evade her. But his father comes right ahead, corraling him.

In Sunday School they study The Acts of The Apostles, the teacher now reading from Chapter 26. "Then Agrippa said unto Paul, Almost thou persuadest me to be a Christian." Hooper has heard it many times but never listened to this verse before. Today the words sound ominous, the words themselves. A premonition. He reviews his father's words. He starts to shiver. Something is closing in.

He feels like yelling, "I don't want to be baptized." Tries it a couple of times, silently. The blasphemy scares him. Add "today" and try it again, louder. "I don't want to be baptized today!" Yes, that is exactly how he feels.

Jo Ann Babcock, sitting behind him, touches his shoulder, whispers, "Hooper, are you all right?" Jo Ann has the biggest chest of any girl in church, impossible to hide even though her mother makes her wear a thick green overcoat to Sunday service, winter and summer. He turns, eyes burning into her bosom. Flames rise to his cheeks. He feels feverish. A victim and a martyr. He will rest his head there on the highest curve.

Worship service opens with communion. From a crisp white

tablecloth trays spread out through the congregation. Toward
Hooper one is passed along the pew, glinting below the skylight,
stopping as each hand raises a small ruby glass and returns it half
empty to its padded hole. Andrew sips, passes the tray to Hooper,
then bows to dwell solemnly on Jesus. Hooper passes it on, quickly.
The touch of it unnerves him, reminds him that Deacon Andrew
Dunlap here assigns the weekly duties. Hooper knows the first time
he waits on communion table he'll drop the tray of glasses. He can
hear the crash, tinkle of their rolling underneath pews down the
sloped floor toward the stage. He hears himself laughing, cursing his
luck.

During two songs and a long prayer the hall is strangely dark.
Through the frosted skylight a gray layer of overhanging cloud en-
courages his dark and fearful, martyr's mood. But now Brother
Dailey is starting for the stage, and a glow replaces the darkness.
He mounts four stairs, crosses to the rostrum, grips its rim and gazes
sadly into the crowd, a long, bony man, Abraham Lincoln without a
beard. The crown of his head is bald. All that remains of his hair
is a gray wreath around the side and back, and while he stands
there a sudden gush of sunlight streams down upon him, a band of
brilliance brightest in the center where his polished dome glows.

Whenever this happens a fine chill grips Hooper, at the coincidence that cannot be explained. He wouldn't call it a signal of
divine approval. He knows such things aren't possible. Yet on
cloudy days he always watches the light, to see which parts of the
service are illuminated, which overcast. He can't help connecting
this sunburst to Brother Dailey's final sermon, can't help thinking
some spirit moves within, around this shiny-headed man.

The preacher's palms lift slowly into whiteness, making two more
brights. Hooper hears the deep voice when it starts to speak. But
not the words. He doesn't want to listen to the words. The sounds
will be enough. The sound and the sunlight. It's just a farewell sermon. He'd rather dazzle his eyes in the light. Upthrust of beckoning
arms mesmerizes him, and sun rushing down to fill void when the
voice dies.

Hooper stares, and lets his mind go blank, and half the sermon's
gone before the words penetrate. He has been trying to get a glimpse
of Jo Ann Babcock's chest, between the shifting shoulders of two
elderly women. A loud silence catches his ear. Then out of the light
a white sword runs him through, pins him to the pew.

The preacher shouts, "One Lord, one faith, one baptism! Ephe-
sians four and five!"

Hand slap on Brother Dailey's Bible.

I don't want to be baptized today!

"*The one Lord, brethren, is Jesus Christ. The one faith is faith in Him. The one baptism is what God tells us about time and time again right here in the New Testament.*"

Gilt-edged pages flapping in the sunlight, and Hooper wants out of here. He knows what's coming next. He dreads it. And he knows it's already too late. This is no farewell sermon, it's salvation talk. Each of these verses is tied to every other verse like an enormous fisherman's net, and he is already caught inside it, caught too behind these poles and sheets of brilliance, and caught by the very jerking of the long body on the stage, like a life-size puppet strung from who knows how high above, sudden pops of knee and elbow, legs snapping, arms darting into the shine.

"*Now let us think what that one baptism means. It does not mean to sprinkle water over a little baby's head. It does not mean to pour half a gallon of water from a pitcher over a young child's face and arms. If we look at the original meaning of this word, if we go back to the language of these scriptures, the Greek of the apostles' day, we find the Greek word was* baptizein, *which literally meant to plunge, to immerse in water. If we go a little farther and explore the word* immerse *we find it comes from the same Latin root that gives us* merge, *which means to be combined or absorbed or swallowed up. Which is why the scriptures tell us we are buried with Christ by baptism, and like Christ was raised from the dead by the glory of his father, even so we also should walk in newness of life.*"

Back of his hand again on the open page, "Romans six and four."

Slap shut the book, sudden quiet. White dome bends out the light, hands clutch the rostrum edge as he leans toward Hooper, kind and grizzled patriarchal face, the voice going low and gutteral for the waiting crowd.

Now isn't that a wonderful concept, friends, to be immersed with Christ, to become one with him, and then to emerge in newness of life? It is God's gift to each of us. And wouldn't you rather take that gift than walk through life alone, in darkness, stumbling down the steps to hell. Look into your hearts, and ask yourself where you stand with Jesus. The Lord himself tells us, in Mark 16:16, He that believeth and is baptized shall be saved; he that believeth not shall be damned."

The white sword twists, carving Hooper's bowels. This is the part he hates. He doesn't have to look into his own heart. He knows he's in the darkness. He doesn't enjoy it there. He didn't understand hell until he was sick once with flu, four hours of violent stomach cramps and sure then that damnation must be the same torment but a thousand times more agony and lasting forever. He doesn't want to go through that. Yet he risks it. He flirts with the chance that he could be swallowed up unsaved while they're driving home from church, because he fears even worse losing his chance for washing away all such darkness from his soul. As it is, he never worries long about his sins. They can pile up, darkness can accumulate toward the time when it'll all be washed away. How comforting to know that no matter what he does or thinks, all will be purified later on. It's an ace he doesn't want to play until he has to.

So he flirts with the darkness. And he flirts, as Brother Dailey just described it, alone. No doubt about that. In this crowd of two hundred he sits the object of their communal gaze. Every eye is piercing the back of his neck. A hail of holy arrows. Every eye except his father's.

Hooper happens to glance at Andrew, and Andrew is watching Brother Dailey, and while he observes the side of Andrew's ruddy face he sees something appalling, yet, once witnessed, entirely predictable. He sees, at least he thinks he sees his father winking at the preacher.

Hooper leans back, breathing deep. Could that explain it? The way things are closing in? Not coincidence at all, but an actual conspiracy? The light, the sermon, the prologue in Sunday School—a plot hatched between preacher, teacher and Deacon Dunlap who knows, though Hooper has never confessed it, how the sunshine weakens his resistance.

He's thankful Brother Dailey doesn't wink back. Too holy for that—weary eye rings, the knees back-snapping as some thread of light yanks upward—holiest man Hooper has ever seen, and somehow this plot is all his father's. Yes, and going on a long time, the looks, the interrogations, launched among holy arrows from all these hovering eyes, a circle of spikes pressing him ever closer to the pool.

It is likely Andrew bribed the preacher to deliver this exhortation, instead of the soothing farewell he probably planned; and bribed the teacher too; and arranged for the clouds to draw back, and stay back, for sunlight to edge the passion of this climax:

"Look into your heart, friend, and if you're not yet one with Christ, and if you want to be, then do not hesitate. Come forward this very day. Repent of your sins, express belief in Jesus, join your life to His by being buried in holy baptism. Look into your heart, step out of the darkness that can only lead to damnation, and step forward this morning to stand in the light with Jesus, as together we all stand and sing."

He bounces down four stairs to stand below the rostrum, right in front of the center aisle, and Andrew fills the stage in his place, catching sun on his straight black slab of hair. With a lift of arms *he brings the crowd to its feet, flipping for page 342.*

Andrew looks a little frightened up there in the floodlight of Sunday morning, announces the number with a voice too loud. Hooper is embarrassed by the look, by the coffee-colored double breasted suit and hard white collar bunching neck skin over the edges. He is embarrassed until his father begins to sing. Then, even if the building were half full and that half fumbling with some unfamiliar verse, as long as Andrew's leading it sounds as if the church is jammed with choristers.

His suspicions dwindle as Andrew sings. He likes to let his father's voice swallow his, make his low notes just as round and full and thrilling, especially when two hundred voices well into a song like this. It is one of Hooper's favorites. The bass line pleases him, and he knows the lyrics by heart, doesn't need a book. Smug, superior to all the page-rustlers, he is that much closer to his father's song. Andrew sings from memory too, coffee arms waving in the sunshine:

Almost persuaded, Christ to believe,
Almost persuaded, Christ to receive.

Brother Dailey sings from memory, and sings bass, and before the first verse is done, Hooper finds himself in a trio with the preacher and his father, shivering when they all hit the same note, pulling in his chin for the low ones, belting loud bars in transcendental unison. Other singers are muted background chorus. Hooper hears only the trio and, concentrating on its overtones, hears some new resonance in its other two voices, a quiver as each note lifts through the pouring light with a plea, a vibration of voices arcing toward his. He feels it rising through the floorboards, and those notes bring to his eyes sudden water. Brother Dailey's eyes are shining, Andrew's too, with the same water. For the first time Hooper hears and understands the words.

Almost does not avail, almost is but to fail.
Sad, sad, that bitter wail—Almost but lost.

He hears it, and a rage starts to boil. His father chose this song. A final stake in Sunday's fence. He stops singing.

But with his own voice silent he only hears more clearly, as Andrew, on the last line, drags his arm through the air to retard the crowd. That final word, lost, spreads into the most hopeless moan he has ever heard, a dirge for his own hopeless soul staggering toward some remote, unlivable catacomb where he will spend eternity weak with flu and convulsed by Satan's stomach cramps.

Arms soar into the sunlight, two hundred voices swoop into the second verse. Hooper is singing again, trying to lose himself in the music.

He can't keep his throat from thickening. He feels so sorry now. For everything. For his father, who has to plot to get his only son baptized. And for the congregation, all water-eyed, warning Hooper about that bitter wail. Sorry then for Brother Dailey's saintly face so lonely and his arms spread to welcome the world, elbows jerking out the tempo on this last Sunday and no one answering his call. But sorriest of all for Hooper, who now wants to be up there bathing with them in that ever pouring light. He thinks of the Transfiguration, Jesus, Moses and Elijah in their reunion on the mountain top, his raiment became shining, exceeding white as snow. *It could be like that.* And he knows if he doesn't join them now he doesn't know when he'll feel this close again. Although if not now, then not much later. Only a matter of time, after all, a matter of choosing the time. He wants to save this moment of washing. But here's the sun still cataracting down on Brother Dailey's dome, and Hooper's eyes are wet in a hall of waiting eyes, and he almost talks himself into it then. He just can't cut loose from the pew to walk in front of everyone. He breathes deep, sings louder, afraid to think, his voice lost in his father's.

Head expanding where round notes tingle, he imagines it's his own voice filling the hall and he never decides to step into the aisle. Later he can't remember walking down. One moment he's singing, the next the light is blinding him, the stage is cracked and tilted bending through the wet he tries to blink away.

Brother Dailey's old face is right in front of Hooper's, tears streaming, smiling, broken-voiced. He takes Hooper's hand in both of his and whispers, "Are you coming forward to be baptized?"

Scarlet nod.

"God bless you, boy."

He asks Hooper to sit. The last notes fade. Brother Dailey announces, eyes brimming, that someone has come forward. Hooper's face is feverish again. The preacher takes his hand, helps him stand.

"Do you believe with all your heart that Jesus Christ is the son of God?"

Hooper had forgotten about that. The main reason he waited this long in the first place, and he'd forgotten it entirely. He doesn't see how anyone his age can believe that. The all your heart part bothers him most. He needs more time to think. He just isn't ready. *I don't want to be baptized today.* But here is Brother Dailey tall in front of him, smile devoutly waiting to spread as wide as heaven. Hooper know what the answer has to be.

"Yes...I do."

"God bless you for that confession," the preacher declares for the back rows to hear, then softly, "You come along with me now."

He beckons Hooper to follow him up onto the stage, through a door behind the pulpit. Hooper hesitates, doesn't want to walk up there. Motionless blue curtains conceal the baptistry. He has watched them open many times, watched the penitent sink into that blue tank, rise dripping, and different. Something happens back there, some weird transformation. People get buried there, Brother Dailey always says the water is warm. That's a comfort. But not enough. Hooper has examined those arisen from the tank. It still baffles him, whatever happens. He doesn't want to change until he's ready.

Too late. His life's in other hands. Behind the baptistry now and he hears his father calling out the page for "Up From the Grave He Arose." Jo Ann's father is back there too. He shows Hooper into a little cubicle, leaves him with a big set of white coveralls made of thin rubber. Hooper takes off his coat and trousers, climbs into the coveralls, looks at himself in the mirror. He's a deepsea diver. He thinks of Brother Babcock's daughter. He has always wanted Jo Ann to get baptized so he can see the wet gown sticking when she emerges. Now Jo Ann will be watching him, in this ridiculous deepsea rig.

A knock. Brother Dailey opens the door, wearing waist-high rubber wading pants, his coat and tie. He explains how they'll stand for the immersion and assures him the water is warm. Then they're waiting at the top stair, gazing into blue water. Brother Babcock holds the curtain cords.

The song ends. He pulls the curtains open with a swish. Brother Dailey wades down, turns, extends the bony hand that will dip him into the cleansing tank. Hooper, the same way he stepped into the aisle, mind blank and feet propelled by hidden forces, follows. Blue water is always warm, it slaps against the tile and plaster, spit spat.

One arm around his shoulder, the other hand, flat, raised, "I now baptize you in the name of the Father, and the Son, and the Holy Ghost. Amen."

Nose pinched, fall back, falling down, into blackness, silence, no more spats or drones or fences. Dark and easy. Hold it. Aaaaaaahh. Plink. The sound of water past his ears. Shreds of blackness fall away. Hooper opens his eyes blinking gray trickles back.

No time to look at the audience. Curtains swish. The crowd breaks into "Only in Thee." Brother Dailey guides him up the stairs, water slapping as they slosh, back to the cubicle, dazed, blind, jelly-legged, stepping out of coveralls and no sense of what to do next, where to go, how to stand or speak. Sit. Listen to the song.

Knock on his door. It opens. In the hallway Brother Dailey stands, head bowed. Someone is praying the benediction.

"We are grateful, O Lord, that this young brother has seen fit in his heart to come forward today to confess the name of our saviour, Jesus Christ, to be buried with him in baptism and to arise again in newness of life. As he goes forth now in his new raiment to do thy work, Lord, we pray that you will bless him and be with him, and be with us all, Lord, until we meet again. Amen."

Newness. Of life. It finally hits Hooper who they're praying about. The way you slap your pockets searching for a pencil, he feels around inside for signs of newness. Next to Brother Dailey, bowing his head at the same angle, staring at the same floorboard, same rubber smell in their coats, he does feel a warmth, a giddiness, a fine bulge of well-being. Detachment. A balloon in the shape of a young man at any moment will simply decide to float away. Is that it? He wants to laugh, grab the preacher's hand, tell him how fine he feels, and how infantile seem all those fears that cluttered his already hazy, disintegrating past.

Like the last glimpse of a man departing into a heavy fog, he sees those long-ago Sundays he prowled these gloomy halls and rooms behind the baptistry, dark stairways to the second floor, corridors lined with frosted glass leading from the church office toward the classrooms. While his parents chatted he explored the labyrinth, crept along, lightly touched the mottled glass, knew every songbook, flimsy testament, map of the Mediterranean, chalk-dusty blackboard, shapeless rostrum, murky rug. Yet each time he longed to find something different, new, and each time his explorations left him unrewarded. At last, back here with Brother Dailey, he sees this corridor behind the baptistry with clear eyes. The tank too. The blue water's mystery is solved. Everything glows with new meaning. He has been blind. Now he can see.

The prayer ends. Shoes scrape. Pages rustle. Voices purr and crackle. Brother Dailey takes his hand. Hooper squeezes, hoping his grip will transmit the wonder of all this newness.

The preacher's eyes are dry now. Hooper's are brimming.

"You've just done the finest thing a man can ever do. You're pure. Beginning again. Believe in the Lord and do his work, son, and don't do anything to stain that purity. It's your most precious possession."

Holy eyes probe his, and Hooper doesn't want this gaze to end. As long as they can stand here, man to man, hand to hand, eye to eye, this giddy elation, this clear vision might never leave him.

The preacher says, "I guess we'd better join the others."

He opens the door. Crowd noises swell in, suck them out onto the stage. The first thing Hooper sees is his father shaking hands with Brother Babcock. The look on both their faces—an oddly conspiratorial smugness, as of some bargain settled—this punctures whatever it is Hooper has been feeling. It begins to leak away. He wants to step over there and read the signals passing between them. But they turn toward him, Andrew red-eyed, his stiff collar pushing at the rhubarb skin. He grabs Hooper's hand.

"Mighty proud a you, boy. Mighty proud."

Brother Babcock turns his tight Texas face into a leathery sideways smile. "We're mighty proud, son."

"Thank ya, thank ya," Hooper says, affecting a slight drawl that seems the easiest way to reply.

These two escort him up the aisle to the rear where a crowd of well-wishers wait to congratulate the celebrity. Among them stands Jo Ann, watching him with a look he recognizes. It is the way he used to stare at those arisen from the tank, the look of the as-yet-unsaved wondering, trying to discover what has changed. His sense of newness swells again. He regards her with superior eyes. It is so warm she has removed her coat and hat, revealing silky hair, white rayon blouse, and Hooper is shaking hands with someone else but aching to use on Jo Ann this new power he wields. He thinks about what he'd do if he could ever get her back to the church kitchen some night after service, help her off with the overcoat. He has never touched a girl's blouse, a girl's skin.

As quickly as it forms, this fantasy dissolves, taking with it all his blood, leaving him hollow veined.

Whatsoever think ye in your hearts, so do ye.

His first sin. Not five minutes since Brother Dailey instructed him about purity, and it's already tarnished. He wasn't ready. Goddam it, he knew he wasn't ready. His chance spent, and now he yearns for it back, if only till he finds the nerve to corner Jo Ann. His baptism squandered, and through the crowd around him he sees Brother Dailey's lean silhouette at the distant doorway, shaking hands, such a holy man, and how disappointed he'll be to learn that Hooper's brand new spotlessness didn't even make it to the vestibule.

Next to Hooper someone shakes his father's hand, saying, "We're all mighty proud, Brother Dunlap. Hooper's gonna make a fine Christian, make a deacon just like his daddy, one a these days." Turning then to Hooper, who has to smile, and shake the hand, and keep blinking to hold back tears that now begin to well.

Something's wrong, terribly wrong. Perhaps he wasn't completely immersed. Perhaps some unwashed, unsaved thumb or nose or knee survived to taint the rest. Or did some essential current low in the *pool fail to swirl up and touch him? How long was he under there? Not nearly long enough. Can you baptize someone again, if the first one didn't take?*

"Sure be nice if Hooper could lead a prayer at the service this evenin', don't you think so, Andrew?"

"I think that'd be mighty nice, Brother Newcomb. How about it, Hoop?"

Strong mechanic's hand still clutches his arm, compels him to look into his father's eyes, sees a fresh shine of water to match Hooper's. But what is he crying about? What has been taken from him? Nothing. Those are tears of joy. The deacon in charge of manning the services has gained himself a prayer leader and a passer of communion plates. The songs they sang, the farewell sermon, the plunging sunlight—Hooper lives through all of it again, and this moment siphons off whatever residue of triumph or achievement or sanctity or lightheadedness he felt. He hates his father for conspiring and betraying him. And that's another sin. His hate bulges. And yet, if Andrew did launch all the holy arrows, Hooper failed to evade them. The circle of spikes, he should have found a path through them, or under, or around.

He wants to excuse himself from the small knot of handshakers still clustering, get outside where he can shout in the street, heap blasphemy on blasphemy till the asphalt cracks and swallows him.

One last tug at his arm. "How about it, Hooper boy?"

I DON'T WANT TO BE BAPTIZED TODAY!

CHAPTER 59

Trips and Voyages: *A Crucial Passage*

*H*ooper touched Jo Ann's blouse, and then her skin, the next summer, at a church camp meeting in the Sierras. Not much else happened. They mashed their lips together several hundred times, nose to nose, tooth to tooth, a practice which continued off and on through highschool, and ended three years later, underneath the pier. After that night, the semen she let soak into his jeans, you might say, came between them. It came between a lot of things.

If he'd been born three hundred years earlier, three thousand miles back, he might have made a passable Pilgrim. Harder out west, where the first thing you do with a girl is take her to the beach and wade together in your bathing suits, where the water's friendly most of the year, and you don't have to work very hard to stay alive, can actually survive off what the average man throws away, as Hooper and Jonas do these days from habit, having learned, one penniless weekend, among other things, that you can live out of garbage cans at Huntington Beach, if you want to, or have to, and eat heartily, and warm yourself against the sand.

Once Hooper started, it didn't take him long to talk himself out of his father's religion. He used the logic he'd been raised on. Many of the verses he had memorized served him well. For instance, Revelations 3: 15, 16, Jesus speaking to the church at Laodicea, "I know thy works, that thou art neither cold nor hot: I would thou wert cold or hot. So then because thou art lukewarm, and neither cold nor hot, I will spew thee out of my mouth."

If you're going to be a Christian, Hooper tells himself, that's the way you have to believe. It's all or nothing. And since he still can't say *all*, it *has* to be nothing. Anything else would be hypocrisy. This is what he tells his father the day after he skips his first Sunday meeting. "I just feel like a hypocrite, Dad."

And Andrew's answer—"We all have doubts, son, but that's not the time to run away from Jesus. His love is like a river, and you can't swim against the current, you can't run away from it for very long. What you have to do is rededicate your life to Him, give yourself up to Him, let Jesus carry you along"—Andrew's answer is a typical instance of how the father, trying to urge his son toward one body of water, somehow shoves him irrevocably toward another.

CHAPTER 60

First things first

*T*he shakedown cruise revealed a leak where fuel line and tank connect. Hooper sealed it with fiberglass and resin. You can still smell fumes after the engine runs awhile, but they only use it powering in and out of the harbor. He also fixed the running lights. They work most of the time. Bass wangled the canvas they need. Now the *Goose*, new rigged, looks invincible. Afternoons Hooper works at Bass's boat supply house. Mornings he takes the boat out, tuning it, readying for getaways, for new beginnings of every size. If only Nona's period would start, the world would be a rosy place indeed.

About a week after their reunion he takes her for a trip into the mountains, to a lookout point you reach by climbing a long flight of wide stone stairs.

"Up here, honey. All the way to the top."

"I'm getting tired."

"Good."

"Let's rest a minute."

"No. C'mon, start jumping."

"It's silly."

"C'mon."

One step at a time he is bouncing, landing hard, flat-footed, gripping both edges of his wide-brim hat, down this windblown mountain staircase. Nona, as if in thrall, takes the first short leap, stone jolt stinging her heels and soles, spurting through bent knees to shiver the pelvis.

"Jump," Hooper yells back, and stops to wait for her to catch up to him, urging her on like a football coach. "You're not even jumping, for Christ sake."

"It won't do any good." But starting to giggle. "My cousin went through this for two months. She tried everything. Nothing works."

"Negative thinking, negative results. C'mon, land *hard*! Jump! Jump! Jump! Jump!"

Giggling, then laughing, they hop thirty-five steps to the bottom and hit the landing just as a touring sedan pulls up to unload. Past the stymied cameras, he makes her hop across the concrete landing and into a clump of bushes to a wooden bench, where they plop down hilarious, breathless, her head on his heaving shoulder.

"Feel anything?" he asks.

"Yes."

"What?"

"My feet."

"Is that all?"

"My shins. My neck is broken."

"What about your . . ."

Shakes her head.

"Another look at the view then."

"It's all silly, it really is. My cousin . . ."

"Your cousin didn't have any imagination. Listen. I have another idea."

Again she shakes her head, this time in such a way—eyes closed, heavy sigh—that Hooper falls silent. They catch their breath.

Her eyes stay closed, and he studies her profile, watches a hand push dark hair from ear and neck, for coolness. He's been doing this for a week, while they sail, while she sleeps, trying to answer the question, Who do you see? The harder he looks, the less he sees, the more she seems a stranger, they way a word gets if you repeat it too many times.

He turns away, again, and they still haven't talked about that day. He knows Nona wants to, probably now, from the way she has forced this halt. He'll leave it up to her to begin. He has, to his own satisfaction, answered everything *but* her question. His own position: actions speak louder than words. Glance and see her lips, on the verge of speaking, framing some sentence with great care.

"Hooper?" Eyes open. "I'm scared."

"Of what?"

"I'm afraid I'm going to ruin everything."

You very well could, he thinks, but says, "It's still way too soon to tell."

"I know my body pretty well. I know when it's changing."

"Well, it doesn't make any difference."

"It *does*, Hooper."

"Listen. If worse comes to worst . . ."

Nona turning toward him with vulnerable eyes, and he doesn't know what to tell her, can't yet say what he prefers. It *is* too early to decide anything. Right now he just wants to change that look on her face, that worry, that weakness.

"If worse comes to worst," he says, "after we take Uncle Jack out sailing a time or two and get a few other things settled, I don't see any reason why we can't take the boat for a good long cruise. I mean, really . . . down to Tahiti or someplace."

He casts her a sly glance. She's starting to laugh, first the mind-reader's smile, then a widening grin, teeth showing, finally her head thrown back and they are laughing together at what is now their own private joke—Hooper's Folly.

"Goddam it, Nona, I've been thinking about this. The *Goose* is just about ready for action. Even if you *are* pregnant doesn't mean you can't sail for six or eight weeks, does it? Then if you're going to have a kid, have it there. We can stay down south a while, little place on the beach someplace, fish, live off the land. You can still learn all those dances. And I'll learn the songs, maybe pick up a little drumming."

191

"We can put an act together," she says.

"That's it. We'll bring back the authentic stuff. You said yourself you didn't want to end up like your grandmother, doing 'Sweet Leilani' all your life."

"It was 'Yackey Hula Hickey Dooley.' She used to sing that one and accompany herself on the steel guitar."

They are laughing again. He hugs her close. "You just stick with Hooper, baby, and he will take you away from all that."

Laughter dwindles. Snuggling she says, "Do you really want to go sailing with a pregnant woman on board?"

"I want to go sailing with you on board."

He likes the sound of that. So does she. They settle back under sun-splattered greenery, and already they are heading south together. Hooper, with his palm now covering the soft shoulder skin, pressing at the thickness, thinks it wouldn't be so bad at all.

The main difficulty is that such a thing would have to be explained to Joe. Hooper, being captain, figures he *could* explain. But it would be tough. Joe has already turned celibate again, sleeping in his truck again, his personal monastery. He has given Goldie her picture back and made it clear that she can hang around if she wants, but don't try anything funny; he's saving himself, conserving his juices again, this time for the inevitable sail to other islands. And Goldie is not included in Joe's idea of any trip. Joe hasn't mentioned this to her yet, since before they go anywhere he plans to borrow as much money from her as he can. In a way Hooper envies Joe his strength in this matter. He wonders what Joe would do if Goldie happened to be pregnant. Kick her in the stomach? Back over her with the Reo? Take her way offshore and make her dive deeper than she's ever dived, down where the nose and ears begin to bleed from pressure? Hardhearted Jonas. And yet, by God, now that Hooper thinks of it, something like that might work.

Nona says, "Hooper, you know I can't really go anywhere, pregnant or not, while Jack's in the condition he's in."

Again his lifting spirits drop. Hard for Hoop to go anywhere either, and leave the old man behind. He says, "Well, first things first. We'll see how he likes the boat. One thing at a time."

He stands up, grabs his hat. "Meanwhile you and I are going to go back to the beach and try some skindiving."

"What?"

"This just came to me, Nona. I've never heard of anybody trying it, but if you think a minute about the physiology . . ."

Again some powerful signal shuts him down. She is a stone figure, some Easter Island statue staring up and past him, and this time it's Hooper who's scared, of some unfamiliar zone she's about to lead him into. She always has that power over him. It's like when he studies her profile so long it snaps out of focus, blurs into something he doesn't recognize. He fears that now, Nona blurring, Hooper blurring, both separately, or both together, out of focus, into unknown zones of no reference.

"Can't we stay here awhile?" she says.

He starts to sit. She takes his hand and stands up. "Let's lie down in the grass."

It's faintly damp there, cool to the skin, and out of the wind, mottled with sun, earth dark below the thick green stems, and Nona rolls up next to him, her lips suddenly soft and open, and the kiss is long and easy while he smoothes a hand across the cotton covering her long smooth belly.

The kiss is enough. He lets her go. She rolls back, their hips and shoulders inches apart, and Hooper, in suspension, waits. Growling muffler of the tour sedan pulls out of the parking lot, travelers back on board, heading for the Pali. The silence when the muffler disappears is like a gong, like a ship's bell marking the hour and a change of watch.

"Can I tell you something, Hooper?"

"Sure, tell me anything."

"It wasn't my cousin who went through all this before."

He waits.

"It was me."

"When?"

"When I was married."

"And nothing worked?"

"Yes. We finally did find something that worked."

"What was that?"

"Al knew a doctor."

A long silence. He turns and see that she is ready to cry.

She says, "I couldn't tell you that before."

"It doesn't make any difference, honey."

"Please stop saying that. Everything makes a difference."

"I mean it doesn't make any difference about how I feel about you. It really doesn't."

He finds her hand. She squeezes hard. "I couldn't go through that again," she says. Then, "It's so *stupid*. People never learn *anything*, do they."

"Jesus, you don't have to panic yet. Plenty of women miss a period and start right up again with the next one. You haven't even been in for an examination yet. We don't even have to talk about that until you get examined."

"I think we have to talk about everything."

"Okay, okay."

"I *am* panicky, Hooper. I am. I admit it. It was so bad last time I couldn't stand to go through any of it again."

"Well, tell me what happened."

"Al didn't want the baby, that's the first thing that happened. I was eighteen and still trying to please him. We hadn't even been married a year. If he didn't want the baby, I didn't want it. Then after the operation he didn't want me any more either. It brought everything to a head, getting pregnant. I guess it always does. So we broke up, and when it was finished there wasn't even the baby left, nothing at all."

She tries to laugh. "He skipped out on the alimony payments, ran off to the mainland, and there wasn't even any money left. That's when I went to work at the Paradise and moved in with Uncle Jack. I couldn't go back home. I was too ashamed of myself."

Tears coming now, and Hooper slides over, holds her close a long time, long enough for another sedan to grumble into the parking lot, unload its dozen visitors, give them time to climb the thirty-five steps, snap a photo, and climb down again, into the sedan, grumble away down the cross-island road.

Finally Nona says, "It's not just the abortion, Hooper. It's the way things change. Sometimes you have to talk about the changes."

"Things haven't changed that much."

"I'm talking about you and me. Or maybe I'm only talking about me. I don't know. Maybe that's what I want to find out."

She rolls away from him again, sits up, hugging her knees.

"When I asked you that question last week, do you remember? about seeing me? I was really asking myself that. I suddenly didn't know if I had ever seen *you*. It didn't matter that much before. But it started to matter a lot. I realized I was still seeing you the way I saw you the first time we went swimming. Do you remember it? I guess I wanted it that way. It was so simple, you know, so beautiful and simple. But I saw that it couldn't stay simple forever, wasn't simple at all, any more, but that I was still seeing it that way."

Her eyes are searching his now. Hooper sits up next to her. "How did you see me?"

"I love the flesh, the body, you know that, the way arms and legs move. I saw your strong-looking face, and the way you walk. It's funny, you know, the way your feet stick out. But it's confident. I saw the way you plant your feet, taking each step confidently, as if this beach you are walking on, just because it's Waikiki and very famous, doesn't make any difference to you, you know what you are doing here and where it can take you. You were my tall brown white man come over from the mainland to make love to me. Not the *first* white man, you understand. But there was something special about you. An honest face, I guess. An innocent face. Not a baby face. An innocent one. You were not guilty of crimes against other people. So I fell for you. And it was beautiful. But things cannot stay that way forever. I wanted them to. They cannot. I didn't admit it until that day at the harbor. Then I got scared. I was afraid you were seeing me in a similar way, and that we had never really seen each other at all."

Hooper is hearing these words, but losing them. They drain off into the earth, with his blood, and he is sitting here hollowed, blinking.

Nona waits a moment, rushes on.

"I probably shouldn't even talk about this. It is the kind of thing that can frighten a man, drive him away. Especially now, if I am pregnant. Women are supposed to be wilier than this, aren't they? They figure ways to make a man do something or be something, but without mentioning it outright. I can't do that, Hooper. My marriage was like that. Full of unsaid pushing and pulling. I can't stand that. It's why we have to talk about this. You see, you are not what I saw at first, and I am not what you saw at first. If we keep behaving as if nothing has changed, pretty soon we fall apart *anyway*. For instance you probably never expected to hear me talking this way, did you. Island girls aren't supposed to do this. Tell me if I'm wrong, but mainland men come over here looking for island girls, or Asiatic girls, because they think the girl will let them be whatever they appear to be, will stay pliable and submissive, make no demands, never make trouble. Isn't that true?"

Hooper closes his eyes, tries to suck them into his head, studies the checkered pattern of reds and purples.

She grabs his hands. "Don't close your eyes. Please. There's only one reason I tell you this. It's much more than whatever is happening to my body. It's because . . . I want things to be right between us. Otherwise, you know, we go on living . . . a sort of half life."

His eyes open. New colors pour in and seem to clear his vision. He looks hard at Nona. Her face is thinner, as if layers of skin have fallen away, or been swallowed. Her eyes burn into his, rimmed in a way he never expected to see, red-rimmed, fire-eyes. Whatever pain they're trying to hide is up to him to remove. And the longer he waits, the more pain they reveal, as if she knows she has made some terrible mistake. Something is expected. His face should, somehow, become like hers, the layers should fall. They don't. He feels, if anything, layers building inside him, along the lining of his stomach, membranes toughening and hardening there. He knows what he should say. Reassure her with a pledge: I love you, Nona, I really do. And send toward her some intensity, some new heat. He can't say it. Something in the words, they don't mean what he is feeling. He can't say her name. Can't even close this space between them by reaching with his arms.

Nona's giving him a look he can't bear. He gets up, walks to the trees, stands staring past them and thinks of Broome, wishes the painful drive away from this place were over and he could pull a chair up next to Broome's chair and play a little music and listen to him talk. Answers would arise from that, just the way he went to Broome the day he couldn't find a boat, and found one. That's exactly how he feels right now, again. Marooned. And Broome? Well, Broome is the veteran of many things, and Hooper knows from experience that Broome will provide.

CHAPTER 61

Meanwhile

*H*is bones know when the mailman is coming, feel him moving up the walkway before the first tread rattles the stairs. He looks around at all his clocks, 8:29, 11:04, 6:51, 2:10, and nods, and waits for the rusty screech, then settles back into red leather, satisfied. He long ago quit paying any attention to the mail, but the man marks a moment in his day.

The next is the second screech, moments later, when Luella grabs whatever's in there. He'll wait for her to scurry down the hallway to her room and then he'll doze a while.

Today the second screech is a long time coming. He shoves his panama back and forth across his head. Twenty minutes pass. He tries to sleep, can't, needs the screech to settle his mind. He gets up, shuffles down the long gallery to his far front window, pulls a drape edge back, peeks out. Black rusted box shut tight. He shuffles to his chair, sits a few minutes, can't stand it any longer, and heads out his door, down the hallway.

On the porch he squints against the sunshine, stands inspecting his empire, finally pulls the lid open, screeeeeeeee, and almost walks back in then, content to know no noise will grate his nap. But he reaches for the box, finds a letter, stuffs it inside his coat sweater without looking, shuffles back to his room, where he grunts bending at the heap of his desk, searching for spectacles, finds them, sits, leans to read the return address: *Office of the Building Inspector.* Inside, the letter begins:

> Dear Mr. Broome,
> As the result of an inspection of your property on January 31 your house was found to fall short of building code specifications in the following areas: plumbing, wiring, foundation, ventilation, drainage, and general safety, e.g., the front yard walk, porches front and back. There follows a list of specific items which must be repaired or replaced, to meet the code. If such improvements are not made within 90 days, your building will be condemned, in accordance with Municipal Ordinance # ....

"Those bastards, those lousy bastards!" Broome is yelling. "Hooper! Nona!"

His head cocks an instant, hearing his own voice echo through the empty house. Every door is open, to dissipate and swallow all the noise he makes. He lurches to his desk, clears it with an arm sweep, scattering jars, papers, ledgers, fountain pens, and calendars. He grabs the phone, listens. Dead. Disconnected. Cursing he heads for the door again, through his frontyard jungle and across the street to a booth. Inside, dialing, he wheezes into the speaker.

The cheery voice: "Public works."

"This is Jackson Broome speaking."

"Yes?"

"I'd like to talk to . . . Staples."

"Just a moment."

CLICK. BUZZ.

"Building Inspection."

"Mr. Staples . . . is he . . ."

"Yes?"

"There?"

"I'm sorry. Mr. Staples is out of the office today."

"Who's in charge of public works?"

"Mr. Harrison. But I believe he's still out to lunch."

"Well, who the hell is on duty?"

"Pardon me?"

"Listen . . ." He tries to hold his breathing down, air dragging at his lungs.

"Yes?"

"I just got a letter from your office that is a goddam slanderous and libelous document, and I'd . . . like . . ."

"Is this a complaint?"

"Jesus Christ!"

"What?"

"I'll find the sonofabitch myself."

He drops the receiver, lets it dangle, heads across the street.

For a year Broome has had a good idea who was after him, but he has never acknowledged them in any way, has not set foot on their parking lot or even tried to learn the name of his antagonists. From forty years of watching Waikiki he knows it's only a matter of time, and rather than negotiate with such overwhelming forces he has chosen to ignore them. And his policy, of course, was right. If he hadn't exposed himself today, he would have lasted another ninety days, at least. But they have finally flushed him out, and here he is, at the attendant's shack, barefooted on the burning asphalt, clutching thighs of grubby slacks, while the sweat oozes under both his aloha shirts, the top one orange and covered with ukuleles, and his feathered panama is no protection from the noon sun which sneaks in under its brim, sending waves of heat up to boil water behind his eyes.

"Who's in charge around here?"

A white-shirted Hawaiian, chair backtilted in the shade, looks up.

"Who owns this goddam parking lot?"

Attendant shrugs.

"Who do you work for?"

"Eddy Chung gives me my check."

"Where can I find him?"

"How come you wanna know?"

"It's . . . a business matter."

"Sometimes he's over in the hotel garage."

"Which hotel?"

"The Paradise. He runs that too."

"Who does he work for?"

"I dunno. Somebody in the hotel. That's where the check come from."

"Those bastards."

"Hey. Take care, brudda. Eddy's a good friend of mine."

Broome's feet are blistering. He scuffles back through his hedge, stands a moment in his own high grass, cooling them, getting his wind. Sweat pouring off him now, and his face on fire, he's on his way to the Paradise, down the tire-blackened incline, cool concrete of basement filled with Lincolns, Kaisers, Dynaflows. Beyond the pumps, beyond the cashier's window, a glass door with Eddy's name on it. Broome heads for that, doesn't hear the man at the window yelling, "Hey!"

He barges in, stands there like a bull. Two men in white mechanic's smocks are drinking Cokes.

"Hey, buddy," one man says, *Eddy* sewn across his chest, "this is a private office."

"You the manager?"

"Yeah."

"Who's your boss?"

"What's your problem?"

"I have to find him."

Eddy looks Broome over—grizzled, barefoot, face flushed, ratty hat—figures him for a drunk. This neighborhood is sprinkled with rows of by-the-week cabins where old men sit tippling port. Eddy gets up, hand to Broome's elbow, tries to ease him out the door.

"He ain't here, brudda. You come back tomorra, maybe you can catch him then."

"Don't give me that shit, young fella. He's upstairs, isn't he."

Eddy shrugs.

Broome shouts, "It's a goddam squeeze play, isn't it!"

Eddy head-signals to his pal and they each take an arm. Broome stiffens, stubby Samson, his flung arms push the two men back. They keep their distance now, watching him. Eddy doesn't want any trouble in his garage.

For Broome the room has blurred, he stands hunched, wheezing, till the shapes come into focus again, the desk, the calendar, two men in white coats waiting to see what he will do. He squints hard, then takes one step back, into the open doorway, turns and heads up the incline toward the sidewalk. Eddy and his pal watch him till he disappears, shake their heads, reach for the Cokes. Cashier pulls a glass partition back, smirking uncertainly. "Who the hell was *that?*"

Broome finds a side entrance to the hotel. It's midday, beach time for visitors. Plush corridors are deserted. A curio shop next to the elevator is closed. The elevator doors are open. Broome steps in, stands unsteadily before the rows of numbered buttons, can't think which floor he wants, stares at the numbers, raises a hand as if to punch one. They blur. He can't remember what he's doing here, feels the line tightening in his chest, the line that knots around his lungs. His hand slams the buttons, looking for support. The doors close with a hush. The elevator lifts. He reaches for the line, to loosen it. But it has him now, around the chest, around the neck, pulled so tight he can't cry out, can't find the breath. It's gagging him. On the floor he wrestles with it, squirms, clawing at his shirt, and the line squeezes ever tighter as numbers blink above the climbing elevator hum.

CHAPTER 62

No shoes, No money

*N*o money on Broome when they find him. No identification. No shoes. Pudgy beachcomber bunched in a corner of the topmost floor. They turn him over to the city, which means the morgue, and that's where Hooper finally tracks him down. In among the derelicts. It's late afternoon of the following day and by this time he has gone a little crazy with the searching and the women's eyes, Nona's, Luella's, pulling at him.

He can't weep at the sight of the corpse. It just fills him with a churning rage. He knows by now pretty much how it happened. He runs out to Joe's truck, and races back to Waikiki, up the hotel driveway, doubleparks there, blocking it, into the lobby, bounding silent stairs to floor three where, behind a door marked TRADE-WINDS, a Japanese secretary tells him Mr. Nolan is out, to which Hooper answers "Bullshit!" and plunges through the door marked NOLAN only to find that the man in charge of developing this chain of parking lots *is* out. So he lifts a teakwood chair weighing a hundred and fifty pounds and hurls it at a floor-to-ceiling mirror next to Nolan's desk, and watches the room fall apart and listens to the chair land, thunk, and glass shards tinkle down on top of the chair. And then he weeps. And waits. While the secretary peeks her glossy head into an absolutely silent office and looks at Hooper's back.

She takes him, once his story erupts, to the hotel's public relations man who, upon hearing it in greater and slower detail, discovers that yesterday's elevator death is in fact the hotel's important neighbor, makes a couple of calls—to Nolan, to the manager—then offers to have the body moved from the morgue to a private chapel out here. The hotel of course will pay for the funeral. And Hooper, now numb, is told not to worry about the mirror. They can work that out at a calmer time.

CHAPTER 63

Obituary

*N*ona's ready for the news. She has already cried, waiting for it, as much as she thought she could. Now the eyes close, as if relieved, and Hooper holds her, feels the slow sobbing start, won't let himself cry again.

It's the first time they've touched since the trip to the mountains, the miserable ride home, and Hooper, glad then to hear that Broome was missing, because Broome had disappeared before, and come back, gladly rushed off to search, and hasn't stopped till now, and you might call this another reunion, Nona grateful for what he's done. Yet they are like two pillars, holding each other up, and hard to say who is holding, who being held—Hooper leans lightly, holds carefully, actually ready to rush away again and just keep moving, away from the look of all these catastrophes. He has never had to hold a woman like Nona. He has never known anyone to die. Except in books. And in the papers. At highway accidents he passed without stopping. No one he ever cared about has died. Among his parents' friends a few deaths he remembers vaguely. Among his own friends, none. And no one in his family has died yet. No one who came west anyway. His father and mother left their families behind, and Hooper grew up outside the skein of generations. Great-grandparents died in Arkansas and Oklahoma, grandparents too, great-aunts and uncles, distant relatives seen once or twice at inland jamborees.

Luckily Luella has locked herself inside her room and hasn't come out since last night. This gives them both someone to tend. Hooper goes back there to break the news, knocking softly.

"Luella?"

No answer.

"Luella?"

No answer.

"We've found Uncle Jack."

Nothing.

"It looks . . . like . . . he's dead."

Long pause. Hooper listens, Nona wide-eyed at the quiet. Then a blood-chilling scream. He hurls his shoulder at the door, bursting in, and Luella's on her bed, in her blue chenille robe, still screaming when the door flies open, suddenly breaking off the scream and resuming what has evidently been her pose for hours, bare feet flat, sitting on the mattress edge straightbacked and staring at the tattoo chart across the room.

Inside the doorway they stand watching, while behind them gather the man in green pajamas, the man who owns the land grant. Nona steps in, sits next to her.

"Luella?"

Lips move weakly.

"Would you like some tea?" Nona says.

A great, breathy inhale. Luella holds it, lets it out. Nona moves to the hot plate.

To the others Hooper whispers. "The old man is dead."

"What? Dead? How? Broome? When?"

In the hall he tells them, and they stand around immobilized till the teapot starts to whistle.

"Well, what's gonna happen?" says the man in green.

"The funeral's day after tomorrow."

"I mean, what's gonna happen to the place?"

"The rooming house?"

"Yeah."

Hooper looks around, squints at the ceiling, hears an enormous silence slowly settling on the roof, sliding into the walls, a silence that grows louder, gets closer, while he listens and the others wait. He swells with an upsurge of righteous anger.

"Don't worry about the place. It'll be all right. We're gonna keep it just like it is, kind of a monument to Broome. You know?"

The man in green pajamas smiles his crooked smile. "Yeah, that's nice. I like that."

And Hooper now is barricaded on the front porch with a shotgun, holding off the enemy, while Jonas in the pergola draws a bead on the hotel windows where invaders lurk. The man in green takes the parking lot side, the women stay indoors loading rifles, cooking food. They will have to burn us out, thinks Hooper.

A whimper interrupts his dream. It's Luella's first remark in eighteen hours.

"I shoulda waited till the mailman came."

Nona, "There was no way for you to know."

"I just ran down to get some eggs."

"How could anybody know?"

"He never could stand any kind of mail. Every piece he ever read would make him mad. I can't understand..."

A steaming cup quiets her. She takes a sip, stares at steam. Nona tells her not to talk, Nona watching the wild hair, the lips moving silently. At the jamb Hooper leans and looks through the french double doors into thick brush that screens the view, Broome's labyrinth, his moat. Behind him the man in green pajamas, the man who owns the Spanish land grant to Malibú, obese in his shoulderstrap undershirt.

Bored, these two shuffle away together, grumbling, green man leading, up the stairs.

As if to follow them Luella rises, walks toward Hooper.

"I heard what you told 'em."

"Who?"

"About saving the place."

"We'll do it, Luella."

"I don't see how. Not now."

"Why not?"

"He didn't leave no will."

"That doesn't mean . . ."

"I talked to him about it a thousand times. You know what a stubborn man he was, never listen to nobody. I told him, Jackson, you got no children, you don't make out a will everything you ever bought or earned just gonna fritter away in court fees and arguments. And you know what he'd do? He'd just turn the music up. Just flat turn the music up and drown me out."

Her voice breaks with snuffles and tears. "Stubbornest man this world has ever seen. Never filled out a paper in his life, nor took his pills, nor eat what was good for him. You'd have to sneak up from behind."

She's pacing now, big flat-footed steps between Hooper and the doors no one has opened for ten years, and calling up all the things she has saved to talk about at just this time, get herself through the first shock. Slowly at first, then babbling, repeating, she talks about the ways he abused her, and about his property, always central to that abuse. Broome's closest relative is a nephew, oldest son of Broome's brother, one of Nona's uncles. He's an assisttant superintendent at the pineapple cannery, who will see no reason in this world not to sell the land and demolish the house. Luella, engaged to Jackson three times and married to him twice, would like to dispute this. But she knows the only papers pertaining to Broome's estate are three affidavits, notarized in 1924, 1927, and 1940, swearing that Luella Pike has no claim whatsoever on any of his real or personal property.

Trying to comfort, Nona says she'll talk to that uncle of hers. But Luella, weeping, says no one but a fool like Broome would keep this house. It's worth too much to keep. "Ain't nothing going to save this house but money now. If we only had some money." she moans, "to buy it outright and fix up all that needs fixin'."

CHAPTER 64

Requiem

Sitting on the bed again, Luella appears to have dozed off, Broome-like. Pale rings around her closed eyes look as if the skin has been soaked in water. Hooper and Nona watch her nodding, rocking. He wants to leave. Nona wants to stay, sit with the woman. And now that Luella's finished, Nona wants to talk. First about the funeral and how they have to keep the hotel out of it. A funeral is a family affair. Trouble is, Broome has no family to speak of. Nona fears no one in her family will care much about his passing. At this, the words break in her throat. He's just been too long away from all the rest of them, hiding here, great-uncle without wife, without children.

Her quiet sobbing shakes the bed. Luella, startled awake, reaches automatically for Nona. Watching their two hands squeeze, Hooper has to get out of here. A little solitude, some place to think, to grieve his own way. He tells Nona he'll phone the chapel right now and see about changing the setup. He steps out into the hall and closes the door.

He walks quickly till he rounds the corner toward the long front-door approach. There he slows down. Something in these hallways always slows him. In the half-light he reaches to touch a waist-high molding, and follows that, playing fingertips along its pitted, painted-over smoothness. At the door he runs fingers over the jewel-eggs and ruby prisms there, drawing patterns in the dust. After a while he turns around, heads back, testing knobs of all these locked rooms, follows that wall around its corner and ends up in the room once his, staring at the amber blinds. Just beyond them, in the space between the window and the blind, hidden in dust, something wispy lurks. He remembers breathing it his first day here, but dares not approach it now. Breath could crumple it.

His barefeet scuff the ragged thready edges of the hallway runner. Up the stairs the runner's worn through. On each step the worn edge tapers as the pattern gives way to unpatterned colored threads and that to matting and matting to the sanded wood. The runner takes him to the attic, full of relics he will use for something, soon, but not now, not this afternoon. So it's back along the hall, past the door to Nona's room. There he looks so closely at the peeling woodwork the paint blurs.

Downstairs again he ends up finally at the old man's door and listens to a silence now sliding past the ceiling, following studs and braces in its slow fall, a shroud of silence gradually enveloping the house. He pushes the door, half expects to see Broome in there, revived, chuckling at this great stunt he's pulled.

But the chair is empty, the lemon light is off, the floor's still strewn with papers, ledgers, bottle caps, 78s. Clocks still ticking. Some have stopped. Above the leather chair, between it and the poolroom shade a fat hole gapes. As Hooper looks, it starts to widen. He wants to fill it. He walks down the row of instruments beyond Broome's chair, runs his thumb across the strings of a dusty mandolin. It rings. He plucks a banjo hanging there. It twangs. He strides along plucking a wall of them—whang, ding, plong, plang, tung, plink. The notes float out into the room, seem to fill it, round notes growing oblong as they find the line of the walls. They ring through all the other instruments, each guitar and uke and fiddle picking up its truest tone and resonating, rich wood vibrates all along the ceiling and baseboard of this one-time banquet hall, setting the high panels too aquiver, the room itself a sound chamber. The whole house vibrates around these jangle notes. They grow and bounce off one another, carom the walls, bulge in and out of instruments, until a bass note lodges in Hooper's throat so large he can't swallow. As he stands here trying to swallow, the cacaphony decrescendoes, dissolves, and dies. The walls stand still, the great hole in the middle of the room's still here. He merely forced those loud notes through it, stretching it some. And he can't stand the silence, can't stand the house or the waiting around in it for whatever is supposed to happen next. Where is Broome? The old man draws him. The veteran of everything now.

CHAPTER 65

Cortege

*B*y the time Hooper phones the chapel its business office has closed. Broome is already being embalmed. Would he care to come by tomorrow to discuss any change in plans?

Yes he would.

The deceased, by the way, will be available for viewing. Would anyone . . .

Yes, that too.

It takes most of next day to get ready. Hooper stalls, wanting to see nothing that will violate his image of Broome alive, yet compelled to see what he's never seen. He tries to talk Nona into going, but she won't, not until the matter of the hotel is cleared up. Half her grief has turned to hate for the men who both hired her and plotted her uncle's downfall. She has already quit her job. The other half has turned to guilt for being gone when the letter came. As if whatever attention she now pays Luella might make up for this neglect, Nona's still sitting with her, in the room Luella refuses to leave.

So Hooper talks Joe into going with him, Hooper the captain, Joe still the loyal mate. The first thing they need are clothes for the occasion.

They find them in the attic. Flowered ties and white shirts. Brown wingtip shoes. For Hooper a single-breasted suit of tropical white linen. For Joe a sporty seagreen pinstripe. They have these pressed at a cleaners around the corner. They shave.

It's four o'clock when they get to the chapel.

The plaque on the door says PLEASE RING AND WAIT FOR ATTENDANT. Hooper presses, listens to the bell-chime in the distance. A slender man in a dark suit answers, looking a little worried.

"Are you here for the funeral?"

"Is he being buried already?" Hooper blurts.

"Who?"

"Mr. Broome. Jackson Broome."

"Oh my goodness, no. Mr. Broome is in the slumber room. Are you relatives of his?"

"Nephews, yes."

"Right this way then. Please follow me."

He leads them briskly, silently across deep rugs to a darkened doorway.

"Will others be joining you here?"

"Not that I know of. But look, is there someone I can talk to? About the funeral?"

"Of course. Of course. But I'm afraid I'll have to ask you to wait just a few minutes. We're in a bit of a fix today. Our organist is ill, and a service is just beginning in the chapel, and . . ." A thin, embarrassed smile breaks the skin across his cheek into four curved lines, his white forehead blushes. "I'm sitting in."

With a nod, Hooper dismisses him. They walk into the slumber room. It has been filled with air so thick that breathing is painful, a room to bring the living as close to the dead as possible. A barely audible string section plays an indefinable tune through speakers hidden behind potted plants. Broome's coffin, lid up, is set against one wall, a spotlight on the old man's waxen face. They have dressed him in a laundered white shirt, with a plain blue tie, a blue coat. His hat is gone. His wispy hair is oiled and combed. The string section fades, and from the chapel come saccharine organ chords.

Hooper gazes at the body, finds himself gasping, turns away, throat thick, whispers, "I can't take it, Joe."

"Neither can I."

Joe's eyes are squinted tight, his mouth contorts.

"It's wrong," Hooper says. "It's all wrong."

Sadly Joe says, "It's no place for Broome."

"We should never have let those guys get within ten blocks of him."

"Too late now."

"No it isn't."

"Waddya mean?"

"We could get him out of here."

"What?"

"I said we could get him out of here. We *have* to, Joe. We have to take him with us. Right now."

Hooper scans the room. No windows. Only the door they came through. He rushes to it. Lobby empty.

"Everybody's in the chapel. All we have to do is get him out the front door. It'll take one minute. Maybe less. C'mon. It's our only chance."

"Oh Jesus. I'm gonna crap in my pants, Hooper."

"Gimme a hand. Take his feet."

Hands under thick shoulders, Hooper lifting remembers other times he's lifted Broome, old man dying since the first day they met and the tears that press his eyes now are for the chance Hooper never had, to know Broome before he started to die.

"C'mon, Joe. Lift!" Hissing. "Lift!"

Between them the body hangs, never this heavy before. The organ music stops. For an instant Joe and Hooper are as petrified as Broome. The maudlin notes resume. Gush of breath as they both exhale.

"We have to walk him out, Joe. Set him down."

Jonas lowers the shiny black shoes. Hooper props one dead arm over Joe's shoulder, stoops beneath the other. They step out into the lobby.

Still empty. The organ music stops again. Behind oak doors a sad voice begins to deliver an undecipherable message. Broome's head has cocked sideways, as if about to speak. His black shoes, pointed back, drag through the plush.

Just as they reach the oak-paneled double entrance, the bell-chime rings. They stare at each other, as if each has recognized his own assassin.

They have no choice. Hooper opens the door. A small woman, heavily veiled, is standing there, looking at the doormat. Her escort, a slightly taller, Oriental man, is looking at Hooper's face, then at Broome's, at Joe's, back to Broome's.

Hooper says, "Pardon us please. Excuse us."

He and Joe come out the door dragging Broome past the astonished man and his sobbing wife. While the man watches, they drag Broome down the walkway, around a corner, and out of sight.

CHAPTER 66

Get ready to jump

*H*ooper flings open the back double doors, they lift Broome inside, onto a mattress. Then Joe is rattling toward the harbor while Hooper, in back, hovers over the body, takes off the blue suit coat, the white shirt and plain tie, re-dressing him in an old aloha shirt of Joe's, and a dirty felt hat they found once on the road out to Sunset Beach, and takes off the polished black shoes and turns the cuffs of the creased blue trousers up above Broome's ankles.

In the harbor parking lot they rip their own suits off—disposable disguises to be worn once and buried—and stuff them under the seat. Waiting for the route to the *Golden Goose* to clear, they break open a can of pork and beans, a can of fruit cocktail, and gobble these with tablespoons. By sundown most of the boat-tinkerers are gone. They move Broome out along the boarded walkway to where the boat is berthed, and hoist him over its rails, down the hatch, below decks, and wrap him in a sleeping bag.

Then it's back to town to tell Nona and Luella what has happened and get them out to the boat, and maybe Goldie if they happen to run across her, and the upstairs roomers, too, if they want to come along. Hooper's driving now—Joe too nervous to hold the wheel—and his plan forms as they speed toward Waikiki. He is exhilarated, feels the future opening in front of him, all things somehow coming into focus and he knows this plan will work. It will be perfect. Sadly late, yet still the way Broome would have wanted it. His last cruise, the one he'd been waiting for, and buried the way Hooper knows Broome would want it to go.

The way Nona will want it too, once she hears how it can be. He's anxious to describe them sailing out a ways, thinking how this will please her, and perhaps change everything, and all he has to do now is slip below decks before Nona does and get at the gas tank. It's sprung another leak somewhere, the rusty fucker, he could smell it when they unloaded Broome, just a whiff, nothing serious, but you don't want gasoline collecting in the bilge.

He is slowing down in front of the rooming house, looking for a place to park, when Jonas spots a black limousine across the street, and in the bright ring of light below the streetlamp next to Broome's hedge, two men in black suits are looking for a way into the yard.

Joe says, "It's the guys from the mortuary."

Hooper shifts into second so hastily the flywheel howls. He stomps the accelerator. It sticks. The engine is racing at full and he can only control it with his clutch. They are bucking down the street sounding like an intersection full of traffic. The men in black turn at the noise.

"Oh shit," Joe says, "they saw us."

In a panic Hooper whirls around the next corner, Joe craning to see through his small back window. The men in black are watching.

"We'd better ditch the truck, Joe."

They are passing the line of taxicabs outside the Paradise. The street in front is empty.

Hooper says, "Joe, I have to do this. Get ready to jump out."

He pulls into the driveway and stops, engine roaring. He commands Joe to hold the handbrake till Hooper says release it. He shifts into second, reaches down and holds the clutch to the floor with his right hand, while he climbs out.

"Okay, let her go!"

Brake and clutch release. Hooper and Joe flip back into bushes, come up running for the beach.

Joe's Reo hurtles along the curved driveway toward a sapling palm. The palm deflects it, sends it across concrete into a stand of young banana trees, which slow it down, but don't stop it. The ground in there is soft and wet and this turns the truck back toward the driveway. It comes out of the greenery, aimed for a cab idling next to the lobby stairs. The startled driver guns ahead, but the Reo catches a rear fender, spins off, takes the headlights of a cab behind, and veers up the carpeted stairway with an infuriated growl. The swinging doors fly inward, showering the lobby with glass. Again the truck has swerved, and it lodges in the door frame, rear wheels spinning above the wide stairs, engine coughing, vehicle seeming so much alive, so angry in its quivering to wrench free that, like a fallen bomb that hasn't exploded, no one dares approach it until the engine slowly sputters out its final snort, last shimmy of rust and rotten fenders, and falls silent.

CHAPTER 67

The getaway

*T*hick traffic on Kalakaua makes it hard to cross. They turn right, shouldering through a sudden throng collected on that corner, then sidestepping, picking up speed as the crowd thins, they are running past shops and nighttime strollers, and Joe shouts, "Here comes a bus! Let's get the fucking bus, Hooper!"

Doors gush open at the corner, old Chinese lady hobbles out.

They leap aboard and stoop to watch behind as it roars away. No pursuers visible.

At the last stop this side of the harbor they jump off. Joe wants to run backward the two remaining blocks, to offer the felony squad reverse tracks. Hooper vetoes this. He can't believe anyone has kept pace with them. Joe sprints ahead. Hooper lopes along, buoyant with escape, running on an air cushion that seems to lift him two inches off the ground, and so lightheaded that when he feels someone coming up behind him, he doesn't turn, isn't worried, doesn't even glance. He keeps his eyes trained on the track he follows and waits to see who it will be.

On silent pads they're catching up, vague shadows come abreast of him. Hooper can scarcely make them out. Men in top hats, men in coveralls, men carrying cutlasses, men on horseback galloping silently, and dusty reins of wornout wagons, leather against flesh, and more leather. He thinks of his father, which is something he hardly ever does, he *never* thinks of his father, yet now it strikes him that his father is back there at the hotel with the doorman and the desk clerk and the plainclothesman who patrols the lobby and the chief janitor and the cabdrivers who by now are incensed, Andrew back there among them shaking his head, with hands on hips, greatly sorrowed by this performance and rounding up some ultimate posse to track down the renegades. But then Hooper hears a soft sound right next to him, diaphanous outline of double-breasted suit, man of middle years striding winded yet immensely pleased about something, and telling him, "Run, boy, run like hell. *You'll* get there. You'll *get* there. Stretch the legs, big fella. And RUN!"

Hooper strides out, through parking lot gravel, out along the catwalks, and leaps onto the boat, quick check to see if Broome is secure, and they are pushing off. Low engine sputter takes them past the night lights, into the basin that catches these rows of light like sparks falling all around them. Sputter out into the empty bay, and on out a couple of miles, till Waikiki is a bracelet in the night, and they anchor there, Broome in his canvas cocoon below, Hooper and Joe on the deck on long lumpy cushions, taking turns watching out for craft that might ram them in the dark.

CHAPTER 68

The world
is full of women

*B*efore dawn a breeze is ruffling
the water. Hooper shivers, not with cold, but with an odd mixture
of gloom and elation. He can't sleep. Stiff, he climbs out of his bag
and weighs anchor, runs the mainsail up, catches the wind. At first
light they're a mile off Diamond Head. Molokai's a dark shape
against the near-dark sky, and Hooper spends a long time watching its bulk grow darker, and its line sharper as the light spreads.
Joe is up now, watching it too.

After a while Joe says, "What are we gonna do, Hooper?"

"I don't know."

"I thought you said you knew what we were going to do."

"Right now we're just going to sail some."

"Where to?"

"We'll cross to Molokai. Maybe make for Lahaina."

"What about Broome?"

"He's all right. He doesn't mind the ride."

"Well, if somebody happened to come looking for us . . . we'd be
a lot better off . . . I mean, if somebody sent out a powerboat or a
helicopter or something . . ."

"Who's going to send out a helicopter? Who's even going to know
where to look?"

Joe shrugs.

"We're in the clear, Joe."

In the clear and steering, Hooper *does* know what he wants to
do. He wants to bury Broome at sea, and sees how he will do it, the
wrapped body sliding past the gunwhale, down its watery chute,
he hears what he will say. Trouble is, he wants Nona to be in on it
and wishes now they'd made a dawn raid on Waikiki, kidnapped
her, brought her along. No car to do it with, though, and anyway
here they are pushing into the Molokai channel. So the only thing
left is to call her tonight at the hotel, from wherever they stop, and
tell her to catch a plane. Aaaah, but she no longer works there. He
might have to send a telegram. Yes. To Nona Kekai, Broome's
Rooms, Wili Wili Avenue. Waikiki. *The body is safe*———No. *We*

stole Broome——No. Jack is with us on the boat. Fly to Maui and meet us at Lahaina harbor. We'll wait until . . . The body is embalmed, he thinks, so it can't putrefy, we could wait a long time. What's the rush? Isn't that where it all started, the big rush about burial, that fear of putrefaction? We could carry Broome around for weeks this way if we wanted to . . . *till you get there. Hooper and Joe.*

Just the kind of scheme that irks her. Half-assed. Everything could go wrong. *You don't really care.* Shit. Well. He has all day to work it out. They could of course stop sooner, at Kaunakekai, on this island they're approaching, and send word from there. But no, Lahaina is the fitting place to stop, old whaling port, one-time capital of all these islands, residue of schooners there, and blubber vats, and chiefly war canoes. He likes the sound Lahaina makes, and knows ahead of time he wouldn't mind waiting there awhile.

Now Hooper feels the breakfast gurgle in his stomach, and it sharpens his mood, this ecstatic sadness, of being both released and carrying such mournful cargo. He knows Joe feels the breakfast gurgle too, and because of it they may not eat for hours, a penance, self-denial test. He couldn't ask for a more congenial partner than Joe, who is grinning in spite of himself as they push out, heading for Molokai's western tip. The sun is up, lifting into a hard-edge sky, just like the day Hooper arrived, except this time the day will be much longer, floating as they are in the bowl of it, rather than so high above, dropping in. You watch the whole day grow from dark to light, skimming across it on your way to the second island.

Watching Maui loom blue-hazed in the distance, and Lanai, like half a coconut off to the south and west, Hooper sees how one island is never enough, you need two at least, so you can sit on one and look at the other, and see beyond it the infinite reaches. Oahu behind them makes four different islands, ridged blue and black, or green where the sun catches.

Joe and Hooper point silently and grin, as if choosing, taking their pick, this island, or that one, exploring the archipelago for what might as well be the first time, for some small bay to anchor in, when the time is right. Like Nona said that first day they went swimming, you get offshore far enough and the concrete intrusions, they melt, the islands rise and drift around you, and this is it, being this far off so many shores you could be skirting any island. These hard green ridges are the very ones Cook spied, and haven't changed that much in a hundred and seventy years, when you're out this far, and this is your first taste of gliding on that same ocean's bosom.

"Hooper, what time do you think we'll hit Lahaina?"

"Sometime this afternoon."

"And what happens then?"

"Who knows?"

"Listen, it wouldn't make any difference to me if we just kept going."

Hoop grins and nods.

Joe says, "I mean we're really moving."

"I know it."

"Well, why stop at all?"

Shrug, grin, shake the head.

"I mean . . . except for Broome," Joe says, "whatever we do with him."

"He's resting easy."

"Why don't we just keep going? Aren't we headed south?"

"Due."

"And that's where we've been talking about going."

"It's a little early in the season, of course."

"We can take our time. What the hell. The main thing is, once you're moving, not to stop."

Hooper says, "We could start with a sail around the Big Island."

"Sonofabitch, Hooper. Listen. I've got cash in the Bank of Hawaii. Yesterday, on a hunch, I stole everything Goldie had, and banked it. And she already lent me a hundred dollars she wired her old man for. And I sold my other board the day Broome died. I'm loaded."

"I've got some in the bank myself. We could withdraw all of it while we're in Lahaina and stock up the goddam boat."

"Oh Jesus, Hooper, I can't take it. I'm gonna crap right here on the dock."

"There's just one thing, Joe."

"What, what."

"I'm worried. I'm just a little worried, that's all. A glimmer of worry in the back of my head."

"About Nona."

"Well . . ."

"Don't let her hang you up."

"I haven't told you this. In fact I haven't told anybody, because it isn't anything like a certainty. But there's a chance she might be knocked up."

"Shit, man, let me tell you something. I know for a fact that Goldie *is* knocked up."

"By how much."

"She is, by her own calculations, about two months along."

"And you don't have any feelings about sailing off at a time like that?"

"I have very *strong* feelings about it, one of which is the feeling that she was not necessarily knocked up by me."

"How do you figure that?"

"If you will think back, those were the days when I was touching no woman, for any reason whatsoever."

"Well then, who ..."

"God only knows. I don't even want to begin to work it out. All I know is, that makes three reasons why I have no desire to go back to town."

"What are the other two?"

"The hotel people for one will be after our asses, mine in particular, once they identify the truck. And the morticians for another. Stealing dead bodies is a terrible crime."

"Let me ask you this. Suppose *Nona* is pregnant. Do you think I can just sail off to the goddam South Seas?"

"Suppose she isn't. Do you know for sure?"

"Not yet. But if she is, I'd feel like hell pulling out on her. Especially now, with Broome gone. And if she isn't, I'd kind of like her to come along on the boat."

Longsuffering look from Jonas, Long pause, while Joe gets his thoughts together. They have never openly discussed this.

"Look, Hooper. You don't take women along on trips."

He knows that, and knows why, but wants the reason confirmed. "Why not?"

"Because it is a male thing, that's why. It's a very male thing. Women just fuck it up. The world is full of women, for Christ sake. When we get to Tahiti, there are going to be so many women we will be beating them away from the boat like sharks. Anyway, we're not going to be gone forever, are we? A few months at the outside. Even if she is knocked up we'll be back in a few months. You are always going to be hung up with a woman one way or another, and if you let that kind of thing stand in your way you are never going to go anyplace you really want to go."

Hooper, musing, "It would be a dirty thing to do."

But Joe knows he has made his point. He falls silent, lets Hooper brood. For a long time Hooper stares at the water rushing past their yellow hull, blue water, churning lightly, gurgling. He doesn't think of Nona, he thinks again of Broome, of how they'll send him into the sea he always yearned for, send him with an incantation. Hooper knows what he wants to say, doesn't quite know why, it just feels right, and yet he feels ashamed to say it, afraid of what Joe will think. *I now baptize you in the name of the father and the son ...* And he would follow that by reading something from the Bible, the way ship captains always do when there's a death at sea. He should have brought his copy along. For that, and for the reading later on. He might finish it then.

The sun is at the bottom of the ocean, sending up dusty shafts of light, and Hooper imagines that the litany is over with, Broome is already buried and wandering around down there among these shafts, and Hooper half expects to see his panama come floating up through one long light beam, beneath it the grinning face, chubby arms treading water. *Heh heh. You can't just throw Jackson Broome over the side.*

The longer Hooper stares, the more he fancies he does see a hat rising. But it isn't Broome's. Some other hat. One he doesn't recognize, a battered stetson, looks like, and below it just the shadow of a face, right under the surface, like those shadows he saw last night, not moving this time, just waiting, several of them now, a black and straight-brimmed preacher's hat, a man in coveralls, vague features flickering, looking at him, waiting for something. They float along next to the boat. He strains to see them clearly, in among the shafts and flickering surface. It's hard not to slip overboard, headfirst tumble down to mingle there, like a skindiver checking out a school of fish.

He blinks. The figures fade. He lifts his face to see the gorgeous day, the sun now high above the slopes of Molokai, and Jonas on the foredeck running up their jib. The wind makes a pillow of it. Beyond Joe's muscled back lie three islands you can sail to. Hooper, steering, has already picked one, has set his course. It's simply impossible not to do.

CHAPTER 69

Down at the

*I*n they scoot, *Golden Goose* with three hands aboard. There has never been a day like it, the day itself is one great wave that doesn't break, sliding down it, down and down, each moment's both a lift and fall, and Hooper, steering, feels the tiller is his arm down in the water, grabbing as they tack.

Mid-afternoon, with Molokai behind them, he starts looking for

216

the spot, the place in this ocean that will be right for Broome. It might be up ahead of them, or somewhere they'll come back to. For whatever is coming next, there is always a perfect spot, if you believe in it, and are willing to wait. Picnic spots, parking places, rooms to sleep in, bench to watch the surf from. Call it a type of *Golden Goose,* something you wait for, and rely on. A matter of belief.

It's sunset when they find it, a couple of miles off Maui, out there between Lahaina and the island of Lanai, five islands visible and Lanai's crater pushing at the swarming orange sky. They anchor there, and Hooper sights the spot, then they stretch out on deck to watch the sun fall, watch mallets of air beat it to a thin gold of time suspended, spread across the water and the sky, gold net of time-lessness dropping around them in a bright haze that only slowly turns to shadow and the gold goes thinner, thinning till the net dissolves with quick falling dusk.

Net gone, the faintest chill shivers Hooper, like a sheet drawn back will cool the skin. The moment you want to last forever slips away, and it's time you wish whatever is to follow had already begun, the time you think most about women. Joe, feeling it, goes below. Hooper sits here, recalling his bus ride of just about this same time yesterday, the leap aboard, then suddenly nothing to do but stand and look around, first time he'd had that chance in weeks, it seemed, and he was gazing down at straight parts of black hair, tops of flared noses, in the middle of a long row of people a foot shorter than himself, Gulliver Dunlap on the crosstown bus feeling no superiority for his size, but a loneliness which made him long for Nona, for something about her he enjoys so much, that size of her, her looking him almost in the eye, like few girls can unless they stand on running boards.

He wants someone to tell him what to do. They'll be ashore soon. Should he fly to Honolulu then? And get her? Or send the telegram and hang around Lahaina awhile? Either one would break Joe's heart. And Hooper owes a lot to Joe. It's Joe who found Broome's in the first place, and thus the boat.

Suppose he gets in touch and she tells him her period finally started. Wouldn't *that* ease things some. Yes. Some. But what about those questions in her mouth? Still can't answer them. And no time now. He needs a plan. He'll wire her that he's phoning, say, Johnny B's at twelve o'clock tomorrow. They will talk things over then. And by that time, who knows, perhaps something will come to him, some *Golden Goose.* Something perhaps as simple as the engine. Joe's down there now, and Hooper hasn't heard a sound, half hopes he won't. The wind has fallen to a dead calm. If both the wind and engine fail, it's out of his hands completely. Cut off from the civilized world, and drifting.

"Goddam sonofabitching cocksucker!"

Hooper says nothing.

"Shiteater fucking pissant bastard!"

"What's the matter?"

"Can you come down here, Hooper."

He drops through the hatch, into murky lamplight, Broome on the floor beneath a bunk, Joe bent into the engine compartment, fumes wafting.

"You flooded it, Joe."

"Bullshit. The fucking thing won't even turn over."

"What's the matter then?"

"How the shit should I know?"

"Here, let me in there. It probably isn't sparking."

Hooper squats, with his jackknife he scratches at the spark wire.

"Be careful," Joe says, "that smell is pretty strong."

Hooper thinks of pilot lights gone out on kitchen stoves, how the room smells when you first walk in, how you open windows, then reach a cautious match toward the pipe, the tiny flame that seems to slowly suck those creeping fumes back inside the stove. He tells Joe to move his shoulder, let in some light. It catches their two stubbled chins, a one day's growth after yesterday's shave, and their gaunt eyes watching. He tells him to press the starter and Hoop will try to make the plug arc.

It works. The spark leaps, igniting not the engine but the air all around them. It explodes with a blue, scalding flash. Cannon roar fills the cabin. Hooper, bending closest, is thrown back against the far wall, the room suddenly blistering his skin. He can think of nothing but escape and collides with Jonas groping for the ladder, claws at Joe, who somehow has made it to the deck and pulls him up. Hooper's shirt is burning, and the heat boiling out through the hatch is chasing him. He hears Joe yelling, "Get away from the boat!"

Fall over the side, splash into this cool lagoon with sudden ease, a net of sponges catching him, one moment to think of Broome and how to climb back on and get him, then his head pops through, half the boat aflame, and Jonas somewhere close yelling, "Hooper, Hooper, can you swim?"

"Yeah, I can swim."

"Then swim like hell!"

The arms lift, the feet kick. But the strokes begin to tear something on his chest, searing split of skin, muscle, chest ripping open and salt sting at his face. He sees an oldtime movie seaman strung up for flogging while the crew assembles, thirty faces wincing with each strop of snake whip across the twitching back. Twenty lashes later, when the wretch is cut loose and thrown against a coil of rope to suffer, his one close buddy comes along with a bucket of just-drawn seawater to spill and hasten healing of the open wounds. Brine splashes on the bloody back. Victim screams and buddy says, It hurts me worse'n it does you, lad. Hooper hears the scream and lifts his own head to cry out, but can't lift it high enough and takes in water, burning at his throat, gagging with it, flailing for the surface in a night so black no telling where the night ends and where the water starts.

Every frantic flail tears the chest, scalding flashes run along his arms. He yells "Joe!" but chokes on the brine inhaled, makes one last gurgle, losing strength. A black twist of terror grabs him. Terror turns to nausea, retching underwater with no way to stop the inward gush. Air he wants, not water, but can't get it, can't find it, legs are noodles kicking for the surface. Then it's there. His mouth flung wide gags again with retching, night air burns his face. "Joe" the gurgle goes. Then Hooper thinks, Jonas never panics. In an undertow, don't waste energy fighting. If it gets you, let it take you where it's going, *then* start swimming back to shore. Under waves you've lost, when there's no way to beat the roiling tumble of the broken wave, roll with it, let it take you black and tumbling toward the bottom, toward the bottom. Roll and wait, and keep flat palms above the head in case of shallow rocks or coral. Go limp. Don't panic. Swirl in darkness, no direction, dizzy head and boiling plunge of dark foam. Lungs burn, and if he doesn't breathe now he'll burst, yet it's another tumble downward, screaming with the pain, and wave after wave is breaking on him, endless set of waves that roar and send billows lunging while he rolls. Down, on down. And how far down can bottom be. Maybe it's beneath the roar. The end of sound would be the bottom.

Plunge and swirl, strain to hear the sound that's fading. He's dropping far below the waves. Yet he could be above them. Colors reverse, like a negative, white walls rising, black boils of bursting foam. He's on a cliff, staring at the sea five hundred feet below, where waves break in slow motion, wondering what it is about this Big Sur coast that makes them lift so long and easy. Listen. It's the silent curl. The sound comes later, after the spume, and that's what slows them down. When you're facing a wave the sound accelerates the breaking, the rising hiss, the readying to roar, and then the roar is coming at you with the water. But up here above the waves, the sound is swallowed, it lags, and the higher you get, the slower they break, the sound is coming later and later, and now that we are high enough, you see, there is no sound at all, just that far-below pattern of slow-curling ribbons lined up in silent rows. The end of sound

His head pops through translucent skin, making one plink in the quiet, floating blackness. Reach for handfuls to pour along the crying skin. Balm. Ease it, wet massage of warm, and drifting, musing, sting gone, gloating in the night's black skin and water resting on him like a feather blanket thick as sky. Calm feather water cover warming cooling *down at the bottom of the*

—SPACER—

We were finished, Hooper said, and I wanted to get up and walk around. I started thinking about movies I have watched, foreign movies where you see a couple starting to make love, and then it cuts to later and they are side by side under the sheets, the girl exhausted, the man half sitting up, smoking a cigarette and letting the smoke float over his eyes. And I really wanted to smoke a cigarette.

I know the feeling, Goldie cries, God, do I know the feeling.

But you know, Hooper says, I never have learned how to smoke.

PART 4

Departures and Arrivals

OR

Nona's Trip, Joe's Voyage, Luella's Exit, Andrew's Spacer, Hooper's Ride

Fifty billion times a year a birth canal is filled with sperm, numberless seeds in every spurt, they wriggle through the darkness of strange waters no one has told them about, dying by the thousands in their swim for safety. One in a million makes it to the egg and lodges there and rolls on down with it to the warm dark home away from home, till the spermandegg grow big enough to spurt again, through the straits with arms flailing, glottis fluttering, yowling at the shock and still wriggling.

CHAPTER 70

One thing
leads to another

*T*here are no funerals for Nona to attend. She and Goldie fly to Lahaina and spend a day in the hospital with Joe. From there Nona flies to Molokai, the island of her birth, to stay with relatives and wait for the baby.

When she mourns it's not so much the loss of *him*, as the loss of *them*, what they might have been if Hooper only were something other than what he was and better able to love some *one*—which Goldie insists he was not, trying, in her tactless style, to soothe Nona by explaining the appropriateness of the way he died. It is a matter, Nona concludes, of commiting yourself to specific people, places, and things, and it is in this frame of mind that she hears, for the first time, something a favorite great-aunt has been telling her for years.

This old auntie, pure Hawaiian, was a dancer once herself. She saw the bones forming when Nona was a child, and made of her a protégée, and tried to hold her back, as someone special who shouldn't have to go into the clubs the way everyone else in the family did. This auntie would have preferred Nona to spend her whole life in the back country studying dances most of the world had forgotten. But Nona left early, of her own accord, once Al the manager discovered her. It is only when she comes back home to recuperate that she finally listens.

Out here on Molokai, which the tourist bureau calls the *Friendly Island*, but which is known locally—because of the unquestionable presence of hurtling fireballs on the roads at night and formations of ancient warriors marching through the full moon—as the *Ghost Island*, listening to this auntie talk about dances she loves but can no longer perform, Nona's mission begins to take shape. She will become a student of the early style. She will not turn out like her mother, who went commercial and never recovered. She will herself preserve some of the pre-Harry Owens Hawaiian music. She will form a troupe of her own and work with gourds and calabash drums, more footwork than swirling hips, her own deep alto chanting genealogies.

She names her son Hooper and lives on Molokai until he's six months old, then moves back to Honolulu, goes to work dancing at the Moana while she starts to put her troupe together. She happens to meet a freelance cameraman there, who's shooting some footage for MGM. He offers to produce a documentary on early Hawaiian culture, and later does, and one thing leads to another.

His name is Bob, he makes good money, knows his job, and works hard at it. They get married at a big luau and spend the next few years living between Oahu and southern California. A perfect setup. Nona can follow her calling, Bob can follow his. When little Hooper turns five they have to settle somewhere, and Bob finally chooses California, for the schooling. He buys a place in San Fernando Valley, within range of the studios. Nona assembles a troupe of expatriate Polynesians who perform all over the state.

Now two more children have come along. She and Bob take yearly vacations to the islands. It all works out well enough, except for the smog, and the traffic, and the prices, and the schools, which are falling apart. Every day she is more like her old auntie, and thinks about moving everything back to Molokai. At least there you can breathe. And there maybe her oldest, young Hooper, could find what he is looking for. She never knows what to do about her son. He has just now told her, in the spring of his seventeenth year, he is going away for a while. He's not quite as tall as his father was, but as tall as his mother, and when she asks where, he answers with soft voice and intensely loving eyes, "I'll let you know."

CHAPTER 71

Get outta the way

*L*uella found another room in a little row of shacks down the street, spent all one day moving her things over there, and walked out the door for the final time the next morning, just as the big tank-tread crane pulled into the yard. The suitcase she carried held her tattoo equipment. She stopped out on the porch and looked up at the startled man in the cab, who thought the place had been emptied. He yelled down, "Better get outta the way, lady!"

"You better get outta the way yourself!" she yelled back.

She set her suitcase down, opened it, started lobbing ink bottles up at the cab, splattering its windows with emeralds and indigos and carmines. A couple of wreckers came running through the grass toward her. She picked up her electric needle, old, rusty, never work again, yet ominous, thrust forward at arm's length. She held four men in hard hats at bay like that until a fifth crept up behind and they hauled her out to the sidewalk yelling and kicking, while the lead ball swung back for its first shot, hung an instant, then came crashing through the room of the man in green pajamas. It swung out and crashed through again, sending a splintered door into the upstairs hallway. The third swing caught what he'd aimed at the first time, one face of the six-sided pergola.

All morning the ball swung. After lunch a bulldozer moved in to start piling up the pieces, leaving tracks in the soil, and swaths the scoop made, about ten feet wide, shiny smooth and level. Mid-afternoon both rigs were rumbling away from a squarish heap of weathered planks and dusty timbers, shingles sprinkled in there, and a few poking corners of balustrade and filigree.

CHAPTER 72

Ride on in

*L*ike a seal will sometimes do when he's sick or injured, Jonas dragged himself onto the beach and lay there in and out of consciousness until a fisherman found him. He stayed in Lahaina while his burns healed. He wouldn't talk to Goldie so she finally flew back to Oahu, where she remained, putting their baby up for adoption, eventually marrying an airline pilot, joining the PTA.

During his convalescence Joe became something of a celebrity on the island. It got him on the crew of another boat that was heading south, this one a schooner in immaculate shape, with plenty of cash behind it. They left in May when conditions were ideal and made the trip to Tahiti without a hitch.

But Joe didn't much like it when he got there. The surf was small, the mosquitoes large, the girls aggressive—three of them, his first night on shore, broke down the door of a hotel room he rented, his blond hair and light skin driving them to frenzy.

A NATIVE SON OF THE GOLDEN WEST

Going south had always been Hooper's idea anyway, not Joe's. After three weeks he caught the French freighter that sails from Papeete to Panama. From there he bussed and hitchhiked his gloomy way up through Central America and Mexico. In Mazatlan he met some surfers down from San Diego. He didn't know them, but they had heard of Vandermeer, now called The Flying Dutchman, or The Van. They gave him a ride north, according him the respect due a man who had survived the disaster of the Maui Channel and also ridden the biggest wave of all time. Side-tripping to a beach south of Tijuana on the way home, they introduced Joe to another batch of surfers, cashing in on the free wine that came his way—guest of honor and his entourage.

Before they crossed the border Joe could smell California coming, that blend of baby oil and iodine drifting off the beaches, the mustardy sizzle-fry from burger bars; exhaust fumes; rotten sweet of canneries. It all came drifting to invade his nostrils, and he despised coming back to it, and loved it, and there was nothing to do but ride on in.

Joe still lives in Santa Monica, where he grew up. He's a life guard there, the only un-tan guard along one thousand miles of coastline. Every morning he paddles two miles on the board with the red cross under his chest. He has more rescues to his credit than any other guard in southern Cal. He lives a moderate life, drinks little, smokes grass from time to time, and tobacco not at all, surfs once in a while, when all the conditions are perfect and he doesn't have to paddle very far. By now other surfers have passed him up, ridden larger waves than his. But Joe's legend lives on, like Lindbergh's.

He lives alone but has all the company he wants. For example, see the man who stops next to his guard stand this afternoon, in the summer of 1970. Stoned. Wearing swim trunks and beads, and shades like Joe's, and stands here in the burning sun for a long time, face pointed at the ocean, says at last, "What a trip, man."

Joe nods.

The man breathes, "Whew," wags his head. "What a *trip*."

In his no-tan and white helmet with a red cross, Joe watches the strollers at the waterside, sepia-toned by his prescription glasses. He hears exhaust blaps behind him.

He turns to speak. The man is gone.

Joe thinks, Shit.

Sitting here.

Hungry.

Try half the tuna sandwich.

Shit. That's gone too. It's three o'clock.

Look for Bernie. Call him back. Maybe he has a joint.

Out of sight.

Watch the girls then. Maybe a young one'll stop. Fifteen. Sixteen. One with blank eyes and nice nips.

Bikini girls.

Accompanied by weight lifters.

Joe watches while they walk. They run. They swim and splash. They do backflips, cartwheels, stand on heads underwater, ride cycles, dune buggies, dance in the sand.

They trip circles around the slower moving gypsy girls in their sand-length purple dresses, beads that click and golden earrings, tangled hair. See the cowboys escorting the gypsies, and the girls from outer space.

See the Garbos, and the hobos, from the thirties. See dandies, and squaws, and Jesuses of every size, and men disguised as women, and witch doctors, and African warriors. Travelers on a summer's day. They pass the time, take Joe's mind off the stomach, and it makes for less rescues when people wear clothes to the beach.

Hometown Eddy Rickenbacker swoops low in his Piper Cub. A mile out some yacht from Newport is scooping wind. Zip goes a kid on a skimboard through inshore flats. And here come six in black leather, four men, two women, black jackets, black gauntlets, black boots moving through the sand with languid step, loosely joined, like the same herd of Angus bulls who gave them this second skin. Black beards, and black hair to cover the ears, and one-way reflecting lenses to flash sun at one another, they drag their boots through the wet sand, fall dead a while next to the pier, hike back to the bikes and blap out through the parking lot. Joe listens to the blapping thunder as they roar down 101 toward Laguna.

CHAPTER 73

Across town.
A year later.

*O*n the screen blue-green fig-
ures plod around in dusty soil. Arms, legs, heads inflated, faceless.
One of them sets a square green box into the dust and stands back.

Naomi says, "What do you reckon that box is for?"

Andrew knows what the box is for. He saw a mock-up of one just
like it when they invited him back to Boeing last year for a tour
of the plant. He doesn't answer Naomi. He is thinking that Hooper
would be thirty-eight this year and imagining that Hooper is inside
one of those suits and what a wonderful thing that would be, and
his heart goes sour.

From the right another blue-green figure enters the screen, swinging fat legs with slow steps, arms out. He swings his torso, looking
around.

Andrew thinks that Hooper probably would have been too tall,
and sees him then, the way he towered, thinks about the last time
he saw him, the last conversation they had. He remembers every
word of it. He remembers every word of every conversation they ever
had. There weren't too many. Sometimes he thinks that is what went
wrong. Or maybe it was the *way* they talked. Often he runs them
through in his head. Sometimes it takes him a day, sometimes a
couple of hours, sometimes they all run through his mind at once, ten
or twelve conversations, with Hooper at those various sizes and ages,
and then Andrew feels most like he is able to put his finger on it,
sees how clearly it was his fault. Seems like it always ended up a
sermon. And yet why *his* fault? A man gives as much as he can.
That's all you can do. You can only give as much as you can.

Naomi says, "You couldn't get me in one a them capsules for
nothin'. They look just like spiders. Big old tarantulas standing
around waiting to jump on somebody."

Andrew doesn't answer, doesn't hear, images flicker in front of
his eyes, his own voice getting louder in his own ear:

"There are opportunities out here that have never existed for
men before *any*where. Right now at Boeing they are talking about
planes that will carry three hundred people. And go a thousand

miles an hour. Can you imagine that? And it's just the start. We're gonna see the day not far off when people can fly to the Hawaiian Islands in four hours, instead of ten or twelve. You ought to wait awhile, Hooper. You could cut that trip of yours by more than half. Why, one of these days we're going to land somebody on the moon, son. That may sound farfetched now. But it's true. And you can bet we won't be stopping there. Fantastic things are coming, fantastic times ahead. We're going to lead the world in every direction, toward the kind of life God intends to make available to all men everywhere. And a man who doesn't prepare himself is going to fall behind. That's all there is to it. I know I can't keep you from doing whatever you're going to do, because you're as bullheaded as I am, in your own way. All I can do is tell you what I know. First Corinthians fourteen and eight, it says, For if the trumpet gives an uncertain sound, who shall prepare himself to the battle? I just ask you to think about that."

Andrew was proud of himself that day, telling his son how the world was going to go. Proud, yes. Puffed up with what he thought he knew. Knows better now. At least knows better than to prophesy. Anyone can do it. Everything comes true.

On the screen the earth appears, between the dome-headed suits and the spider-legged capsule, a blue rearview mirror beyond the luminous rim.

1974:

Galloping on

*I*t's the same in every town they come to, Bakersfield, Sacramento, Redding. You pass Uncle John's Pancake Parlor, King Arthur's Pizza, Daddy's Deep-Fried Chicken, Woof-Woof Lunchroom Number 2, MacDougall's DriveInnBurger, Taco Amigo, and LeRoy's Instant Doughnut. All send off the same glazed formica reflections and interchangeable steely corners, brass rods from the ceiling hold oval lamps designed for easyclean, and everything's encased in plastic bags. You drive on, thinking, although you already know this road too well, that there must be something else. A dim spot in the stream of overhead neon lifts your *hopes—a laundromat closed, a bodyfender shop, a scoured empty lot waiting in the darkness. Then lights again, not blinking. The lights don't blink any more, they're steady, hot, harsh, low, and steady, dragging you along. And you're passing Farmer Tom's Pancake Palace, Alpine Pizza Number 4, Chicken City, Woof-Woof Lunchroom Number 12, Take-a-taco, MacDaniel's BillionBurger-ShakesandFries, and Captain Doughnut staring at you through the hole in a doughnut four times the size of your car. By squinting you can see what you already know: Aunt Ida's Pancake-o-rama is five blocks away. It's all starting over, and there's nothing to do but park next to Captain Doughnut's giant pegleg and glinting cutlass and step inside the plastic cover where, with elbows bracketing your coffee cup, you become a cutout, a silhouette edged by formica glare for the motorists still out there making their decisions.*

Nothing but that, unless you choose to just keep going, and that's what Scott intends to do, and makes a lesson of it as they leave the freeway outside Redding and take 299 toward the high country, yelling back to tell young Hooper and the others that no matter how big the fire, no one will burn down Chicken City or deflate Captain Doughnut's plastic frigate. No matter where the war or what else makes it through the seventies, these will prosper and endure.

Hearing that, Hooper relaxes for the first time since they left Los Angeles. He finally believes what Scott has been telling him. Secretly he has been clinging to this idea that by blowing up one building you could somehow blow up them all. But it is clear that Scott really does know what he's talking about, and Hooper now is unreservedly glad he came along.

See him sitting here, brown-eyed, brown-skinned, looking a little like an Indian, but of no tribe anyone could name. Something has softened the tautness of his Indian skin. His hair is what Hawaiians call ehu, black hair that shines auburn when the light hits it right. His nose is straight, his chin is strong, he wears a scraggly black moustache that makes him look younger than the seventeen he is.

Mackinaw, heavy wool shirt, levis and boots, sitting in the lead bus of three VW's and a cattle trailer caravaning to Idaho where Scott has a place picked out. A man Scott calls "a wealthy sympathizer" has given them permission to use it. Scott has been there before, tried to settle there before, and failed, which is probably why he talks so much, still convincing himself that everything he knows is true. But Hooper trusts him now, completely. The theory about burger bars and chicken palaces somehow has persuaded him.

They are going to grow food when they get there, and drink pure water, and breathe mountain air, and it is the only thing that makes sense to Hooper, the only thing now that seems worth struggling for, or fighting for, if it comes to that, as Scott says it might, unless they are very careful and very lucky. Each bus carries a rifle. Hooper hopes it never comes to that. He looks forward to the work and to the time after work when he can find a place in the forest, a lonely place. A holy place. Yes, that's the only way to think of it —a holy place where he can purify his mind by dwelling on the silence. You can't do that where they're coming from. No such thing as silence any more. A man needs silence to purify his mind. And good food to purify the body. And good water to purify the skin. And it is not easy to have these things. That's why Scott failed the first time. No one realized how hard it would be. Scott admits it himself. But he says the spot is perfect. What you need to do is plan. He says this time he has planned for everything. He boasts about it, and this nettles Hooper some. But he has learned that whenever Scott brags about something he has done in the past, it always turns out he actually did do it and did it well.

On the fourth day Scott, leading, turns off the asphalt onto a graveled road that becomes a dirt track after the first mile. It carries them through deep forest toward the Salmon River. After six more miles they break past the tree line onto a pasture that slopes some seventy-five yards to the bank of a stream. This joins the Salmon half a mile down. A couple of trees rise from the stream bank, then forest again on the other side. Plenty of timber for building, rich soil, and space to run animals here. They're already unloading chickens from the last bus, and the cow from the trailer, and turning the dogs loose. The travelers are getting out of the buses slowly, savoring the discovery, and awestruck by the way Scott's predictions match the look of this land. They wrestle the dogs, they stretch out in deep grass, they walk to the tree line.

Hooper and Scott and Scott's woman walk down to the stream, and kneel and drink from cupped hands, and Hooper says, "What do we drink in the winter, Scott, when the stream freezes over?"

"We dig a well, man. We do that first. Today. Tomorrow. Then we build a house over the well, so it comes up right into the kitchen. And we sit around in the kitchen in the wintertime drinking water till it's running out our noses."

Hooper laughs. Scott laughs. Scott's woman, next to him, laughs and looks at Hooper drinking. It is a way Nona sometimes looks at him. She is twice Hooper's age, this woman of Scott's, and looks at him now with that mother's smile of affection, but affection oddly kindled, as if seeing someone else besides himself.

Scott sees the look and stands up, commands them to follow him *back up the bank to a spot thirty yards from the stream's high-water mark, and declares in a deep voice that is both patriarchal and mocking the patriarchal, "We will build the first house here," planting then a long staff through the grass, into dark earth.*

Hooper, avoiding the face of Scott's woman, says, "I'll start unloading the bus."

Creditaphs

There were no epigraphs to open this book. They have been saved for the end, epigraphs being in themselves a kind of credit. At movies most people get up to leave as soon as the story is over and don't wait to read credits run at the end. And that's all right. The story is the main thing. But for those who are interested

COSTUMES were inspired by Thomas Paine:
> Government, like dress, is the badge of lost innocence; the palaces of kings are built upon the ruins of the bowers of paradise.

MAKE-UP, Robert Browning:
> ... Notice Neptune, though,
> Taming a seahorse, thought a rarity,
> Which Claus of Innsbruck cast in bronze for me!

MANNERS, Miguel de Cervantes:
> I would have you know, Sancho, that it is a point of honor with knights errant not to eat once in a month; and when they do eat to take what they find nearest to hand.

PACIFIC SCENES, Herman Melville:
> For as this appalling ocean surrounds the verdant land, so in the soul of man there lies one insular Tahiti full of peace and joy, but encompassed by all the horrors of the half-known life. God keep thee! Push not off from that isle, thou canst never return!

TRAVEL CONSULTANT, *The Guinness Book of Records:*
> The record distance for firing a human from a cannon is one hundred fifty-five feet, in the case of Miss Victoria Zacchini in the Ringling Brothers Barnum and Bailey Circus, Madison Square Garden, New York City, in April 1959. Her muzzle velocity was 140 mph.

BACKGROUND MUSIC was provided by:
> Django Rinehart and the Quintet of the Hot Club of France.
> Eddie Lund and his Tahitians, on the Brunswick LP, LAT 8233, *Your Musical Holiday in the South Seas.*
> Fats Waller and Harry Brooks, who wrote "Ain't Misbehavin'."
> A. J. Piron who wrote "I Wish I Could Shimmy Like My Sister Kate."
> Bud De Sylva who wrote "Minnie the Mermaid."
> Jack Palmer and Spencer Williams who wrote "Everybody Loves My Baby."

Jackson and Baxter Broome who wrote "You'll Never Go Hungry in Hawaii."

And Phillip P. Bliss who wrote "Almost Persuaded."

GENEALOGICAL REFERENCES, Ezra Dunlap, M.A., F.R.S.G.:

Many Dunlaps were prominent members of the clergy, both in the British Isles and in America, the Reverend James Dunlap (1730–1785) being one of the most notable. Trained at the Divinity School of the University of Edinburgh, by the age of thirty he was ministering to the largest Presbyterian congregation in Glasgow. Rather than pursue position and prestige, however, he left this achievement behind and volunteered to serve in sparsely populated northern Ireland, where experienced and devoted clergymen were sorely needed. His gravestone, which still stands outside the church in County Antrim where he spent his last years, bears this inscription: "My cup runneth over."

from *A History of the Dunlap Family*, 1920.

SURFRIDING IN THE HAWAIIAN ISLANDS, Lieutenant James King:

The boldness and address with which I saw them perform these difficult and dangerous maneuvers was altogether astonishing and scarcely to be believed.

from *Cook's Voyages*, Vol. III, 1779.

CURRENT EVENTS, Shirley Temple:

I think this country is in trouble.

San Jose Mercury News, August 30, 1967.

SPECIAL EFFECTS, Billy Graham:

Utopia is coming (Channel 11, same night)

OVERSEEING THE ENTIRE PRODUCTION, Hart Crane:

Here waves climb into dusk on gleaming mail;
Invisible valves of the sea,—locks, tendons
Crested and creeping, troughing corridors
That fall back yawning to another plunge.

Santa Cruz, California
September, 1970

234

ABOUT THE AUTHOR

James D. Houston was born in San Francisco in 1933 and has spent most of his life on the California coast. He has published three previous books. *Surfing, The Sport of Hawaiian Kings* (written with the anthropologist Ben R. Finney) is a non-fiction history of surf-riding in the Pacific Islands. *Between Battles*, his first novel, was released by The Dial Press in 1968. His second novel, *Gig*, which Dial released the following year, won San Francisco's coveted Joseph Henry Jackson Award in 1967 while still in manuscript, having been written during a Wallace Stegner Creative Writing Fellowship at Stanford. Stories and essays of his have appeared in *Holiday, Playboy, Cavalier, The Year's Best Science Fiction*, and *Stanford Short Stories*, as well as in numerous little magazines on the West Coast. He has worked intermittently as a musician playing string bass and guitar and has taught writing at Stanford and at the University of California at Santa Cruz. Married in Hawaii, he and his wife live in Santa Cruz with their three children.